In the soul of every artist the murderer's ghost lives on. Some make an honoured guest of him; some chain him, and bolt the door, but know that he is not dead.

—Mary Renault

Est ubi gloria nunc Babylonia? Where are the snows of yesteryear? The earth is dancing the dance of Macabré; at times it seems to me that the Danube is crowded with ships loaded with fools going toward a dark place.

—Umberto Eco

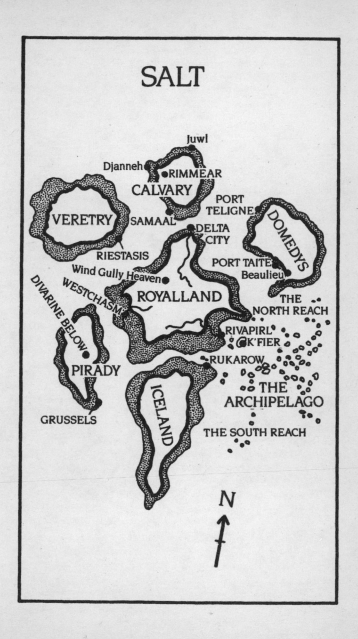

One

Beau knelt a little way off, smashing his head methodically into the dry-stone wall. Silky white curls tumbled over his forehead every time it hit. His lavender eyes were squeezed shut against the pain.

"It won't do any good," Humi said. She sat in the shade of a stunted oak with a torn shift in her lap. Though she'd been pretending to stitch as Beau talked and raged out his despair, at sixteen years old she wasn't callous enough to watch him hurt himself any longer. "The scars will only make you look exciting."

She got up and crossed the dell, dragging him away from the wall. The short grass scratched her legs as she pushed his hair back. There was no blood, only bruises, livid on the dark, grainy skin beneath his golden fur. He would have no scars, though she had spoken the truth: they couldn't have detracted from a beauty like his.

"I shan't go." His voice was nearly inaudible. "Humi, I won't. I won't die."

She squeezed him. It was hard not to let slip how desperately she longed that he could stay. "You've got nothing to say about it! How can you even think of disobeying the flamen?"

"I won't disobey. I'll make him take back his choice! He won't want me with a smashed face!" He pulled against her arms, but she held on. In a moment he relented. It was late summer; the sun stood midway down a sky the translucent blue of an aquamarine. The temperature was as high as it ever got in Westshine, this western province of the continent Domesdys. Humi gazed over the top of Beau's head across the low, dry valley, to a

slope which had been desolate ever since time began. It
was too close to the salt for anything to grow. The grass
on that side was copper-colored, sparse.

Above the ridge, over an expanse of other barren
ridges, a long, thin glitter sparkled. It was like the sea, but
it was not the sea. It was the salt.

"You know what Mum would've given for a chance
like this, Beau?" Humi said. "You know what *anyone*
would give to've been born like you?"

To her, he was just Beau. Betrothed, childhood companion, worst enemy and best friend. But when he was
born, the sight of him lying like a squalling, unearthly little vision next to his mother, Mercy, had driven all other
expectations out of the minds of his family. They asked
nothing of him beyond his face, which knew no such
thing as a bad angle, and his body, which moved like fur-
covered steel. They knew they would get their love's
worth out of him later on.

Now that investment had been returned. The traveling
flamen Godsbrother Sensuality had chosen Beau to be a
ghost, a beautiful statue of himself for the gods to enjoy
however they wished. In return, the Garden family would
get two hundred sheep, sixty shillings' worth of metal
tools, a cask of Royalland wine, and festival clothing for
the whole family. All of Westshine would envy them.

It was like being told that the gleam at the bottom of
your well *is* gold, as you've always hoped. There was as
much laughter as tears.

That Beau was not equally overjoyed did not matter.

His ambition was to marry and have children, to be a
farmer like his father and uncles. But no one suspected
him of such ordinary desires. He was too beautiful. Last
night, he, Humi, and their older cousins Brit and Emper
had been roughhousing around the fire in the courtyard.
Forgetting their grown-up dignity, Brit and Emper had
teamed up to take their two smaller cousins down. Gig-
gling hysterically, Humi had caught a sudden glimpse of
Beau—his face reddish on one side from the firelight and
ghostly pale on the other from the stars—and fallen silent.

She did not usually notice his beauty, but right then he seemed to have become a god.

And huddled by the flames with his leman at his feet, Godsbrother Sensuality had lifted his head as if his blind, salt-encrusted eyes could see. He had stared in Beau's direction for a long moment. It was said that flamens *could* "see" the gods to bow to them. Mightn't the same be true for a beauty not quite divine, but almost? (Humi had never seen a god, though one was said to have appeared to her great-grandmother. But she was sure they were as beautiful as the statuettes that her father and uncles carved. More beautiful, in their perfection.

The Divine Balance swung. Beau's life dropped down, down, down, out of sight, while his beauty was exalted to the sky.

And Humi went up into the hills to cry by herself. Without Beau she had no future here in the hamlet that her family had farmed for thousands of years. Since the time when Domesdys had been a land of stupid, heretical peasants, since before the Divinarchy came into being, the traditions had been the same. Humi would be an inferior being if she did not marry. And Beau was her only cousin anywhere near her age. Even if the others hadn't had wives or sweethearts, they would not have taken her, for she was not pretty. Her hair and face and body were all the same dirty tawny shade; her grayish-black eyes were the color of blood, her figure only passing. It had even made Beau ill-tempered about betrothing her at first, for he did have a streak of vanity, slender though it might be.

She wanted to leave Beaulieu. But where would she go? The outside world was a colorful blur of tales that the lemans of wandering flamens had told her. In it, the gem that was Delta City gleamed like a diamond. That was where the Divinarch sat and ruled over Salt. The Divinarch. God of gods. In Royalland.

Lesser gods were supposed to frequent the saltside, to appear to lonely girls tending sheep on the hills and give them strange, furless children. But those were only stories. Humi knew what she would really be when Beau was gone—old maid, work-ox, nurse for little nieces and nephews. The hamlets of the saltside strained every muscle to drag their living out of the thin earth. No one was spared. Even Beau was only worked more lightly than the others.

Humi had sunk so deep into her own misgivings that she scarcely noticed when Beau began to smash his face against the wall again. When she did see, she forestalled her impulse to grab him. Maybe that was where she'd gone wrong last time. And indeed, just when she thought she'd have to stop him before he killed himself, the sharp movements in the corner of her eye stopped. She kept her eyes down. A moment passed and another; then a heavy, painful weight came crashing down onto her feet.

"Gods' blood!" she whispered.

He stood over her, breathing shallowly. One cheek was a black mess of blood. He had dropped the stone in her lap. Wincing at the shooting pains in her ankle, she stood up. He wiped his eyes. "It's a lot harder to hurt yourself than you'd think."

"You *are* going to have a scar now, Beauty Garden."

"Made you notice, didn't I!" The leaves mottled the blue sky behind his head. The sun shone through a gap in the foliage onto his blood-smeared golden face. "Humi, you've got to come with me. I can't stand to go on my own."

Her breath jammed in her lungs. In the instant before the world turned the right way up again, her thoughts flew free of Beaulieu, out, out into a universe that was brighter and deeper than she would have dreamed possible. In Royalland, the lemans said, everything was green.

Is it true that in Delta City, the gods walk the streets every day? she wondered.

Will I ever see a god if Beau leaves me here?

What will I see?

It was agonizing to let go of those fantasies.

She had cherished hazy dreams of getting away ever since she was nine, when the outside world intruded upon the hamlet like the fanged mouth of a predator, in the form of a flamen, Godsbrother Transcendence. He had taken Humi's little sister, Thani, away to be his leman. A five-year-old chatterbox with white-blond fur, Thani had skipped away by the Godsbrother's side, leaving Humi looking after her. That was when she had first realized that it was possible to leave. And there was Humi's mother, Faith. When Humi was one year old, Faith had nearly been chosen to be a ghost to decorate the inauguration of a new Heir in Delta City. Humi knew that if her mother had been chosen, she would have gone. And Humi, growing up in someone else's care, would never have forgiven her for it.

"You've probably got chips of wall in that cut, Beau." She probed it with dexterous fingers, wiped it with a fresh oak leaf, avoiding his eyes.

Bruises were puffing his other eye shut, but he seized her shoulders without fumbling. His hands were calloused, and strong from manual labor. She couldn't writhe free. "If I have to die, I want you there with me. Come."

"Beau, you're crazy. What would I do in Delta City?" *After you die*—she could not say it.

"When the flamen told me I was chosen, he said I could take a companion. 'It is an acceptable practice, if the companion is content never to return,' he said. Now listen, why would you want to return? There's nothing for you here! Aunt would never let you farther away than Butterfly Cote to marry, and there's no one there, nor in Garden Vale. D'you want to live under her eye for the rest of your life? Working for Brit's and Emper's and Gent's families?"

His voice was rough. They were unused to expressing their emotions to one another. Her nose stung with imminent tears.

"Come with me."

The sun lay on his perfect lips. She watched them shape the words. Her fantasies fluttered round her head, blinding her. "Come with— "

"Stop! I'll ask! But she won't let me!"

"Yep," Beau said in satisfaction. "She will."

* * *

In the saltside every acre was precious. The low stone walls which marked out cultivated property stopped well short of the beginning of the salt. But sheep and goats wandered on the unclaimed brown slopes, and from time to time, parties from the hamlets ventured into the salt itself, seeking transparent berries and fruits. They wore cloths pulled over their faces. It was dangerous to go out in the salt when there were no clouds, or even at night if the stars shone brightly. The glare of every color in the rainbow at once could blind you. And even if it didn't, sooner or later a salt blizzard would come scudding over the wasteland and whip particles into your eyes, where they would take root and form crystals that grew until they filled your eye sockets.

That was how lemans became flamens, if their masters died while they were still in service, and if they rejected atheism, choosing instead to follow their masters into the flamenhood. They took pilgrimages of many days out into the salt. Returning with the salt crystals growing in their eyes, they were hailed as full-fledged Godsbrothers and Godsisters, possessed of the power to work miracles.

The salt symbolized the divine, the unknowable. The flamens' histories of the time before the Conversation Wars, when the whole world was an unmapped sprawl of barbarian kingdoms, showed that the salt had never lain farther than a few hundred leagues from the coasts of the six continents. Only the rivers of fresh water emerged from it unscathed. And it had never been explored, not even by the Wanderer, the first flamen, who had gone in sighted and come out blinded; so no one knew how large the continents really were. In terms of inhabitable country, Royalland was the largest and Domesdys the smallest, except for the Archipelago, where each island was either all salt or all soil, and people lived on fish.

The gods came from the salt. The myriad, nameless gods of wondrous appearances in the grandparents' tales—and the Delta City Incarnations, the Sage, the Mother, the Striver, the Maiden, the Heir. And the Divinarch. When they tired of living in Delta City, they returned home to Heaven, to have their places taken by others. Heaven lay in the depths of the gleaming, teeming wastelands: the abode of gods, the mecca of souls. But no one alive in 1352 had been there. Only two men had ever gone there and returned. The Wanderer, and a thousand years later a disillusioned leman, Zeniph Antiprophet. Antiprophet was devout and generous-minded, and he was so pious that when his Godsister passed away, at the age of fifty-eight, he ran crazy with grief. He swore he would seek out heaven and reclaim her from the gods.

He didn't find her on the great barren tableau in the middle of Royalland, though he traveled up the Chrume, the great river of Royalland, and searched the salt for so many months that his death was deemed certain. But he did find Heaven. All children, even the most pious, knew the tales he had spouted when he came back down the Chrume. That the beings all Salt worshiped were not any more gods than he was. The gods themselves had told him this, he asserted; that was nonsense, of course. Humi would never have dreamed of falling for it. But many people did believe him. Including many young, impressionable lemans.

When Humi's grandparents were young, there had been three flamens in Nece town. Her great-great-grandparents had been married by a flamen who lived in the hamlet itself, in a round stone hut that was now the silo. Now only one flamen lived in Nece, and all the services that the others had provided were done by wandering flamens. These Godsbrothers and Godsisters had followed the example of those who, over the past hundred and fifty years, had uprooted themselves in an effort to tend to all the outlying habitations that had had flamens of their own but no longer did. To wander, they gave up their political positions of local government. The exchange was altruistic, but it had a downside. What with this, and the increasing frequency with which lemans relinquished the flamenhood to become lords and ladies, the flamenhood had lost its iron grip on much of the world. Now it had to vie undignifiedly with the atheist nobles for power. And it seemed set to lose more still, as the Divine Cycle wound to a close and the Divinarch grew more and more tired. A hundred and ninety was old for a god.

Humi and Beau sat in the dell for a long time, hugging each other. When the sun dipped toward the glittering horizon, they got up and walked home. Though the hamlet was only a couple of miles distant, a long arm of salt lay in the widest valley they would have to cross, and it was still too bright to venture across. Holding hands, they followed a goat path through the furze around its tip. Humi glanced down every now and then at the salt. Iridescent shrubs and flowers glittered red in the last of the light. Chitinous insect wings flashed.

Beau's face was set and his hand sweated in hers. But her own composure astonished her.

She could taste the difference in the air as they crested the last ridge. Less salty. Below, firelight flickered. The fields and outbuildings of the hamlet were arranged so that they formed a different but equally pleasing pattern from each hilltop: a flower, a star, a face. For centuries it had been slowly mutating. Whenever the Garden men planted a crop, they considered its aesthetic impact on the whole valley, often hesitating for days between, say, flat oats and the slightly darker ringers. They made frequent trips to the ridges to judge and rejudge. Humi usually felt a tingle of appreciation when she saw it all laid out below her—aesthetics was the one topic on which she could communicate with her father and uncles. But now, in the dark, she and Beau hurried down the hill.

The hexagonal courtyard of the hamlet lay right across the road to the salt. The Garden women flurried to and fro, transferring a meal from the inside pantry onto the trestle tables that stood in an oxshoe around the fire. Six chanticleers hung spitted over the logs. Godsbrother Sensuality was ensconced in the only chair, halfway along the oxshoe. His Calvarese leman Miti sat in his lap, reporting the activity in a hushed flow of words. For a moment after Humi and Beau appeared, his voice was the only sound besides the hiss of the fire; then the women's tongues loosened again. But the tension didn't leave the air.

Beau's face drooped as he noticed it. But he said nothing. "Gent wants to settle with me about my fowls," he whispered, and strode off with his brother. Joy, Humi's youngest aunt, sent her inside with a smack to change her dirty skirt. She had to look pretty for the flamen, though he could not see her. "Inside" was the Gardens' side of the courtyard, as opposed to the oxen's side, the kitchen, or the fowl's. An unbelievably cramped four rooms. While the darkness and head-height rafters were comforting, no one could spend a day on the hillsides and not be stunned by the smell. She breathed shallowly as she fumbled her only dress on. When she came out, tugging her hair free of the neck, she went in search of her mother.

Faith was stirring a giant pot over the fire while Tici, Humi's grandmother, turned the chanticleers. Faith clung jealously to the good looks that had made her a near choice for a ghost. Her hair was like a mass of leaves, her fur chestnut brown, tinged ruby by the flames. Humi took up a position at Faith's side and locked her hands behind her back. *"My manipulative little murderess"—watch and see if she doesn't call me that,* she thought. The scathing nickname was only half fair, for Humi had never tried to manipulate anyone. But the whole world would despise her as a murderess if they knew about the Awful Thing she had done when she was nine years old. She did not want to think about that. Why had she remembered that— "Mother?"

Faith glanced up. The familiar half-annoyed, half-scared look came over her face. "What?"

"Mother, I want to go with Beau." The enormity of the thing hit her again even as she spoke the words. Her grandmother, who was deaf, turned the spit tranquilly. The fat dripped off the chanticleers; light spluttered up the far walls of the courtyard.

"You want to leave?" Faith said at last. "Why?"

It came out in lumps and spurts—the persuasive, logical reasons that she and Beau had dreamed up. Beau had convinced her, but she doubted her ability to convince Faith in turn. She twisted her fingers behind her back.

"There's no one else I can marry—" It wasn't working. She knew it wasn't.

Faith drew a deep breath, stirring the stew violently, mechanically. "I bore two daughters, Humi. Neither of them was beautiful, though of course I can't say what Thani might have become. But I bore no daughter who wasn't so much greater than me that she could have lived out her life here without going mad."

"Mother? What do you mean?"

"You can go!" Faith stirred fiercely. "Now get away from me!"

Humi backed away. Eventually she bumped into a bench, where she collapsed and sat with knees drawn up, staring around at her family. Maybe they saw the look on her face, for not one of them enlisted her help for anything until the time came to sit down at table.

Faith took a seat a good way away from Humi, next to her friend Emish, a widow from Garden Vale, half a morning's walk over the hills. She was staying at Beaulieu "to help with the harvest." Humi could not look at them—she was still stunned. But she was aware of how they kept glancing at her over the fire pit.

Godsbrother Sensuality rose to his feet. Miti hopped down to stand beside him, and his voice grew suddenly audible: ". . . fresh-baked bread, chanticleers, and I think it's a vegetable stew. The table is suitably decorated with small statuettes of the Divinarch."

"That will do for now, Miti." The flamen had a deep, unsweet voice. "Brothers and sisters, the gods thank you for your faith and your hospitality toward their servants. And especially tonight, they thank you for your gift to them. The flower of your children, Beauty Garden, to be preserved forever as a ghost."

Humi realized that Beau's mother, Mercy, was crying. She sat next to Humi with tears flooding down her face. Her husband, Perance, held her tightly, but she did not take her streaming eyes off the Godsbrother.

"The councillor to whom Beauty is to be given is an atheist lady," said the flamen. He said it as casually as if he were saying Beau would be given to his spinster aunt.

Not that flamens had spinster aunts, Humi thought in a flash of illogic. The Gardens sucked in their breath in horror. An opponent of the flamenhood? It was as bad as if they had been told he would not be a ghost after all.

Beau himself, whose sole consolation, Humi knew, had been that his ghost would gratify a god, looked like a caricature of shock.

"Councillor Belstem Summer—surely even here you have heard of him?—plans to inaugurate his daughter, Aneisneida, in a seat on the Ellipse. She is replacing Godsister Purity, who died in an accident with her leman, leaving no successor. There will be great pomp. The ceremony will be decorated with the finest ghosts Salt can offer. Your son, Beauty, will be an example of the virtue which we flamens can still find in Salt." Humi couldn't believe that any of her family dared to raise their voices, but her uncle Cand spoke, choking on his indignation. "Godsbrother, why do the gods disgrace my nephew by giving him to one of the nobility? Why do they smile on the atheists?"

The flamen turned his blind head toward Cand's voice. The crystals in his eye sockets took on a fanatical gleam. "The wish of the Divinarch is that Aneisneida be honored like any flamen who becomes a councillor. We do the gods' will. Now be silent before I forsake your table and your hospitality, Godsman."

Cand bowed his head. The food steamed, growing colder, while no one dared to move.

At last Godsbrother Sensuality rumbled, "May the gods take pleasure in the food we eat," and sank into his chair. Thankfully, Cand's wife, Prudence, leaned around him to carve a chanticleer. Humi mentally heaped the chattering voices on top of her head, waiting for her trembling to stop.

After the feast was cleared away, and the flamen established in the only "good" room in the courtyard, Faith and Emish volunteered to watch over the sheep. Admitting that Emish had to earn her keep if she was to stay at Beaulieu much longer, Humi's father, Reng, let them go.

They bobbed away in the darkness, the dogs leaping around them.

Larger salt animals tended to keep away from the human country, with one notable exception: the predators. These beasts with their rows of fangs, their talons, and their innocent, heart-shaped faces, had no matches for bloodthirstiness in the salt or out of it. And they had developed a taste for humans' livestock—and whenever possible, humans themselves. "Guarding the sheep" had two traditional implications. One was that of the most dangerous work on the farm. The other was that of a lovers' rendezvous. In this case, the latter applied.

Hours after Faith and Emish left, Humi's eyes were still dry. She lay next to Tici in the backmost curtained-off section of the house, on their scratchy pallet under a feather quilt too hot for the season. Tici whuffled softly. A few feet away on another pallet, Joy and her husband, Uth, slept deeply after having coupled. Six-year-old Merce and their baby, Asure, breathed more quickly.

Overhead, a predator screamed. Humi sent the gods a quick prayer for any sheep that Faith and Emish might have missed when they gathered the flock into the fold. If once the predators got a whiff of their blood, they wouldn't survive long.

But no predator could smell so delicate a scent as blood through the heavy odor of Beaulieu.

Humi knew it was the last time she would lie wrapped in this thick, stuffy darkness, surrounded by people who cared about her. She made it last for as long as possible by keeping herself awake, seeing how many fingers it took her to weave braids in the frayed edge of the quilt. But the threads were short—she couldn't get it any lower than two fingers, and those on her right hand.

TWO

The next morning, Godsbrother Sensuality worked a miracle. The wandering flamens who visited Beaulieu didn't by any means always repay their hosts with miracles: it was too taxing, not only for the flamens themselves but also for the gods.

Breakfast was cold meat and barley porridge, eaten in the courtyard. Over in the feed that Gent had scattered, the chanticleers, quails, and pigeons which were no longer Beau's responsibility sang their shrill morning music. Beau sat directly across from Humi, looking like a lamb that knows it is mutton. He kept trying to catch her eye. She stared devoutly at the statuette of the Divinarch on the table in front of her. Her body felt chilly in the breeze. The sky was the hue of a chunk of glass shivered inside; the ridges reared bleak and brown against it. Her family finished eating and stood uncomfortably around the courtyard, gazing anywhere but at the Godsbrother, who still champed at his porridge. Miti's dark eyes dared anyone to stare.

Humi mustered her courage. "Godsbrother? My name is Humility." She got the syllables of her hated full name out as quickly as possible. "Godsbrother, has my mother spoken with you about me coming with Beau to Royalland?"

A dead silence fell. It seemed that even the birds of the mountain stopped singing. "Ah, yes," the Godsbrother said, pushing himself back from the table, wiping the fur around his lips. "A young woman loyal in your attachments, who will well be able to survive on your own. Hardworking, determined, imaginative. Observant of

Dividay, respectful to your elders, well able to bear children. Useful around the house."

"Humi—" Reng came up behind her and clasped her shoulders possessively. "Daughter, what is this?"

Before she had to answer, a disturbance came from behind the oxhouse. All eyes turned toward it. Grim-faced, putting the dogs away from stained skirts, Faith and Emish came down the road from the salt.

"There's been a killing." Faith's voice carried thinly across the courtyard. "Right under our noses. Eight— *eight!*—of this year's lambs. The predators know they are tenderest, I swear, and pick them out."

Humi's father dropped his hands from her shoulders as he turned to find out the extent of the damage. She stepped back from the babble of questions, signaling Beau that they should go collect their belongings. Indoors, they wordlessly stuffed clothing into flaxen sacks. Humi listened to the splash of blood being scrubbed off hands in the dirty dishwater outside the door. Emish's soft voice described the massacre.

She looked up at Beau. "Why don't I care? I watched the lambs that're in those predators' bellies being born. Why don't I care?"

He looked as though he hadn't slept a wink— glamorously hollow-eyed, desirably vulnerable. "Dunno."

Prudence's voice rose: ". . . they're in the house. Beau! Humi!"

All the family had formed a circle on the bony earth of the road. When Humi saw Godsbrother Sensuality take the center alone, she knew what was coming. Cand said respectfully, "We're sorry to ask this, Godsbrother. But those dead lambs mean the loss of this year's generation. Of course we'll be getting the—compensation—but we may starve first. We'd been reckoning on the little ewes—"

The Godsbrother cut him off curtly. "I understand." The Gardens bent their heads in attitudes of prayer. Silence fell, as profound as if the world had stopped. Humi had watched miracles before: she didn't expect to see anything beyond the way the crystals in the Godsbrother's eye sockets bulged a little, and the sweat started out on his skull. Minutes passed. Two roosters flew at each other over by the fowl house, and Prudence peeked from behind her fingers, obviously itching to flap her skirts at them.

Finally it was done. As the larger rooster, victorious, preened his blue neckfeathers, a shrill *maa*-ing floated from the high end of the valley.

The circle broke up. Laughing, adults and children craned upward to see. Eight little flecks of white on the bleak hillside, standing out like snowballs in summer. Humi sucked in her breath as she watched them straggle downhill. Miti put his arm around Sensuality—odd to see the child half-supporting the big man—and guided him to the permanently ajar gate. "Come on then, you two!"

Faith said, "Daughter."

The three of them stood before her: her mother, her father, and Emish. There were wet splotches on Faith's dress where she'd scrubbed off the blood, but she had taken time to scrape her hair back neatly. She hugged Humi tightly, kissing her forehead. Humi swallowed and clutched her, wanting desperately not ever to have to let go. When Reng joined the embrace, she felt that she couldn't have been happier in Heaven. "Oh, Mother, Father, I don't want . . ."

"Yes, you do. My little girl. Oh, but I love you so much!" Faith whispered. Humi couldn't name the catch in her voice—was it grief, or relief?

Reng pulled her aside. "I shall settle with your mother when you're gone. She acted out of her place. You're the only child I have left—and that means a lot to a man—and you were always a good judge of the beauty of the crops."

Those words helped Humi stay dry-eyed as her cousins and aunts and uncles and in-laws came up and embraced her. Little Asure was the only one who threatened her self-control, chuckling at Humi's solemnity. Beau, too, was running the gauntlet.

"Beauty, you couldn't have done us more honor if you'd started your own hamlet."

"You've made your aunt Faith happier than anyone else in the world could have." (That, viciously, from Reng.)

"You'll come back if you make your fortune, Humi, won't you?" said a small voice.

Humi was walking backward along the road, Beau at her side. "Good-bye!" she called, waving her arms above her head.

"Good-bye," Beau muttered. He whirled around and tramped beside her, head down. The breeze set wisps of hair dancing around Humi's face and lifted the fur on her forearms. The flamen and Miti walked so fast that she had to skip backward to keep up with them. They were talking together as if they witnessed the sundering of families every day. Her family was no more than a collage on the long, low stone wall, spots of all shades of brown, the reverse of the eight miracle-born lambs on the hill above them.

They slept on the road. Miti carried a light knapsack which held all of his and the flamen's earthly possessions; Beau and Humi's flaxen sacks seemed heavier each morning. Five hamlets later, they reached Nece town. Humi and Beau had come a-fairing here every spring and autumn ever since they could remember. Summer Fair was only three sixdays off now, and the quiet little backwater was beginning to gear itself up. Before Humi was born, not only ale but also wine had flowed at festivals, and the craftsmen's doorways had fluttered with bunting. But now the merriment had a somber edge to it. The Divine Cycle was ending. Black ribbons decorated the biceps of the children playing in the road, and the sleeves of the good-wives sweeping their steps. Black Divine Seals (little icons of the Throne) were tarred onto doors and windows. It was symbolic grief, but tinged with very real apprehension: traditionally, with the end of the Divine Cycle came upheavals. Nece citizens bobbed their heads to Sensuality and stared openly at Humi and Beau.

They departed along a country road the same afternoon. Humi and Beau craned their necks to see into the backyards of tanner, blacksmith, sculptor, cobbler, wood-

worker. Dust and steam puffed out from holelike doorways in the hill; on the bare ground outside, oxen
switched their tails and women gossiped. They marched
through the last of the mountains and into the flatcountry.

All over, the harvest was being brought in. Nevertheless, the travelers always found accommodation, for the
people here were as pious as saltsiders. They tended their
sheep, oxen, goats, chanticleers, bantams, pullets, har-
vests, and children with religious stoicism. The little ones
stared at Beau; the adults said that proximity to him was
remuneration enough for everyone's board. When Humi
told them that they were betrothed, they looked at her
with barely hidden jealousy.

They were only three months on the road.

At the beginning of winter, they neared Port Taite. The
little country road merged with a highway which led from
Port Taite to Port Teligne, Domesdys' capital, in the
north. They walked among carts and wains along the
broad, dusty road raised above fields larger than any
Humi had ever seen, toward the break in the cliffs and the
incredible vista of black, sparkling sea.

The city lay below.

"This is *nothing*," said Miti in one of the rare moments
when he condescended to speak to Humi and Beau.
"Why, the population's no more than two thousand. You
should see Port Teligne, or even better, Samaal." Miti had
been born in Calvary, the blazing northern continent
where everyone worked the metal mines the way
Domesdians worked their fields. No doubt his early memories glamorized Samaal, Humi thought dismissively.
How could there ever be more houses and people gathered together than there were here? "Or you should see
Delta City."

The Port Taiteans were Domesdians, with fur and hair
of a thousand shades of brown, yet they weren't country
folk, and they didn't gape at Beau with unashamed awe as
the hamleters had done. As Miti led them into the heart of
town, Beau stared up, down, and around curiously. His
apparent liveliness lifted a weight from Humi's shoulders.
At least a dozen times on the journey, she'd caught him

trying to wreck his beauty. Once she had come on him
kneeling facedown in an oxtrough, silky white curls floating.

She knew she hadn't been paying enough attention to
him. She should have been with him all the time. Instead
she had been talking to the hamlet folk, finding out what
they thought, what they considered beautiful.

Wonders such as coffee bars, couturiers' shops, an Icelandic bathhouse, and a curiosity shop slipped past. The
black ribbons of mourning hung everywhere, twisting in
a little breeze. Port Taite was a pious city. It was one of
those iridescent early-winter days, disconcertingly cold.
The sun shone brightly on ragged clothes and unwashed
heads, on gaudy pictorial signs and the frilly coats of the
well-to-do atheists, on the window boxes overflowing
with winter-blooming flowers.

"Hey, *saltside kids*! Get out of the *street!*" Someone
grabbed both of them by their jackets and shoved them
back against a shopfront, just before a huge-wheeled carriage thundered through the spot where they'd been
standing. "Sorry, Beauty!" the man said, abashed, as he
saw Beau. "Couldn't see your face in the sun. Sorry."

"That's all right." Beau was dazed. Dust rose between
them and the oxcarts which still trundled placidly along
the street. "What was that?"

"One of the young atheists. Watch, 'n'—" Another carriage hurled itself along the narrow street. This time
Humi noticed the animals racing before it, attached not by
a yoke but by reins that glowed red against their dark fur:
draydogs, sleek hounds the size of cattle. "That's the fellow he was racing."

"Wait," said Beau, looking around in consternation.
"Godsbrother Sensuality's gone."

Humi thought it a happy development. "We can find
him later. Or he'll find us. He won't want to lose *you.*"

Beau turned back to their rescuer. "Godsman ... did
you see where that flamen and leman went, the ones that
we were with? A heavy man with light brown fur, a
Calvarese boy about so high ..."

"Godsbrother Sensuality!" The man slapped himself on

the breast. "Don't tell me you are the ghost! Why, the town's abuzz with rumors about your coming. And you are everything they say." He made a tiny bow.

"I—I—" Beau gasped.

Humi pulled his ear down. "He's not telling the truth. If everyone knew about you, you would've been spotted before now."

"The flamen is taking a room on Finilar Street. That is common knowledge. I can lead you there." The man started off along the crowded concourse. Beau beckoned Humi to follow. Annoyed, she caught up to him and whispered, "I don't trust—"

"Nonsense! He knows who Sensuality is!"

But as they hurried along, the man eyed their spindlespun clothing speculatively. "Not much farther now . . . The Silver Boat is the name of the inn Sensuality frequents. The owner puts him up for free." He led them into narrower and narrower streets, where garbage moldered outside closed back doors. Humi walked carefully, wishing she had more than one set of eyes. Two cats flurrying from a window nearly stopped her heart.

Suddenly the man halted. "Here we are!"

"The back entrance?" Humi said sarcastically as she placed herself in front of Beau. The man wheeled around and plunged toward her. The knife in his fist glinted in the sun which came down the alley.

The world slowed down, like a scene viewed through glass. Humi whirled out of the way. Beau rolled away, grunting in astonishment. Eyes darting, grinning confidently, the man turned on her. As she wrenched aside, he thrust past her and lost his balance. Catching his arm, she was on top of him in the grit, her knee crushing his throat. Broken syllables of pleading came from him; but all she knew was a terrifying desire for justice, or was it gratification?

Blood trickled and pooled. Blood bubbled like red spit out of the man's throat, soaking his collar.

The knife fell with a dull clatter. Humi stared in horror. Beau yanked her back, clamping his hand over her eyes. He muttered rhythmically as he dragged her away down

the row of back doors, "You didn't mean to. He would
have killed us. He thought we were helpless. He thought
we had money. You didn't mean to—" over and over, till
Humi shoved him away from her. They pelted on until
they were exhausted. In the relative safety of a crowded
thoroughfare, they examined each other for traces of the
crime.

Luckily, not a drop of blood had stained their clothes or
their fur, apart from Humi's hands. Those were soon
cleansed with spit and polish. She glanced around. Her
whole body was trembling. "It was just here we lost the
Godsbrother."

Beau gazed at Humi for a long moment, and then
crushed her to his chest, right there in the flow of people.
His heart beat fast within his chest. "Humi, I have to
thank you. That fellow would have killed me, too. Think
how awful it would be to die on a pickpocket's knife
when I am destined to die as a ghost in Delta City!"

"Don't speak of it! Don't say it, don't say it, don't say
it—and for Heaven's sake don't *thank* me—"

By taking one life she had saved two. Of course it was
worth it.

*But once you start justifying taking human life, where
do you stop?*

A cold breeze chilled her neck.

I've killed. Again.

She was nine; her grandfather, Old Cand, was fifty-
five; he knew he was dying. She couldn't see why the rest
of her family wouldn't admit it. They treated death as
something to tiptoe round and euphemize, while Humi sat
long hours with Cand and discussed what would happen
to his body when he died, and how his soul would travel
from Beaulieu to Heaven-in-the-salt. Eventually the old
man brought their conversation round to the topic of poisons.

She could still smell the bitter pungency of the cup she
had held to his lips. He had gulped thirstily, eyes starting
out of his fur. As Humi slipped away, stifling the panicky
weeping which came from knowing—too late—that she
had done an Awful Thing, Faith had spotted her. But by

the time Faith found Cand, slumped half out of his bed, it was too late. And after that nothing was the same between mother and daughter. Now she had done it again—

A long shadow fell across their embrace. Beau pulled away. It was Godsbrother Sensuality.

"So my vagrants have found their way back. How was your outing?"

Another figure stood against the lead-paned window of the inn. As Beau stumbled through incoherent excuses, the figure swung, and Humi saw a tall, knife-faced woman in a flamen's robe. A little boy hovered by her side; sunlight glowed deep in the crystals jutting over her cheeks.

Godsbrother Sensuality said with an air of satisfaction, "This is Godsister Decisiveness. She will take charge of you from now on, Beauty."

Regardless of how they'd slept on the road, it would have been out of the question for Beau and Humi to share a bed tonight, though she'd badly wanted Beau beside her to comfort her. Instead she had Godsister Decisiveness. Before they blew out the candle, Humi saw that the flamen was flat-chested as a man, with two anomalous little flaps of fur. Thankfully, the mattress was hard enough that they didn't roll together when they lay down.

When Decisiveness's harsh breath had evened out, Humi lay awake on her back listening to the rowdiness downstairs. The wine served in an inn, Miti had informed her, was far more alcoholic than ale, and the pipes had other things in them besides tobacco.

Look what the city has done to me, she thought, *in a single afternoon.*

In the middle of the night, a nightmare of blood brought her bolt upright in bed, teeth chattering. A thin line of yellow under the door focused the blackness, turning the world the right way up. The sleepy, nightgowned silhouette of the flamen rose in front of it. Scarcely knowing where she was, Humi gave herself up to the cool hands pushing her back to the pillow. Decisiveness's fingers drew away the tormenting sights that replayed endlessly in her mind. For the rest of the night she slept dreamlessly.

They ate breakfast in the inn's dayroom, where sunlight shone dustily through leaded panes and the food tasted of silver; then they went down to the harbor. On the way, Humi noticed that Decisiveness had gained Sensuality's subtle awareness of Beau's whereabouts. The docks consisted of two quays jutting out into the bay. Since it was the windy season, dozens of ships clustered along and between them, so many abreast that in places you could have hopscotched from one quay to the other. Fishing clips rubbed shoulders with shorebound careaks and intercontinental clippers that were so top-heavy with their masts it was a wonder they didn't topple over onto the smaller vessels. Embossed luggage and crates of imported goods lay in heaps outside the holds of these tall ships. The men and women tripping down the gangplanks sported ruffles and sequins that made Humi's mouth water.

Sensuality guided his charges around the fishermen, who were unloading squirming, sharp-fanged netfuls of pickering, to a clipper whose figurehead was a mass of iron petals.

"The *Regal Flower*. Passage for four is booked. She sails with the tide."

Several fishermen, their fur stiff with salt, were bawling at men unloading baggage from the *Flower*. "Wharf's not wide enough for all of us!" Humi expected the lemans to use their unchildlike authority and reach up to touch the men, politely requesting that they lower their voices for the flamens' comfort, but Miti and little Cor merely glanced at each other and shuffled closer to the water. The wavelets knocking the sides of the ship were green-black. There was something sharp and wild about *this* salt. Overhead, terns wailed and dived.

"I shall regret you, Beauty," said Sensuality. "But when you are a ghost, I shall come visit you in the lady Aneisneida's apartments. And I shall see you with my own eyes in Heaven."

Miti's lucid dark eyes rested on Humi. Suddenly, she

found herself hating the thought of his pilgrimage into the salt. If Sensuality lived till Miti was an adult, the flamen would choose a new child leman, sending Miti out into the world to make a life for himself; but if he died before the boy grew up, Miti would have the choice of flamenhood or athcism. To be a Godsbrother or a lord?

She knew which he would choose. His piety was pure and unquestioning.

"Good-bye," he said sweetly. If he knew what she'd been thinking, he didn't show it. Exemplifying the paradox of leman and child in one body, he hissed, "You'll never visit as many cities as *I* have, Humi! But just wait till you see Delta City! Then you'll know Port Taite is nothing more than a heap of rotting wood!—Come on, Godsbrother." They wound away down the pier between the thrashing silver mounds of fish.

Humi had expected nothing from the Godsbrother, but he might have been sorrier than *that* to leave Beau. After all, Beau was probably the greatest beauty he would ever come in contact with. Then she saw a thin black line of blood on Beau's cheek. And she understood. The flamen had *embraced* him—as Humi had never known a flamen to do—and one of the salt crystals had laid his cheek open.

The planks of the *Regal Flower*'s deck were interwoven like threads in a piece of fabric. They gave under Humi's feet, sending her bouncing into the air with each step. This was a Domesdian ship, all made of wood, unlike the metal-hulled and -masted Calvarese clippers berthed alongside. A bristle-faced sailor directed them belowdecks. "Here and here. At yer service, Godsister."

Decisiveness listened to Cor describe the tiny, hatchlike doors. "Only two rooms for us. Well, the ship must be crowded with Domesdian nobility. There are not usually so many lords and ladies mincing around Port Taite's wharves as Cor has described today, I assure you. We shall repeat last night's sleeping arrangements."

Humi shot a worried glance at Beau's face. Could Cor stop Beau from trying to kill himself? Would the child recognize the signs of his suicidal state of mind in time? "Very well, Godsister."

The harbor was crowded and maneuvering difficult. The crew of the *Regal Flower* wouldn't let them upstairs again till the square-rigger had passed the cliffs at the bay's mouth. But then Humi and Beau hurried up to the aft rail.

Domesdys' coast had already spread out into one long vista of cliffs, topped with tufts of winter color. Humi stood beside him in silence, just watching, as the land sank lower and lower until even the black hollow of Taite bay was lost under the glaring winter sky.

Three

On the fifth day out, Humi lay high in the ropes, jolted by the movement of the mainmast. It was a single whippy tree trunk, and as the top lashed to and fro, shudders traveled down it, detouring through her body. A feeling of guilty freedom made her reluctant to climb down. The winter wind blew powerfully; the *Regal Flower* sheared through the foam-topped waves so fast that Humi felt the spray up in her perch.

Now that nothing was visible in any direction but a horizon where the black brine ended so sharply that it might have been cut, her own insignificance thrilled her. The moving, roaring cocoon of sails afforded her regularly spaced glimpses of that horizon. Made of common spindlespun, the sails were literally miracles: they thrummed in the wind, and Humi could see the fabric distending at every stress point. They wouldn't have lasted twenty minutes had it not been for the words which a flamen had put on them when they were made, protecting them against all storms.

She didn't hear the commotion below until one of the sailors monkeyed up the ropes to fetch her. "Young Godsie!" she read on his lips. "There's an emergency!" The look on his face told her what it was. She followed him down the ladder. The ringing in her ears did not allow her to hear his explanation, but she guessed what had happened. She felt sick.

Beau had tried to hang himself from his cabin ceiling. This was his first attempt since they had been on board, and his most serious. Cor had come on him and, being a leman, had not screamed or run but had cut the rope before any severe damage was done. Yet Beau would not or could not speak. Humi slipped down the passenger ladder and held on to it, swaying with the *Regal Flower,* rubbing the brightness out of her eyes. Finally she could see. "We've taken young Beauty in Lady Hempwaite's chamber," said the sailor worriedly. "Girl, hurry, do, he's been asking for you—"

Swallowing bile, Humi followed him to the last chamber on the corridor. Lady Hempwaite, a Royallandic woman, went by the invented name of Zerenella: she was of that breed of nobility rich from skimming the profits off their provinces, taxes which the flamens they had replaced would never have deigned to collect. The cabin was equipped with a double bed. Tall, pale-green-furred, Lady Hempwaite stood at its foot, thin hands covering her mouth.

Beau lay in a fetal position, face toward the wall. Humi lifted the curls away from his neck, fingers trembling with care, and the awful necklace of bruises leaped out from beneath his fur at her. Each bead spread into the next, a swirl of damson and vomit. "Beau!" Her voice wobbled in and out of a whisper. "Cousin, betrothed . . . ! Why did you do this to yourself? I don't understand! Don't you care for me any longer? How could you deprive not just me, but our whole family, of your honor?"

He shifted, and the violet pools looked up at her, but they were so bloodshot she could make out no expression. "They've already got the compensation."

"Oh, Beau." She lay down next to him on the feather mattress. He strained to tighten an arm around her.

"I'm sorry." The words were slurred as if he hadn't used his voice for a sixday. "I didn't stop . . . to think . . . about *you!* Love you . . . just *forgot*—"

It was *her* fault. She'd known she wasn't spending as much time as she could with him, and since they had been on the *Regal Flower* she'd been even less attentive. "It's my fault, my fault!" she whispered. Remorse racked her. He managed to turn his face toward her. Though the smile he gave her was more than half a grimace of pain, it was so loving that Humi felt dirty. They hugged, sobbing against each other's shoulders. "You want to cheat the gods out of their due," she gasped. "You didn't care that they've already paid for you."

"Yes. It was selfish of me."

"But natural," she whispered. "So natural."

He took a deep breath, wincing. "I ought to resign myself. Even if I didn't have to be a ghost . . . no one would ever have loved me for anything except my face."

"Don't think that," she whispered, nearly crying. "*I* love you just for being Beau! And I'd marry you—and—and have your children. No flamen in the world could take that away from us. If we wanted to keep it."

There was a long, long pause. Waves crushed against the hull. "You mean, if we were to . . ."

"Escape." She said it very quietly, into his hair.

He shuddered. "It's . . . impossible."

"No! Once we get to Delta City, we could just slip away—we could have done it in Port Taite." She was scandalized at her own blasphemy. "We could live together. We could get married. Raise crops. Children."

"Gods, Humi, I—"

Zerenella Hempwaite, in front of the porthole, turned sharply on her heel. It hit Humi that her taut posture had expressed not fear for Beau, but avid interest, like someone standing outside a cage.

"Pious little saltrats," she said in her sweet singsong accent, and went to the door. "Even if he *is* to be a ghost, and sacred and all that, someone please see they get off the bed before they tear the coverlet."

She felt herself pulled up, out of Beau's arms. Her head whirled. In the salt-caked daylight from the porthole she could make out no features, but the steely grip on her arm belonged to one person—and it wasn't Lady Hempwaite's maid Wenina; it was Godsister Decisiveness. The tip of the flamen's hood bumped the cabin ceiling. She smelt faintly not of the ship but of solitary meditation, a quiet perfume like dried lavender.

"Humility."

Her voice was gentler than Humi had ever heard it.

"Godsister?"

"I must speak with young Beauty. This is not the first such incident, is it?" She clicked her tongue. "Well, I am not Godsbrother Sensuality, all heavy-handed bullishness, to let a thing like this go by the wayside in case I make it worse."

Beau whispered through his swollen throat, "Godsister?" The cracked wind instrument of his voice gave out. He raised himself painfully on one elbow.

The Godsister set Humi on her feet, straightening her as if she were a doll. But she wasn't paying attention to her anymore. Her voice resonated in the small cabin. "Beauty, I see it is urgent that I speak with you."

And Humi found herself outside the door, leaning her forehead against it, tracing the ornamentation.

She never knew what the flamen said to Beau. But one thing was certain: from that terrible gale-driven afternoon on, nothing was the same between them.

The voyage lasted three more sixdays. Every night as heartbreak pressed in on her, she lay stiffly beside Decisiveness, fists clenched. The Godsister gave sermons every Dividay: Humi forced herself to attend them, sitting among the sailors on deck to hear tales of meshed history and religion like the tale of Waywardness Flamensdaughter, who had defied her mother, a flamen councillor in Delta City, and come to a bad end. Humi was sure Decisiveness was aiming the tale at her.

After the first such sermon, she screwed herself up to speak to Beau. "You've hardly said a word to me in the past sixday. I don't understand."

He closed his eyes, tipping his face up to the blue sky as if for inspiration. "Humi, I have to be a ghost. I know it. That's what I was born for. I did ... those things ... because I couldn't face my destiny. But I have to. This is what Godsister Decisiveness told me: the only way people can show their appreciation of beauty like mine is to preserve it. And just think what a waste it would be ..." He laughed wonderingly. "If I got old!"

"What has she done to you?"

He looked at her, puzzled.

Scarcely daring, Humi put out her hand to touch his face. The rough-silk sheen was the same as always. How could she have ever grown used to living with the most beautiful youth in the world? How could she ever have dreamed of having children by him?

"Please don't ask me to escape with you again," Beau said softly. She started. "I'm having a hard enough time coping with it as it is. I keep forgetting, and then wanting to deprive them of the satisfaction of having me, when I remember that one way or another I have to die."

Humi let out a harsh sob and pushed her face into his chest. He ran his hands inside her blouse collar, stroking the short fine fur on her shoulders.

"I don't understand!" she muttered over and over. "I don't understand!"

He did not answer. She fancied that he had receded so far from her, inside himself, that he could not hear.

She spent a lot of time after that clinging in the tern's nest, losing herself in the giddy, rolling vista that made her feel so small. Finally the sailors allowed her to take watches alone.

It was from the height, perched above the screaming sails, that she first saw Royalland.

Four

Thirteen and a half centuries before, a man whose real name was soon forgotten became the first to sail the Chrume to its source. He was the Wanderer. Some said that the first miracle ever was the fact that his fragile bark completed the journey. But whether by chance, or that the gods had a hand in it, he was alive and in possession of his faculties when he reached the top of the river, having survived rapids, salt desert, and the predators who worried the Chrume like a strip of wet ribbon. He was a tenacious man. When the river vanished underground, he started up the salt mountains. But soon the slopes leveled off into a tableland, utterly barren, where not even an insect moved. The voices of the wind sang in the formations sweetly enough to make him weep for the home he would never see again. It blew salt particles into his eyes. Eventually he collapsed from exposure and starvation. It was then that the gods appeared to him, and while he slept, they bore him to Heaven.

More than a year later, he arrived back in Delta City, blinded by the salt wind but recompensed by the gods with the power to perform miracles. In the years to come, the salt crystals would not discriminate between rich and poor, half-wit and genius; they would bestow the miracle power on every leman with the dedication to seek it. But, perhaps because he was the first, the Wanderer was phenomenally strong. After his miracles failed to convince his people of the gods' existence, he persuaded a party of his friends to come to the salt to see Heaven for themselves—men and their wives and their children. They roamed long and fruitlessly, deep into the barrens.

More than once they came close to mutiny. At last the gods took pity on the Wanderer's pleas, giving the party permission to enter Heaven—but only if the adults let themselves be blinded.

When they returned to their homes, the glowing tales of the children who had been their guides, combined with the power the adults now wielded, gave birth to the flamenhood. This is how women, who had been as badly off as slaves in the Wanderer's village-city on the Chrume delta, gained access to the all-powerful flamenhood. Men and women together, they spread across the world. Before the Wanderer died, he heard that an army of militant lemans had marched to the edges of the world: to the verdant forests of Veretry, to the earth-sprinkled rocks of Domesdys, to the snows of Iceland, to Calvary, whose north coast burns on the equator. The Conversion Wars were a crusade against the worship of straw dolls and underground fires, but also against ignorance and barbarism. But they should not have been called wars. Rarely did the army have to kill anyone in order to make clear the advantages of the flamenhood's arbitration. Soon the last barbarian had sworn piety, and the world became the Divinarchy. The Divinarch himself, with his Divine Guard and his five Incarnations, came to dwell in human lands.

He paved the way for fifteen successors. Over the centuries, more than one hundred and thirty gods personified the Incarnations. The Guard changed so many times that not even the flamens, each of whom memorized an entire history of religious tales as soon as his or her eyesight went, could offer an exact count. The flamens were conscientious shepherds; their miracles could right anything they believed to be a wrong. Until 1208, not one generation of their human flock veered off the path that their parents had trodden. How much the gods themselves had to do with this "dark age," no one knew. But there is a limit to the time for which any entities can hold a world frozen, once they have graced it with even such an impenetrable nugget of knowledge as the miracle power. Stability breeds influences to wreck itself from within.

And all during the centuries of the Divinarchy, there were worse contrasts between the provinces of Salt than ought to have existed. The flamens would have had it that no man live better than his neighbors, even his neighbors on the other side of the world. That was a good and fair system. But they couldn't enforce it to the letter—and that margin of human error was the source of its failure. When Zeniph Antiprophet made his revolutionary declaration that the gods were not gods at all, the gap between classes widened drastically. He showed *some* Saltish—the ex-lemans—the skills which he said he had learned from the gods. Most revolutionary was the method of inscribing speech on paper. His disciples snatched at this invention he called literacy and used it to write proclamations that they hung up in city streets where no one could read them, announcing that their "coins"—another idea Antiprophet claimed to have got from the gods—would be the new medium of transactions, that they carried more power than anything the flamens could invoke.

And it was true, as the flamenhood's numbers dwindled, so did their abilities. It was as if they drew on some pool of energy which was gradually being drained.

Also shrinking were the reserves of able, trustworthy children whose parents would let them take a leman's vows. Even these children, when their flamens died, were often enticed away by the promises of nobility—despite all they'd sworn, despite their friends' pleas. The carefree life of the city peer who let his bodyman or-woman do all the work for him; the power held by the atheist who settled down to head a province; the responsibility-free roamings of an itinerant lord—all were intensely attractive.

No place glowed brighter to the new lords and ladies, in 1352, than Delta City. It sparkled in the constellation of Salt's cities like a firework. And every devotee and atheist in the city knew what an eager part the gods played in its decadence, renewing their role every evening as the sun went down.

White confections of sails had been dotting the horizon for days. Now the *Regal Flower* came into the thick of them. The vessels hailed from every country in the world. Local fishing careaks, crewed by brawny, green-furred men, tacked between the greater ships, but they were outnumbered by the transcontinental clippers. Humi could not believe the height of some of the ships crossing the *Flower*'s bow. Whenever they came close enough, she strained to see their figureheads: fish, birds, gods, flowers, women, insects.

But for size and intricacy, the city ahead topped them all.

Straight ahead, the gleaming brown highway of the Chrume swept out into the sea. This was the main channel of the river. Thousands of lesser canals had already opened off it to form a vast marshy delta, hilly with grass and rock islands of all sizes. A salty smell of fetid grass and fresh blood came to Humi's nostrils. Far, far away beyond the dank winter marsh, she saw a patchwork line of littoral.

Completely covering the rocky island they were built on, Delta City's buildings seemed to project sideways like barnacles over the mouth of the Chrume. As a whole, the city had a queerly agile balance, gripping the rock with its claws like a huge feathery bird.

At first it seemed as though they were headed straight for the tall, rocky cliff itself. But the river's current shunted the *Regal Flower* sideways into the lee of the island. And the *Flower* slipped farther west, caught in the sidewash of the river. By the time they actually reached the cliff, it was gone, and they were among the wharves.

"Oh, gods," Beau murmured, "make me strong."

Humi remembered that this was the city where he was going to die. A tilting forest of masts surrounded them. Flocks of gray and black gulls shrieked overhead. Deltan voices curled from quay to quay, cajoling, threatening, pleading in the names of all the gods. Waste rocked on the water. The girth of each stilt supporting the quays could have contained a small house. Men hopped frantically, very near across a gap of oily water, yelling for ropes. The sailors of the *Regal Flower* sent them whistling across the open space. There was an interminable delay while the clipper maneuvered into its berth; then the gangplank was thrust out and made secure.

The rest of the passengers had still to go below and pack their luggage, but Cor, Beau, Humi, and the Godsister carried their light sacks on their shoulders. They were the first off the ship. "Good-bye, Ollit! Bye, Rate, bye, Cidity . . ." Humi called back to the sailors as she followed Godsister Decisiveness.

From the docks, the city rose into at least six stories of wood and stone. Washing lines, and catwalks, and hanging gardens spanned the streets. Since each story overhung the street further than did the one below, they passed through many stretches of artificial darkness where the top floors had met and melded. None of the streets were more than half the width of Port Taite's, which Humi had thought oppressively narrow.

She didn't see how she could ever get used to living in a maze like this. And these were the main concourses. The roads (or tunnels) writhing away between the houses were even narrower and duskier. She hadn't imagined that her first experience of "the land where everything was green" would be like this! The only green in sight was the Deltans' fur.

Waste skidded under their shoes as they trudged along. Not one oxcart or dog carriage could be seen, though many big-wheeled sedan chairs bruised their way through the crowds. The noise was even worse than it had been at the docks. "Hold on to your bags tightly," said Decisiveness over her shoulder. As she spoke, a man slammed into her and hurried on without apologizing. None of these Deltans seemed to have any respect for the flamen. They shouted carelessly in her face as they did in everyone else's, advertising their wares or fighting or courting in slipshod, nasal accents. Humi tapped Cor's shoulder. "Shouldn't—shouldn't the city be in mourning? I don't see any black streamers—"

A shadow passed over Cor's small face, and he raised his voice to be heard. "This is Christon District. The commoners are mostly atheists. Another district, Marshtown, holds the only concentration of devotees left in the city. Maybe there the people care that their Divinarch is dying. Here no one does, or at least not openly."

Humi stumbled over a root growing out of the central gutter. Cor put out a hand to catch her, and she smiled wanly. Smells of food drifted past her nostrils; moisture dripped from the tunnel roof they were passing under. She stuck out her tongue and caught it. Luckily it was only the condensation from someone's hanging garden.

"Here," murmured Cor to Decisiveness. "Here!" said the flamen over her shoulder, and vanished up a tiny flight of stairs. Beau, whose face had been turned despondently groundward the whole trudge, followed.

As Humi put her foot on the first tread, curiosity struck her, and she craned back to squint at the sign over the door. It bore a crude drawing of a bed and plate. For some reason her relief at seeing that the place was only an inn incapacitated her. She had to wait at the door until her heart stopped pounding. But then she looked up again, and the misshapen plate didn't look so much like a plate. In fact, the longer she stared, the more it came to resemble a badly drawn head.

"Humi!" came Godsister Decisiveness's voice. "Do not stay outside! It is perilous here even during the day!"

"Coming!" She scrambled hastily up the stairs. The twisty stairwell opened into a candlelit hall where Beau, Decisiveness, and Cor stood facing a stranger.

"Godsman Larch." Cor reached up to grasp the strange man's hand. "This is Humility Garden, the companion of our ghost. Humi, Godsman Larch."

"I am entrusting you and your cousin into the Godsman's care, Humi," Godsister Decisiveness said. "I am assured of Larch's worthiness. He is the head of a company of beauticians who have served the flamens since the dawn of the Divinarchy."

"You make it unnecessary for me to introduce myself, Godsister," Godsman Larch said with a twinkle in his eye. He bowed over Humi's hand. "We are the House of Larch. We are just one couturier's establishment in a city which supports dozens, but there is a long-standing bond between the House of Larch and the flamenhood. I mean that whenever the flamens choose ghosts, they are brought here, where it is our honor to ensure that they die in style." He chuckled at his own pun. "The house has cleared out the rest of its customers for the duration of your stay. Godsie Garden, I'm sure your cousin and I shall find each other stimulating."

Stimulating!? Humi thought in disbelief. She said, "I—I'm sure you shall!"

"I am glad you have taken to each other." Decisiveness lifted her head, and her salt crystals caught the light. "I must leave you. We will meet in Heaven, Beauty." Like Godsbrother Sensuality before her, she enfolded Beau in her arms. *He's going to have more scars than he could ever have given himself,* Humi thought wryly.

But then all thought fled her mind, for the Godsister's robed arms came around her, sharp edges pressing into her cheeks, and the harsh voice murmured, "I am sorry, girl. Sorry that I had to take him from you. You've survival instinct enough for two: you would have persuaded him to escape, I think. And you would have done well together. But this is the way it must be." She gave Humi a last squeeze, then departed, flapping away down the corridor like a great hunch-shouldered bird, Cor at her side.

Humi fingered her cheek. She had not felt any pain, but her fingertips came away wet, the fur slick and gleaming.

"Marked!" Godsman Larch said cheerfully. "Some say it's good luck. For your sake, I hope so!"

Five

The other five ghosts who had been chosen for Aneisneida had already arrived at the House of Larch. A Veretrean girl, three Royallandics, and an Icelandic who was probably the only youth in his country with a slender build (Southerners were famous for their layers of blubber). None of them could hold a candle to Beau except the Veretrean, though for the first few days they all dazzled Humi. But since exactly six had been chosen, there was no question of competition—though how the news of choices crossed oceans to reach itinerant flamens in the depths of the countrysides, Humi would have liked to know.

There was a lot she would have liked to know about the House of Larch. As the days passed away, she came to be intrigued by the sheer existence of an organization devoted to producing beauty—and the knowledge that it was but one of dozens in the city. She had nothing else to think about. She felt frustrated, secluded—wrapped in soft wool, with nothing to bump against. Beau had been given a room on the top floor, where winter light came through a window in the ceiling. Here, no one objected to their sleeping together, even in the same bed. Every day, Beau had evaluations and fittings and lessons with Godsman Larch's team of beauticians. Neither of them was permitted to go outside, so Humi came along to everything. At first the beauticians and couturiers and hairdressers ignored her, as they did the other two companions; but she slid closer along the floor until the Royallandic boy Rain moved aside to include her, and there she was, in the circle of living, breathing ghosts, the six most beautiful youths and girls in the world. She did not know why the beauticians tolerated her presence—she was only grateful that they did. Perhaps they found her amusing. Certainly she was not like the other companions, the Veretrean girl's husband and the sister of one of the Royallandic boys, both of whom sat mute and tragic in the corners of the mirror-lined rooms.

Humi loved the whole business of beautification. Along with Beau, she learned how to walk and seat herself in every kind of chair and to pose in doorways or at the head of stairs. She learned how to make an entrance. She learned all over again how to smile and frown. She learned how to flatter her face and body with clothing, how to choose it from the drawings the couturiers unrolled before them—although unlike Beau and the other ghosts, she wasn't actually given any new garments. Most important, she learned how to alter her face with dusts and shadows so that no one, looking at her, would have guessed her to be Humility. The beauticians laughed and clapped when she turned from the mirror, simpering and flashing bespangled eyes, flipping elbowfuls of skirt. After that, some of them went so far as to single her out for attention, whereas before they had simply permitted her to listen. They dallied after sessions to satisfy her greed for knowledge; they chatted with her in the corridors. On one memorable occasion, Godsie Bareed, a young Calvarese couturier, took her out to a nearby tea bar. The Christon streets hit her like a barrage of sound, smell, and sight after so many days locked in pulchritude.

The beauticians even taught her things which Beau did not learn. For example, the method of inlaying a small metal filigree into a cheek—Beau's. One shaved a small patch of fur, then administered an anesthetic. When the head rolled to one side, one began to cut with a scalpel, just deep enough to draw needle-thin lines of black blood. One worked the filigree into place in the cuts, then applied sealant. When it was peeled off some days later, the scars had been transformed into white spiked leaves radiating from behind a white iron flower.

In such a fashion the beauticians made the best of everything Beau had. Yet they didn't change him so much as they *polished* him, replacing instinct with studied elegance. He had never looked more vivaciously alive.

"If it were possible for your ghosts to be extracted from you while you lived," Godsie Bareed said, "you would not have to die. The killing is the most objectionable part of making a ghost. I shall not touch on the issue of your piety now, but I know that for one reason or another, you are all willing to die." She paused in her pacing of the circle of ghosts to crack a smile. "You all understand what conditions permitted you to be born looking this way, and the necessity of satisfying them. And none of you shirk that necessity."

Humi knew she meant, Not even the three of you—two Royallandics and the Icelandic boy—who are atheists. But Humi didn't see what difference it made, any more than it mattered whether they were going to be given to an atheist lady or a god. Being chosen as a ghost was still just as much of an honor—or tragedy—just as profitable for the family left behind.

"Now, let us make your choice of neckline for evening dress a little easier. Grace, your eyes are far apart. It is easy to place too much emphasis on them: one must at all costs avoid the heart-shaped face which will recall the visage of a predator. We are aware of the righteous distaste our gods bear for predators, and even though you are not to be given to a god, they will still see you, and might be offended . . ."

Humi listened, spellbound, storing every word in her memory.

That was a trick she had perfected by the age of twelve. When she chose to, she could relive every bite of the supper at which she had been sitting when the sixdays of practice finally fell into place, and her family's words, instead of arrowing into her ears and hanging for an instant before the next sound tumbled in and overrode them, sank into her memory as if into quicksand. It had been the fat time of autumn. Tici had cooked a great stewpot full of red beans and teajuice. There had been a clotted bottom-of-the-pot crust broken up in each helping, which Humi

had relished because she thought it was oatpudding. Later
the combination of excitement from her discovery and
finding out that it had been blood from the ox that died
had made her vomit. She could remember that too.

But the food at the House of Larch was always good.
She and Beau ate alone in their room. Or Humi ate; since
they had arrived, Beau had barely consumed enough to
keep himself alive. It was part of the interior process
which honed away every cell of excess flesh, erasing every hint of brutishness, turning the muscular farm boy
into an aristocrat. The ring of cutlery was the only sound.
They no longer had anything to say to each other. Beau's
remarks, though obviously intended to indicate an interest
in Humi's life, were so superficial that they hurt. When
they finished eating, they would lie silently under the
blankets until sleep shuffled over the roofs to the leaded
skylight and threw itself down on them, sprawling like a
wanton over their faces.

She woke at night only once during the sixdays of their
residence in the House of Larch. Shouts from somewhere
along the corridor penetrated her sleep. It was Rain, the
ghost from Westchasm with the warm smile whose sulky
sister screamed her desperation at him whenever they
were alone. *That kind of companion shouldn't be allowed
to come,* Humi thought. Evidently the girl had finally
cracked his protective shell, and he was shouting back.
He'd been looking haggard the past day or so—small
wonder, if he had come to fear for his beauty—

His voice spiraled into unintelligibility. Wide awake,
Humi wondered suddenly why she was so hot. The odor
of sweat enveloped her. Springy curls of fur tangled her
eyelashes. She was in Beau's embrace, hugged fiercely to
his chest. He breathed with shuddering slowness into her
hair.

The scent of two people's body smells mingled together was completely new to her. She felt dizzy. She
eased his arms open and rolled to the extreme edge of the
bed. The night was warm—the wool blankets were unnecessary. Her grandmother Tici, right now enduring an icy
Domesdys winter, would have been glad of them. But no.

The Gardens had two hundred sheep now. Tici would certainly have a warm bedjacket.

Humi folded her arms behind her head and gazed up into the stars through the skylight. Far, far above, one bluish dwarf stared down at her through the mist of the constellations.

The next morning Beau gave no indication that anything had happened. And the incident was never repeated. For as it turned out, that night was the last they ever spent together.

"It's time," said the servant who brought their breakfast. A scrub-furred young Deltan whose duties around the House of Larch were multifarious, he had often provided companionship for Humi when she could no longer stand the ghosts' silence. The tray rattled as he set it down. "Get out your finery, Beauty. You're to choose what to wear."

"I *am?*" Beau put one hand to his breast in a studied gesture which said, *Dear me, I have been longing for this chance for many sixdays, but I really don't trust my own taste, or at least I don't want you to know that I do.*

"It's a test," Quen said. "And if I was you I would eat a good breakfast. The palace banquet are *un—*" he planted a kiss on his fingers—"*un*describable—but it's all a test. Ghosts aren't allowed to eat."

Beau glanced at the tray, the steaming bowls of gruel and the tropical fruits opened out like water lilies, sitting in their own orange blood. He obviously had no intention of touching it.

Humi followed the young man out the door. "Quen. Do you have any news concerning me and the other companions?" She'd carved out a routine for herself here—and now it was over, just like that. She realized abruptly that she had not really given a thought to what would happen after this. "What am I to do when they go to the palace?"

"You're to go too, of course. And stick with Beauty till he's chosen. That's what you're here for. To look after him."

"Chosen?" Humi pounced on the crumb of information. "Again? By whom? What's the palace like? Oh, tell me!"

She seized Quen's hands. The empty tray clattered to the floor. "What do the streets look like now? Is there festival, with a procession, and dancing, and food?" She was drawing on her memories of festival time in Nece.

Quen stood stock-still, looking down at her. His hair hung over his eyes in curved green bangs. "Humi," he said at last, "this isn't my place or yours."

"Oh." Mentally scolding herself, she retreated. "But tell me, please—what are we supposed to *do*?"

He tucked his hair behind his ears. His eyes slid away from her face. "Palace gatherings are only for palace initiates. It's not like it was in the days of the flamens. Nobody knows anything that goes on in the palace district now. Anybody that wants to see the new ghosts has to go on a tour. My mum and dad took a tour when the Heir arrived here fifteen years ago, when loads of ghosts were made. They had to wait for hours just to be hustled through the suite where they were stood."

"But Quen, what happens to the ghosts between leaving here and—and being stood in that suite? How are they going to die?"

"Can't tell."

"Why not?"

"Just can't. Its being secret is the most important thing about it. Hardly anyone knows. There, I already let something slip! Every minute I've known you, I've been scared—" Quen's fur quivered, muddying as his dark skin became visible—"you'd ask that question, and I'd answer—"

"Why?"

"Isn't it plain? Has there ever been a companion like you?"

"You mean you were afraid you'd help me because you *like* me?"

"I never knew any ghost's companions before." Shadows moved across his facial fur.

"Then will you help me?"

"I have to get these trays down to the kitchen! Go back to Beauty, Humi!" And he plunged into the next bedroom as if into safety.

Humi stood in the hall while the sweat dried on her palms. Quen had told her enough. A vague plan was forming in her mind. Beau needed her—but for once she didn't go to him. It was only her dress sense he would want now, and she had to have that for herself.

Hope rekindling inside her like an abnormal little flame which refuses to be doused by water or dirt, she went downstairs.

A hush gripped the entire House of Larch. Footfalls far off in the warren of passages creaked like the voices of the house itself, grieving for its latest litter of children.

Humi found Ministra Bareed in the wardrobery, among racks of costumes sewn to fit long-dead youths and girls. Candlelight splashed their racks with gold. For a moment Humi watched the couturier pace restlessly; then she went in.

"Humility! Hasn't Eloquence ordered you to stay with Beauty?"

She hadn't known it was an order. "No, Godsie."

The couturier was a flexible woman, made of night-colored fur and bone. She swayed edgily to and fro. "That boy must be disciplined. He is forever failing to do what we ask of him, because he believes that as a servant, it isn't his station to talk to companions and ghosts. He won't learn that in a pious establishment there's no such thing as a *servant*! Go back upstairs."

"Godsie, don't discipline Quen, please." Humi's voice sounded fragile and false even to her. "It was my fault. I asked him a lot of questions—and he wouldn't answer. Godsie, please tell me what's going to happen."

Ministra's surprise was clear. "You are a companion. I can't tell you."

"You haven't been *treating* me like a companion!"

"We haven't, have we?" She sighed. "We've never treated you as what you are, nor told you how we are failing you in not doing so. To some people it seems reckless of human life to treat a sibling or betrothed or beloved as merely the wings which bear the bird aloft, valuable during flight, to be clipped and thrown aside when the time comes for the bird to be caged. Disrupting two lives to produce one ghost seems unnecessary and even unfair."

"What do you mean—*disrupting?*"

Ministra's fingers traced the embroidery on a coat sleeve. "Look at what has already happened to you. And what is going to happen to you next is the result of being alone, penniless, and grieving in Delta City. You decide what that is."

"Do you mean you don't help me? That's not fair!"

"Whenever the question of the companions is raised, it returns to the flamenhood. And the Godsbrothers and Godsisters will always bow to tradition. It is the only thing on their side nowadays, which makes them a little hidebound. If they disregard it, they knock the ground out from under their own feet."

"Go on," said Humi in a tone designed not to stem revelations. She had perfected it over the past sixdays.

"Belstem Summer and Goquisite Ankh want to revise the entire chain of ghost choice, to make it more efficient and humane." Now Ministra's voice held passionate contempt. "They want to turn us into an *operation. They* want to select the ghosts for ceremonial occasions instead of letting the flamens do it. But we haven't yet yielded one handspan of ground."

"And I . . ."

"Tradition has never made any provision for the companions of the ghosts. Because for you, it's a voluntary thing to come here. Like suicide. There are no laws against *that.*" Her shirt rippled over bony shoulders as she shrugged. "You were told that this involved self-sacrifice on your part. It was assumed you were willing."

"I didn't know it meant being *abandoned!*" *I'd give my eyeteeth for something to hold over the cold bitch.* "I thought you were my friend, Godsie—"

Wrong move. Ministra Bareed's voice went cold. "The friendship of companion means no more to me than the friendship of a ghost. What if I denounced you for defying tradition?"

"Then I would denounce *you* to the flamens." Humi swallowed. "I would call you to account for treating me differently from the other companions, giving me false hopes of getting out of this."

"We should have treated you like them. I agree with you there. But before you denounced us—" her voice held just a faint, traitorous tremble—"I would make sure you could never say anything again."

If threats were the weapon of choice, Humi could best a hint of mutilation any day. Oddly, she felt exhilarated—at least she knew what she was dealing with. "First, I'd kill you with the scissors from your belt. I'd drive them into your throat, and watch your blood gush onto the floor. I'd . . ." She went on.

The room was silent. She could smell the other woman's horror.

"There, that's what is waiting for you if you don't help me! Well, Ministra?"

"I—I accept. Humi, you are not what I believed you to be." Humi could not believe it. She had swallowed the confabulation.

"Tell me what you want me to do for you."

Six

The House of Larch was one of the highest buildings in Christon, commanding a view of the sky from the skylights in the penthouse. A lemon horizon in the west faded spectacularly through green into night. Godsman Larch entered from the stairs, pulling on a frockcoat. "None of you thought to turn on the lights?" he scolded the gloom-shrouded figures. "So modest! Don't you wish us to see you in your finery?"

He was the only one who laughed. Each ghost stood with a fan or purse or decorative dagger in motionless hands, close enough to the others to feel their body warmth, yet alone. Their breath whispered like an unending sigh.

Finally the last candle hissed into life. "There . . . we go!" Larch surveyed his charges, hands on hips. "Strike me down, but you all look stunning!"

His cheer was monstrous. *Is it possible to practice in the House of Larch too long?* Humi wondered.

"Line up, line up so that we can see you. Companions by the sides of your ghosts. It doesn't matter that you're wearing street clothes. No one will take offense—they'll know what you are."

No, they won't, she thought. *Gods grant me luck, and they won't!* She let her eyes drift. Only the soft, ruminative click of Larch's tongue let her know that he had realized what was wrong.

Seven ghosts. Seven ribboned, jeweled, dusted beauties, all with the same blank smile of allure—and only two drab little companions in spindlespun. Oblivious of tension, all seven ghosts gazed blindly and gracefully at nothing.

As the rest of the beauticians entered, Larch's face told them what was wrong. Frightened glances shot from man to woman. Their eyes darted along the row of ghosts. Black spots trickled across Humi's vision. She didn't know how much longer she could remain motionless.

"Well, I see nothing wrong with any of you," Larch said at last. "We should have been in the palace by nightfall. But it will do well to be fashionably late. We'll make all the better an entrance."

And the beauticians fell to chattering and laughing among themselves with an edge to their voices that was far more than relief. A decision had been made. They did not have to act. They did not have to question the premise of intrinsic beauty on which the entire ghosting process was based.

"They look superb!"

"I told you Wella would choose the violet dress—didn't I?"

"I suppose I must pay up."

"Are we going to give her a chance like this?'

"Never bet with a couturier, Godsie!"

"She deserves it. I've never seen a companion like her, and I've been here forty years this Midwinter."

"But who helped her? It must have been . . ."

"One of us. But not me."

"Not me."

"It wasn't me."

And one by one, their eyes went to Ministra Bareed, who stood by herself, gripping her arms, her face as muddy as if smeared with earth.

Beau thought, *What am I doing in this ridiculous hourglass of a coat?*

He couldn't remember. All he knew was that it was crucial to wear it with grace. On the open roof outside the penthouse, sedan chairs waited to take them away. Twisty little alleys led off the open space between the roofs.

Beau was vaguely aware of lights coming from around
the corners of the passages.

His keepers looked like strangers in their court regalia.
Beau could not remember seeing any of them before, although he was sure he must have. They herded him and
the others into the sedans like sheep into the slaughtering
ring. Squashed beside a pale-furred girl whose name he
had forgotten, Beau endured the bumping journey stoi-
cally. Every now and then the porters carried the sedan
down another flight of stairs.

At last they settled to the real ground, not a roof or a
catwalk. A porter hooked back the curtain. It was sheer
luck that Beau kept his balance as he stepped down, for
torchlight blazed into his eyes, disorienting him completely.

Humi glided up to him and breathed exultantly, "Don't
look now, Beau! But they're admiring you!"

They were the focus of a hush spreading through the
entire crowd, stopping men and women in the middle of
their business, attracting every eye. Beau felt his body as-
suming the pose to receive adulation. After a second,
Humi copied him. Her mimicry was flawless. Only a
small part of his mind knew or cared what she was doing
anymore, but that part saw that she had dressed herself up
as a ghost and was parading around with him and the others. It was wrong—wrong! But he didn't know quite why.
She was beautiful: her cheeks were flushed, her eyes
sparkled. Surely she deserved as much honor as he?

He could not anchor his concentration on the question
any longer. A smear of rotten fish was soiling his boot.
This annoyance occupied his mind until it was thoroughly
scraped off against a cobble. Then he tried to take in his
surroundings. The great marketplace in which the sedans
had set them down contained a sprawl of food stalls and
drinking booths. Crowds of green-furred Deltans stood ar-
rested in the middle of eating, shopping, fighting, while
several pickpockets took advantage of the distraction to
go roaming. The air smelled of alcohol. Torches flared
everywhere, turning the sky to soot. As if in a dream,

Beau heard fountains gushing, and far-flung droplets landed on his face.

"Antiprophet Square," he heard one of the couturiers say to another ghost. "Used to be the holiest place in the city. It was called Suvret Cat Square, for the first Divinarch. There were nine flamen councillors in the Ellipse, and they all lived here."

But it's not a square, it's a pentagon, Beau thought. Each side was a garden in which an ornate mansion nestled. The largest mansion of all had no garden in front, but opened straight onto the square: it resembled an overblown six-tier conch shell of gray stone. Its yawning doors looked more like a black maw the closer he came. Colored costumes seemed to flow into each other in the doorway. As Beau mounted the steps, to the stares and chatter of the crowd, his body took over. Studied poise came into play. The colors were all around him. Fingers tugged at his clothes, twitching, pulling. A voice belled out from somewhere beyond, and they withdrew, but only for a second, descending again instantly like harpies.

Behind him, there was a *clomp* of stone. The doors had shut.

It felt as though they had shut the unseasonably warm night in with them. He felt himself begin to sweat, but he knew his body was coping, smiling and bestowing kisses on cheeks, meeting no one's eyes. Dresses and tailcoats and gossamer shawls swirled. A thick stone passage created a moment of cool. Then he was standing in line with the others, Humi next to him—her breath was so quick, her eyes flashed so brilliantly, she had none of the cold, distant demeanor of a ghost! Did no one see? Maybe no one was close enough. Finery ringed them at a distance, and murmuring talk battered against the ceiling of the great room like hosts of birds. An aisle gaped slowly open between the guests, and a man and woman strolled leisurely down it. The torchlight was so brilliant that Beau could see grains of badly applied facedust in the fur around the woman's nose.

The man was hugely overweight, a Royallandic,

dressed in such flagrant bad taste it could only have been intentional. "Seven."

The whole gathering was silent.

"Seven, a good number, Godsman Larch. It would have been too obvious to send six, would it not, Godsman Larch, for the number of Aneisneida's Council seat? I applaud you."

Behind the ghosts, the couturiers relaxed.

Step by step, the man led the young woman along the line, stopping her to peer over her head whenever he saw something that pleased him. "Wish we could stop them sending these little rats," he muttered when they passed Wella the Veretrean's husband. And, "That's the pick of the lot, Anei, you mark my word," as they paused before Humi.

At that unfortunate mistake, Beau realized that the man must be the atheist Belstem Summer. And the frail, pale-furred young woman must be his daughter, Aneisneida.

Beau's future owner.

Beau had no conscious wish to follow her with his eyes, but a tiny part of his mind throbbed: danger.

Don't be absurd. That feeble bundle of nerves couldn't kill a flea!

Then who would?

"A remarkable bunch!" Summer dropped his hands with offensive joviality on Beau's and another ghost's shoulders, peering between their heads. "Remarkable. Simply captivating! Gods' blood be spilled, your bunch have surpassed themselves this time, Larch!"

A ripple of pleasure ran through the beauticians grouped behind Beau. Larch emerged, bowing profoundly before the Summers. "Always my pleasure to serve you or your friends, milord," he murmured deferentially. "And especially—" he brushed his lips across her hand— "your beautiful daughter."

"Not safe to be too beautiful around here!" Summer said crudely. "You old snake, Larch! Let's be glad she isn't in any danger! Haw!"

The whole gathering broke into laughter, even Aneisneida, even Larch—even Humi, in obvious disbe-

lief. Ice encased Beau's muscles, but he broke it to elbow
her in the ribs. Summer was plainly the most dangerous
man in the room. The gods only knew what would happen
to Humi if she exposed herself.

Perhaps the fact that she'd sparked his attention
shocked her silent. She shut her mouth and straightened
her fan. When the guests surrounded them again, a crush
of flounces and flutters, touching, feeling, she played the
ghost admirably, keeping her dignity at the same time as
she let them finger her. Beau kept one eye on her: the fear
had shaken him back into himself somewhat.

At last someone exclaimed, "Why are we standing
here? We should make a tour! Myrthesa, bring that dear
girl along and I'll bring this one. Take her arm. Now, off
we go!"

"The harpsichord salon, Selenie?"

"No, the indoor lily-pond! There's that stunning Icelandic ghost in the centre, you must remember, dear—"

Beau had never seen a ghost. So he was unprepared for
the shocks that awaited him in nearly every room of the
mansion. Ghosts posed clothed, naked, introspective, absorbed in obscene acts, staring arrogantly over the heads
of the crowd. Each hair on their bodies was textured like
diamond. So were the fashions of previous days that they
wore. Visually, they had a curious impasto texture, fur
and clothes and eyes alike, as if they had stepped out of
paintings into three dimensions.

Surrounding each one was an aura of intense, unearthly
cold which ranged from a finger's width to an armspan
deep. But when Beau forced himself through it to touch a
hard, perfect sleeve, expecting the diamondine to cleave
to his hand like iron, it was no colder than wood. And
pure, uplifting happiness dizzied him like wine.

When he touched the next one, he was gripped by a
sexual climax so intense he knew he must be dying. This
ghost was arched over backward, naked, one hand clutching her crotch. The next was in use as a candelabrum.
Wax dribbled down his arms. From him Beau got screaming muscular pain, meant perhaps as a rather romantic reminder of what goes through the household objects we

use every day. He felt sick at the thought of touching any more—but he could not tell the atheists so, and they pushed him willy-nilly into their embraces.

Now they were in a room done in typical Veretrean decor—large, with colored mosaics let into the ceiling at random places, rough-floored, chairs and tables worked in colored glass. The woman named Selenie had encircled Beau in an arm cased in so many layers of silk it might have belonged to a doll. "Of course, Aneisneida will not stand you in any of these rooms, I'm sure. She'll have you in her bedroom or her private sitting room. But isn't it nice to know your *context*? The Summers keep the ground floor for receptions. This chair set was imported from Grussels only last month—admire the scrollwork! The red coloring is, I believe, derived from boiled feathers. I have a similar set in my parlor. My husband's family holds one of the oldest lordships in Delta City. Our patriarch was a disciple of Antiprophet himself."

Humi said in a clear, disgusted voice, "Why, your family is only two hundred years old! *My* family has lived in the same valley since the barbarian years before the Wars!"

There was a brief silence. Another woman tittered, "It talks! Shed the gods' blood, but it talks!"

Missing the point altogether, a man said pugnaciously, "What does it mean by 'barbarian' times? Those were the golden days, when all the world lived free of the flamens' tyranny, and I'd have it respect this house that it's in!"

"You haven't a clue what you are talking about, Lord Moore," said the pure, bell-like voice which Beau had heard before. "Let ignorance keep quiet until it learns sense!"

In response to the voice, a glass dauphin sang a sweet, thin burr against a table. If the voice had not been scaled down to fit the room, the ornament would have broken. "Whose was the voice that slandered the flamens, my pets?" the voice asked pleasantly. As the guests fell away, Beau saw him.

His skin was pale, rainbowed in the torchlight, and furless, yet the effect was not nudity but daring. He was taller than the best man present, but preternaturally slender, light muscles defined under his shirt; his face was sharp and as perversely attractive as an undernourished child's. His eyes were enormous, one brown and one blue.

The muscles at the bases of his wings worked rhythmically; the silk edges of the slits in the back of his shirt lifted and caught in the folds of the muscle casings. The silk tightened across his chest. He scanned the knot of atheists who had taken possession of Humi, his wings caressing his shoulders like a semitransparent mantle.

This being Beau recognized from countless effigies, though they had been carved in wood, without the scintillating coloring. This was the Striver himself.

One of the Incarnations.

A god.

"Pati," someone muttered deferentially.

"I come to see what you've done for your little *sociale,* and find you insulting my people. Ah, well, you do it to our faces as well. Why should I lose sleep over it? Where's Belstem?" The Striver—*Pati*?—tapped one bare foot on the floor. Talons protruded from his heels like spurs. "Not here? Why, I thought he would have stayed to make sure none of you steal his daughter's birthday presents."

"It's not her birthday, Pati," someone said sullenly.

"Well, it ought to be, the blameless child, she deserves a birthday once in a while. Where are they? The ghosts, that is." Pati assumed a mock oratorial stance. "Too often am I misconstrued among you slow-witted humans. It is better to run the risk of overclarification than to fall into the trap of being misunderstood. Where are they?"

When the god mentioned the ghosts, Beau thought he heard a hint of emotion creep into Pati's voice. Out of the corner of an eye he saw Humi push her way to the front of the crowd, staring at the god with heedless avidity.

"I heard one speak just as I arrived," said Pati. "A ghost, giving tongue, now when they are so close to being silenced forever!"

Behind him, the air crackled and turned itself inside

out. Beau had the impression that he was watching a pair
of rapidly expanding sunspots. Then two gusts of hot air
whooshed toward his face, and there was a smell of burning sulphur. Two more beings stood on either side of Pati.

No one screamed or fell. The Striver swung round to
the newcomers with perfect aplomb. "How is business?
as our friends here would say. Belstem hasn't come on the
tour. I'm surprised—he likes to show off his acquisitions.
And his minions quail at showing me the beauties. Can
you believe their impudence!"

One of the gods was shorter than any human. She wore
no garment that Beau could see, and had no wings. An
abundance of dark blue hair poured to her knees, cloaking
her body. Her face was an aggregate of sharp angles: she
had huge, night-colored eyes. "Pati, you're tormenting
them." She minced up to a Royallandic and straightened
his waistcoat with elfin hands. Then she slid in among the
guests, pushing her way between skirts, dropping to the
floor and calling "Coo-*eeee*!" from inside wired flounces.
Some women giggled nervously and danced on their toes.
But no one seemed to resent her intrusion the way they
did Pati's rudeness.

"What are you doing, Broken Bird?" Pati sat down on
one of the glass chairs and idly picked off the scrollwork.
His fingernails must have been as sharp as files. "Are you
cuckolding some poor woman while she stands right next
to you? I know what you get up to, and at the most inap-
propriate times."

One of the ladies glanced at the bits of glass on the
floor and sighed. She called, "Milord Heir! Can't you
make them stop? Dinner will be growing cold!"

As Beau craned, trying to see who she was speaking to,
Broken Bird popped up in front of him. She had used the
same trick of transportation as before, but it was not the
blast of warm air which made him flinch—it was her tiny
blue face pushing itself fiercely up into his. Her hair rose
up to wrap his wrists, and she called piercingly, "I've got
one! Patience! Charity! Here's one, and he's a lovely!" As
she backed out of the crowd, keeping hold of Beau with
her hair, she trod on someone's foot. Judging by the

shriek, her talon had gone straight through slipper and flesh to the tiled floor. "Oh! Oh, by the Power—" she spun, hair lifting itself out of her eyes—"Lady Minnowquay, your daughter's foot! I am so sorry—"

She knelt and began gently to remove the slipper. Someone else grasped Beau by the hair and tugged him into the open.

"Oh, *yes*," his new captor breathed. "Delicious."

"Seldom if ever do I agree with you, Arity," said Pati, eyes misty behind semitransparent violet lids. "But on this we are in accord."

"Mmm . . ." The third god let Beau go. Swinging his leg over another delicate chair, he rocked to and fro, grinding his pelvis into the seat. Then he stopped and considered Beau. Beau could do nothing but smile blandly at them. "I swear that the flamens still choose the best ghosts of all."

"And you envy them in more ways than one, Arity," said Pati quickly, like a knife thrust.

Arity flinched. "I intended that as a compliment to your people, and indirectly to you. You do not deserve a clarification, and you won't get one."

"Clarification is the tool of he who harnesses the masses."

"So you see yourself as a mass, Pati? And myself as your master? I am flattered."

Pati flushed. It was a queer sight. Since he had no fur, he couldn't muddy, but his skin darkened as if blood were rushing into it, and his wings whirred. Arity smiled the tight little smile of a man who has gotten his own back, and he turned again to Beau. His skin was a muted, mossy green. It was stretched over bones less finely drawn than Pati's, and his body was stockier—more like a human's. While he had sharp cheekbones, chin, and eyebrow ridges, his face seemed more capable of human expressions than Broken Bird's or Pati's did.

Yet for all this he couldn't possibly have been taken for a Royallandic man. Besides his naked skin, his shoulder blades were long and streamlined; his bare feet were six-toed, embellished with talons that left scratches on the floor; and his finger claws could have taken Beau's eyes out with a single twist. His hair was a strange, soft purple-brown which a human would have assumed was dyed. Beau thought with a sudden flash of enlightenment: *Now I know why the gods value beauty so much. They're not beautiful themselves. That makes sense . . . doesn't it?*

"Well, Beauty," Arity said, "you certainly have style. Let me compliment you on this coat. Can I have it after you are dead?" He plucked at Beau's sleeve. Beau already regretted choosing the ludicrous garment. The brocade was the color of unripe corn, with white lace spilling from beneath it at cuffs and lapels. The collars, stiff as sepals, framed his face like a flower, deepening his golden fur to ochre. He had enhanced his eyes with violet sap. *Oh, well.* He posed, presenting Arity with the full effect.

"Oh. Oh, strike me down." The god stroked Beau's cheek. "Little boy, will you go to bed with me? I want to fuck you and fuck you—"

Pati had recovered and was violently finishing off the chair he sat on. "Shut up, Heirloom. Don't make the poor thing sick." He turned to Beau. "Go away! We don't want you!" And to the rest of the gathering: "All right, get out! Go eat your banquet, drink your wine, indulge yourselves like hogs!"

Broken Bird tied off a bandage around the foot of the girl she had injured. "I can't *tell* you how sorry I am to spoil your evening, darling. But go to Lady Summer and ask for proper care. Then maybe you'll be able to dance." She smiled, brushed a kiss across the foot, and was gone in a *pouf* of air. The girl and her mother hurried out.

Pati guffawed rudely at their backs. "Erene!" he shouted into the next room. "I know you're there somewhere, but you've done a hell of a good job on your face this time. I didn't spot you in all of ten minutes!—Go on, Beauty—"

And Beau bowed, turned, and went, as fast as was graceful. "Don't break things just to relieve your boredom, Pati," he heard Arity say. "I can do anything I want without resorting to destruction." And he balanced on the back of the brittle chair, making it spin round and round, graceful as a butterfly.

Humi was waiting for Beau at the door. The lumidust on her bosom was marked: she must have let the Deltans touch her to satisfy their curiosity, as docile as a true ghost. She was staring with such absorption at the gods that she hardly saw him.

"What are you waiting for?" Beau hissed. "They'll guess you're not really a ghost!"

Her face went blank and her mouth opened. Amazing how she had made her lips look full and pouty. But, oh, yes! He shouldn't be speaking! The episode with the gods had jolted him completely back into his own body.

"What's that!" Pati was peering toward them keenly. "Another ghost? Is *this* the one that I heard talking?"

"Don't be ridiculous, you half-winged throwback," Arity said. "Let the poor things go! You can't get anything out of them—they're dead on their feet."

But Beau felt the Heir's keen gaze fix them for a moment before Pati garnered his attention with a dig which would have cracked human ribs. That image of them stayed in Beau's head for the rest of his life: the most revered creatures in the world perched twirling on the backs of chairs, in an empty room with blood smears on the floor, quarreling over the metaphysical qualities of human ghosts.

"Seafood, dear?"

Humi let her eyes drift over the plump fingers extending the fork. The slice of flesh was white and flaky, but dense like beef. Mutely she turned to look at the lady.

"A water porcupine. Very slow and ungainly, my dear. The young men train dauphins to catch them. Of course, there are hardly any left in the marshes, so this is a real rarity."

Humi shook her head slowly.

"Very well, then!" The lady—Arolette Meadowlord, her name was—flicked the slice of porcupine onto her own plate. "But my dear, you've not eaten much!" She gestured vexedly at Humi's plate, which was littered with samples of this and that. Humi had in fact not eaten a bite, though she was hungry. She realized that earlier, in the parlor, she had been inexcusably reckless. Now she would have to be on her guard. Death might be in the water porcupine or the salicornes, the sea rice or the finger rolls. She dared not risk finding out how the atheists had chosen to kill her.

Lady Meadowlord fell to conversing with her other neighbor. Lady Meadowlord had, it seemed, paid cash for the privilege of sitting next to Humi, and she was angry that she couldn't make her talk.

"You coarse new nobles!" the old lord on her other side said vituperatively. "You are not accquainted with palace etiquette. You made your money raising deer in the snow!" With their white fur and heavily built bodies, the Meadowlords were patently Icelandic. "What does a herdsman's wife know of ghosts? Ex-lemans such as myself know that they are not *supposed* to eat, my dear enlightened lady, any more than they are supposed to talk. I saw the ghosts that were chosen for Arity's inauguration. Look at her: she knows her place, even if you don't!"

Humi had dropped her gaze to her folded hands. She'd buffed her nails and painted little designs on them. The lumidust on her hands made her fur look like gold-and-silver plush instead of dead stubble.

After a while she dared to look up again. The banquet hall was the largest space she'd ever seen enclosed under a roof. Frescoes of gods and men cavorted all over the vault above her, dim under a layer of grime. The tapestries which ornamented the ribbed walls were stained and motheaten with age near the top, but grew steadily richer as they descended toward the flagstones. The voices of the guests rushed like a river under the vault.

She was sure that behind his dreamy eyes, Beau, at the next table, was far more alert than he should be. And it was her fault. Why had she given him cause to worry? The chink of silver and glass filled her ears. A procession of servants carrying trays blocked her view of him. There was Wella at the next table. There were Cienci and

Telli—at least she thought it was they. There was Ameli, the petite, pious Royallandic girl whom Belstem Summer seemed to have appropriated. Against all custom, he was forcing her to talk and laugh with his daughter. Anei-sneida looked as though she were in worse pain than the little ghost was.

Torches flared over the exits. In the arched passage opening directly across from Humi stood a plain young Calvarese woman in a cherry-colored gown, holding Rain's hand. Her unsubtle gestures suggested that she wanted his company. *But my sister,* objected Rain with vague obstinacy, uncurling a hand toward the hall.

His sister stood like a green stain between the best tables, noticed by no one except the scurrying servants, who ducked around her. Her hands wrung her skirt. Staring around for Rain, she looked wild with fright.

Leave her, the Calvarese woman gestured impatiently. *Come on.*

Rain went. His sister scanned the guests ever more desperately. As people began to notice her, she picked up her skirts, chose an arch at random, and pelted into it. Humi shivered, clasping her empty goblet tightly. It was the skull of a salt wolverite, the gaps sealed with silver.

"Excuse me," said a voice at her shoulder. "I've been observing you with fascination, milady ghost, and I couldn't help noticing you've drunk nothing but water. There's no custom forbidding ghosts liquor. Some ladies hold that it's kindest to give them as much alcohol as they'll take; though I don't believe this, I would like to pour you some wine. May I?"

Humi turned slowly, controlling her movements right down to the eyelashes. It was her other neighbor, a young Royallandic man with a deferential, attentive manner. His hands were large and knot-muscled. She pushed her cup toward him, and he poured. "I am a merchant," he said, "born in Westchasm."

The wine eased like red oil toward the lip of the goblet. She nodded for him to stop. She thought she liked him. Where was the overfamiliarity with which atheists like Lady Meadowlord hid their curiosity? On the other hand,

where was the nervous revulsion that others displayed?
Until lady Meadowlord gave up on Humi, the merchant
hadn't tried to attract her attention, but he didn't seem
ghoulish, like those whom she had seen staring at her
from corners with greedy longing. He was treating her
like an ordinary person.

"My aunt is the head of the merchants' union in
Westchasm," he said. "She sent me to negotiate a trade
agreement with the lords of Delta City. The road is dangerous, especially these days when so many people are
leaving homes that are no longer hospitable, and we
needed to arrange security for our caravans. I was eager
to see the capital of the world—and it has not disappointed me."

She nodded for him to go on. The torches burned down
and were replaced. Belstem Summer's laugh roared out
more and more often as he grew drunk. A party of musicians entered the hall and, without commanding attention,
began to play. Arias leaped up into the vault, echoing so
that it sounded as if fifty men rather than a dozen were
playing. Bows darted across violins, cellos, and basses;
fingers walked the keys of cornets, french horns, and sax-
ophones. One by one, couples rose to glide between the
tables. The change in the atmosphere was magical.

"Ghosts often do not wish to dance," murmured the
merchant. "But, my dear, they are allowed other plea-
sures. I do not hold out much hope—but I swear you've
captured my soul."

Dishes and white cloths had been swept together from
the tables. The banqueters who had overindulged relaxed,
watching the dancers drift between the tables in open
spaces that seemed made for the purpose. The merchant's
hand rested lightly on Humi's sleeve.

This did not seem right somehow. But she heard her
tongue betraying her. "Yes!" Lady Meadowlord stared at
them, agape, as the merchant stood to give her an arm. He
was taller than she had supposed, with the muscles of a
fisherman beneath his rust silk cutaway coat. Lace cuff
brushed lace cuff as he took her hand. They wove between the dancers toward one of the far arches.

"The Summers' mansion is very large," the merchant whispered. "Surely not all the rooms are occupied."

Humi laughed. She felt electricity wriggling between their joined hands. *It's the custom,* she thought euphorically. *The custom!*

But not one possible retreat in the Summers' labyrinthine mansion remained empty. More often than not, the alcoves were occupied by other couples, faces buried in each other's necks, oblivious to the world.

"I think we shall have to return to my lodgings," the Westchasm merchant whispered to Humi after they had tiptoed past the third couple engaged in actual coitus. "If you do not mind, milady?" She nodded. "I hoped that we should not have to go outside. But it isn't far. I'm lodged in Marshtown."

They left by a back entrance and picked their way through a brick-walled cleft in the building to the square. The merchant hailed a sedan and gave the porter a complex string of directions. Inside, in the jouncing dark, he began tentatively to kiss her. Could he tell that she had never kissed before—except Beau, once, when they were fourteen? The touch of mouth on mouth had been an unarticulated taboo between them which kept them chaste. The young merchant nibbled her lips, and his tongue licked her teeth. Abruptly, he pulled her over onto his lap.

The porter knocked on the side of the sedan, then drew back the curtain. Humi allowed herself to be led up to the front door of the house before which they had stopped. The street was a dark, canyonlike curve of shops and tall houses, all shuttered, all quiet. The porter's white livery glowed like a target where he stood by the sedan. The stars shed a misty glow over everything. When the merchant unlocked the front door, it released a dusty whiff of perfume and spices and dust.

"Up here, sweet ghost," breathed the merchant. He led her up a wide, crooked flight of stairs. At the top, she heard somebody screaming like a hare, on and on behind a closed door. The merchant grimaced and hurried her on. "The other lodgers. I shan't stay much longer—the house is not of such good repute as I thought when I came here." At the end of the hall he pushed open another door.

Two torches burned on either side of a large bed. Cascades of soft, thick lace curtained the windows, and a vase of giant speedwells stood on the floor, suffusing the room with fragrance. An empty doorway revealed further cluttered rooms.

"Oh," Humi breathed, forgetting herself, "oh, how beautiful! Milord—" she caught his hands—"Milord, I'm a virgin. Please be gentle . . ."

His throat jumped. He smiled tenderly down at her. "I'll be as gentle as I can. It will have to hurt a *little,* but I hope that if you are in enough pleasure, you will not feel the pain."

She pressed her forehead against his incongruously powerful shoulder. "Milord . . . what is your name?"

After a moment he said, "Ziniquel. My name's Ziniquel."

She whispered it time after time as he began tenderly to undress her. She shivered when her dress slid down past her breasts and then past her crotch. Thank the gods she'd taken the time to rub lumidust all over her body, not just on those parts which showed outside the dress. She thought with a thrill of pleasure that she must look like a statue in gold. Ziniquel caught his breath. "Little ghost, how corporeal you are! And how exquisite!" He pulled off coat and shirt, lace collar and boots. She could see the bulge in his silken pants, but he didn't remove them yet; smothering one of the torches with a cloth hung below it, he swept her expertly off her feet, laying her on the bed.

Later he whispered, "Here . . . hold this flower. I want to see how it goes with your fur. I see you in both bronze and gold as the torch flares—" By this time it was almost burned down. Sated, sleepy, she knew that most of the lumidust must have rubbed off. But perhaps he didn't notice in the low light. Perhaps he was no longer looking at her objectively. Her body was sore, yet more supple than she could remember ever having felt. He closed her fingers around a giant speedwell. "Hold it to your nose. No, don't ... I see you as a wild little thing, brimming with very real violence and passion ... fling out your arm like this. Raise your hips. Oh, for a few scratches ..." He seemed to be talking to himself. "May I?"

Where had that little knife come from? She didn't care. She was happy to please him, and it didn't even hurt when he started slicing the skin of her chest as if preparing her for a metal filigree. He dropped his head to the slices and licked, smearing the blood artfully. "Ohhhh ..."

And his lips were on hers again, and she hardly even noticed when he drew suddenly away from her and the air rushed between their bodies. She twisted her hips, begging wordlessly.

And he was reaching below the bed, his eyes receding into a chill, untouchable distance. In his hand was—

"No!" she screamed, writhing away from the snakelike jab of his hand. The speedwell's petals scattered as she threw herself off the bed. He came on, eyes like frost, all signs of desire gone.

They fooled me after all. So this is how I am to die—"I'm not a ghost! I can wash it all off!" She backed into the open doorway, casting around for water. "I never knew my disguise was *this* good! I'm not a ghost!"

Water. A sinkful, ledges littered with bottles and brushes. She snatched up a sponge and doused her face. *Why* had she rubbed the dust in so well? As Ziniquel reached her she dropped the sponge, breathing hard, fur spiked and wet. Drops turned black as they reached the blood on her chest and mingled with it. She tucked her hair behind her ears—she could do something as ungraceful as that, for she was Humility again, the illusion of beauty dispelled. "See? I'm not a ghost, am I? You can't believe it now! Look how ugly I am!"

Slowly, Ziniquel came back into his eyes. He lowered the syringe. For a moment she thought she would collapse. She grabbed a towel and scrubbed her face dry. "C-c-can I g-get dressed?"

"Yes! Yes, by the gods, put some clothes on!"

Unsuccessfully she tried to do up the falseribs of the

dress and keep an eye on him at the same time. He shook
his head briefly, then came and stood behind her to fasten
it. He had put down the syringe, but all the same it took
all her courage not to shrink away from him. "What—
what was in that?" she asked.

"Oh. Salt aconite, for intense but fleeting agony." He
finished the hooks and eyes, then moved away from her
to light more torches. "I'll probably still have to kill you.
Don't get cocky. My reputation will never survive my
having been tricked like this. You're very homely; a pity
you are not a little thinner, then that bone structure would
show—but you'd lose your figure."

The room blazed with light. It must have been close to
three in the morning. Whoever had been screaming,
downstairs, had been reduced to moans. Ziniquel made a
face. "Hear that? That's Mory at work. She is the cruelest
of us all. I don't know that I *should* kill you—there might
be a better way . . ." He cast his eyes over her.

She'd sidled away until her back was to the wall. Now
she edged nearer to the vase lying on its side.

"Don't even think about it." Ziniquel sat on the end of
his bed and began to dress. Not just his manner, but his
voice had changed. No longer was he the gentle, romantic
merchant from Westchasm. Now he was a matter-of-fact
killer. No longer handsome—far more dangerous. "I
could kill you with my bare hands. But I have to think
about it. That was a good disguise. It had to be, to fool
me. That's got to be worth something."

"I don't understand." Humi failed to keep her voice
even. "You made me believe in you, and then you tried to
kill me. You *did*, didn't you? It isn't all just a dream?"

"Wish it was." Ziniquel nipped shut his boot buckles.
Then he looked up. "And I bet *you've* killed, yourself!
Only another killer would have guessed what was coming. This has *never* happened to me before. Don't deny
it!"

Humi knotted her hands, feeling her lips go dry. Was
she mad to trust this man? "Murderess. That's what my
mother used to call me. Manipulative little murderess."

She wondered if she had just lost her last chance to

live. Survival would be enough for her right now. She'd be happy to be on the streets, where Ministra Bareed would have sent her. *Oh, gods! Pati, Broken Bird, Arity!*

Ziniquel Sevenash leaped to his feet and hugged her. Stunned, she held on as he capered around the room, cannoning into the coatstand, skidding in the dirty water. "Erene, Mory, I'm on my way now!" he crowed. "Girl, what's your name?"

"Humility—"

"Hmm. I bet they call you Humi. See, tonight we thought all but one of us would get a ghost, and then there turned out to be seven of you—enough for us all. But praise the day that I drew the short straw! You're going to be a ghostier."

"A . . . ?"

"There are seven of us. Each of us holds a seat on the Ellipse. Where do you come from?"

"Domesdys—"

"Marvelous. We haven't got a Domesdian as either master ghostier or apprentice at the moment. Oh, Humi, I'm going to show you everything!"

"You mean—you make the ghosts? *You?*"

"Isn't that obvious? Of course!"

"My cousin is a ghost. If you're telling the truth, then he has been—*chosen*—by another of you." *Beau! Was that you screaming?* "I have to see him. Take me to him."

"Erene has him," Ziniquel said annoyedly. "Do you have to?"

"Please!" she begged. "You can't *not!*"

"Oh. Oh, strike the gods." He blew out breath. "It would have to be Erene. She and I are not the best of friends. But if you must—you are going to be my apprentice—we should not start by disagreeing—"

He placed a hand in her back, where the falseribs cinched her waist so small he could have circled it with two hands, and guided her into the hall. It was still dark. They mounted two more flights of rickety stairs to a landing where starlight came in through skylights of thick, flawed glass. There was only one door. Ziniquel pushed it open.

Another bedroom, but far more opulent than Ziniquel's—obviously a woman's boudoir. Feathers nodded from the torch brackets. The circular bed was strewed with little puff pillows in jewel hues, and rugs of painted skin covered the floor.

The door clanged shut behind them. In the adjoining room, something fell to the floor and a woman let out a sharp exclamation. *"Hell!"* The voice had an edge of exasperation so raw it scraped the ears. Ziniquel slid to the doorway, quick as a snake. Humi, following, dug her fingers into his shoulder. The next room was large and messy—a workshop like Ziniquel's. Something whitish spattered the boards next to a dropped syringe. In the far corner Beau crouched, nude, shaking. The woman turned on Ziniquel, furious. "What the hell?" Steel-colored hair slid from an elaborate, half-undone coiffure. Her gray-furred face was wrathful. In one hand she gripped another syringe. "I'll deal with you in a minute!" She began to edge backward. The sheer, deliberate stealth of her motion made Humi's spine crawl. Beau did not see how close she was coming until she tensed, ready to whirl and leap on him, and—

"Beau! Ware!" Humi screamed shrilly.

Beau scurried further into the corner, letting out tiny noises of terror. The woman let the syringe fall and stood up. Her rage seemed to drop away from her like a series of husks. Underneath, she was a small woman. Her dress was crumpled off one shoulder, showing the breast. "Ziniquel, once again, what are you doing? What was the very first thing Constance taught you—could it have been never to interrupt a master at work?"

Ziniquel leaned an elbow on the doorway. "Nice job you're doing here, Erene. I can feel those waves of positive emotion coming off that ghost."

"Don't start. Just don't start. Who is this? Where's *your* ghost?"

"This is my ghost."

Humi edged out from behind him. She didn't want to get too close to the woman. Was there any way she could reach Beau?

"She doesn't look like much." The woman flicked an eye over Humi. "The flamens' standards must have dropped considerably if they chose *her*."

Ziniquel sighed resignedly. In a few well-chosen words, he told her everything Humi had told him about coming to Delta City as Beau's companion. He ended: "And I'm taking her on as apprentice. Since we're going to have a long, productive relationship, I thought I would begin by indulging her wants. This ghost is her cousin. She wanted to see him before he dies."

"You're taking her on?" the woman Erene said. "Ziniquel, is she good enough? Or is it just that you're so covetous of an apprentice that you think happenstance is providence?"

Ziniquel's moss-green fur bristled. "Erene, you don't have the right to ask me that. I'm a master ghostier, just like you. But I'll answer anyway: no matter what else I might sacrifice, I'd *never* put my art in jeopardy. You, of all people, should know that."

"All right. She's good enough. I'll trust you on that." Erene put her head on one side and gazed at him. "All the same, I don't know whether you're ready for an apprentice, Zin, especially one only two or three years younger than you. You're just too raw."

Ziniquel stared straight at Erene, challenging her. "I was as ready as anyone ever is."

She stood silent for a long minute, as if trying to remember. Finally she nodded. "Yes, you were."

It was a painful admission, Humi could see.

"But that's not what matters here. This business of apprentices is trickier than you may think." Her eyes moved to Humi.

Summoning boldness, Humi stared right back. Erene was old enough to be Humi's mother—but her soft gray fur covered any lines that might lie in her skin as smoothly as a layer of mist. Her dress was the pink of blooming roses, looped over beige underskirts. Her fingers on Humi's face felt unexpectedly gentle. "Well, girl, a murderess, huh?"

Humi nodded, gazing up into Erene's face. Nothing to

be done except stick it out. No use to protest that her grandfather had wanted to die and that she hadn't meant to kill that man in Port Taite. Not good to remember that timeless moment when she had looked down and seen him lying in his blood.

"Would you like to watch me work?" Erene gestured toward Beau, in the corner. "Actually, it might add a nice edge. I was planning a masturbation scene—the implicit force in his body is extraordinary. It's not too often we get ghosts who've done physical work all their lives." She spoke now to Ziniquel. "This handsome, powerful young man, who should be able to snap his fingers and have girls come running, spending his energy touching himself alone. I had it, I was on the very edge, when you came in."

"Gods, I'm sorry!" Zin said sincerely.

"I planned him like this—" Erene arched her back, throwing out her arms.

A shared passion seemed to bloom between the two ghostiers, transcending their hostility. Ziniquel said eagerly, "But if he's gazing at her—dreaming of their being together—it will add another dimension to his emotion! The piece will have much more depth!"

"We were never lovers," Humi protested, but they paid no attention.

"I'll do it!" Erene exclaimed. "What's her name? Humi! Sit over there. On the stool by the window. Gaze at him, meet his eyes, beg, *plead* with him to come to you. Don't worry—he won't be able to." Her mouth curved. She dusted her palms on her skirts. "You say you're a murderess. Prove it."

"Hah! Nice, Errie!" Ziniquel dropped to the floor. "I have faith in you, Humi! Do it!"

Humi felt as though her heart were being shredded. Agony filled her. *Beau!*

What could she do?

Could she save them both?

No.

Could she save Beau by sacrificing herself?

Uncomprehending and wild-eyed, he had flattened

himself against the wall. His teeth showed. Yet he hadn't curled around his private parts, as an animal would. He seemed to be unconsciously daring Erene to return. There was no way he would be able to pull his mind together to make an escape.

Could Humi save herself by sacrificing him?

She heard herself sob. Hardly knowing where her feet were taking her, she stumbled toward him. A strong, salty smell hit her several armspans away, but ignoring it, she collapsed at his feet. "Oh, love—"

It was clear that he didn't really recognize her. His hands buried themselves in her hair and came away, pulling strands out. His mouth vacillated, and his eyes wandered the room dazedly. The only reactions left to him were to danger and safety.

Crying, she hugged him. "I love you. I'll always love you."

She backed away from him and stumbled to the window. Hating herself, she collapsed on the stool. Like any other warm-blooded creature, she had no control over her instincts: she would do whatever was necessary to save her own skin.

Seven

The ghosting lasted till dawn crept under the curtains. First Erene had to bring Beau back to the peak at which she had had him before Ziniquel and Humi interrupted her. Then she merged in the new aspect of her piece, the longing for Humi. This was where Humi herself came in. She had to make herself cry, she had to kneel near Beau, extending her hands in all-too-real yearning. Ziniquel directed her in whispers. He seemed to know what Erene wanted as well as the older woman did.

Finally Beau's hand was moving steadily between his legs. His eyes held Humi's like bits of violet glass.

Erene stooped over him and ran her hands through his hair, disarraying it artfully. Ziniquel approached, watching like a predator. Erene was on her knees. She gripped her refilled syringe lightly yet firmly. "She likes robe root—it works more thoroughly," Ziniquel breathed to Humi.

"Humi!" Beau cried, speaking for the first time since she had come in. "Humi!" And his other arm curled out with the pure, fluid grace he had learned in the House of Larch, straining toward her. Ziniquel's breath sizzled. Erene's eyes did not flicker. But as Beau climaxed, head cracking back, she sprang. The needle entered his outstretched arm near the wrist. He sank to the floor, mouth opening, legs loose and apart. The stench grew worse. If Humi had looked, she too would have been sick. The catharsis held for a long moment. Then Ziniquel plunged, grabbing Beau under the elbows and backing rapidly. A brown stain followed them.

Erene did not move. Her eyes were shut tight and her whole body seemed to quiver with tension.

"Open the curtains!" Ziniquel hissed.

Stumbling over her feet, Humi obeyed. The view caught her eyes and held her there. She had forgotten that they were on the top floor. Beyond gray-tiled shoals of roofs, she could see the marshes: a vast net of canals and islands, the water pink in the first rays of light. The sun was just rising over the far-off shore, behind the grassy islands. Black flurries of birds crossed its orange disk. Their calls came peacefully over the roofs of Marshtown, harmonizing with the sounds of water and the air.

She let out her breath. Thin, cool air chilled her lungs. Below in the street, somebody called brokenly, "Wait for me, boys, wait for me! This is ghostiers' ground! Don't leave me—" She looked down and saw a brightly costumed young man throwing up in front of the townhouse. The local children, the first Marshtowners to rise, gave him a wide berth as they prodded their animals down the street. His coughs and miserable curses reached her ears clearly.

"Hello!" she called. "Did you have fun last night?"

He started and stared blearily around. Finally he looked up.

"Were you at the Summers'? I recognize you, I think. Young Lord Meadowlord, from Iceland?" She could have dropped a copper into his open mouth. "I know your mother! Give her regards from me, the ghost she sat with last night! Tell her she may see me again soon—but next time *she* will be the one in danger!" Humi laughed, an ebullient sound that careened off the windows opposite.

The young man stared for a minute longer, his horror growing. Then he picked up his coattails and ran. His first step took him skidding in a puddle of pig piss: arms flailing, he dropped his hat and left it lying as he vanished around the corner. Humi chuckled, and turned around.

"Nice," said Erene. She slumped in a leather armchair in the far corner. "You have a tongue in your head, after all." Rolling her eyes up to Ziniquel, she smiled provocatively. The other ghostier leaned in the doorway, arms folded, his face dark with battened-down fury.

Beau's body was gone. Only the various stains remained—and the smell. And the empty syringe. And the cold, radiating from the center of the floor.

Erene's voice was happy with anticipation. "Humi. Move out of the light. Now look at the middle of the floor."

Humi squinted at the spot where she could still see Beau in her mind's eye, poised as he had been at that last instant. And she *could* see him. She blinked. Like a figure blown from transparent glass, tilted over on his back so that one foot stuck stiffly into the air, like a human soap bubble. How could she have missed him for an instant? He cast a shadow on the floor, fuzzy-edged and watery but as real as her own.

She ventured toward him and touched his crystal hair. She flinched from the burning shock of cold. There was nothing else. No emotion such as there had been with the ghosts at Belstem Summer's palace. He had died exhausted, mentally burned out.

"She can see him, Zin!" Erene gloated. "Scowl all you like, it will do no good!"

Humi dragged her eyes away from the delicate figure. She looked confusedly from one ghostier to the other. "He's so cold. But I don't feel anything else. Just a sort of exhaustion. Why?"

"A new ghost is imbued with whatever emotion it felt at the moment of its death," Erene said. "Not only the paint on them, but the emotional content, is contributed by the ghostiers who make them. That's our most closely guarded secret. The world sees ghosts as shrines to the departed, whereas we see them only as art. Now that you know that, you have to stay. You can't leave."

Ziniquel's face was as dark as a rainy evening, his arms tightly folded. "What methods, Erene! Threatening her!"

"Ziniquel?" Humi appealed. "Why are you angry?"

It was Erene who answered, her voice revealing no signs of exhaustion. "Because he's still a child, and he can't help showing it. He's too young to take on an apprentice, especially one as promising as you—but *I* am in sore need of someone to carry on my craft. So I have decided to claim you. I have the right. Whatever else I may be, I am still senior ghostier, and I can claim my privileges. We will do very well together, Humi." She crooked one finger. "Come here."

Bemused, Humi circled the nexus of coldness in the center of the floor.

"Sit down."

Shrinking from Ziniquel's wrath, she obeyed.

Arthritically, as if it were a great effort, Erene stroked her head. "Save the gods. I only ever had one apprentice, and he left me. That was the worst day of my life. But this is the best, and it is only just dawning."

"Stop rubbing it in!" Ziniquel erupted. "How dare you pull this! She was *mine*, Erene!"

"It wasn't *I* who was fooled by a disguise no cleverer than one of my own! I don't think a man as naive as *that* should be allowed to have an apprentice at all, Ziniquel!"

Humi held her breath, waiting for his retort. But he flung around and stormed out of the suite. The door slammed violently.

Erene laughed like a peal of little bells. "Humi, darling—" her fingers twitched on Humi's sleeve—"I want to remember what I'm like when I have an apprentice. I want to become that woman again, because I think she's better than this one. But will you forgive me if occasionally I slide back into being the senior ghostier who no longer truly deserves her position yet clings fiercely to it?"

"Why . . . why was Ziniquel so angry?"

"I took him down a few pegs in front of you. And I confess, I haven't been exerting myself to get along with him recently. But with you I will be different."

"Wait!" Humi felt panic rising. "I haven't agreed to anything! What if I don't want . . ."

Erene's voice hardened. "Don't even *think* of leaving without my permission. Quite apart from the secret I revealed to you, there is the blood on your hands. You helped us make a ghost. And that blood never washes off. I can have you tracked down."

Humi's throat felt dry. "If you're trying to threaten me, it's no use. I've lived with blood on my hands since I was nine years old. If I wanted to leave, that wouldn't stop me."

"Ah," Erene said after a lengthy pause.

Silence fell. With a sort of gladness, Humi saw that the gray eyes were troubled. So she had managed to throw her off balance.

"Well. Are you willing to be my apprentice? Or not?"

"You're making fun of me," Humi said bitterly. "I can't refuse." She felt terribly alone, a thousand miles from Beaulieu, with no one to turn to for help. "I have nowhere else to go. I would be stupid not to stay with you. And—" perverse pride flared—"I'm not stupid. Whatever else I am."

"No," Erene said at last. "You're not."

The sunlight glinted off Beau's ghost, catching her in the eye with flashes of violet, green, orange. Humi wanted to cry. She wanted him back!

"Well, then," Erene said, and paused. Humi was silent. "I need to get out of this chair. I need some nourishment. And I expect you haven't eaten anything for at least one day. You're a country girl—I take it you can cook." Humi nodded drearily. "You'll find a fireplace, flint, tinder, and pots in the next room. Dried meat in the compartment at the bottom of the sink, oats in the closet. Why don't you make us some breakfast?"

It wasn't hard figuring out how to use the Deltan cookware and hearth. In silence Humi mixed up a hearty breakfast of oatmeal and salt pork. The food restored Erene's energy. She stood up and stretched her legs, complaining of the bruises Beau had given her. It was almost noon. The ghost of Beau glittered in the middle of the floor, easily visible in the midday light. "I suppose I must take you to meet the other ghostiers. Do change out of that dress, girl. It makes your fur look so drab."

"It looked good with gold and silver," Humi said sullenly. "And my natural fur is drab no matter what I wear." But she was glad to escape the cinch of the falseribs. The spindlespun skirt and blouse Erene offered out of the enormous wardrobe in her bedroom were much more comfortable, and they fitted well, as Erene was exactly Humi's height. Round-hipped, Erene had small breasts, and her bones showed around her waist and in her forearms. By no stretch of the imagination could she be considered beautiful, but she had a wide mouth and aggressive eyes. She was a Piradean, born of a rocky, unkind land.

"We'll have to get you some clothes of your own," she said. "And gowns for your appearances at court." She let her dress fall in a heap. Humi watched her search, naked, through the sea of garments on the floor of the bedroom. The apartment on the other side of the workshop where she had ghosted Beau comprised this bedroom, a sitting room, parlor, guest bedrooms, dining room, and bathing room. It was furnished in Piradean style, which meant a few pieces of stone-leaf furniture softened with cushions and draperies. The gorgeous boudoir that Humi and Ziniquel had first entered was simply a front, decorated for Erene's ghosts, not Erene herself. This was her sanctum. But Humi had the feeling she did not spend much time here. Several skylights in the sitting room were cracked, and a leak in the parlor ceiling had ruined a tapestry. When Humi pointed that out as they walked through the apartment, Erene had been shocked. She ran her hand over the blended colors and sagging threads like a woman noticing a wound in her body for the first time.

But at last she said that done was done, she never noticed that kind of thing until it was too late. And, complimenting Humi on her sharp eyes: "Look over the rest of the place if you want. If you like Piradean glasswork, there are some nice pieces on the dining table." But one of them had rolled to the floor and shattered to pink dust. Another had old, smelly wine lees in the bottom. Spiders scrabbled in the ceramic tub in the bathroom.

Puzzled, Humi returned to the bedroom. Erene was plucking garments haphazardly off the floor and putting them down on the wrinkled, dampish bed. "I take these to the washerwoman when I want to wear them—*if* I can find the one I want. How miserable it'll be to make this place habitable again. Perhaps I'll have to let Algia in at last—she's the only one of us who likes cleaning house. But how I hate to give in to her. Oh, well."

Fastening her dress as she went, she pushed along the wall and opened a door, revealing another landing. The hall and stairwell were cruder than Humi had noticed last night, under the influence of Ziniquel and wine. The construction looked hasty and raw—either that or very old indeed. As old as Beaulieu, so old that carpentry had been markedly more primitive. And here, unlike in Beaulieu, nobody had taken the trouble to sand or paint or limewash in a dozen centuries.

But the stairs didn't creak as Erene and Humi descended to the ground floor. Daylight shone in the cracks around the front door. They crossed a bare, dusty antechamber and stopped before the single door, whose rudely carved knob bore a patina of many fingers. Erene stooped, felt in a crack under the skirting and offered Humi a glass mug. "Here. Like this. I expect they're talking about us—we'll get the jump on them."

Humi put her ear to the bottom of the glass. She gasped. She could hear the voices inside perfectly.

"You can't blame Erene." It was a man's voice, rich and confident. "She's thirty-five. That's almost too late to start training an apprentice. Zin, you'll find another precocious little girl—maybe even another companion. Now that that trick has been thought of, more will try it. Don't sulk."

"You always defend Erene, Elicit!" Ziniquel burst out. "Last night I was tricked only because I'd never conceived such a thing could be done. Next time we'll all be on the lookout, and such a trick won't even get past the beauticians. I tell you, she's an apprentice you'd all covet!"

"Well, I wish *I'd* seen her disguise!" A woman laughed. "I hardly believe an untutored child could fool you, Zin!"

"She fooled even the gods. I was standing in the crowd. I saw Broken Bird pass her over."

"So when are we going to meet this extraordinary female?" The voice was so high and nasal that it rendered even that innocuous question offensive.

"How should I know, Owen?" Ziniquel asked. "You can't trust Erene. For all we know, now that she's got her hands on an apprentice—the last thing she needs *us* for—she'll move out altogether and leave us lying like her cast-off gowns. I wouldn't put it past her to take Humi to live with Goquisite in that frilly social crossroads of a mansion!"

"Never," the woman said instantly, and several others agreed with her. "No one has *ever* moved out of Tellury Crescent for *any* reason. Erene wouldn't go that far."

"Anyway, the strength of her position lies here." The new voice was crisp, elderly, a breath of reason. "Her Ellipse seat springs from her status as senior ghostier. She wouldn't jeopardize herself by leaving us."

"Oh, yes, she would!" Ziniquel flared. "She's screwing herself up to do it! That's why she's been so miserable these past months—all she wants is to spend all her time with Goquisite, and to hell with her political career!"

Humi realized in a flash of enlightenment that she knew who "Goquisite" was. She was Goquisite Ankh, the Ellipse councillor, commonly mentioned in the same breath as Belstem Summer.

"That isn't fair, Zin." It was a soft, husky, woman's voice, but a few words quieted the uproar which had broken out. "You're skewing things, as usual. Erene cares deeply about politics. Goquisite is only one part of her dilemma—she sees the future, and she's trying to drag us toward it. It's not her fault we're so heavy."

"What's this, Mory? Are you turning traitor too?"

"No. But I can see what Erene sees. I can sympathize with her."

The man who had spoken first—Elicit—said, "Let's not dissect poor Erene like this! We all love her—yes, even you, Zin!—and we won't turn out backs on her, no matter what she does. *That's* what the strength of her position is, if you want." He was clever, Humi thought. He meant to defuse their anger at Erene by making them feel as though she owed everything to them. "We've been looking after her since Hem left, and we won't stop now. Let's have an end to this, Zin. If she wants the apprentice, for the gods' sakes let her have her."

"But we *can't* let her have her! She was mine, and Erene simply stepped in and took her!"

"It's within her powers."

"Zin is right. she *shouldn't* use her powers like that." This must be the fourth woman ghostier. "Most of them aren't meant to be touched. They're for show, like ornamental daggers. And as for the practical ones, their use is dictated purely by decency and friendship."

"Then everything's all right!" It was the effeminate-voiced man, Owen. He sounded as though he was enjoying a last word on the affair. "Because everyone knows that Ziniquel and Erene *aren't* friends! And so they can do whatever they like to each other!"

"Gods, you'll trivialize anything to get your digs in, Owen!" Zin roared. There was silence.

Dazedly Humi opened her eyes. Erene's mouth trembled. That last exchange must have been loud enough for her to hear even without the glass.

Several dreadful moments passed.

"That's horrendous." It was a teenaged girl's voice.

"But true. Isn't it? Consider, Emni."

Some distance away a door slammed. Then another, closer by, and before Humi understood what was going on, Erene had yanked her to her feet and dragged her back from the door.

"Zin. Zin, what are you doing?"

"You can't suspect—"

When the door thudded open, they were standing side by side a respectable distance away. But Humi still had the glass in her hand. Ziniquel's eyes locked on it. He looked up at Erene, betrayal in his eyes. "I didn't think you really *were* listening. Never in a million years."

The senior ghostier breathed fast. Her hand tightened painfully on Humi's. Ziniquel's agate eyes spoke volumes. He took a hesitant step toward Erene, as if trying a bridge.

Erene wrenched her hand from Humi's, turned on her heel, and fled.

"Damn," sobbed Ziniquel. "Oh, damn. Oh, Erene. I can't go after you anymore." He leaned against the antechamber wall, face buried in his hands, shaking.

"That's the apprentice," one of the ghostiers said from within the room.

"Go speak to her."

"What's her name again?"

Humi listened, staring at the dusty reddish wood floor, not at Ziniquel. Eventually she heard him stumbling past her, up the stairs.

A knobbed finger touched her chin and eased it up. An elderly man, thin and graceful, with green Royallandic fur, stood beside her. "I'm Fra Canyonade." The old man's voice sounded crisp and assured. But his face was troubled. "That must not have sounded very well to you. It is possible that Erene and Zin could become irrevocably estranged. Erene's taking you wasn't the last straw—no, I'm sure it wasn't—but we have just been reminded that a split is possible."

"Would . . . would that be so unthinkable?" Humi asked tremulously. "It doesn't seem to me that they like each other very much, anyway . . ."

Fra guided her into the large room. It seemed like a lounge, with crude old paintings on the wall, cushioned chairs, and a great fireplace. Fifteen or so people sat around the room, some with plates neglected on their laps, staring silently at Fra and Humi.

He put his arm in hers and escorted her toward the table. He didn't move like a grandfather. If his steps were slow, they were light. "Among the ghostiers, our unity is our strength. The slightest crack in our solidarity would be unthinkable."

They stood up to greet Humi. There were Piradean, Royallandic, Calvarese, and Archipelegan faces, and one Veretrean woman, who extended a hand to Humi. She was middle-aged, with a scrubby brown apple-cheeked face and a warm smile. "Don't take it too badly, Humi. You're not the cause of the trouble, only its latest installment. Hard of Erene to do this to you, I think. I am Rita Porphyry, and this is my apprentice, Owen Phyllose." Humi didn't need to hear Owen's voice. His smile was enough to warn her that he was the cynical, soft-voiced one.

"I'm Beisa," said a plump, motherly woman in a blue dress. "And these are my apprentices Sol and Emni." They were a teenage boy and girl, with white fur and black hair identical to Beisa's. *Archipelagan*, Humi thought. Thus they didn't have to be related. All Archipelagans had the same coloring.

"I'm Mory," the Calvarese woman said. With a start, Humi recognized her ... not in this patched skirt, but in crimson ...

She had enticed Rain out of the banquet hall last night.

"And this is my apprentice Tris."

"Trisizim Sepal," the boy said in a precise voice. He was Calvarese too, about fourteen years of age.

"Elicit Paean," said the remaining man. His voice identified him as the man who had defended Erene. A tall, intelligent-faced Piradean, his hair was cropped as short as fur all over his scalp. "And my apprentices—" he snapped his fingers. A pale nonentity of a woman came around the table, hustling a girl of seven or eight in front of her. "Algia and Eternelipizaran." He lifted the child up into his arms and planted a kiss on her cheek. "My little prodigy!"

Wriggling out from under the kiss, Eternelipizaran complained, "I thought you'd be younger, Humi."

Everyone laughed. Elicit jogged the little girl up and down. "Maybe the next new apprentice will be your age. For now, we like Humi the way she is. Isn't that right?"

"I know we'll be friends," Humi said to the child, and there was an uncomfortable silence. She should not have spoken! She longed for Erene, or even Ziniquel, to be a buffer between her and these strangers.

"Oh, it's too bad of Erene to go off and leave the poor thing like this!" Rita burst out. "I don't think *she's* any readier to take an apprentice than Zin is!"

"Done is done, Rita." Mory, the Calvarese, squeezed

the older woman's arm, keeping an eye on Humi. "All we can do is prepare her to cope with Erene's—vacillations."

"It's very easy, isn't it," Elicit said mildly, "to blame Erene for our own inefficiencies and outdated traditions?" He put Eternelipizaran down, then stepped behind Humi and gently massaged her shoulders. She wanted to wriggle out from under his touch, but she stopped herself. "Child, it's not as bad as they're making it sound! You're one of us now. We'll stand by you."

The sequence of events was too convoluted for Humi to comprehend. All she had to hang on to was Erene. Erene, at least, had expressed in no uncertain terms that she *wanted* Humi. Not that she was having her foisted on her. She twisted around to look at Elicit. "No need to take care of me. I'm Erene's apprentice, and she promised me I'll be safe with her!"

He laughed delightedly. "Oh, what a fine ghostier you'll make!"

"What a love!" Beisa said, and hugged her. The Archipelagan woman's fine perfume was incongruous with her homely dress. That inconsistency spoke of money, and plenty of it, but no self-centered vanity. The ghostiers were commoners so rich that they didn't even bother to furnish their houses. Now, as if Beisa had broken the ice, they were all crowding around, reaching to touch Humi. She was surrounded by bony, muscular, soft, hard bodies and a dozen different perfumes. It was frightening—until she relaxed: and then a wonderful sense of acceptance pervaded her. Maybe they really *did* want her, after all. Emni, Beisa's girl apprentice, hung an arm around her neck; Mory hugged her. Fra kissed her on the cheek with his old, dry lips. "If Erene ever comes back," he said, "she'll take you to see the Eftpool. It's the ritual for new apprentices."

"*Imrchu,*" Emni said caressingly. The word was strange to Humi, but it sounded like a term of endearment. "Would you like some custard? We were just having lunch—"

Eight

"No outsiders are allowed to enter our houses," Emni said after lunch, when they were in a sedan, riding through Marshtown. "We don't put ourselves up on pedestals, but we have to have some indication that we're not just like the neighbors. So we have a rule that anyone who crosses our thresholds without permission incurs a dreadful punishment."

"Unless he's a god," said her brother Sol quietly. "You can't keep the gods out." The sedan jounced and jolted, curtain swayed, and outside voices discussed groceries, piglets, childbirth, theology, and a dozen other subjects, in snatches. Sol and Emni sat across from Humi in the half-dark.

"Don't nitpick," Emni admonished her twin. She turned to Humi again. "You live in Albien House with Zin, Mory, Tris, and Erene. It joins onto the Chalice, which is the ghostiers' original house. Thaumagery and Melthirr were built later. Look out the window and you'll have a good view of it as we go round the bend—you must not have had time when we were hustling you into the sedan."

Humi peered through the curtains. "Oh," she breathed in delight. The many-windowed building to which Ziniquel had brought her last night was instantly recognizable. Most townhouses tended to grow slender and crooked, even in Marshtown; the only exceptions were the mansions of the palace district. But Albien House was a pleasantly proportioned building snuggled between a glassblower's shop and the taller, equally ancient structure that was the Chalice. It had a certain immovable dig-

nity. Humi felt proud that *she* was one of the few
privileged to enter it.

"Sol and I live a little way up the street in Thaumagery
House, with Beisa, Rita, and Owen," Emni said as Humi
let the curtain fall and turned around. "Fra, Elicit,
Eterneli, and Algia all live in Melthirr House."

"Who is Algia again?" Humi asked, trying to get them
straight.

Emni glanced at her twin. Sol was a stocky boy, stingy
with words, who wore his black hair shaved up the back,
with long bangs. Humi had yet to see him leave Emni's
side. "She *would* be the one you forget. She's the pale-
furred Deltan with no chin. Officially she's Elicit's apprentice. But all she does is play mother to Eterni."

"Shush!" Sol said sharply.

Emni giggled. "And clean house for us all. One of the
disadvantages of keeping our houses off limits is the
dirt—we can't have servants."

"Erene's apartment is a disaster," Humi said.

"Oh, Erene. She won't let Algia, or anyone at all, apart
from Elicit, inside her apartment. I don't think there's any
big secret . . . I think she's just ashamed of how dirty it is.
It's been more than a year since I went up there." Emni
rolled her eyes. She oozed camaraderie. "She hardly goes
there anymore except to work. Most nights she's away.
She only sleeps at home if Goquisite is out of Delta City."

"Shut up, Em!" Sol said sharply. Emni's long black
hair flew into his eyes as she twisted toward him. She
buried her face in his neck.

Humi glanced dubiously from one to the other.

"All right!" The curtain was thrown back, and there
was Owen, smiling unhealthily. "Here we are! Not very
far after all, was it?"

The porters had stopped the sedans in the upper end of
a small, steep Marshtown street. The smell of salt and
reeds rotting in winter came to Humi's nostrils. On this
side, the island sloped to the level of the marshes; the water could not have been more than a stone's throw away,
on the other side of the buildings that lined the thoroughfare at the bottom of the hill. The parked sedan chairs

spread out of the mouth of the narrow street, blocking traffic. The dull-garbed pedestrians glanced up curiously and then continued on their way, unsurprised.

Humi slid between the sedan chairs to Erene's side, where her master stood with Elicit and Rita. Elicit stopped speaking—but not before Humi caught her own name. "Shall we go in?" Rita said diplomatically.

Erene looked as though she was having a hard time battening down her anger. Without bothering to answer, she rapped hard on the plank door. It opened to reveal a plain woman with two furry babies, one on her back, one slung on a hip. "Gods' greeting, Godsie. Who . . . ?" her green face wrinkled.

Erene muddied violently.

"Oh, dear," Rita whispered.

Elicit stepped past Erene and cleared his throat.

"Ohhh! Godsman Paean!" The woman's smile lit her eyes, and she peered past Elicit into the sunlight. "Gods grant health to my children! You've brought *all* your fellows!"

"Indeed." Elicit ducked into the house and pulled the woman after him. Humi heard him muttering urgently, presumably to save Erene's face. But before he finished, Erene touched Humi's arm. "Come on," she said. "We can be the first in. When the atmosphere has only just been broken, it's really something unique."

Humi bit her lip and nodded. She followed her master straight through the house. Erene pulled her through a door, into the sunlight again, only now it was muted. Multicolored patches of light drifted over them.

"Oh! Oh, it's beautiful," Humi said involuntarily.

Erene nodded pleasedly. "It's the very repository of beauty."

The top of the dome was lower than the house, so that it would be invisible from the street, visible only from top-floor windows in the surrounding houses. Inside, metal rods branched up from the brick sidewalls to support a weight of glass that must be immense, for all that the dome looked so airy. It was a geodesic greenhouse, each triangle of glass a different brilliant color. They seemed to shift into a new pattern every time Humi looked up. Dark, fronded plants grew around the bases of the walls, drops of humidity trembling on the tips of the fronds. The air was so heavy that Humi found it hard to breathe. A pool of black water was sunk into the middle of the floor: though they had not touched it, ripples ran away from Humi's and Erene's feet.

"The atmosphere's going," Erene whispered. "The more people come in, the less it can hold out." She knelt on the brick path and reached down to the water. The reflections of the dome in the pool shook with violent queasiness. "Quick! You too."

The bricks were worn smooth as the boulders of stone walls by centuries of feet and knees. Humi's finger seemed to vanish as it entered the icy water. Something sharp and small shot past beneath the surface. The underwater gust of its passing played with her fur. She gasped.

"It touched you? Good. They're not afraid. If the efts are afraid to touch an apprentice the first time, it means that he will always be striving miserably for goals beyond his reach. Owen was one such. You have met him. My first apprentice, Hem Lakestone, didn't feel them either. But he cares nothing for a ghostier's goals now ... Perhaps there's nothing in the superstition." Erene was silent, moving her hand in the water. "Here. Here, Telitha. This was the most beautiful ghost I was ever privileged to make. She's more than ten years old now. Telitha ... ahhh."

Slowly, Erene lifted something out of the pool. As the surface of the water broke, Humi smelled a sudden waft of *badness*, ennui like nothing she had ever felt before— like dining rooms where meals have sat congealing for years, chambers hung with cobwebs through which ancient, obsolete men and women limp drearily, circling. The thing in Erene's hand thrashed wetly against her palm. Erene closed her fingers on it. "Hello, Telitha. How have you been?" She waited a moment, as if for a reply. "Oh, don't give me that."

For a moment Humi sensed the desperation of the invalid who tells her relatives again and again how the nurse is abusing her, and she cannot get out. Cannot get out.

She quashed her misgivings. "Can I hold her?"

"Better not. But isn't she beautiful?" Erene held the creature up to Humi's eyes. It had silver scales and a long, transparent-edged tail like a tadpole's.

It had a woman's face.

She gasped and wrenched away. Although she hadn't heard the door open and shut, the ghostiers were crowding around her. Beisa gripped her, stopping her from falling. "Throw that thing back!" she said to Erene. "It's more than a decade old, it must be starting to rot!"

"I can smell it." Mory knelt and deftly tweaked the wriggling eft out of Erene's grip. She lifted one of its scales and poked. Again Humi smelt rotting meat. "Ugh. Erene, for the gods' sake." Mory tossed the eft back into the pool. Ripples traveled back and forth, hitting the brick walls with hard *clops*.

"Quick, Humi, call your cousin," Erene said. "Beauty. Just say 'Beauty.' "

"She'll be in danger with that, won't she?" Rita said worriedly. "Gods know how many farmers call their child after his primary virtue, and how many of those have lived up to it all the way—"

"Don't be ridiculous, Rita," Erene said. "The efts will know who she means."

"Beauty, Beauty," Humi whispered. "Beau! Here!"

"That's not loud enough!" Ziniquel said in a clear, ringing voice. "You know how difficult it is to hear with your ears underwater, don't you?"

"The other day I called for a ghost of mine named Happiness," Rita said, "and you'll never guess what I got. I closed my fingers around it and brought it up into the light. I could see its *skeleton*. Its eyes dangled, yet it managed to look up at me. It must have been as old as a god."

"Rita, by the *gods*—"

"Beau!" Spray flecked Humi's face as she leaned out over the water. "Beau!"

He threw himself into her hand, alive with pent-up energy.

Their eyes met. His face and its frame of curls were stuck onto the end of the fish's body like a mask.

She was stricken with a crippling sense of guilt. "I'm sorry, Beau!" she whispered. "It was both of us, or just one! Please forgive me. It's not like it's done me any good. I don't know what I'm doing here with these people. I wanted to see the world. I wanted to live in Delta City. But I think I've got more than I bargained for." She choked tears down fruitlessly. "I want to get away."

Humi, you were born to become a ghostier. She thought she heard his voice. It sounded just as it always had, but with the added solemnity of some unguessable knowledge. *Just as I was born to be a ghost. You did right by me, betrothed.*

"What are you saying?"

You are blameless. It was my destiny.

"The Godsister did that to you!"

Destiny is destiny. Don't believe me, if you won't. I just wanted to ease your mind.

"And is this my destiny? Do I have to learn to live without you? Can't I just go—" she swallowed tears—"I want to go *home*—"

You have to live without me. Nothing can change that. And you'd be a fool to go back to Beaulieu! Even if you could get there! For a moment the voice was the old Beau's, country-inflected, making fun of her for her foolishness. *Humi, this is what you wanted all your life!* Then it went solemn again. *Are you going to throw it away now that you have it in your hand?*

"All I have in my hand is you," she whispered.

It's a game of souls. Don't you remember the thrill that ran through you when you saw my ghost in the sunlight? The feeling of power when you saw my life slip away? Don't you want more power? And more?

He flipped out of her hand like a dauphin.

"Beau!"

But he arrowed below the surface.

Destiny? Imagination? Or the Godsister's influence? Could that last beyond death?

Rita helped Humi to her feet. The air was fairly whipping around inside the dome. "Are you all right?"

"I . . ." She swallowed.

"I know, dear. It's hard."

"You don't understand." *I have to stay here. I have to stay with you.* Humi gave a sob and buried her face in Rita's scrawny, comfortable bosom.

Gently but firmly, she found herself pushed away. "Erene," Rita said, and sighed. "She's yours. Apparently you promised her you'd look after her. Well, do it." Without looking at Humi, she took her place in the ring of ghostiers around the pool. Elicit came through the door and stood beside her. The ferns lashed, the air dashed and boiled about the dome as if it were a giant arena of sky. White crests formed on the waves in the pool.

"They're going to stay to see the storm," Erene said. "Let's go." She grabbed Humi's arm and pulled her out into the corridor. The cool air flowed into her lungs like milk. A child had drawn with charcoal on this side of the door: stick figures standing in a ring, rivers of hair blowing around their heads. Humi was too dazed to speak. "Good-bye," Erene said magnanimously to the Godsie as they passed her. She was sitting in the doorway, giving suck to one of her babies. The baby's wispy fur and suction grip on the nipple reminded Humi fuzzily of her little cousin Asure. Asure, whom she would never see again. She stopped to pat its head.

"It's Elicit's." Erene laughed unkindly. "You can see it has his hair—or lack of it."

The woman muddied. "Don't speak so, Milady Gentle. Xhil will be back any minute, and he doesn't want to know about Godsman Paean and me."

"I should think he'd be happy to have all these children to raise," Humi said. "Godsie, you're very fertile."

The woman laughed. "Only this one is mine, love."

"You might as well tell her the rest, Soulf," Erene said. "Then she won't worry about getting in a fix."

The woman shifted the baby to her other breast and looked up to meet Humi's eyes. "Love, the ghostiers can't raise babies in the Crescent. And they're wise enough to know it. But just like you said, any other women would be more than happy to have extra babes. So they foster them out. I belive there are five of us foster mothers, scattered throughout Marshtown—isn't that right, Godsie Gentle?"

"Rita has two daughters. Constance had one—the girl must be nearly old enough to marry now. Beisa has a son and a daughter, and then there is Mory's son. That's right."

"And I have Ines and Virtue, Godsie Glissade's daughters, and of course your Tessen, milady. Would you like to see him?" She turned as if to call.

"No!" Erene's voice came out strained. "No, don't! He's probably at some game."

"With respect, I should think not. They all help me about the house, and so learn to spend their time profitably, milady."

Humi looked from one woman to the other. What a strange concept! What kind of woman would give away her own children? The light slanted in the front door and lit Soulf's green-gleaming breast. It was almost sunset.

They had spent hours in the Eftpool.

"We must be going," Erene said. Humi could hear the faint shrill of panes of glass vibrating in the wind. "Lady Garden and I are walking home."

Soulf nodded composedly. "As you will, Milady Gentle."

Down on the throughfare, the shopkeepers were rolling up their awnings for the night. Children drove animals along the street, leaving the scent of manure in their wakes. None of the passerbys paid any attention to two women dressed modestly in spindlespun. As they climbed uphill, Humi asked: "Erene—who is the father? You're not married, are you?"

"Gods! No, I am not married. Tessen is Hem's. He was my first apprentice. But that was a rather gauche question, Humi."

Humi did a dance step to avoid a pile of pig dung. "I'm sorry. I thought . . . I thought I could ask you anything."

"You *can*."

"Then—who's Goquisite? Is she Goquisite Lady Ankh?"

Erene's eyes blazed. But this time Humi stopped dead, refusing to be intimidated. Deltans pushed past them, laughing, swearing by all the gods at once. "She's Lady Ankh the councillor. And she's my friend. And to be blunt about it, Humi, she does not have a great deal of intrinsic strength, and she is standing on a razor's edge between audacity and treason. *And it's my fault.* There is a matter of business between us, that is even more important than our friendship, but I have asked the others not to tell you until I want you to know. All I can say now is that you are to be my helper. Goquisite will trust you because you're my apprentice, and maybe that will take some of the pressure off her."

Knowing she was going too far, yet unable to stop herself, Humi said: "Is *that* why you wanted me, then? Is that why you took me from Ziniquel? An extra support on which to stand this business with Goquisite?"

"You—you—" Erene stood stock-still, eyes burning with a fury beyond anything Humi could have guessed. Then she slumped. "Partly."

Humi could not believe it. She could not believe Erene had actually said that. *Well, I'll become a ghostier too,* she thought furiously. *Like you, cold and manipulative. After all, I already am, aren't I? I'll use you, just as you plan to use me.*

For you, Beau. I'll make it up to you.

Nine

Erene Gentle loved the time-consuming job of painting ghosts, especially ghosts as outstandingly handsome as Beauty Garden. Whatever other concerns might occupy her mind, this was her vocation. The seclusion with her work was like a cleansing by fire, a test of her abilities. When a ghostier over thirty years of age looked at her hand holding the paintbrush and saw that it had begun to shake, she was finished—as a ghostier, at any rate. If she had any sense, she would retire. Constance, Ziniquel's master, had loved her work so much that she had kept on and on. And it had cost her her life. But Erene hoped that she herself was years away from that yet.

Erene watched Humi like a predator for signs that the girl was weary of sitting in the corner and running errands. During this period when the master ghostiers did nothing but paint, boredom was inevitable for the apprentices. But if Humi had misgivings she hid them adroitly. It was Erene herself who felt unsure whether she had been wise to apprentice the girl. Alternately, she regretted and congratulated herself on that split-second decision made out of vindictiveness against Ziniquel.

But as Humi's patience, aesthetic taste, and self-control became apparent, Erene realized that once again chance had been kind to her.

One night, coming back from Elicit's apartments, Erene halted in the doorway, watching Humi move hesitantly across the paint-stained floor toward the ghost. She picked up Erene's palette and bush. Erene opened her mouth to stop her. The process of painting was inextricably melded with the emotional coloration of the ghost, so that no one could say where one stopped and the other began. Strictly off limits to new apprentices, both processes.

Humi knelt sucking the hogshair for a minute, forehead creased in thought. Steadying her hand on the ghost's as-yet-unpainted nose, she blocked in several more of the hard, icy curls with white. Then she made a face. Laying down the brush, she crept back to her corner, shivering with cold. She had on only a spindlespun dress, whereas Erene, like all ghostiers while they worked, wore woolens.

Erene reached behind her, slammed the outer door, and came in. "I brought you something to eat." She tossed Humi an egg-stuffed roll. Humi caught it with only a slight fumble, but when Erene looked closely, she saw that the girl's lashes shimmered like fringes of jewels around her eyes.

So she *did* feel pain. She just was not showing it to Erene. And that was good, because Erene could not hug her. Would not surrender to the maternal instincts that were growing in her every day she lived with Humi.

Erene had to set an example of hardness. She could not even congratulate Humi on her talent, although she could tell that now, now that Humi had touched it, this was going to be the best ghost Erene had made in years. The girl was a born ghostier. Her emotions flavored everything Erene had put into the ghost thus far. It might even be her best ghost since Hem left.

How long? How long was that? Erene thought. Tessen would be seven soon, wouldn't he, and it was the news of her pregnancy which had caused Hem to break with the Crescent. He had not understood why she couldn't raise their child. Or give it to him to raise. He had not understood that since they were unmarried, and she was his senior in years and rank, then it was *her* child and she would dispose of it as ghostiers always did.

So he'd stamped out of the shocked assembly of ghostiers in tears. And for two years Erene hadn't known where he was.

He had been traveling the world. Now he was back in Delta City, managing a shop that sold curiosities from the depths of the Veretrean forests, from the nomadic Iceland-ers, from the barbarians in the reaches of the Archipelago. On one of his voyages he'd found a wife, and they had two children. The shop was in Temeriton, the whorehouse district—a dangerous place to raise children, but subject to none of the rules of piety that bound Marshtown, for sure. Hem's clients were rich, atheistic, and increasingly seedy. He could not have removed his life farther from the Crescent if he'd moved to the wastes of Iceland.

All was forgiven and forgotten between Erene and the Lakestones, at least on the surface, and she sometimes went to visit the family, bringing presents for the children and a bottle of fine wine.

But lately she had been spending too much time in Antiprophet Square to go to Temeriton.

I must take Humi to meet Goquisite. Gods, what is Goquisite going to think? Erene was not looking forward to that confrontation. How would Goquisite take this ev-idence that Erene's trust in her was less than total? Erene had sent a letter with the news that she had taken an ap-prentice, but had received no reply. Probably most of the atheists knew by now. Ah, well—they could not be too upset. In Ellipse, an apprentice, like a leman, was no more than an unimportant appendage of the councillor to whom he or she was attached.

They would have to revise that assumption later, after Erene had trained Humi up.

But first the girl needed quite a bit of refinement. Erene had made the appalling discovery that she didn't know how to read—didn't even have a clear idea of what writ-ing was. But perhaps that was unsurprising. Zeniph Antiprophet had introduced the alphabet only a hundred and fifty years ago, and Humi, living in the saltside, might never have seen a book. But it should not be diffi-cult to teach her everything she needed to know, from sightreading to social graces. Erene had only to slip a fact into a casual discussion to have it thrown back at her later. The girl was so quick to learn that Erene felt as though her child was growing by leaps and bounds, out of all control.

But though Humi seemed to have an almost unnatural appetite for learning and she was always there when Erene needed her to mix pigments or wash pans, often when Erene woke from a nap, Humi would be missing. Erene would pretend to sleep again, and a few minutes later, Humi would sneak in, breathing hard as if she had been running—or making love.

Erene suspected Ziniquel. Unscrupulous as ever, he was probably bored to death with being the one idle ghostier. He'd nearly ghosted Humi, so presumably they had already had intimate contact, even if they had not actually done the act. And she could very well envision him seducing Humi just to get his revenge on Erene.

One day she called Humi to her. Painstakingly, she explained that she didn't want Humi getting involved with any of the ghostiers. Erene herself had a long-standing relationship with Elicit, which had evolved over years—but she did not mention that. Besides, she *needed* Elicit. If it weren't for him, she would have no supporter when she needed one, no bed to crawl into when she was lonely. Humi had Erene. That should be enough.

Erene didn't disclose that, at one point or another, she had been intimate with all the adult ghostiers. She couldn't chance it that Humi might do the same. She couldn't chance it that Humi might realize that underneath their workaday exterior, all the ghostiers had an essential bond, that of *imrchim,* which was practically impermeable. (It was almost enough to make her cry, remembering how close they used to be, remembering the laughter.)

No. Erene needed the girl for herself.

So she only told her that intense relationships detracted from the energy necessary for one's work. This held true throughout a ghostier's life, but was especially important when she was first apprenticed and had so much else to cope with. Therefore, she finished, giving a little laugh to lighten the mood, squeezing Humi's hands, she really would advise against spending so much time with— whoever it was.

Humi looked at her with enormous black eyes. They

had no age or emotion, only a deep, dry canniness. Erene felt suddenly uneasy. "I wasn't with anyone," Humi said.

Her hands were dry, not sweaty. "Then where do you vanish to every time I turn around?" Erene snapped.

"I've been in Marshtown. Down on the jetties. I watched the punts come back full of live eels. I watched the young men slide their dauphins out of the tanks into the marsh, and I waited with them for the dauphins to come back with water porcupines in their beaks. I sneaked out on the private jetties and watched the atheists play champions in the deep-water pens. They use every animal that can swim, and some that can't, and they bet on them all. I went back to Christon, and stood outside the House of Larch, thinking that I ought to go get my belongings. But I didn't do it. Stupid bit that I am." She grimaced at her own inadequacy. "I walked along the shopping concourses, and I went to Antiprophet Square, and I ate hot pancakes while I watched the lords and ladies go in and out of the mansions. I went up on the roof roads and talked to artists, courtesans, young atheists living rough, sculptors, and scribes. Did you know—" incredulity lit her eyes—"did you know that there are people who practice that alphabet thing you're teaching me for a *living*?"

Erene smiled, but inside she felt misgivings. Humi would have to learn that such a naïve, all-embracing outlook had no place in the life of a ghostier.

"I went down to the wharves and watched the ships unloading cargo," Humi was going on. "They're all in a tearing hurry right now, because the trade winds are going to drop off in a couple of sixdays. It makes you feel like you have to do something and go somewhere right this *minute*, just standing down there. I've been in the waterfront bars—"

Erene held up her hand. "Sweetheart. Knowing the city is essential to a ghostier's life. So is meeting people. But so is something else. What is that?"

Humi shrugged.

"Politics. The Ellipse meets every four sixdays. All of us missed the session last Sageday, so we will have to go to the next session, which is two days from now. *That* is what you ought to be thinking about."

"How can I—"

"Wait." Perhaps she should not be so harsh. "If you and I hurry, we can be finished with Beau's ghost by tomorrow and have a day to ourselves. All alone. So we should get to work right now." She cuffed the girl lightly. "I tell you, you are never going to want to see blue again after you have mixed me the exact color of your cousin's eyes."

Humi said, "If the efts didn't turn silver, we could go make a comparison."

"Mix that pigment!" More danger—"You are not even to *think* about going back to the Eftpool until you have made a ghost of your own. It's forbidden."

Humi bent into the cupboard to get a mortar. Her tawny hair fell forward, almost hiding the muddy color of her face.

"You have been going, haven't you?"

Humi straightened up, standing with her back to the sink, small and sturdy as a carving of blond wood in her paint-stained dress. She held her head high, but there was a tremor in her voice as she said, "What if I have?"

"Oh, child," Erene laughed sadly. "Child, I went too, when I was Molatio Ash's apprentice."

Humi said nothing.

What can you expect? Erene asked herself. *You killed her betrothed. You haven't exactly created a friendly environment for her. You haven't trusted her enough to tell her very much of the truth at all. What kind of caretaker are you?*

No kind of caretaker. A master.

A little more truth, she thought angrily to herself.

"Do you know why I took you away from Ziniquel? I told you back then, but you probably don't remember. I am getting old, and I must have an apprentice for the sake of my art. That is the first and foremost reason. That is the *only* reason."

Humi tossed her head. "You told me that wasn't all."

Erene could not bring herself to say the rest: "For you,

too." She could hear Humi silently pleading for it, but she could not say it.

Hem's desertion had left such deep scars. She had not even realized—

"Give me that mortar," she said. "Now! And I need chalk, white, and lake pigments, and a dab of moss essence—"

When Erene took Humi to collect her flaxen sack of belongings from the House of Larch the next day, she discovered that Humi had made her first enemy. The ties between the House of Larch and the Crescent were old and hoary, steeped in the conviction that each institution had the other to thank for its existence but dared not acknowledge it. Favors tended to be repaid in full, and grudges lived long, mischievous lives. Erene was friendly enough with Ministra Bareed; it was shocking to see the way Ministra and Humi circled each other like cats.

As they walked back through Christon, Humi explained with rare effusiveness, "I outbluffed her when I was persuading her to help me put one over on you. She realizes that now, and she's seething."

"The House of Larch are the best of their kind," Erene said. "Everyone who was anyone used to patronize them, up until about fifteen years ago. Now there are hardly any rich devotees left in the city, and they have a shortage of customers. They're terrified that they'll have to either revise their precious traditions—in which case they would lose the flamens' business—or close down." She thought with pity of all the beauticians living their lives on tiptoe in that dark, rickety townhouse, living for those moments of glory before the court, one every fifteen years or so. She looked sidelong at Humi. "They're just drudges, trapped in tradition. There are really no similarities between them and us at all."

"They see beauty flower under their hands, like us. That would make up for anything," Humi argued. "I would be a beautician, if I wasn't going to be a ghostier."

"Yes!" Erene laughed, relieved that Humi had passed her impromptu test. It was almost a miracle how the girl surpassed every standard Erene set her. "I believe," Erene said, "in the irresistible lure of beauty. I think if two rival ladies could be given a ghost to work over, they would be fast friends afterward. And both ghostiers and beauticians have more sense than ladies. The ghosts will always unite us." But thinking of scheming fools like the Ladies Nearecloud, Gulley, Crane, and others left her with the unsettling thought of one particular lady, shrewd as a barnyard hen, with delicate bones and soft black hair. *Goquisite.* A greater lure even than beauty united the two of them. Freedom. Freedom from the crushing, stifling weight of piety.

She asked abruptly, "Who was your first enemy, Humi?"

Taken off balance, Humi gaped for a moment. Then her eyes went flat. "My mother."

"Oh, love." And Erene embraced her right there in the street, between wafts of fishmongery and the hot, raunchy scent of a leatherworker's shop. "You'll do. Yes, you'll do." Incredibly, Humi let herself be held. The crowds pushed around them. Erene was astonished to find that the fur below her eyes was wet. This was the moment of commitment. This was when she brought herself to say, "Humi, the Erene Gentle who deserved her name and position is coming back. And it's all due to you. I've needed your presence for longer than I've known. I think—" She swallowed. "I think I could love you as if you were my own child."

Humi shifted uncomfortably. "I don't need a mother! Didn't you hear what I just said? I need a friend and a teacher. But not any more mothers."

Erene's head whirled. As the daughter of a Grussels merchant, she had rebelled against the idea of children, but it was so long since she'd been that cosseted, overeducated girl. So long since she'd shed fierce tears over the fate from which she could see no escape— marriage to a stranger, children, a life lived in an old rut. So long since the ghostier Molatio Ash had arrived one day to buy some gold lichen pigment and visit with her father—those were the days when ghostiers could travel, when they didn't have all they could do to keep abreast of events in Delta City—since, magically, he and thirteen-year-old Erene had each known that the other was the one they had been searching for.

Ignoring Erene's father's anger, Molatio had spirited her away.

Erene had been naïve, precocious; Molatio had been like a second father to her. For a long time now she had harbored a secret dream to play mother to another child. She wanted to teach that child all she knew—not just ghosting, but how to cook for a hungry man, and old wives' tales, and how to embroider cloth and write beautiful calligraphy. It was a treasured fantasy.

But Humi was not that child.

Humi, Erene saw now, would chafe against any relationship that implied the existence of an adult and a child.

"Very well, my—apprentice," she said softly. "No mothering." A gang of young men pushed past. In the lingering whiffs of their perfume she let go of Humi. "But that doesn't mean you will be unloved."

Humi looked down, smiling tremulously, and touched her cheek as if flicking off an itch. "It won't be difficult for you to love me more than *my* mother did."

Erene was struck by a pang of adoration. "Oh, by the gods. You poor thing." She hugged her again. Humi quivered like a bird in her arms. She had long lashes, for all they were so pale. Long, graceful lashes. Erene laid her face against hers, just holding her, until the fishmonger stamped out of his shop and told them they were making a spectacle in front of his window.

Ten

Strangers thronged Tellury Crescent. The locals lounged in their upstairs windows, commenting loudly on the visitors, dropping pipe ash on their heads. "Court business," Erene had warned Humi, "always takes place at night." To her, the Crescent felt like a river of embers, a glow of lantern-light shadowed with eddying bodies, hot and pungent. She held Erene's hand tightly, shuffling by her side wherever the crowd carried them. The lantern light hung so bright in the air that she could see the bluish clouds of smoke sinking from the Marshtowners' pipes. One by one, the ghostiers carried the ghosts downstairs and posed them outside Thaumagery, Albien, and Melthirr Houses, and in the shallow, railinged strip of yard before the Chalice. This was the only time the public would be able to see them, so socialites condescended to rub shoulders with merchants and commoners. Little Eterneli marched before each ghost to clear the way, blossoming under the attention she received, flirting with the strangers who tousled her heavy green curls. "Algia was like that too, once," Erene said quietly to Humi. "But she's been here a long time now. She has lost her stomach for everything except Elicit. He overwhelmed her with love. And he will do the same thing to Eterneli eventually. But he can't help it—he expects so much of them."

At least his safety is assured, Humi thought. *Maybe he's just canny. Maybe he doesn't want to end up dead. Like Constance, Ziniquel's master.*

They drifted with the flow of the crowd. There was Wella the Veretrean, standing on the threshold of Melthirr House, her mint-pale fur glowing in the dark doorway.

She clasped an armful of flowers to her breast. Diamond tears sparkled on her cheeks; but through them, she was smiling. Elicit had let her die in happiness.

Rain was another matter. His rib cage had been opened up like a shellfish, and he had been tortured until only his beautiful, pain-racked face remained human. Humi remembered Mory leading him into darkness, demure in her cerise dress . . . his sister running, crazed with terror and bewilderment . . .

The last ghost in the line was Beau. Lanterns nodded like the bolls of bog-cotton above his head. Voices muttered and hummed, pointing out details. Sweat prickled over Humi's body in hot and cold waves. There he sat on the ground, manipulating himself in front of all these people, degrading himself and her and all the Gardens for years to come. Unwashed bodies hemmed her in so tightly she couldn't escape. She stood stiff, fists clenched, ears ringing.

But before she had to break, a man in the white-and-gold Summer livery elbowed her aside. "Milady Gentle?" He bowed before Erene. Behind him, several teams of draydogs were forcing a path through the crowd. "Lord Summer. The ghosts."

"Show's over," someone muttered. The crowd began to disperse.

Erene looked the man up and down with cool disdain. "Give my greetings to your master. You will find one of those carts unnecessary."

"Pardon?"

"Are you deaf? You'll need only six carts."

"Milady." One by one, the other retainers were loading the ghosts onto the carts and draping them with sheets. "Dammit, you're right!" The head retainer regarded the last cart. Humi had a sudden, awful fear that they would pick her up and sling her bodily onto it. But he shook his head and called out to the others to move. The carts creaked to the mouth of Tellury Crescent, their drivers blowing on fingers that were numb from touching the ghosts.

As the crowd drained, Humi breathed a sigh of relief.

All day the ghostiers had been irritable with weariness, yet unable to rest because their task was not yet over, and now their spirits seemed to rise like hot air balloons. They joked and roughhoused, caring nothing for the gaping stragglers. The Marshtowners chuckled tolerantly as they closed their upstairs windows. The ghostiers were *their* children, though precocious and wayward.

And then sedan chairs rattled up to the Chalice. Five—six—seven. As Ziniquel tickled her, Humi stopped laughing, dismayed. One after another, the preposterously liveried porters fell to a halt, turning out their calves and stiffening their spines. The leader stuffed a hat on his sweat-damp hair, only to sweep it off again. "Greetings from the Divinarch, miladies and milords!"

Erene smiled unpleasantly. "You almost arrived in time to see our ghosts, Merisand. Belstem's retainers have taken them to the palace now."

The other ghostiers held their breath. But the man's expression remained implacable. "The Divinarch hopes he was correct to assume you would appreciate the use of his sedans."

"We appreciate it greatly," Elicit interjected quickly.

Erene sighed. "Come then, Humi. The night is not over yet. Though I had not expected the Divinarch to be quite so prompt in calling Ellipse. The sun has only just set."

Obediently, Humi followed her into the sedan and sat back in the sumptuous cushions. On the curved wall, a candle burned behind a faceted-glass shield. The sedan started to rattle over the cobblestones. Erene gestured ahead. "Humi, the man who is pulling this sedan is Afet Merisand, the head porter at the Old Palace. He is one of the few humans the Divinarch will speak with face to face. He's also one of far too many humans who know about our conspiracy."

"What—what conspiracy?" Humi's heart dropped sickeningly.

Erene sighed. "I'm reluctant to tell you ... somehow, it feels as though our holiday together is ending." She touched Humi's knee, letting her hand linger. "But you won't understand anything at Ellipse tonight unless you know about the undercurrents. The fact is that Goquisite and I are conspiring to bring down the Divinarch."

Oh, gods. Conspiracy. Against—against the gods?

"We want to win freedom from their rule. All the Ellipse councillors know what we are doing, and all of the ghostiers have had to acknowledge it, however reluctantly. So I think it is time that you know, too. And I want you to understand. We are not fools. We are deadly serious. And we are the product of an ethos which has been fermenting as long as there has been atheism."

"You—you're an atheist?" *I though she had told me everything!* Humi thought wildly. *How much more is there?*

"I have been an atheist for some years," Erene nodded. "It is quite difficult to remain pious when one interacts with the gods face to face, day by day. A flamen's piety is—*blind*—and the rest of the ghostiers . . ." She shook her head. "I don't know how they do it. They are some of the most intractably pious men and women in Delta City. They don't see that the gods' rule is over and that it is time for mortals to rule themselves. The flamens' arbitration has degenerated into positive injustice—if it was ever fair—and Goquisite and I have bound ourselves to oust the Divinarch, and all the gods in the Ellipse along with him."

She sprawled on her elbows in the cushions, relaxed now that she had hit her stride. Humi heard Reason in her voice—Reason, that persuasive devil who has brought down monarchs before and would not hesitate to stoop to a senior ghostier. But her mind rebelled against it. The Divinarch was *divine!* What kind of temerity did it take to dream, much less actually plan, to oust him?

"We won't make our move for quite a while yet, of course," Erene said. "The Divinarch is surrounded night and day by the Divine Guard. All we can do is test the waters around potential accomplices and, when we're sure of them, enlist them in the cause. Belstem is our strongest ally—in fact, many people think he is the ringleader. Our moment will come just after the Divinarch's death, before the Heir assumes the Throne. While the world mourns, we will strike. The Throne will never have another occupant. It was built for gods, not humans, and our world has no use for another dictator." Erene clasped her knees, and her eyes shone. "The Ellipse will take on the power of arbitration. Our votes will become law all over the Divinarchy. The disparity between rich and poor is growing, and that alone should give us more to do than any Divinarch has had for centuries. But that is as it should be. The Conversion Wars can't cast their shadow down all of time. We are finally emerging from that blackness."

The hubbub of the palace district swirled in blips around the sedan. Merisand's leather-shod feet thudded outside the shell.

For some reason, a memory of home kept running through Humi's mind. Every Dividay, if a wandering flamen was not there to preach, the Garden family took a statuette of the Divinarch and stood it on a wood pedestal on the middle of the courtyard. Then they knelt in a circle and prayed. Humi remembered her uncle Cand's rough, reverent voice rising out of the courtyard, floating to the ridges. *Bring us rain, but not too much ... let lambs be born, but not too many ... send us a flamen, and soon, to heal the canker on Mercy's thigh ...*

"Erene, what will people do without the Divinarch? Who will they pray to?"

With an annoyed expression, Erene leaned forward and rapped a complex rhythm on the paneling. Merisand's footsteps slowed for a moment, as if in response, then picked up again. "Soon even the saltsiders will be atheists. That problem will not exist."

"But if the Divinarch and the Incarnations are gone, people will pray to their new rulers. To believe in rulers," Humi said, suddenly sure of herself, "people have to think they're superior to themselves. Before you know it, Erene, *you'll* be a god, along with the other councillors. Do you think you're better than the rest of us?" Erene opened her mouth to reply, but Humi rushed on. "And you know what else you're leaving out? Miracles. If the flamens go, miracles will go with them. I'm a saltsider; I know how one miracle makes the difference between a good year and a year when your middle sticks to your spine in the winter and you wonder if living on salt rabbits, will allow you to see spring. In Calvary and Iceland, the weather is so harsh that people couldn't live at all if not for miracles."

"The lords of those provinces will provide for their people," Erene said firmly.

"The flamens will resist."

"But they'll lose. Because they're too decent to kill. And if *we* have to, then we are ready."

"Not more wars," Humi said.

"Gods' blood, no!" Erene shook her head. "One clean strike, like an amputation—cutting down only those who are determined to die for the Divinarch—and the new regime will slide easily into place."

"Who's going to do the killing?"

Erene shook her head.

"Is it the other ghostiers? Are they part of this too?" The prospect seemed horrible. She had always known there was something different about Erene—but if the other ghostiers turned out to be atheists, that would undermine Humi's whole world—

"Gods, no!" Erene seemed shocked. "I told you they're pious! I have no illusions that they will ever join the cause. Most of them refuse to know even as much as I have told you. And let me warn you that you should not try to make them understand. It will only drive a wedge between you. I know how difficult it is not to share things with them—it can be the most difficult thing in all the world. But now you understand why I told you not to get too close to any of them. We are on different sides."

Humi twisted her fingers together. It seemed so strange that she had lived with them for a month, and gotten to know them so well, and never known that they were on different sides. It was quite clear to her where her loyalty lay—but it saddened her. Trust had come so hard between her and Erene. She could not ruin it over this. She would not. "All right," she said. "I'll keep it to myself."

Erene kissed her cheek. "That's a darling. It's not even a matter of secrecy, really, just etiquette. The Divinarch himself, and the rest of the gods, know everything, and they must have told the flamens, so that everything we plan is known to the whole Ellipse. Nobody can keep anything from the gods—there could be one of them hidden away in even the most secluded meeting room, listening. They can come and go at will. *You've* seen that. They are powerful in and of themselves. Goquisite and I often ask ourselves what they are going to do when they decide we are a real danger."

Humi's bowels froze. She failed to see where there was any question. *Surely they'll crush you, take away all your privileges and exile you to the farthest island of the Archipelago—if they don't kill you!* "But—but what are they doing now, if *they* know everything?"

"Nothing." Erene's breath puffed out in frustration. "The Divinarch takes no action to stop the eroding of his power. In fact, he takes no action at all. *And we do not know why,* unless it is just that he is old and half-mad. I am sure some of the Incarnations would act against us if he let them, but they can do nothing without his consent!"

The sedan swung hard left. A new surface resounded beneath the wheels. Erene uncrumpled her skirts, reached out and twitched Humi's neck ribbons straight. "We are here." The sedan stopped. Erene scrambled out, tucking wisps of hair behind her ears. Humi followed.

The sight of the Old Palace crowded her confusion out of her mind.

Afet Merisand had set the sedan down inside the gate of an enormous courtyard. Oases of fountains and greenery dotted the cobbles. Outlandishly costumed humans crossed the open space; household animals snorted and played. The other sedans stood empty by the gate. Flocks of night birds held raucous court on the surrounding roofs. Humi could hear the sea, somewhere below, it sounded like. The tang of brine in the air overpowered more normal smells of dung and food and fuel, but she could detect quite a powerful smell of burning sulphur.

The seaward side of the courtyard sprang up into the night like a fountain of wood, a fantastic edifice bearing torchlit balconies like cups of flowers. Far away, a pair of enormous, three-man-high oaken doors stood ajar.

"Farewell," Erene smiled to Merisand. "Propel not thy chariot into mischance, you sly old fop." She started to walk across the courtyard. Belatedly Humi realized that she was seeing as many gods as humans. *Members of the Divine Guard.* The strange faces. Each god's body seemed cast in a different, unique form. She was too dazzled by their strangeness to tell their genders. Their intense, pure voices rang out louder than the mortals', louder than the birds, effortlessly, like melodies over the sound of the sea.

A sharp fingernail meandered down her spine. She yelped and spun.

"Hello, Humility," Arity, Heir to the Divinarchy, said. "You were the ghost that spoke, weren't you?" There had been no whiff of sulphur; he must have arrived the ordinary way, by coming up behind her. His face glowed a smooth green in the light from the lanterns in the nearby oasis. He turned to Erene. "You're late. The entire Ellipse is milling around, waiting for you. Where have you been?"

"I had a thing to talk over with my apprentice," Erene said smoothly. "I told the porter to take us by a longer route." Humi marveled at her demeanor. Arity might have been a friend Erene had just met in the street—never mind that he was a god. Never mind that seconds earlier, Erene had been plotting to deprive him of his throne. "What is the Heir to the Divinarchy doing out in the courtyard," she asked, "when assassins may lurk around every corner?"

"Picking dandelions," Arity said shortly. He began to walk towards the palace, his heel talons clicking on the cobbles. Then he shot a glance back at Humi. "What do you think, little ghost?"

"It's—it's beautiful—"

"There used not to be any humans living here." They passed into the racket of the lobby. "That was before the Ellipse passed an edict stating that human servants had to come and clean every two sixdays, because it was dangerous to the Divinarch's health. And now there are many humans living in the Divinarch's household. But there used to be stalactites of tallow below the torches, and stalagmites dripping to meet them. Hundreds of years old at the bases, I should think. And a smell of soot, mixed with the perfumes of generations of Divine Guards."

Arity himself was wearing perfume. Humi sniffed. It reminded her of the salt near her home.

"It was quite repulsive," Erene said.

"If you do not like to breathe the past."

"It still looks rather dirty," Humi ventured, trying to make peace. They mounted a wide stairway. Cobwebs hung from the ceiling of the stairwell, and dust obscured the features of the ghosts which stood in niches in the banister.

Arity stopped and looked at her with a half-smile. "I seconded the edict."

She blinked. "Milord—"

"*Gods,*" Erene spat angrily. "Can you not make sense for *once,* Arity!" She seized Humi's arm and hurried up the stairs, leaving Arity behind.

"I do, only not to you, Milady Gentle!" he called after them. The flow of humans and mortals eddied around him, giving him a wide berth. As Humi looked over her shoulder, he winked out of existence.

I will understand, Humi thought, shaking her head to rid her eyes of the blind spot. *I have to understand.*

Erene left her apprentice at the door of the Elliptical Chamber, directing her to one of the little alcoves from which, like the other apprentices, she could watch the session through a peephole. Apprentices could not enter the chamber. Only councillors, lemans, and the Divine Guards that accompanied the Divinarch. It was at the Old Palace's heart, buried like the yolk of an egg in concentric ellipses of rooms: an enormous bare room with a ceiling black-dappled above the chandeliers and wooden panels gleaming with age. No skylights or windows. But it was only ever used at night anyhow. The gods slept during the day, and it would be unthinkable for Ellipse to meet without the gods—at least, officially. In actual fact, most of the Ellipse's decisions were made in Antiprophet Square, in Goquisite's or Belstem's parlor.

It was near impossible to accomplish anything in session these days, what with the schisms between the councillors and the Divinarch's increasing reluctance to attend. The twenty-first seat always stood empty, as a reminder that no Divine Seals would be given out. Erene herself, as the most powerful councillor, had come to shoulder the task of arbitration to some degree; but the pious councillors, and the Incarnations, did not accept her authority.

Everyone seemed to be present, talking in groups clearly divided along political lines: nobles, ghostiers, flamens, gods. Heads turned to acknowledge her arrival, and they began to drift toward their seats. Goquisite broke off her conversation with Marasthizinith Crane and hurried over to Erene. Her round dark eyes lit up. "A pleasure to see you, my friend." Her voice overflowed with warmth.

With a laugh, Erene gave her a swift embrace. "It's been too long!"

"What is this that I hear about a new apprentice? I thought that when Hem left, that was the end of that nonsense."

"Goq," Erene said. "You hardly *knew* me before Hem left. And right afterward, it was natural for me to be disenchanted with the very idea of apprenticeship. But I *have* to have an apprentice. Ghosting is the be all and end all of me." She wished she was still as sure of that now, in the chamber, in Goquisite's presence, as she had been while she painted Beauty Garden's ghost. "Without it, I wouldn't *be* here in Delta City." That was the truth. "I wouldn't be on the Ellipse."

Goquisite's round arms went around her neck. Erene shut her eyes, praying that Goquisite would accept that easy explanation. Goquisite awakened protective urges in her like those that Humi did, only subtly different. *Please believe me. I just want to spare you.*

"Will you partake of late supper at my house?" Goquisite asked. "I think it's time—" She whispered, her voice giggly with secrecy, "I think it's time that we work on Marasthizinith."

Oh, gods. Erene had planned to take Humi back to Tellury Crescent tonight and go over the Ellipse session, laying out whatever important arguments had cropped up, telling her what she should take seriously and what she should not. Nuance of voice and face, especially with the gods, would often prove vital. She had planned for them to share a cold supper, with wine, and then sleep as long as they both wished in the bedroom that Algia had rendered so clean.

"Of course I'll come," she said. "I'll bring Humi. She won't be any trouble."

Goquisite pouted. "I suppose I ought to meet her."

"Shall we begin?" Erene said loudly to the assembly. She walked around the council table to her seat, number 20, taking care not to catch Goquisite's eye as Goquisite sank into seat number 4. They could not be seen to favor each other once the Ellipse changed from a social gathering to a political machine. Erene was glad she was wearing a fine violet dress with a low-cut back—that frivolity might decrease suspicions that they had been talking of the conspiracy. She took her time gathering up her skirts and arranging them over the chair before she sat down. "We will wait for the Divinarch. Patience please, everyone. And—" she let a note of sarcasm creep into her voice—"let us maintain a respectful silence."

"Pfuh." In seat number 14, Belstem Summer sat like a sack of wheat, uncouth in a bright yellow tailcoat and hose. The other nobles' seats were all in the low numbers: Aneisneida Summer's was 6. On either side of Belstem sat the ghostiers, and between Fra, in seat 13, and Erene sat all five Incarnations: Pati the Striver, the Maiden Hope, Broken Bird, the Sage Bronze Water, and Arity the Heir. Broken Bird and Hope were actually numbers 1 and 2, but they had brought their chairs around so that they could converse privately with the others. The five of them whispered together like bosom friends, controlling their voices so as not to make Erene lose face by openly disobeying her request for silence. No one would have guessed that they belonged to two bitterly opposed factions.

The division within their ranks was even commoner knowledge than Erene, Goquisite, and Belstem's conspiracy was. If not for the Divinarch's refusal to react to the atheists' growing power, and presumably to let the others react, Erene thought, she would have had real rivals in Pati and Hope. Broken Bird and Bronze Water were no threat—as far as she could see, they agreed with the Divinarch's philosophy of inaction. But Pati and Hope were different. Together with most of the Divine Guard, they had proclaimed themselves warriors in a battle against all things atheistic. Outside the Elliptical Chamber, they were as harmless as the others—Erene supposed she had the Divinarch to thank for that—but when the gods lost the confrontation which they knew full well was coming, would Pati step down from his post with grace? Or would he stage a recoup, a debacle which even Erene, ghostier and sometime torturer, could not imagine?

She did not know.

Beside her, Arity sat with his elbows on the table, absently braiding three fat, wormlike strands of Broken Bird's hair. If there was one being in Delta City who disquieted her more than Pati did, it was Arity. As the main beneficiary of Pati's crusade to keep power in the hands of the gods, the Heir ought to have backed the Striver all the way. But every stand he took in Ellipse contradicted the one before. And no other god would dream of putting himself out to palliate a situation rather than to worsen it. When the other Incarnations faced off, two against two, as inevitably happened, Arity was the peacemaker.

If *only* Erene knew what was going through his mind.

A purplish-limned patch in the air—

The whoosh of heat made Erene blink. When she opened her eyes, one sunspot had become two realities, standing on the table beneath the chandelier.

"The Divinarch!" announced the tall young Divine Guard, his hair rising of its own accord. The Divinarch of Royalland, Calvary, Veretry, Pirady, Iceland, the Archipelago, and Domesdys, et al., straightened up. He was no taller than a ten-year-old child. His bones showed through folds of naked, gray-pink skin like sculptures draped with a silk curtain. His blond curls were now no more than white wisps on his skull. The living mustaches which had once reached his waist had shriveled: they twitched constantly, like snakes hung by their tails. His once clear blue eyes were cloudy. He was 191 years old.

He looks worse than last time, Erene thought with pity. Presumptuous to feel sorry for him. But who could help it when they saw this?

"Greetings to the Ellipse." His voice was still strong, and he did not bother to moderate it. "Tonight's topic is the inauguration of Aneisneida Summer, and what it means not only to our Ellipse but to our whole world." He coughed. Erene moved her hand away from the spatters of white blood that landed on the table before her. "The precedent in question is, Should it become customary for Ellipse seats to be hereditary, or should we name Aneisneida an exception and devise a method for choosing the successors of councillors who are to be succeeded by neither lemans nor apprentices? I beg you to discount the fact that Aneisneida's predecessor was a flamen, for as we all know Godsister Purity and her leman died together, caught in a fire, leaving the seat open to the most appropriate candidate." The Divinarch caught Belstem's eye with his cloudy one, and Erene saw Lord Summer flinch slightly. "I am unwell. I shall not stay. I await your decision, and at the end of the session I shall pass a verdict—or maybe I shall not. Sunrise, my friend, let us go."

The Guard shut his eyes for a minute, mustering his strength, and then they went.

"What's the point?" Ziniquel sighed from the seat number 12 in the aftermath of their departure. "We all know there'll be no verdict. We're just going through the motions—"

"Order!" Erene said sharply. Ziniquel muddied, but she did not look at him. "I announce this session open!"

"Should we revise the laws of succession, you will hold the unenviable position of precedent, Aneisneida,"

Godsbrother Puritanism said immediately. "I should like to hear your position." Aneisneida was pale—not unusual for her—but her hands gripped the table, trembling. Puritanism's leman, Auspi, murmured in his ear. Puritanism pursed his lips. Where the salt crystals grew in his eyes, they flooded out of the sockets onto his forehead and cheeks. It gave him a fearsome look, as if his eyes were flaming with white fire. "Aneisneida?" he said.

Her eyes darted to her father's in a wild plea for aid. Erene mentally commended Belstem for his silence. He must be going through anguish right now, keeping himself from jumping in to help her.

The Maiden, Hope, said in a voice like a length of satin falling to the floor, "Go on, Councillor Summer. We're listening."

Aneisneida rose shakily to her feet. Erene ground her teeth as she heard snickers. "Councillors," Aneisneida said, "I am the first mortal councillor ever to accede to the Ellipse without passing through either lemanhood or Tellury Crescent. I feel that I am the first in what should be a long tradition of noble councillors. As the youngest councillor, I hope before I die to see a full eight seats around this table occupied by men and women like me."

Puritanism went rigid. "Summer! Why have you put this inflammatory nonsense into the mouth of your child?"

Belstem protested self-righteously, "She composed every word of her speech herself!"

"May I go on?" Aneisneida's voice trembled.

"We shall have words!" said Puritanism. "We shall have words, Summer!"

"I am Summer too," Aneisneida said, more strongly. "And the winter is over." ("How precious," Pati muttered sardonically.) "The tradition of passing seats from master to apprentice, or flamen to leman, is outdated. A master and apprentice come together late in life as compared to a parent and child. They may be of such different temperaments that the focus of the seat is changed when it is passed from one to the other, and thus the balance of the entire council disturbed. There can never be a really close relationship between two people who will consider murdering each other for personal gain." That was a direct jab at the ghostiers. "The younger can never fully understand the older, nor respect his position.

"I speak of all crafts, all positions. Children are chosen as apprentices by craftsmen who are no relation to them. They are taken as cabin boys on ships. They are apprenticed to traders who travel up and down the country with the seasons. Separating lines of succession from bloodlines ignores one of the most valuable treasures we humans possess: our racial differences. The combination of a master from one continent and an apprentice from another cancels out the unique perspective which each of them brings to the craft. Over the thousands of years since the Conversion Wars, this practice has wiped out the indigenous languages of each continent, each province, so that we all speak more or less the same tongue. Many people do not even know that there used to be many languages.

"There is also a problem with our lack of records. Even in Delta City, most of the important families have come into being in the last two centuries. They are cut off from their ancient history by the severance of their founding member, usually an ex-leman, from his or her family. They know nothing of their heritage. Families are the natural warp of history. By chopping them up to make one child a leman, another a ghostier's apprentice, a third a cabin boy, we destroy the sense of nuclear *community* which each province, each town, and each household ought to hold dear above all else.

"I propose a law detailing changes in these objectionable customs. It would be foolish to try to correct centuries of wrongheadedness at a stroke, but it is high time we councillors gave birth to a beginning. I believe that I am she."

There was dead silence as her chair scraped again.

Far below, the sea lapped against the cliff.

Belstem tipped back in his chair, laced his hands on his stomach, and began almost inaudibly to hum.

"*You* composed this speech, Belstem," Erene said icily,

breaking the silence, "because it's what you've been wanting to say for a long time—and you thought we would not be as hard on Anei as we would on you." Her mind boiled coldly. When she did not admire Belstem, she despised him. Right now she could have ground him under her heel. *No truly close relationship between two people who will consider murdering each other . . . No?* Some detached part of her mind was whispering, *Humi, Humi.*

"The peace within and between the continents is the flamenhood's greatest accomplishment. I acknowledge that freely. Their custom of choosing lemans in one place and setting them down in another is a vital ingredient of that peace. Do you want to upset everything that centuries have proved to be wholesome, just to consolidate your triumph over the flamenhood?" Elicit's voice cracked as he said, "How high have you set your sights, man? Are you *insane*?" Words appeared to fail him.

But words never failed Pati the Striver. "You spineless worm, Belstem," he said silkily, "you slithering, crawling ground thing that harbors longings to be greater than the *gods*. Your arrogance comes dangerously near to treason, and I'll see you recant or I'll see you thrown out of Ellipse."

But by the end of the session, that goal was not realized. Belstem held the floor alone against Pati, Broken Bird, Bronze Water, Hope, and all the ghostiers, including Erene. Usually she backed Belstem, but this time she knew he had gone too far. Pietimazar Seaade and Marasthizinith Crane had swung back and forth, not wanting to alienate themselves from anyone. Erene hadn't let herself hope that Goquisite would not back Belstem, no matter how preposterous his scheme might be; when Lady Ankh first voiced her disagreement with him, Erene had hardly been able to keep from rushing around the table to hug her.

It was a measure of Belstem's phenomenal powers of argument that by the time everyone else in the Chamber was exhausted, and Erene finally called a halt, he hadn't yet been put at a disadvantage. Next session they would end him, Erene thought as the councillors straggled toward the door. Goquisite took her arm, saying that she had told her porters to wait at the Ferien entrance. Erene's mind still lingered on the session. *Surprise was on his side tonight, but we'll prepare an argument for next time and finish this madness.*

She would not let herself wonder whether, once the conspiracy succeeded, Belstem might swing permanently to this extreme end of the spectrum.

We'll make him see sense.

Eleven

Alone in the juddering sedan after the session, on the way to pay a visit to Goquisite Ankh's mansion that she had not anticipated and did not want, Humi struggled to understand the thing that had happened to her during Ellipse.

Spark and clash, her memories flowed, fusing with each other like pieces of a divine jigsaw.

The first: the Eftpool.

The second: Several days ago, as she wandered alone along the roof roads, a terribly drunk young man staggered up to her. He grabbed her collars and breathed alcoholically into her face: *"I see ... I see ..."* Then in a voice which might have belonged to a different person, "Godsie, if you don't stop me I'm going to be taken with prophecy. It's happened once already, and I'm afraid, deathly afraid. Slap me, hit me, please—"

He winced and let go of her, his arms jerking like windmill blades. More out of fright than anything else, she hit him hard across the face. He blinked—spasmed—heaved a shuddering sigh.

"Thank you ... Can you take me over there? I would be obliged ..."

The discreet wooden sign, swinging in the breeze, denoted a hard-liquor daylight bar. Wrinkling her nose at the smell blowing from the door, Humi half-supported him to the threshold. "Won't you have a ... a ... a glass of wine?" he asked. "A glass with me? I'm a leman. I'm perfectly safe—"

Drunkenness didn't attract her, not in others or in herself. Since he was a leman, that made it even less excusable.

The whole episode frightened her. She excused herself with the truth, saying that she had to get back before her master woke up. It worked like a charm. She had never seen him again.

The third memory: She sat in a soft, musty-smelling armchair in an alcove outside the Elliptical Chamber. She had long since forgotten the sweetmeats that had been left for her refreshment. She pressed her nose to the glass of the peephole, captivated, as Pati leapt up on the table, commanding the Chamber. Belstem, on his feet, tried to shout him down. The glass reduced their voices to squeaking, but if Humi strained her ears she could make out the words—

A soft *thump,* and a gust of warm air hit the back of her neck, bumping her forehead against the glass. She smelled burning sulphur.

The Divinarch stood by the chair, his presence too intense for the tiny room. A tall, crop-haired Guard held him with one arm. The Guard sneezed, looked over what was left of the sweetmeats, and took a piece of marchpane.

The Divinarch's voice threatened to drive the air from Humi's eardrums. "Mortal girl Humility. As misnamed as my *firchresi* Patience."

"Y-yes, Milord God?" Determined not to be at a disadvantage, Humi got to her feet. She towered over the Divinarch.

But he turned his face up toward her, and the papery skin slid back from his nose and the clustered fangs in his mouth. "Of late the land has been riddled with prophecy. The lemans who are taken by it spout all kinds of ominous sayings, which are most often taken to prognosticate the end of my reign. The like of which prophecies I do not need." He laughed. Instantly the Guard handed him a square of linen bleached so white that the new blood he coughed up was nearly invisible. "Most recently taken," the Divinarch continued when he got his breath, "was Lexi Treeborn, leman of the councillor Godsbrother Joyfulness. Whether he is to be believed or not . . . that is up to you. These were his words to you, and he called you by name, though afterward he remembered it not.

"You lean out the window with the ghost of your childhood companion behind you, and look towards the sunrise. And your body longs to follow the birds across the marshes. You shall follow them, yea, and to Heaven. You shall receive the highest honor the world can bestow upon you. Yet you shall live a life of deception. Your heart shall be heavy as a rock veined with iron. And the truth is ineffable. Not even the gods know it. You cannot know it. You must learn to face it. It is ineffable.

"Tell me, child, what am I to make of this?"

And of course, Humi had already met Lexi. And he had nearly prophesied again.

In the sedan, Humi shivered. Brilliant, frightening pyrotechnics ignited in her mind. She wondered that they didn't shine through her skull and light up the dark. Brilliance: she caught glimpses of the meaning of the prophecy. But she could not understand it, any more than Lexi had.

"I don't know," Marasthizinith said. "Honestly—I couldn't commit myself to anything so—so—"

"Dangerous as openly affiliating yourself with us?" Goquisite suggested sweetly.

"No, no!" Marasthizinith's eyes were wild. "No—it's just—that I am timid, you know that, and a delicate character! How can I successfully engage in—in—subversive activities?"

Erene leaned back into the luxury of the overstuffed loveseat, wine cup suspended between thumb and forefinger. She enjoyed these exercises in persuasion. "Pieti has given us his allegiance. Did you know that?" She was anticipating an event which had not actually happened, but which she knew would soon. "I assure you nothing undue will be required of you. You're the only councillor left whose allegiance we are not sure of. You must join us—or . . ." She lifted her cup to her lips and with delicate lasciviousness sucked the dark red liquid.

"Or," Goquisite picked up her cue, "we shall have to ... reconsider. One suspects you of piety, Maras. Is this justified? Or are you just scared?" She slid a glance full of secret laughter to Erene, and her hand stole out across the arm of the loveseat. Hooking little fingers with her, Erene luxuriated in contentment. (She refused to remember Humi, who sat alone not twenty feet away, in the unlit corner of the sitting room.) Maras couldn't possibly hold out against both of them. No matter what their weaknesses, together Erene and Goquisite formed an inquisition machine that could reduce far more sturdy prey than Marasthizinith Crane to quivering pudding.

"I—I don't know ..." With a shaking hand, Maras poured herself more wine. When she put down the decanter the one-legged side table rocked and nearly toppled. "What would I have to do?"

"I told you. Nothing," Goquisite said patiently. "Except refrain from betraying who is at the center of the conspiracy."

"You and Erene." Myopic brown eyes skittered from one to the other. "I thought it was Belstem."

"So do most people. And so do those abroad who guess that something of this sort is afoot. But this way, if by some mischance Belstem should *not* outlive the Divinarch, all would not be lost." Erene hoped she managed to keep spite out of her voice. When pressed, Belstem had confessed to writing Aneisneida's speech. But he had demonstrated no penitence.

"We are enlarging our network of supporters all the time," Goquisite said. "But you won't have to worry about that, Maras—it's Erene and I who probe the allegiances of the lesser nobles, who search out the accounts of the Wars that will help us mount our coup."

"Perhaps that is where *I* could be of help," Maras burst out eagerly. "I daresay I am the most knowledgeable among us on the subject of history. For a long time, I have taken an interest—"

Erene suppressed a smile and sipped her wine. They had her now. It was only a matter of careful reeling in.

* * *

All right. They've got her. Humi sat in the corner, arms folded, glowering at the candlelit circle of sofas and lounge chairs. She wasn't tired—the tea she'd drunk when they came in had seen to that—but she was sick of Goquisite and her befrilled parlor and the thousands of meticulously dusted figurines on shelves. She was weary of Erene's making cow eyes at the woman. She was so obvious! The motion of her head above the back of the loveseat betrayed a slight but perceptible tension. Humi took a vindictive pleasure in that. Maybe Erene thought she'd put Humi out of sight and mind; maybe she thought that as soon as they left here, she'd be able to hold out her arms and Humi would come running. But it wasn't as easy as that. Humi could already tell that she would never like Goquisite. The inattentive way Lady Ankh had looked her over when they were introduced—she had been talking to Erene and twirling a wineglass at the same time—had made her feel like an animal, a poodle or a salt cat, a pet.

The far door swept open. The three in the candlelight started. A figure clad in a dark cloak strode in, shaking out his moss-green hair. Drops flew. A candle hissed. "Milady Ankh, Milady Crane, a pleasure. Erene, I've come for Humi. Do you know it's three in the morning? She's a ghostier, not a hired servant! She ought to be at home in Tellury Crescent, in bed."

Humi levered her stiff body up and hurried toward Ziniquel. "Here I am!" she called with a relief that she'd meant to conceal.

"*Imrchu,* I wouldn't dream of letting you sit in a corner all night," Ziniquel said. As he brushed past Erene and Goquisite to meet her, his dripping cloak slapped Erene's face. She remained silent. Ziniquel ignored her tacit plea for peace. "I have a cloak for you, Humi. Here. We're walking. I couldn't get a sedan at this ungodly hour."

"It's perfectly possible," Erene said. "Goquisite has three porters regularly detailed for the night shift, and more on call."

Ziniquel guided Humi toward the door. He spoke without turning. "I don't think it's wise for a porter in Ankh livery to be seen bringing *anyone* home to Tellury Crescent at this hour of the night." His tone gave the last phrase a meaning unsuitable for polite company. Erene's face went muddy gray.

Ziniquel's rudeness emboldened Humi. Her irritation boiled to the surface. "Good night, Erene! If I see you at home, until then. If not, until tomorrow!"

Ziniquel shut the door on a ringing silence. "I wonder how they'll smooth *that* over." He chuckled. "Goquisite is not very deft at dealing with situations once she loses control."

Now that she was alone with him, Humi felt suddenly shy. The last time they had seen each other privately, she had been dressed as a ghost. It made her muddy to remember what had happened that night. But he seemed to feel no awkwardness.

The angular spiral stairwell was lined with ghosts. "Goquisite is an avid collector, especially of ghosts canted towards the darker end of the spectrum. She admires your cousin's ghost greatly. Erene has dedicated several of her works to her."

Footmen struggled to conceal their surprise as Ziniquel and Humi passed between them, out into the night. Icy rain roared like a sea on the tropical garden which rambled around Goquisite's mansion and up its walls. The scents of bruised greenery rose around them as they ducked under broad magnolia and rhododendron leaves. Antiprophet Square glistened. An occasional light reflected on the cobbles, but as they left the palace district behind, these petered out, and the muffled sounds of carousing gave way to barking dogs and snuffling pigs. Marshtown laid itself silent, bare, to the rain.

"We're home," Ziniquel said abruptly.

Humi had not even recognized Tellury Crescent. Albien House looked more forbidding than usual, heavier, a scarecrow-roofed shadow against the night. The door was unlocked, as always. A single light burned in the hall that the Chalice and Albien House shared. It was as bare of furnishings as ever, but right now it seemed to Humi that it would be a crime to place anything here besides their feet. "Talk about *wet*!" Ziniquel said. "Humi, do you want a hot drink?"

Caught in the middle of wringing out her hair, she nodded. "I'd—I'd be glad."

Their wet footprints followed them up the stairs. "How about chocolate?"

"What's that?"

"You don't—gods! Your manners are so sophisticated, sometimes I forget you're just a saltsider!" He grinned at her. "It'll be a rare treat to introduce you to chocolate. Cacao bean, no honey."

Humi hadn't been inside his workshop since she had posed as a ghost. The lace-curtained bedchamber awakened disturbing memories. Shivers ran up her spine. In the middle of the workshop floor, cross-legged in the midst of scattered palettes, pigment pots, and brushes, sat another ghost.

It was Wella's husband.

Humi sprang back halfway to the door. "Gods! What—why didn't you send it with the others?"

"What?" Ziniquel followed her eyes. "It's just a ghost."

"I was a companion alo- along with him." Her teeth chattered in the cold as she sidled forward. "He was Elic-it's ghost's husband." The Veretrean boy looked peacefully absorbed in a book. She couldn't believe his silky sheet of hair was diamondine until she brought herself to touch it. Cold—cold, and hard. So were the pages of the book. So were his lips, whose dark-sheened flesh looked so tender, caught up by one pearly tooth. When she touched the diamondine, she felt no despair or desolation, only the steady, peaceful zest for life of one who is studying what he loves. None of the other ghosts she'd seen tonight compared to this one for technical excellence. But she knew that he came of tree-farmer folk, like his wife, and that he could never have felt such an emotion in his life.

The ghost's spell dissipated.

"What are you going to do with it?"

"I don't know yet." Ziniquel stood watching her.

"Probably give it to one of the flamens. Joyfulness, per-haps. He loves books—he gets Lexi to read to him, even though it's an atheist thing."

"But it would be wasted on him. A flamen can't see."

"The art of ghosting was conceived for blind men. He can *feel*. And he won't cache the ghost away in his home, as the Summers have done with the commissioned ones—he'll put it in a tavern or public place, so that common people can feel it. Maybe he'll even send it abroad. That's why I give my ghosts to the flamenhood. I want them to be used, not coveted." He stopped, then shrugged, seem-ing a little abashed at his own passion.

"Then most of the ghosts that you make—they *aren't* commissioned?"

Ziniquel snorted. "The last time anyone commissioned ghosts was for Arity's inauguration. Fifteen years ago. If we only worked once every fifteen years, we would soon lose our credibility in the Ellipse."

"So how do we find our ghosts? How did you get hold of this one?"

"Usually—well, usually, we seduce them. That's an-other talent ghostiers have to have."

Humi remembered Mory leading Rain out of the hall ... Erene with her dress torn off one shoulder ... She would *never* be able to do that! "Not me!"

"I wouldn't have thought you had any potential as an apprentice if I hadn't seen that you could," Ziniquel said. "It's not as hard as it sounds. All I do is sit in my favorite haunts—in disguise, of course—and the ghosts find *me*. And I hear from Emni that you're already learning the technique." Humi flushed. Did her explorations through the city count as practice for ghost-hunting expedi-tions then? "All the runaways in the world come to Delta City. A good many of them are penniless when they get here, and those are generally the youngest and most beau-tiful. Here's the manifesto." He recited, "*Ghosts must rep-resent every part of Salt. They must be young. They must be beautiful, which means that they must be instantly and constantly pleasing to the eye. And unless they be ex-tremely exceptional, their beauty must conform to some degree with fashion as dictated by the present court. The ghostier's eye having fallen upon a young man or woman conforming to these standards, it is up to him to judge whether the decay of his or her beauty is exigence sufficient to weigh heavier than his or her life in the Divine Balance.*"

"Oh," Humi said. "Erene hasn't told me any of this."

Ziniquel laughed unpleasantly. "She hasn't told you much, has she?"

"She hasn't exactly had leisure to teach me lately." Humi rose to Erene's defense. "She's had other things to worry about."

"Oh? What could be more important than the tutoring of an apprentice?" Ziniquel's eyes were hard as green ice.

"Court business," Humi spat, "that wouldn't be difficult for her to accomplish at all if it weren't for the rest of you sitting in her way like *stones*—"

"Humi! You're not responsible for her. You don't have to defend her to me. And I—" He stepped forward and closed his hands on her shoulders. "I shouldn't shift my anger onto you. The rift is between Erene and myself. I apologize."

Humi found herself trembling.

"I don't think you understand. Do you understand?" Gently, he lifted her chin with one hand.

Horrifying herself, Humi burst into tears. "She's my master. I depend on her goodwill! I'm on her *side*!"

Ziniquel shook his head disbelieveingly. He pulled her close and held her to his chest, rocking back and forth. "What has she been telling you? Your talent depends on us—*all* of us! You can be on her side and ours both at once. The rules of ghosting aren't like those of other crafts. If she died or moved out of the Crescent, you'd have the choice of staying in the Crescent and being taught by one of the other masters. She knows that, and it probably influences her decisions. So in a way, *you* have power over *her.*

"But that's not the point."

His cloak smelled of rain. Steadied in his arms, she began to relax.

"What I mean is that—" he paused, as if searching for words to describe something he took for granted—"there are thirteen people who would make you welcome if you crawled into their beds late at night. You will never want for someone to care for you, to love you. There isn't *just* Erene. We are all your family. In the language of the gods, there are no words for father, mother, brother, sister—but there are a hundred different words for *friend*, and one of them applies specifically to ghostiers." He moved her away a little and looked into her face. "The gods don't like people to know that they have their own language. Or that they created a word especially for us. So we only use it among ourselves."

"Tell me," Humi said, fascinated, her tears slowing.

"We are *imrchim*. You are my *imrchu*. I am your *imrchi*."

. The word was redolent of embraces and whispers. Humi felt a sense of awe. *The language of the gods* ...

"Our companionship is essential to our art. You must remember that. Never reject your *imrchim*, or your talent will fade away too."

"What about Erene?"

"I didn't say anything about her," Ziniquel said brusquely, and moved away. Humi hugged herself, suddenly cold in her wet clothes. "How about that chocolate?"

His apartment was as higgledy-piggledy as Erene's, but in a friendlier, lived-in way. Hearth fires smoldered in every room. The furniture was dark with age. The small kitchen held a far wider array of foods than Erene's did (even now that Algia had put it in good repair). Humi watched as Ziniquel prepared the chocolate; then he led her into the living room. "It's so homelike," she said sincerely.

He shrugged. "The others use their apartments to remind themselves of their origins. So do I, and I'm Deltan."

"But these must—" She stopped. Then she said, "These must have been Constance Searidge's rooms before they were yours."

"She was Icelandic. I changed them completely."

The fire had died to embers, its heat intensified by the humidity in the room. The windows dripped condensation. The imported pine wood logs released a sharp scent of resin. Ziniquel stared into the fire.

"Will you tell me about her?" Humi said softly.

"You must have heard by now. It's only one of our stories."

She shook her head.

"Gods . . . Why is it falling to me to tell you all our secrets? I'm not your master." He sank back on the fleece rug. "Sorry. I didn't mean that the way it sounded. Really, I'm happy to speak for the *imrchim*. And I suppose I'm a good spokesman, because I'm not ashamed of anything I've done." He stared up at her, hands behind his head.

It seemed impossible that this hot-tempered, cold-blooded creature, dangerous as an unsheathed knife, would talk to her. Impossible that he trusted her with his secrets. But then, she was his *imrchu*. "Tell me," she said.

The story of Constance Searidge's death was a drama which the ghostiers reenacted many times per generation. In fact, only two of the current master ghostiers had got where they now were by their own masters' natural deaths or resignations. He wouldn't tell Humi which they were. One had to respect the fact, he said, that some of them were secretly ashamed of their deeds, and of the hunger for power, an essential component of the ghostier's character, that had brought them to commit those deeds. Ordinary people would have been dogged by guilt all their days. The ghostiers' talent lay in their ability to shrug off almost all of it. The more, the better the ghostier.

Ziniquel's murder of Constance Searidge had hinged on her refusal to acknowledge that she was old and her heart weak, on her confidence that Ziniquel would compensate for her weakness and ask nothing in return, and on the bodies of several infants. Ziniquel hadn't killed them. Babies died by the dozen every day in Delta City, victims of disease and poverty. While Constance was out, he turned the room into the scene of a massacre. It had been furnished all in white, with textural paintings and fleeces. The blood stood out as if something had been savaged on the snow. "It was too much for her to take, murderess though she was. Ghostiers aren't hardhearted, you know—we're just able to direct our compassion where it matters. We do have our vulnerabilities. And I knew Constance's."

So ridiculously easy. Humi closed her eyes.

"She looked much older after she died."

"What did you do with the body?"

"I locked the door on the whole ugly mess and left it. There was an Ellipse meeting that night. I invented an excuse to come into the Chamber, and I claimed Constance's seat. I was safe then. I brought the others here and showed them what I had done."

Humi shivered. Her imagination provided color for the scene, most of it red. "All that for an old chair with '12' carved on the back. It seems so pointless."

"Haven't you felt it yet?" Ziniquel's voice was quiet, but it made Humi shiver. "Ghosting *is* power. Our god-given license to kill extends to *anyone*, Humi, anyone at all, provided that we can make a beautiful enough ghost out of them to swing the Divine Balance. That's where we get our seats in Ellipse. Because right back at the beginning of civilization, the gods made us the most powerful people in the Divinarchy."

"Is power that important? I thought art was the key—"

"Oh, no. *Oh*, no." Zin smiled mirthlessly. "Power is all-important. And for many of us it doesn't stop with ghosting. It doesn't even stop with the Ellipse. Many of us, throughout the ages, have been consumed by ambition. They've let the ice into their hearts. Erene is one of those, I think."

"Are you?"

"Not me." He gestured around the room. "I'm content. I wouldn't even miss the Ellipse, were you to take it away from me, as long as I could still ghost."

She felt the heat of the fire, imbuing the air with its sweet pine scent. But the ice was there. It was outside in the rain, waiting. She felt something else too, like a current running invisibly between her and Ziniquel. The near-obscene things which he had done to her sixdays ago, in that lace-hung chamber.

She slipped down to the rug and snuggled against his side. "Ziniquel."

"Mmm?" He stroked her arm, smiling down at her.

"Do—do *imrchim* make love to each other?"

"They do indeed." A log crashed in the fire. His hand picked at the nubs in her sleeve. "But not you and me."

She pressed her face into his shoulder, unspeakably embarrassed. His bones were prominent under the linen tunic, his flesh hot from the fire.

"Wait," he said, laughter in his voice. "Let me explain. You're a virgin, right?"

She nodded.

"And you're only sixteen! You're not ready for that."

"Erene told me not to," she said into his shirt. "But I thought you said you loved me."

"I do. *Making* love is different. I think Erene was right this time, much as I hate to admit it—it's too early for you. You want to find your feet among all of us, not get hopelessly attached to one person. Specially not me." He squeezed her. Disappointment washed through her like a tide. She had a feeling of a giant, irrevocable step taken—a crossroads left behind. It had to do with more than just Ziniquel. It had to do with Erene. Obeying her. Loving her. The business Humi had promised to help her with. The things the Divinarch had said to her, for her ears alone. But she did not want power or recognition; she only wanted someone to hold her and kiss her tenderly. She wanted this man.

"Who were your other lovers?" she asked.

"Erene. Mory. Elicit. Owen. No one right now. But I suppose you can tell I have my eye on Emni. If it wasn't for her attachment to Sol, she and I would be lovers. I'm pretty sure of that."

"You were *Owen's* lover?"

"Yes, I'm a lover-of-men at times." He looked down at her face. "Is that taboo in Domesdys?"

"What—no, that's not what I meant! Oh, Zin." She

snuggled against him. "I don't want anything more from you than love."

"You've got that." He sounded vaguely puzzled. She was reminded, with a sudden feeling of age and wisdom, that he was just nineteen, and that this was the only life he'd ever known. "From all the others too. Never doubt it. You are our *imrchu*."

She fell asleep there, lying with her head on his shoulder.

She dreamed of Beau, and efts circling in clouds of bloody water, and Constance Searidge lying dead with her head in Ziniquel's lap. Ziniquel howled silent grief. The Divinarch's mouthful of fangs grinned solemnly in his pinkish-gray child's face. *Curiosity is our worst flaw,* he said to Humi. *As a race, we gods have always been victim to it. Now our decline falls upon us soft as snow, because we delved too far and uncovered the Great Irony which we never should have known. Stunned by it, we let ourselves drift. And the current of time carries us downward.*

Follow the birds, Humility.

Gold streamed in the window. Outside, sparrows and starlings swooped and fluttered, darting across a strip of bright azure sky. For a moment their warbling tore at her heart. But then all was hidden beneath the bright reality of waking.

Her cheek rested on a feather pillow. A multicolored blanket snuggled her in warmth. The fire crackled cheerfully.

"Good morning!" Zin called, opening the back door of the apartment. "I've brought breakfast!"

She could smell apple pastries and hot chicory.

"Fresh from Frivalley's bakery! How did you sleep?"

Twelve

That day, over the lunch dishes, Humi talked to Owen. In the afternoon she spoke long and earnestly with Emni. And gradually the ghostiers' complicated shorthand of affection and death opened up to her.

The spice of constant danger raised their companionship above the mundane. These men and women whose vocation was so closely tied into death were spoiled for anything else, like sugar addicts whose palates find all other foods dull. The possibility of the hidden syringe lay in each embrace: and so apparent betrayals were really fair victories. And what looked to an outsider like murder was only a lapse of wariness on the part of the victim.

Keeping this in mind, Humi saw that it was impossible for them to be merely fellow craftsmen. They became *imrchim.*

Rita was living in the shadow of the axe, just as Constance had. But *she* was canny enough to be aware of it. That was the reason she took such joy in life. Her every day was borrowed from Owen. "I'm just taking my time. Soon that seat is going to be *mine,*" Owen boasted to Humi. But later, Emni told Humi that he had already made several attempts which Rita had sidestepped.

Every master was in danger from him, for the ghostiers' law of succession was nonrestrictive—but Rita made the easiest target, since she and Owen shared living quarters. She held seat number 11 in the Ellipse—inferior only to Fra's, Ziniquel's, and Erene's among those held by the ghostiers.

Emni and Humi sat on the lip of the twins' big, sunken bed in their white-walled bedroom. This apartment was a model specimen of what Humi doubted she and Erene would ever have: a family home. The walls were scattered with the Archipelagan ink paintings for which the twins and Beisa shared a talent. Bubbly as always, Emni seemed happy to gossip. "Algia's twenty-seven. That's almost *too* old to become a master. Elicit thinks he's safe from her—and I agree." She laughed. "She's just too watery. Any potential she *had* is all gone."

Privately, Humi thought Elicit had displayed a keen eye for apprentice material when he picked Algia. Several times, she had surprised a sneaking look of red danger in the woman's eyes.

"Me and Sol aren't fully trained yet, of course," Emni said. "We've only been here four years. And Beisa teaches thoroughly and slowly. Seven years is the minimum which makes a master ghostier—we'll likely take longer. Zin did it in just under six, but he shouldn't have. His accession was fair but not really welcome among the rest of us. Even if Constance was past her prime, she was as astute a councillor and as brave a friend as anyone."

"Isn't that rather the point?" Humi asked. "She was past her prime as a ghostier, so she had to go."

Emni grimaced. "Yes. You're catching on fast. That's what Ziniquel said. But I thought he was just making excuses for his own ambition—he's very unscrupulous."

"Do you like him?"

Emni looked at her, puzzled. "Of course. I love him."

Do you know he's attracted to you, though? "Em, I'd like to know about you and Sol. You grew up together, didn't you?"

"Yes."

Humi waited. Emni poured both of them more watered wine. As she relidded the pitcher, she said carefully, "Sol and I are complete opposites. Beisa has told us both, privately, that only one of us has the potential to be a master ghostier. But she wouldn't say which. And I don't suppose we'll ever know, not until she starts to fail, or until one of us gets impatient. *Then* we'll see which of us stood up in the womb and which lay curled around his or her ankles."

"What a horrible thought to live with," Humi said sincerely.

"We manage." Emni gulped wine. "Don't tell anybody that, Humi. I—I never told anyone before. And I know Sol hasn't either. He wouldn't like it if he knew I'd told you." Humi nodded sympathetically. "It'd be easier," Emni said with a trace of anger, "if we only knew whether Beisa took him along as company for me—or me for him. And only later started treating us equally. But she won't tell."

"Maybe she doesn't—"

"Supper, Em!" Sol put his head around the door. "Oh, hello, Humi." Grinning, he seemed perfectly friendly. "Erene's been back for a while. She was looking for you. But now she's helping Rita serve up." He paused. "You'll find them in the Chalice kitchen."

Humi recognized a hint when she heard one. "See you in a bit, Em," she said, and levering herself to her feet, she went out into the hall. When she heard the door close behind her, she came back and put her ear to the crack.

"What did you tell her?" Sol's voice was harsh.

"Nothing you wouldn't have told her yourself." Emni's self-righteousness quailed into defensiveness. "Don't worry, Sol! She's sweet! I love her! I want her to be our friend!"

Sol said bitterly, "She'll split us apart. She can't possibly understand how it is between you and me."

"We're brother and sister. She could *never* split us apart! Besides, she has other things to worry about. What's it going to be like for her as Erene's apprentice?"

"See! Your mind's already full of her concerns!" There were rustles, and a little gasp. Sol said roughly, "It's just that I couldn't stand to lose you, Em. Do you see? I couldn't stand it."

"I love you too!" To Humi's horror, Emni began to weep. "I promise I won't talk to her anymore!"

Silence. Or nearly.

Humi felt a loneliness open up inside her. Intellectually she did not envy their closeness. But for some reason she wanted to cry. She hurried through the apartment. Beisa

was sitting in the last of the light, sketching two
Marshtown youngsters squatting in the window opposite,
sharing a pipe. As Humi passed, she looked up and
smiled, the smile of a sorely tried mother who is glad that
her children are making other friends at last.

Thirteen

Erene got the summons from the Divinarch that morning, by courier dove, as she tried to dress in the cramped bedroom without waking Humi. It said to come alone. Erene did not know why she had asked Elicit. Maybe she needed to share something with him. She felt they were not so close as they had been. Once, they had been two Piradean ghostiers, bound by trade and ethnicity, so similar in their likes and dislikes that they could finish each other's sentences. When they lay together in bed, she had the strangest feeling that they were one complete person, that she could not move without moving Elicit's body, too. That kinship had started the day Erene arrived in Delta City, young and bursting with life; it had weathered Hem, Erene's atheism, and even Erene's friendship with Goquisite. But it seemed as though it might not weather Erene's snatching Humi from Ziniquel.

So she had brought him today, to show him that she trusted him.

They swept to the end of the hall, where a queue of vacant-eyed Deltans ended before a pair of oaken doors. "We have a prior appointment," she said kindly to the first woman in line, and they entered the Throne Room. The guard pulled the doors shut behind them. Jeweled chandeliers shook sprinkles of colored light over the walls. The vastness of the hall made the Throne look diminutive. Human-made, it was a thousand-year-old tribute to the first Divinarch, less a chair than an enormous, elaborate setting for the Divinarch's tiny body, trimmed with age-blackened bits and bobs and fetishes from every corner of the six continents and the Archipelago. On a dozen pedestals built into it stood Divine Guards, Arity, Pati, Hope, Broken Bird, and Bronze Water among them. *Even Incarnations have to do whatever duty the old idiot feels like assigning them!* Erene thought disgustedly.

She squeezed Elicit's hand as they bowed to the Throne. "I am sorry we are late, Divinarch. Several streets in Christon were blocked by beggars. They had overturned produce carts to loot them. It is disgraceful how many paupers there are this year."

"It is the same from Samaal to Rukarow," the Divinarch said. Unlike most gods, he made no attempt to moderate his voice for the sake of human ears. "Many, many of my subjects have sunk to destitution who before were able to eat."

He yawned tremendously, stretching his little body until it quivered, and leaped down from the Throne, a wizened pink monkey child with enormous fangs and eyes. His mustaches jerked spastically. He appeared to be having a good day. "You may all go now," he said, looking around at the gods on the pedestals. "All of you."

The gods' voices sparkled like fireworks.

"Milord!"

"And leave you alone with a ghostier and an insurgent? We're not going anywhere, Old One!"

"Er-serbalu, iye fash graumir?"

"Yes, I am going to make you leave! Go away. Go on. Even you, Pati!"

"Do you think he's cracked, Errie?" Elicit whispered.

"He's not mad," Pati answered from the Throne, his white face glassy, his wings thrumming. Gods had sharp ears. "Just deluded. I don't know what he's planning. Both of you had better be on your guard." He vanished.

One by one, shooting distrustful glances at Erene and Elicit, the other gods followed. Erene blinked to clear the spots from her eyes.

"Good," Divinarch said, rubbing his hands. "I can still make them do my bidding. When I get too old for *that,* it will truly be time to die . . . ! Lady Gentle, I have been wanting to talk to you alone for a long time. And you, Godsman Paean, you might as well hear too. The *firim* would make such a to-do if they heard what I am going to tell you." He perched on the base of the Throne, drawing his knees up. "So, Lady Gentle, why do you think there are so many beggars in the streets this autumn?"

"It is the taxes," Erene said cautiously. "Belstem Lord Summer has raised them again."

"And why did he raise them last year . . . and again this year?"

"To improve the economy, Divinarch." Why did he want to hear this? He must know already. "To put power in the hands of those who have the capital and therefore the influence to use it effectively. To give the lower classes an incentive to better themselves."

"Glib!" The Divinarch steepled his fingers. "Answer me. Why do you and Belstem want the common classes to better themselves?"

"Everyone should desire to better themselves."

"Aha. Now we come to the rub. The flamens believe that all mortals should be equal, and equally content. Whereas, if I hear you right, Belstem does not believe in contentment. He thinks that mortal society should have a dynamic, preferably an upward dynamic, though as in the case of the beggars, it can so easily be a downward one. He believes in constant movement between the social strata. I seem to recall that his word for this change is 'progress'."

"With all due respect, Divinarch, you know the atheistic position as well as I do." Erene bobbed her head. "You're leading up to something. What is it?"

"Watch out!" Elicit breathed in agony.

The Divinarch's voice rang with satisfaction. "In my opinion, Lady Gentle, Godsman Paean, Lord Summer is right to raise the taxes."

Elicit gasped.

"It *is* time for mortal society to *progress,* to outgrow the constraints imposed on it by the flamenhood. We the gods are no longer relevant to you. We can share in this progress, or not, as humanity dictates. Erene, you and Belstem are geniuses, pioneers, as great as the Wanderer and the Antiprophet. I salute you."

Oh, gods, Erene thought. *No. He's joking, but this is it, this is the end with Elicit. He'll never trust me again. He'll think I set him up to hear this.*

And, sure enough, Elicit thrust himself to his feet and stepped forward, staring at the Divinarch, his hands clenching into fists. "Lord god, that's not possible. You and Erene are enemies! You know perfectly well that she wants to prevent Arity from taking the Throne when you return to Heaven!" His voice cracked as he begged, "You want to stop her!"

"Wrong!" the Divinarch sat up, claws on knees. "I do *not* want to stop her! Of course, in order to keep the peace, I cannot act to help her either. But she need not fear my retribution. In fact, she has my blessing, whatever that is worth." He laughed. *Perhaps he is not joking.* Erene scarcely dared to think it. Blood spattered his trousers, mingling with the gemlike bits of light from the chandeliers on the white cloth. "Lady Gentle, I have undermined the peace my ancestors maintained for generations. I have made a philosophy of my deeds. I am supreme among bunglers!"

"He's mad," Elicit muttered. "He must be."

"No. I am not." Erene shivered at the tone of relentless cheer in the Divinarch's voice. "*This* is what I pride myself on: all my life, I have made my own choices. Alone among gods, I have followed my whims instead of the traditions set up for me by others. A hundred and fifty years ago, when I lived in Heaven, I found a lost, half-dead human. I took him in. While he healed, he explored Heaven—and unlike the Wanderer, thirteen hundred years ago, he understood Heaven for what it was. He absorbed our secrets, learning everything he needed to bring mortal society neck and neck with ours. And he developed the concept of equality that he called atheism." The Divinarch chortled. "I sent him back to the world of mortals. I did it! I was the instrument of your receiving those secrets that helped you to understand that we are no more gods than you are!"

"No," Elicit whispered. "I don't believe a word of it."

Erene's heart bled for him. At the same time, she listened, hypnotized. "Go on, Divinarch," she breathed.

"But even I was not expecting the rapidity with which atheism spread." The Divinarch sighed. "Our race was only ever superior to yours because we had existed for so much longer. But our civilization hasn't changed since time before time. And once we gave you humans a hand out of the bog of barbarity, you drew equal with us in what is, compared to the length of our history, no more than a day and a night. In a few minutes, you will draw ahead." He shook his head.

"Yes?" Erene breathed after a long pause.

Bronze Water reappeared suddenly, standing on the Throne above the Divinarch. "We *should* have expected it," the Incarnation said. "We should have known, from our experience with the Wanderer, what one lone human could do to the gods. Even before the Wanderer—when we watched primitive ghostiers at work, and for the first time fell in love with something human—we should have understood. Ghosting is the only craft you invented that we did not. It illustrates what is human: the ability to bring something out of nothing with only faith and heart for tools. Like the miracle power."

"Divinarch," she said helplessly, her heart overflowing. "Bronze Water—I want to thank you—you have justified everything I believe in—"

Elicit was shaking, his face hidden in his hands. She could see him struggling to make excuses for the gods within his mind. She suppressed her own pity.

"I thank you, and I think I understand. You believe we are due to take precedence over you. Broken Bird is of your persuasion, I would guess. But the younger generation have reacted to your signing away their birthright, asserting that they are superior to humans and have the right to rule over us."

The Divinarch and Bronze Water stared at her, two sets of unreadable god eyes. "I really think that we have explained ourselves," he said gently. "I think you should go now." He slid down off the Throne and began to hobble away. Bronze Water followed, like a burly father going after a child. The Divinarch's mustaches bounced like springs, but his gait was arthritic.

The windowless hall felt huge, yet unsafe, as if the sea were trembling at the doors, waiting to roar in. What was she to do with this? This license to revolution? The Divinarch had given her an edge not only over enemies but over friends as well. He had as good as picked her over Belstem to head the regime that would replace the Divinarchy after his death. She could now state her own position in so many words, both in Ellipse and in social situations, without fearing punishment. No one would understand her daring, and so they would respect it.

But she could not share the knowledge, not even with Goquisite. To tell Goquisite would be to tell Delta City. The masses would not understand: anarchy loomed, a fulminating specter.

Lucky the Divinarch had picked *her* to hear his stand, instead of some noble with a loose tongue!

Lucky she had brought no one besides Elicit, who would die rather than remember what the Divinarch had said, much less pass it on!

The whites of his eyes were blood-veined. She looked at him, unable to speak, unable to tell him how much she needed him, that she would not have hurt him for the world—"You don't actually believe him, do you?" His voice was ragged. "He's mad. Or he's playing with your mind. Gods are intellectual demons. He could trick you as easily as snapping his fingers."

For a moment doubt gripped her, but then she shook her head. All the Divinarch had stated was his personal beliefs. And she was sure that everything he said, he believed.

I did the deed! I sent Antiprophet back! he had said.

And what other explanation could there possibly be for the gods' inactivity but that they were all obeying him?

"Let's go home," she said almost inaudibly. "Please, Elicit. Let's go. Let's not fight again."

He started to move, then stopped. So tall and gray, like a rock showered by water as the bits of light from the chandeliers danced on his fur. "We used to be more than *imrchim,* Erene. Not even Hem came between us. And you know I never cared for Algia or Eterneli or Soulf one-tenth as much as I care for you."

Oh, Elicit! "I—I love you—"

His face hardened. "I used to paint your likeness on my ghosts. You never saw, but they were all you. I used to dream about you even on the nights when we slept in each other's arms."

She imagined throwing herself at him. She imagined it so vividly that she smelled the camphor on his seldom-used court clothes. "Can't you just love me?" she whispered. "Does it have to be this that comes between us? Does this have to be the last thing?"

"Erene, it wasn't you who was forsaken for a clique of fashionable monkeys spouting blasphemy. I can't sacrifice my integrity. Not even for you." She could tell he was very near tears.

"Next!" a god's voice howled faintly from outside, and a draught from the waiting hall blew in as the great doors swung open. Erene saw the sentinel's confusion as he registered on two lone mortals and an empty Throne.

"Don't let the petitioners see, Orange Bracken!" The air exploded in a spot of color. Pati appeared between Erene and the Divine Guard. His wings churned as he began to shove one door shut. Elicit took Erene's hand in a rough grip that could have been anything except intimate, pulling her toward the doors.

"Thank you, Striver. Just let us out . . . We're finished here. Yes, quite finished."

For several nights in a row, Humi had slept alone at the top of Albien House. Last night her pillow had been wet with tears. Erene appeared to have left the Crescent. Humi would have given a year of her life to take back her rudeness the night of the Ellipse. Since then, her relations with Erene had been normal. But now there was this. What else had she done wrong? Who else could have caused this disappearance?

The other ghostiers looked at her sorrowfully. Though she knew she could have gone to any of them for comfort, she would not. She wanted Erene. She had not known it was possible to miss someone so much whom she had known for only such a short time.

Finally Erene returned for dinner. After the meal, the *imrchim* left Humi alone with her in the Chalice. *Now or never,* Humi thought, and gripping her goblet of mulled wine tightly, she asked Erene where she had been going every night.

The senior ghostier remained silent a moment, tracing the raised silver design on her cup with her thumb. "I have my own room in Goquisite's mansion," she said at last. "A canopied feather-mattressed bed, a girl ghost that my master Molatio made in a niche, a pet piglet with its own basket by the fire, and Goquisite's room just down the hall. Every morning, we meet in her room and cuddle up under the comforters to order breakfast. It is convenient for me to stay there, because I conduct a good deal of my business at court late at night."

"But what about me?" Humi said. "Where do I fit into that?"

Erene drained her cup. "Get me some more wine."

Humi pattered down into the kitchen, poured more from the saucepan on the range, and silently tendered Erene the refilled cup.

"I told you I would be a good master," Erene said. "And I meant to stick to that. I still mean to. But I have been slipping. I know where my priorities lie. And I have been avoiding it."

"Where is it?"

Erene hesitated. "I've been a coward. I waited to tell you. And everyone. They aren't going to like it. But it can't be helped."

"What is it?" Humi asked with a sense of dread.

"You and I—we're moving out. We're going to establish ourselves at Goquisite's. Goq and I have arranged for an entire wing of her mansion to be decorated as a separate household. The only thing we won't have there is a workshop—and of course we will be coming back here to work."

But when are you going to find time to teach me? I

have to learn to ghost. She felt the need like a hunger pang. *I have to.* For a fleeting moment, she thought about asking if she could remain in the Crescent and take lessons from Ziniquel or Fra. But she remembered how much she had missed Erene. And she remembered, as if it had been a lifetime ago, the promises they had made as they stood in a bustling Christon street.

Erene wanted this to work so badly. Humi could see it in her eyes. Probably to her it looked like the perfect solution.

And Humi had the power to *make* it that. *If you don't have time for me, I'll teach myself,* she vowed silently. *You won't know anything is wrong. I'll stand up for you.* "It sounds wonderful, Erene," she said. "Let's tell everyone tonight."

"Oh, darling," Erene said, and hugged her with the wine cup still in her hand, hard. Wine sloshed onto Humi's shoulder. "I knew I could depend on you, sweetheart. I knew I could trust you."

Fourteen

Thani and Godsbrother Transcendence lay in the small stone hut which the village kept furnished for wandering flamens. Night outside: a herb-scented candle burned in a sconce. In Calvarese style, the bed was made up of a heap of felted throws on the floor, soft and snuggly, but Thani chose to pillow her head on Transcendence's bony arm. Her whole body felt shaky with the aftermath of tears. Transcendence's fingers moved through her hair, soothing her. "Sssh. Sssh. I have to tell you your prophecy."

"I don't want to know," she whispered. If she could have undone the whole day, she would have. Prophecy killed lemans if it took them too often, she knew that, and she was afraid: even though this was her first time, she had never experienced worse pain. It had started with a few twinges while she led Transcendence through the village this morning. They had just arrived at the oasis at dawn, after a night of hard walking, and so they had not yet seen any of the Calvarese sick who awaited their help; somehow Transcendence had managed to do three miracles on no sleep and a breakfast of black chicory. Thani longed for his selfless endurance. She herself had thought she might fall down at any minute.

Perhaps her exhaustion had made her an easy target for the prophecy. (She thought of it as a dark little cloud of foreknowledge drifting through the air, looking for a leman in whom to spend its malice.) It had felt as if all her limbs were being torn apart. Unbearable stresses racked her joints, and nearby villagers ran to her as she fell to the ground, arms splayed, teeth clenched. As clearly as a judgment, she saw the sun blazing in the middle of a circle of dark faces before it went out.

She had come to right here, in this hat. A Calvarese woman old enough to be her grandmother was bathing her face. Thani could not remember her own grandmother: had her name been ... Tici? The woman cooed gently to her. Thani knew she could not afford to be perceived as vulnerable. She pushed the woman away and screamed for Transcendence.

Now she shuddered and sniffled, snuggling into the hard, angular curve of his body. When adolescence had first started to usurp her body, she had hated it, for flamen and leman moved from oasis to oasis too quickly for her to become comfortable enough with any other woman to ask her what these changes meant. But now, at thirteen, she was comfortable with herself. This way, she could be close to Transcendence as never before. "Tell me, then," she whispered, marshaling her courage.

"You said: *We must go to Royalland. To Delta City. There is a thing to do. Danger to the Divinarch. Danger to the Divinarchy itself. There is a traitor to kill, a figurehead of piety who has turned. I must obey the dictates of the gods.*" Transcendence paused. Thani held her breath, dreading a name. "The rest was gibberish."

"It was incomplete, then!" she cried in relief. "We can't obey it!" The very thought of going back to Royalland made her queasy. Like most lemans, she had been to Delta City once, right after Transcendence chose her, to learn her duties, and that was enough. She loved Calvary. She loved the sun on sand and crags, the skeletal towers of gears which lowered men down the mines, the way they reared black against the brazen sky. She loved eating the spicy, soupy messes that set your mouth on fire, just so that you shouldn't forget, in the evening, how hot the blazing sun was that would rise to greet you on the morrow.

"Leman," Transcendence said sternly, "did I hear you suggest that we disobey the prophecy?"

With difficulty Thani swallowed tears, hiding her face in the pelt of white on his chest. "No! I meant only

that—we can't! Until we receive clearer guidance from
the gods. I mean, how are we to know who we have to
kill, unless—" she hated to say it, but she had to—
"unless I prophesy again? Surely the duty that we *know* is
more important? I mean, we're expected at Firoun next
sixday—and after that, Samadh—we can't deprive them
of the miracles we would do there—"

"Child," Transcendence said, "we go on. For now. Rest
assured that the gods will tell us what we must do. Prophecy is their least ambiguous voice, but I also know their
bidding in my heart, when it is imperative."

"Do you know it now?" she asked.

He sighed. "No. But it will come to me, or else to you.
We have been chosen for this deed, Thani. It is a test of
our faith. Somehow they will let us know how we may do
their bidding—and until then we will watch."

She nodded, hardly registering the words, hearing only
that for now, they would not go to Royalland. He would
not be able to see it if she nodded, so she gave the rote
obeisance that to her was anything but a platitude: "Yes,
master. I obey you, and through you, I obey the gods."

Outside, one of the oasis hounds barked. High overhead, the scream of a predator trailed thinly down the
night wind. Transcendence held her close, as if any noise
which evoked the existence of a world outside the little
hut threatened their togetherness. When all fell quiet, he
rolled her gently onto her back. His fingers traced paths
from her collarbone to her pubis, circling each nipple. A
tingling warmth grew inside her.

He was her life. And he knew what she looked like
only through touching her.

Strange to think he'd never seen her face. She could
itemize his in every detail. He had stridden into her baby-
hood home along the road to the salt, like any other wandering flamen, hood thrown back so that he could enjoy
the mild Domesdys rain. Even then his hair had been
white. He was alone: his first leman, a girl then nineteen,
had gotten married the sixday before, to a boy who lived
in Nece. This he told Thani's sister, who was feeding the
poultry in the courtyard. Humi ran out to the cornfield,

where Thani was helping Mother glean the last stalks, and called out that a flamen had come alone. Not joyfully— Humi had not, Thani remembered dimly, been a joyful child—but with a face like stone.

Thani pushed her face into Transcendence's mop of white hair. She caught his stark-tendoned wrists and pulled him down on top of her, entwining her legs with his. Heat grew between their bodies. "I love you," she said passionately as he caressed her. He smelled of salt and sand and cumin, of the desert.

Fifteen

Mell slumped on the tavern stool, weary but satisfied, paying no attention to the sailors from Westchasm wrangling as they pushed in out of the rain. It had taken him months to get here from Calvary, sleeping his way from ship to ship (and he'd had a *hard* time of it before he learned to pick out which sailors were lovers-of-men at first sight) but finally he had arrived. Delta City. He'd longed to come here ever since he could remember. Now he felt a warm sense of lassitude—and he was sweetly conscious of the attention he was already receiving. The boys at home had been right. Ragged clothing *couldn't* disguise beauty. The woman in the expensive cloak, in the corner, had been staring at him for fifteen minutes. She seemed like his best prospect at the moment. Mell felt more comfortable with men, but he would sleep with a woman if it paid well, especially one as pretty as this one. You got introduced to both sexes rough and early in the bronze mines, and you learned to appreciate whatever came your way.

A snaky-looking fellow by the bar eyed Mell too. Mell suspected that *he* had very different intentions. A pickpocket, maybe, who kept his eyes open for tenderfeet fresh from the country. Or a cruising pimp. Plumped in the middle of a stinking marsh the way Delta City was, everyone had to arrive via the docks, whether they came from overseas or upriver, and many of them hadn't a clue what they were in for. Many greenies would fall victim to that fellow. Even now he was straightening his collar, popping a sprig of basil into his mouth to sweeten his breath, and preparing to mince over to Mell's corner.

Not a chance, friend. Mell swallowed the last of his beer and got up. Donning his best smile, he wove gracefully between the tables to the woman in the cloak. "Milady," he purred, "it's raining very heavily, and I am fresh out of lodgings. How would you say to a trade? Me, in exchange for the sharing of your bed tonight?"

She stood up and held out a hand to him. The candle over her head flared green. It smelled pungently of sap. "Indeed, you may share my bed," she said. "Indeed."

Familiar now, the darkness of her room, once the damp bedroom in Erene's apartment at Tellury Crescent. Erene did not mind her sleeping here instead of at Antiprophet Square every once in a while—so she knew she was not missed. And there had been no question of sneaking Mell into Goquisite's mansion, for gods-knew-who might have seen her and stopped her. Or at least let him know what he was in for.

Familiar the pillow-scattered bed. Familiar its scent, the floral perfume she had picked for a signature mixed with the smell of ink from the treatises on beauty she read at bedtime. Intoxicating, the slim body in her arms, his accomplished kisses. She hoped he couldn't tell how inexperienced she was—as a lover, but also as a ghostier. Solo ghosting was forbidden to apprentices. But somehow she knew she was ready. Since she grew confident of her place at Tellury Crescent, and knew that they would not throw her out no matter what they caught her doing, she had been itching to break a few rules.

She had decided to leave it up to chance—go to a dockside tavern and see what happened. And Mell Cujegrass had happened. He was handsome as only a Calvarese could be, his sultry good looks sizzling with sexuality. He wore his hair long, with a miner's forelock. One of his temples bore a shiny burn. When she saw him across the tavern, that tiny imperfection had struck into her eyes like a knife.

Ziniquel had been right, when he said that all she had to do was wait and the ghosts would come.

Panting, momentarily spent, Mell rolled away. "Do I

satisfy you? Are you pleased with your choice? Many courtesans can be found on the docks, you know, milady. But I warrant I am the best."

"You ... hh ... you are ..." She knew he was not in fact a courtesan, but fresh off the boat. So proud. So young. So fiery. And doomed to die. She *knew* that, were it allowable for her to tell him what came next, he would accept no compensation such as the flamens had paid the Garden family. He would give himself to her, welcoming the glory of having his beauty admired for ages to come.

It was just that this way it felt like cheating. She closed her hands on his arms, pulling him toward her. "The cold's getting under the covers. Come here."

"Mmm ... ahhh, that tickles."

"You sound so surprised when you laugh."

"I grew up in the bronze mines. There's not much to laugh at there."

She traced his collarbone with her teeth. The fur in the hollows of his neck still tasted of metal. "You're superb."

"Let *me* taste *you*." He dragged her away from his throat as roughly as if she were a small animal. "Come here, little one—" He drove his lips against her mouth and his arousal between her thighs. Then he penetrated her. Caught up in her dreams of ghosting, Humi had practically forgotten her virginity. Pain shot through her like a dart. She wondered if he could tell that he was her first lover.

Four in the morning, and it was all over, and Humi felt nauseous. The mirror in the bathroom showed her tousled hair and a face the color of gravemud. An hour ago, she had woken up and realized that she would die if she did not replenish her body. Single-mindedly, she had dragged herself to the pantry cupboard and wolfed down everything in sight.

Before that ...

The beginning of the night—after Mell had pulled away from her, looking down at her face with the first stirrings of doubt, and she had realized that *now,* now she had to do it—swam back into her mind like a nightmare.

She remembered patching together the clues that Erene had dropped over the months. Finally understanding that infuriating vagueness at the heart of everything Erene said.

Ghosting was indescribable.

Death was the flight of a soul from the material plane. As Humi drove the knife into Mell's ribs, she had understood the sheer, staggering psychic force one had to employ to block that flight. At last, she had felt the sickening slackness as the soul despaired of ever getting away and dropped sideways, slipping out of her grasp like a fish. She wondered why she had ever wanted to do this. She was alone in the apartment with scores of candles blazing and she wanted to die. How could she have done it? How could she ever have let herself be beguiled into a profession that required her to kill human beings?

He had trusted her. That was the worst of it.

I killed him. I killed him. Oh, by the gods.

The basin's china rim was cold and sharp. It left red trenches in her palms. A little pinkish water remained in the bottom. She splashed her face, toweled her fur with the sleeve of her blouse. Two rooms away, the body sprawled beside its ghost, slack and foul. She could not even remember how she had posed the ghost. She dreaded to go and see whether it had come out well. "If it's a mess, I'm damned in the eyes of the gods. It has to be beautiful enough to weigh more than Mell's life in the Balance. Why did I do it before I was sure I could do it well?" She sat on the hard marble floor, whining softly. "Overconfidence! Damn!" The legs of the basin stand rose to a dizzying height above her. She had committed a crime worthy of a predator. No excuse—no escape. No going back. No excuse—

The bathroom door opened, footsteps circled her, and a hand touched her shoulder. She yelped and wrenched away, scrambling to her feet. Only belatedly did she realize the touch had been gentle.

The Heir to the Divinarchy stood in the doorway, slim, barefoot, clothed in black.

"That is an inspired ghost you have made."

His purplish-brown hair blazed like a fire of dead leaves.

Humi shivered. She was too wretched even to be surprised at his appearance. "Milord Heir, don't say things you don't mean! Do you realize what a crime I've committed?"

Arity hitched himself up on the basin and swung his feet. It bore him without breaking. He must be lighter than he looked. "All the usual qualms." Humi could not take her eyes off his face. She had not seen him at close quarters since that first evening at the Old Palace. She had forgotten how beautiful he was. His eyes were abnormally large, but unlike those of the other Incarnations, they held compassion that Humi could only label human. "From what I can make out," he said in a clear, textureless voice scaled down so as not to destroy the bathroom, "you think you have killed for no purpose. You cannot imagine what possessed you. You hate yourself for your heedless arrogance." He shook his head and laughed. "By the Power, girl! If you want to feel guilty, visit the Eftpool! The eft will tell you that it wants its life back, or that it thinks its death was justified, whatever impulse comes out on top. But does it really matter?"

"He wanted to live," she whispered. "There was that vitality in him. Not like Beau."

"It doesn't matter! By the ghostiers' standards, you have pulled off a coup! Here, let me show you." Beckoning with his chin, he led her to the bedroom.

She looked down.

He sprawled on his back on the white fluffy carpet, mouth open. Blood filled his mouth and trickled down his dark cheek to the ear. His hands clawed, frozen, at the stab wound under his ribs. The body had taken some time to die after the spirit fled.

The ghost stood erect, contraposto, beside her bed, the fingers of one hand in his mouth as if he were licking them. His eyes crinkled in surprise and wonder. She had caught him just as he was beginning to laugh. That streak of childlike innocence showed plainly.

Arity took her arm and ushered her into the brightly lit

living room. He sat her down on the cold stone floor by the dead hearth, then leaned forward and shoved the embers with the heel of his hand. They sputtered into flame. "You made your ghost reflect the subject you drew it from. None of the other ghostiers do that. They construct artificial works of art out of their own imaginations. You, because you chose an incredible subject, have made one of the most powerful ghosts I have ever experienced. And it's not even painted yet!"

"But—but I didn't even know what I was—" She could not keep her eyes from filling with tears. Then she sobbed and sagged forward into his arms. He caught her and held her, supporting her weight with the kind of gentleness that is born of great strength. His chest felt like an unbreakable stone shell. His body heat was twice that of a human. Sobbing, scandalized at herself, Humi thought wildly: *He's a god! A god!*

But he had made it all right for her to go on living.

"Thank you, thank you, milord—"

"My pleasure," he said gently. Then his voice hardened. "But don't speak to me that way. If you love me, don't."

She pulled away and looked at him.

He shook his head slightly. "Don't use the word *god,* if you want to please me. That's all."

Fear moved in her. "Why shouldn't I call you a god? That's what you *are*—" He sighed sadly. "I'm sorry. Milord." She ducked her head, the shorthand of worship coming back to her. "It's not my place to ask questions. I won't call you a god anymore."

"Damn! By the Power, you mortals are impossible!" It exploded from him. She brought her eyes up. "Impossible!" Then he took a deep breath, his shoulders quivering. She could see that his smile was forced. "All right, Humility. I would not force you. Call me whatever you want." And he vanished.

Later that night Humi watched stolidly as Erene circled the ghost, her court slippers tapping on the workshop floor. She reached out and fingered a transparent eyelash.

Her face was cold, gray, unreadable. Humi hitched one hip on the windowsill. Outside in the Crescent, the sky drizzled with dawn. Of course Humi wanted Erene's approval—but it did not seem to matter as intensely as it had when Erene was the only person who *ever* saw anything she did. A feeling of weightlessness buoyed her up. Now that Arity the Heir, the ultimate authority on beauty, had approved of her ghost, Erene could not destroy her happiness.

"You are not a master ghostier," Erene said finally.

"How could I be?"

"If anyone were to know about this ghost, you would be severely censured."

Humi shook her head. "Erene, they wouldn't."

"Don't get clever with me, girl! I don't mean the ghostiers!" Erene turned on her. "I mean the nobles, especially Goquisite! Be sure that they have all learned the rules of ghosting, so that they can use them on us. And I hope it comes as no surprise that Goquisite would count it as a victory to have you disgraced."

Humi swallowed. Maybe she had been stupider than she thought.

"So, how is this? We will say he is mine." Erene touched the ghost again, her fingers lingering on his diamondine chest. "I'll present him to the Divinarch. That is always a graceful gesture on the part of a ghostier. And this time, I have a special debt to the Divinarch that I have not been able to think how to repay."

"But—" The memory of ghosting tingled in Humi's fingers. Like plunging your hands in a basket of knives, holding on to the soul until it slipped down into the Eftpool. She had put so much pain into this ghost. She wanted the credit for it! Ashamed of her own selfishness, she turned and said to the street, "I would have liked to give him to Arity."

"What?"

Humi turned back to the room. "Nothing. But—but Erene, what if I make another one? What will we do about that?"

Erene's brows drew together. "Haven't I made it clear

how much trouble *this* one could cause? Are you seeking to jeopardize us both? For the gods' sake, Humi! It's against the rules!"

She swallowed. How could she put it without seeming rude? The muddy, salty scent of the drizzle invaded the room. "We've already broken so many rules, you and me, Erene. Does this really matter? Don't you want me to be the best ghostier I can be? And besides—" She remembered the feeling of power. The knowledge that she could create beauty that weighed even more than life in the Divine Balance. "I'd be a liar if I told you I would never do it again."

Erene rubbed her face. When she took her hands away, the palms were silver, and dark gray patches stood out on her cheeks. "Humi—" she cracked a smile—"I seem to have forgotten to tell you how proud I am of you. It is a marvelous ghost. Any one of the *imrchim* would be proud of it."

Humi let out a shaky breath she had not known she was holding.

"You must just understand how hard things are for me right now. Belstem will not give ground over the wheat levies from Royalland." An edge entered Erene's voice. "Did you ever hear such a thing? I do not know what he means to do with the money, but he insists that the Summer establishment must get a double share, now that there are two councillors in the family . . ." Her voice slowed down. "Anyhow, obviously I didn't make a ghost last night. And you did."

"It'll be years before I'm as good as you are now," Humi said loyally, because she felt the current of death pull between them. The air of the room shivered like moving water. The undertow tugged at her. Mentally, she slapped it away, terrified.

Erene seemed not to notice the tension. "All in all, you exceed my wildest hopes, darling." She held out her arms.

Humi hung back, glancing from Erene's peach-colored dress and silver-dusted breast to her own paint-stained skirt and blouse. "I'll muss your—"

"Silly girl." Erene laughed tenderly. "it's time I took it

all off anyhow. I've been up all night at court. We'll celebrate your first ghost by sleeping here today."

Thankfully, Humi stepped forward and laid her cheek on the senior ghostier's shoulder. The metallic tang of Erene's facedust cut her nostrils. She thought, *I didn't even care about Beau as much as I care about Erene. I lied—I would have given up ghosting if she had asked me to.*

And she could not help remembering how Arity the Heir had felt in her arms: hot, hollow, unbreakable as stone.

Sixteen

Months stretched into years. Summers and winters soaked Delta City with the flavor of the sea. Humi found that she was spreading herself thinner and thinner in the attempt to strike a balance between Tellury Crescent and Antiprophet Square. At first she retreated back into the ghostiers' shelter as often as she could, but it was very difficult to resist the pull of court society. Goquisite, Erene, Marasthizinith, Belsten, Aneisneida, and Pietimazar, and their backstabbing, glittering circle of acquaintances sucked her in almost unstoppably. They did not want her in particular—she was only an apprentice—but they would have her anyway. Attend one *sociale,* and she would find six invitations on her pillow, all of whose senders would be offended if she did not appear.

Her solution was to gradually drop out of sight. All ghostiers disguised themselves from time to time, for their forays into the city demanded anonymity, but by the time Humi turned nineteen, she disguised herself so often that Humility Garden scarcely ever showed her face at the Ankh mansion. She had become a recluse, devoted to her art.

Meanwhile Humi went about court in facedust, hairdust, eyepaint, and full costume, as any one of a dozen different personas. What with the height spurt Humi put on in her eighteenth year, Goquisite often took her for a stranger when she was herself. Her tawny fur had got a green tinge from her wearing facedust so much of the time. When Goquisite *did* recognize her, she treated her like one of the guests who dropped in and out of the mansion at all hours—polite, friendly, bestowing confidences and kisses that were no more sincere than her glowing, all-purpose smile.

Humi perpetually failed to understand how this shallow woman could provide adequate companionship for Erene. She reminded herself that Goquisite had been a leman when she was a child, like all the first-generation nobles: there must be some keen edge, some perceptive capacity, hidden under the satin ruffles and soft flesh. But she still could not fathom their friendship. All she could do was watch in wonder as they took down their opposition like predators taking down sheep. For Erene's part, Humi knew that her commitment to Goquisite was extraordinary. When Humi and Erene were alone, Humi often felt that her master was talking not to Humi but to a semblance of Goquisite that sat in Humi's place. She tolerated the indignity in silence. She knew how much Erene depended on her.

When they returned to the Crescent, Erene relied on Humi to shield her from the other ghostiers' tacit disapproval. (Ziniquel did not bother to hide his contempt. He would not even sit in the same room with Erene any more. Humi dreaded the day when he would not be able to restrict his dislike to Erene.)

She tried to convince Erene not to upbraid herself over the loss of their confidence, but to accept it as a fair exchange for her freedom to move about the court. For that was essentially what it was. But at the same time Humi understood that no ghostier could let this loss pass without rage and grief. For without her *imrchim*, a ghostier simply was not. Moreover, the ghostiers' political clout sprang from their unity: and even as the nobles' conspiracy extended its tentacles into the provinces of Royalland and overseas, Erene was jeopardizing the base of her power at home, in Ellipse. At the moment, all the ghostiers still voted with her—but how long could that last?

Humi felt the fabric of their life stretching, stretching, fraying at the edges.

Thus, Erene certainly had no time to consider Humi's tender feelings. She had no time to wonder if Humi might have developed political motives beyond loyalty to her, and put them into play. (Humi had not, but she knew Erene was foolish not to take the possibility into account. For that was what apprentices were supposed to do.)

Apprentices were not supposed to ghost. But Humi needed ghosting the way addicts needed their opiates. At the end of each day she spent encased in lace and facedust, helping Erene take care of her business in the salons of the city, she went hunting or she escaped in a sedan to Tellury Crescent. She ran upstairs, tore off her gown, dropped a sweaty, loose old dress over her head, and threw herself into the aesthetic dilemmas of her latest ghost as if into sweet oblivion.

And energy that she could never access any other time, not even when she needed it, welled up like clotted urgent speech in her fingers.

She guessed that it was partly the sexual links between her and her ghosts that provided this energy. But that was forbidden. When it came down to the act, ghostiers were supposed to keep themselves apart. That way, they did not completely lose themselves in their art. But Humi had started by breaking that rule, and now she could not stop. The other ghostiers knew, of course; they shook their heads at her but did not stop her. And there was one thing they did not know—the reason she never became lovers with any of them. The illicit air of the lovemaking made her tense with a wild ecstasy she knew none of her *imrchim* could duplicate. The ghost boys' and girls' caresses licked her body like whips. And painting them, afterward, fulfilled the need that that generated. It was a vicious circle.

When she finally collapsed in her boudoir, Arity would come.

After that first ghost, he visited her regularly. She soon stopped trying to guess why—he was a god, and therefore his actions were impossible to analyze. He would *teth* into her room on the top floor of Albien House, and they would sample cold delicacies which she filched from the Chalice kitchen. He devoured them hungrily, sitting with her in the soft, feminine boudoir that she had constructed out of Erene's old living room. Here, she both brought her ghosts and slept herself on the nights that she spent painting.

Her early conversations with Arity seemed stilted to her, more awkward than anything else. Hopeless of his favor, she wondered why he kept coming. But then, about a year into their friendship, while comparing garments, she made an accidental discovery. All over his body, talons grew in clusters. Thick, brown cat-claws like those on his hands and feet, bursting painfully from green skin. He reacted with outrage when she dared to ask him about them, and she did not see him for several sixdays; but when he returned, their friendship seemed to have deepened immeasurably. He trimmed them regularly, he said, so that generally there were only flat brown circles on his flesh. Just sometimes, he missed some. She was enchanted. It was as if he no longer felt he needed to keep up his godlike, insouciant front before her. They could now sit in silence without his having to make witty, pointless remarks. Sometimes he came to her in blind furies which drove him stamping and hissing the length of the room, and she cowered from him until it blew over. Then he would sink down with his head in her lap, and smile.

In return for this new trust he placed in her, she started to volunteer her own worries. Her fear that people would discover Erene was not making her own ghosts; her fear that Belstem was getting too extremist to be tolerated. And other, small day-to-day things.

And Arity seemed genuinely to care. He listened with furrowed brow and gave advice which, though occasionally facetious, was generally well meant. If he saw that she was exhausted and fretful, he would become solicitous, humoring her mood until she started to laugh.

She found herself telling him all her woes. Once in a while she would make herself cry with worry, and he would pull her into his arms and hold her the way he had the first time she ever cried in front of him. The sheer strangeness of his heat, and his muscles sliding like butter over his rib cage, stopped her tears, like a blow to the face. She was reminded just how different they were: that Arity was, after all, preternatural.

No matter how often he came, she knew nothing about him. He never told her where he went when he vanished into his sunspot. She never saw him except in her apartment. In public, he behaved like a bawd and spoke in ciphers, like all the other gods; she wondered if this could really be the same person who lay with his head in her lap, talking of aesthetics and fashion. In Ellipse, he seemed possessed of an ability to bring about resolutions when it seemed the Incarnations would not ever agree, though often these made for short-term peace rather than long-term efficiency. Sometimes, as she watched through the peephole, her gaze resting on his slim back, she wondered whether he was consciously preparing himself for the role of Divinarch. Was that why he sometimes acted so distant?

The Divinarch. The Old One. *Er-serbali aes hymannin.*

Though he did not know it, in dropped words and phrases, Arity was teaching her the language of the gods.

"I am so tired," he said, leaning against the headboard of Humi's big white bed. "I fell asleep in Ellipse last night. I don't know what to do about it."

Humi lounged on a pile of cushions at the other end of the bed, her legs curled up in the chenille pool of her evening gown. Her hair was red and her fur gold: she was young Lady Fellwren, who lived a couple of days' journey up the Chrume. She had returned from a midnight *sociale* at Marasthizinith Crane's and was just mustering her energy to change, when Arity arrived. "Perhaps it is because the flamens of the city are doing so many miracles this summer," she said. "Perhaps they are draining you. Have you been to Shimorning yet? Or Temeriton? The heat is worst there. Flies everywhere, and such a smell of the sewers. Belstem and his famous police force, of course, do nothing to help." She heard her voice go acerbic. "The flamens have all they can do to keep the people alive."

"That wouldn't have any effect on me, Humi," Arity said.

She yawned again. "Whatever you say, milord."

Though she had propped all the windows in the apartment wide, letting in the fetid stink of the marsh that no perfumes could disguise, the boudoir was hot. This summer was sopping with humidity. Foul water had brought disease to the city, and shortages provoked crime, inspiring Belstem to place rewards on the heads of the underworld crime lords like Gold Dagger and the Hangman, who headed rob-and-resell operations. The famine on the mainland had brought the predators swooping as far as Marshtown at night. "I think each summer has been hotter than the one before as long as I can remember," Humi said, at the exact moment when a predator screamed long and thin overhead.

Arity cocked his head, listening. Then he looked back at her. "You know, Humi, I think you should be able to see by now that I'm not a god."

"Oh, don't be silly," she said, quenching a spark of fear. She always dreaded his bringing this up. "If you're not a god, what are you?"

He sat still, legs crossed, green ankles bare, his gold earrings glimmering in the dusky tangle of his hair. "We're not divine. I can tell you that. Among ourselves, we speak your language as much as we do ours, but we don't call ourselves gods. We call ourselves *auchresh.*" She had never heard the word before. It had a hideous sonority. "In your language, that would be *exotics.*"

"Exotics? *Auchresh?*"

"Yes. And our language is *auchraug.* The flamenhood made us into gods seventeen generations ago, with little or no encouragement." He rocked forward and said with a strange intensity, "Some of us are ready to step down. But we cannot. Partly because so many mortals base their lives on worshiping us and partly because some of us still won't give up the privileges that come with being gods."

"Shut up," Humi said. "I don't want to hear."

"I never thought of you as willfully ignorant."

There was no answer to that that would let her off easily. She swallowed a lump of apprehension.

"I want you to understand." He glanced down at his ankles. "I want you to know why I am the way I am."

He *never* mentioned the talons that sprouted randomly all over his body. Not even by implication. Suddenly the room seemed darker. The mechanical clock on the wall of the boudoir struck two.

"Do you want to know the truth?" Arity said carefully. "I'll show it to you. Can you take it?"

She could not reply. Fear crippled her. How humbling, to have the scared little devotee inside her exposed! She'd thought that she had left that little girl behind in Domesdys. How naïve, to suppose she could escape her childhood so easily.

She stared at her hands. On each nail was painted a little crown, the symbol of the Throne. Goquisite had started the trend, and a woman like Lady Fellwren followed every trend that came along. But the crowns were chipping off. Humi needed to repaint them before tomorrow. She needed to select a gown for the lace-knitting *sociale* at Lady Haricot's. Erene needed Humi to work on Lady Haricot . . . "I have so much to do, Arity," she said. "Is this really the right night for a grand revelation?"

His face darkened like water before a squall. One hand flew out in frustration, the thumbnail catching her cheek. She feared he was going to erupt into one of his unpredictable rages. "Is there *ever* a right time for truth? Truth isn't a welcome guest in this city! One has to force it in wherever it will fit!" But then he must have caught sight of the blood oozing through her fur. He enveloped her in his arms and rocked her fiercely, subliminating the violence. She felt his tongue licking her cheek, rough like a cat's. The heat of his body scalded her through her falséribs and her gown. "I'm sorry!" he hissed. "I'm sorry!" Her blood smelled salty on his breath. "Hang on!"

And she felt nothing. His arms vanished from around her. She was neither hot nor cold, submerged in a boundless currentless ocean the temperature of blood—

And then—

Starlight.

On her other side, bright panels like windows.

Her eyes hurt as the pupils expanded. No, it wasn't just her eyes, it was her whole body, and by the gods it hurt!

She was expanding from a superdense speck to her proper size and by the gods it *hurt*—

Warm wind washed over her. She staggered, and caught onto a balustrade. It was still dark. Stars danced in sparkling mists overhead, and away before her spread another immense glittering.

A man's voice came close by. The world snapped into focus. That glittering was the sea in starlight, so far below that Humi might as well have been standing on a cliff. No, not a cliff, a balcony, with a solid house at her back, and Arity standing a few steps behind her. She could see nothing of the city. This was the high, rocky, southern prow of the island, beneath which the Chrume slithered like a great, gleaming lizard of water.

"Arity!" she called in panic, pushing her hair out of her eyes as she spun around.

"I haven't betrayed you, Humi." He was right there, squinting against the wind. "This is Hope's house. You didn't know we had houses in the city, did you? Those slatted windows behind you lead to the rooftop dining room."

"How did we get here?" But she knew before he said it.

"That was *teth˜tach ching*."

Her tiredness had vanished, extracted from her by the wind like a string of scarves from an illusionist's sleeve. The rumble of the tide colliding with the river came faintly to her ears. "All right, then, Arity. What are you? Not a god. Not a mortal. What?"

"An *auchresh*."

"But what's that?"

"I knew you wouldn't believe it from me. That's why we're here. Hope!" he called. "Come upstairs!" I've brought you a visitor!"

Footsteps inside the house. One of the slatted blinds rattled up, and a winged silhouette, her skirt swirling about her ankles, stepped into the window. "Pati! Is it you?"

Humi caught her breath. Not even Arity, in his most unguarded moments, had ever sounded as *human* as this.

Certainly she had never heard the Maiden, who epito-
mized feminine timidity and modesty, sound so nakedly
yearning.

Hope must have seen Humi the minute she stepped out
through the window. Her face went closed. Her wings
snapped open behind her like upside-down, ragged fans.
"What the fuck, Arity!" She dropped into the language of
the gods—*auchraug*—speaking too fast for Humi to follow. Arity listened, arms folded. When Hope stopped for
breath, he asked a quiet question. Silence held for a moment. Then Hope spat strings of gutteral syllables at him.
Humi blinked, gazing from one god to the other, the fact
that they were arguing over her growing less and less relevant.

Finally Arity turned to her and said, "It'll be all right,
Humi! I'll be back soon! Trust me—" He turned to the
window and ducked inside under the blind. His shadow
dwindled on the bright slats.

Hope took a measured pace forward into the starlight,
her mouth a thin line. Even with her golden hair loose
around her face, wearing a shapeless gored dress that hid
her figure, she was transcendently lovely. Humi stood feet
apart, arms folded, staring at her.

"Well," Hope said at length, "Arity says you are Erene
Gentle's apprentice. But I don't think I've ever seen you
before."

Humi raised one hand and dragged it across her face.
She teased the front locks of her hair clean.

"Ahhh. All right. I've seen you among the *imrchim*."

False confidence was the only way to bluff this out. "I
would hardly have recognized you like this, either."

"Ah, yes." Hope rubbed the flawed silk of her sleeve
between thumb and forefinger. "I was expecting another
visitor, one who does not judge me on my wardrobe ...
I do not know what Arity thinks I am! He expects me to
tell you something that we do not even mention among
ourselves!"

"Don't, then."

"But I am curious now. Can the barrier between
auchresh and *hymannim* can be abolished? Arity thinks

so." *I thought we already had abolished it,* Humi thought. But Hope was continuing, "Pati would say that the barrier is sacred. But surely not even he would object to finding out if it is possible." What was her relationship with Pati? Humi wondered. Before, she had sounded like an expectant lover. But it had never occurred to Humi that two gods might be sexually involved with each other. Like two mortals. Hope raised a thin golden hand to her mouth and spoke through her fingers. "Why did Arity choose *you* to hear this?"

"Why not?"

Hope shook her head. "You *hymannim*!" That meant mortals, humans. "You think so differently."

"Would one of you automatically think you were unworthy, then?" Humi frowned. "Arity never seemed—"

Hope laughed. "Arity is the most discontented of us all! But Pati and I are proud of our race." She drew herself up in her loose dress. "We are determined to make a future for ourselves, though the world has united to deny us our place."

"What about Arity, then?"

"Arity ... poor Arity. If he had his life to do over he would choose to be mortal."

A queer, potent disappointment washed through Humi. *There, then.* She stared at the far-down river. *There's the attraction I hold for him. So there is nothing else.*

Hope was pacing to and fro along the balcony, wing edges fluttering behind her. From the clawed elbows above her head, the wings fell to her knees, like a golden carapace, and her skirt swirled under their trailing edges. "We believe in the Power that is all around us," she said. "It is greater than any of us. It carries us along like a tide. And I think it means me to speak truth tonight, even though the words burn my tongue." She looked straight at Humi. "We are predators."

"What?"

Hope nodded.

"Predators." Humi felt the world going black.

"All of us. Everyone."

Predators. All my life I have worshiped predators.

Then common sense kicked in.

"No, you're not. You can't possibly be. Predators have more sense than animals but less than humans. They just scream and hunt and kill. And you're coolheaded, sane, intelligent beings, whether you have souls or not! You don't live on fresh meat! You can't fly! You don't ... come from the salt ..." Her voice trailed off.

"But we do," Hope said. "We're the reject predators. The deformed—"

"Hope, I'm—Hope?" A tall, thin figure materialized in the shadows. His eyes gleamed like metal as he glided out into the starlight. "Hope, it's a mortal! What is it doing here?" Humi cringed, but he did not turn on her. She herself seemed no more important than a stray dog. "What have you been telling it?"

Hope's beautiful face was white with horror and her hands clamped onto each other like vises. She spilled out a stream of *auchraug*.

"You haven't," Pati said. "Oh, by the *Power,* Hope!" His voice hardened. "This is some scheme of Arity's, isn't it?"

"I knew I shouldn't have let him persuade me!" Hope moaned.

"Did she believe you, Hope?" There was a gust of sulphur, and Arity balanced on the balustrade, feet wide. "Well, well. Pati." His hair blew around his face. "Throwback."

"No," Humi whispered desperately.

The gods had voices greater than any human's, and hearing like bats. Pati swung toward her. "Mortal!" His voice dripped contempt. "You can't possibly understand what is means! So lose your mind denying it! We're beasts, dangerous beasts with nothing godly about us. Just like our parents! Hideous, fanged monsters!"

"But we're *not* like our parents," Arity said. "They cast us out at birth. In the salt there is no creature who can kill a predator—so they have to control their own numbers. Each litter contains one strong, able, flighted predator, and the exotics. The flightless, weak *auchresh*. They roll us out of their lairs and drop us down the crags. Baby *auchresh* die on the salt, in the sun. But just like their flighted brothers and sisters, they can move and cry and put food in their mouths. Most die, but some crawl off the smelly mountains and survive. Eventually they find their older siblings in the Heavens."

"I don't understand," Humi said desperately. *I don't want to understand.*

Hope pushed around Pati. Her face was set. "The reason why there are so few women among us is because any species needs more females than it does males, and so fewer of us are born deformed. And we are weaker than the males, so we die in greater numbers. Ugly facts. I do not know why you want to hear them."

"Every one of us is sterile," Arity said. "We depend on the predators for our existence."

"But our brains have conquered the world," Pati said. "There's justice for you, mortal! What did you weaklings do with your ability to reproduce? Nothing except roll around in the grass like pigs, until we came and organized you!"

Humi could not stand it any longer. Their faces, their strangeness, their shouting. *My family worships predators.* She scrambled up on the balustrade, kicking at Hope's hands, leaning on the warm pillow of the wind. Swaying dangerously.

"You are the first human to learn this since Antiprophet!" Pati shouted. "What are you going to do with it?"

Antiprophet! Her ears hurt from their unmodulated voices. Arity tried to take her in his arms. She fought him. "Don't touch me! What did you ever befriend me for? Why are you putting me through this?"

His voice hissed. "We cannot fly. Instead, we have this."

And he stepped off the balcony.

The glittering turmoil of tide and river spun upward. They were weightless. Nothing pulled them down, they weren't falling, but the water was zooming up to meet her. Black waves, silver, a roaring in Humi's ears—terror—

Nothingness.

* * *

Warmth, and comfort, and well-being.

She lurched to the surface, and found herself lying beside Erene in bed. The gray walls of the Gentle suite, with their rippled pattern, seemed to hang at a distance like sheets of cloud. Sunlight fluttered in rectangles on the floor. Insensible to conventional decorating tactics, Erene had tacked linen curtains over the skylights at the start of summer and let them fill with crisped insects. She said she liked the patterns.

Groggily, Humi rolled over. Erene breathed with trancelike slowness, her dark hair a coarse tangle over her face. Tenderly Humi parted it and dropped a kiss on the ghostier's ear. Erene did not move. *She must be exhausted,* Humi thought. *When did we get back last night?*

Then she remembered.

She thrust herself up, her heart beating so fast that black spots danced across her vision.

And a piece of parchment slipped to the floor. She leaned over the edge of the bed, scooped it up and read the flawless script in a glance. "Sundown, tonight. Your boudoir." And the little hieroglyph which meant "Charity, Heir to the Divinarchy."

The door cracked open. "Erene?" Goquisite's head came in. "Oh, Humi! I thought you spent the night at the Crescent."

"Erene's sleeping. Perhaps you could come back later."

Goquisite padded into the room. "Actually, Humi, I have been wanting to see you." She wore a petal-pink camisole that bared her shoulders and ballooning harem pants, with a gauzy robe over the whole ensemble. "Oooh, these tiles are so cold!"

"That is my favorite touch in this suite," Humi said, watching Goquisite pick her way from rug to rug. "It reminds me that my feet are on the ground." Lady Ankh's gaze dropped to Humi's chest as she came to stand beside the bed.

"May I ask why you're wearing your evening gown?"

Humi had not even realized that she was still fully

clothed. *Thank you, Arity,* she thought angrily, *for making me look like an uncouth idiot in front of her!* "I—I was too tired to change. What did you want to ask me?"

"Actually, it was about Erene." Goquisite appeared to study each detail of Humi's gown with interest, but Humi sensed she was trying to put her concern into words. Finally she looked up. Humi was shocked by the worry in the small black eyes. "Humi, she is terribly unhappy. Maybe you have not noticed."

Humi closed her eyes for a second, trying to swallow a lump in her throat. "I've noticed."

"And I think I know what is wrong with her. She hasn't made a ghost in a year and a half. Because she passes yours off as hers, no one knows that she has let months and months go by without making any of her own." Goquisite wrung her hands distressedly. "I have to help her!"

Humi had never let down her guard in front of Goquisite, and she would not now. But the urge to relinquish the burden of responsibility was undeniably powerful. She had known for too long that something had to be done about Erene's dry spell. And she had done nothing. She had not even gotten around to asking anyone else's advice, as Goquisite had.

But now danger threatened. If Goquisite had made the connection between Erene's failure to ghost and her depression, who else, knowing the symptom, might suspect the cause? The linen curtains over the skylights shook as a breeze blew. The dead flies rolled and bounced. The rectangles of light on the bed jumped, and for a moment Humi had the impression that the ceiling was breaking apart like a dying flower, that the life she and Erene and Goquisite had constructed so carefully on a foundation of deceit and disguise would come sliding down on their heads.

"You surprise me, Goquisite," she said in a low voice. "I did not think you would understand."

"I understand Erene," Goquisite said. "And it's breaking my heart to see her like this. You have to do something, Humi. Help her."

I? I have to?

But in matters of ghosting, Goquisite would be worse than useless. It was to her credit that she understood that.

Humi heaved a sigh that made her ribs hurt inside her falseribs. "What do you suggest?"

"I ..." Goquisite looked at her, puzzled. "I thought you would know what to do, once I brought the matter to your attention."

If I knew what to do, I would have done it a long time ago! "But of course I do!" Humi said. "I was just testing you. Of course I ..." Then it came to her.

Who else knows her as well as I do?

Her old apprentice.

"I think it would be better for you not to know," she said, confident now.

Goquisite glanced down at the stone-leaf night table. "What's this?" She picked up the parchment. "Meeting a secret lover, Humi?"

"No!" Humi snatched the parchment and folded it small, tucking it into the bodice of her gown. She took the opportunity to dash two tears from her eyes. Something had to give way; something had to go. She could not be at Tellury Crescent at sundown. Not with this new concern. She could not allow a minor part of her life to usurp center stage, not when Erene was dying in the footlights. She hoped, swallowing hard, that Arity would not think she had betrayed him—or, gods forbid, that she was *frightened* of what he had revealed to her—

But if he wanted her full attention, he should have picked someone whose time hung heavy on her hands!

He just used me to test his theories about hymannin, she thought to herself. *When I started to unload my worries on him, gods know why he didn't find someone else! Well, Ari, maybe now you'll stay away from us! We* hymannim *are pale creatures compared to you, and predictable in our loyalties.*

She swung her legs out of bed. The weight of the chenille hem dropped around her ankles like a circle of chain. She bent and started to unhook the dress at the back. "I will arrange things today, Goquisite."

Goquisite smiled with unmistakable relief and obvious, childlike confidence in Humi's abilities. She turned to go. "Send Erene over to me when she wakes, will you, Humi? We have guests for breakfast."

"Certainly."

The door closed. Humi hung doubled over, unmoving. Under the coverlet, Erene slept on.

Seventeen

Delta City broiled in a thick, smelly, diseased soup of heat that afternoon. Scarcely anyone was abroad in the Lockreed Concourse, though it was the main concourse of Temeriton, the district that lay behind the docks at the northernmost end of the island. Stepping from her sedan into the shade of an awning, Humi took pity on her porter. "You may go. Return for me in . . . oh, shall we say a couple of hours?"

"Yes . . . Milady Garden. Good to serve you once again, Milady Garden." He rested in the traces for a moment, head hanging, then shambled away to turn in at the first pub he passed.

The awning announced, "Delights and Diversions." All along the concourse, decrepits clotted the shade. A beggar with a gangrenous leg who dozed beside the shop door looked blearily up at her, sticking out his bowl.

Humi tossed a copper into the bowl and bent to adjust her hat in the window. The dull green-tawny hue of her fur made her wince. Every time she saw her own hands today, she panicked, thinking that she had somehow forgotten to disguise herself before coming out. She felt uncomfortably vulnerable. But she guessed that it was better not to deceive Hem in any way.

"You and I have never met, milady," said a low, rumbling voice. "But I take it that you are Humility."

An immense man with a mane of black curls stood in the doorway of Delights and Diversions, nearly filling it. His eyes were the yellow of the sunlight on the cobbled concourse.

"A fine young lady. Dressed fit to *be* a ghost rather

than make them. How old are you—twenty-two, twenty-three?"

"Nineteen." Humi found her voice. "And that's old enough. If I were still in Domesdys, I'd already be a mother twice over."

"I'm sure you would," Hem said implacably. "I'm sure you would. Well, I expect you have come about Erene." She gaped. "Come in."

She followed him into the waft of cool air. The door shut with a jingle. When her eyes adjusted, she saw a small, dim room lined floor to ceiling with books, knick-knacks, effigies, statuettes, dried butterflies and salt flowers, and so forth. Racks laden with more stuff stood on the floor. Mobiles and wreaths turned slowly from the ceiling. Behind a counter sat a Veretrean woman with fur the same green as old copper. A small child curled on her lap, languidly mouthing the woman's black braid. A hint of pride crept into Hem's voice as he said, "Humility, this is my wife, Pleasantry Lakestone. Leasa, this is Humility, Lady Garden. Erene's new apprentice."

"Call me Humi, please, Godsie."

Leasa smiled. "We knew Erene had taken another apprentice, of course, but none of the merchants' wives from whom I get gossip are quite sure of who's who in Antiprophet Square, so we did not know your name. Or whether you were old or young, Calvarese or Icelandic." She held up the child. "Humi, this is my daughter Sensitivity . . . Ensi."

Humi put down her hat to shake the child's chubby hand. Ensi smiled at her, a sudden, heart-stopping beam of toothlessness, and tightened her fingers. Humi couldn't remember how long it had been since she last touched a child. She'd never gotten into the habit of visiting the ghostiers' children in Marshtown as the other women did, mainly because Erene had no real relationship with her son, Tessen. But she had never before regretted that oversight.

She turned to face Hem. "Godsman Lakestone, it is hard for me to admit this—" she dimpled—"but I need help." She had to get it out. "Erene has stopped making ghosts."

Hem visibly flinched.

"I—I don't know what to do. Should I confront her? Should I ignore her pain? I can't do that. Is there any precedent?"

"Why didn't you go to Tellury Crescent?" Hem was recovering. "This is a matter for the ghostiers, not for a shopkeeper!"

"The ghostiers would use the information to persuade the Ellipse that Erene is not fit to hold the twentieth seat," Humi said simply.

"So it is that bad," Hem said at length.

The door jingled. A Deltan woman in smeared yellow facedust puffed in, with a sweating lackey waving a fan over her head. "Leasa!" she cooed. "How are you today?"

Hem pulled a quick face at Humi. "Greetings, Milady Catgut . . . Humi, shall we go within? Ensi!" He hurried them around the counter and through a door. In the narrow back room, which was furnished with a sofa and a low table, a few toys lay on the floor. Small, high windows showed the other side of a back alley. Hem delved into a cold-closet in the wall and produced a bottle of red wine and a dish of water-gateaux. Ensi climbed on the bench next to Humi, murmuring quietly to her doll. Hem poured the wine. It was chilled, delicious. Sunlight from the alley made a long, narrow grid on the wall above Humi's head.

"I know very little of palace affairs," Hem said. "Only hearsay. I knew I was leaving it all behind when I opened Delights. Our customers are avid socialites, and as atheistic as any, but since none of them have the palace entrée, they have no information to speak of. And Leasa and I are not in the habit of scrounging for gossip on the streets."

"Then this will be a long story," Humi said.

"She has knotted a real cat's cradle this time, hasn't she?" Hem said when Humi finished.

The sun had gone down. The wine bottle had grown sweaty.

"What advice have you for me?" she said.

He pursed his lips. "Believe me when I say that for five years, I loved Erene just as much as you seem to. She was my sun and moon. I think it is in no way a disadvantage to be able to give one's heart completely, as you and I can—rather, if we give it into safe hands, we can become the happiest men and women alive." A smile tweaked his lips as he looked down at his little girl, who had gone to sleep with her head in Humi's lap. "But if I learned one important thing from my life with the ghostiers, it was this: Nobody can live more than one life. You cannot manage anyone's affairs other than your own—mine, the affairs of Hemlock Lakestone; yours, those of Humility Garden. That is the danger of disguising oneself. One risks taking on more responsibility than any of us can handle—which is surprisingly little if one wants to live a good life."

"Nonsense!" Humi sat forward, momentarily forgetting about Ensi. "That is patently untrue. What are the greatest leaders of men but those who take responsibility for thousands of lives?"

"Those are the men and women who die young. Just think: ghosts, in their beauty, exemplify the aesthetic excellence of our whole race. And they must die for it. Already, by making ghosts for Erene, you are living for her. Stop now, here! Let her correct her own negligence, or die her own death!" His wineglass squealed as he turned it in his powerful hands.

"How can you say that?" Humi asked. "You know I love her the way you loved her. I cannot possibly untangle my life from hers." Humi looked down at the little girl in her lap. She fingered the soft green down around Ensi's ear. Ensi's pink lips were mushed against Humi's skirt, and she breathed in little snorts.

And the Balance swung. Humi took a deep breath. "Shall I take her up to bed for you?"

Hem looked annoyed at the change of subject. Humi wormed her arms under the rumple-furred child, picked her up, and carried her out. On the staircase, she met a boy of ten or so, stinking of sweat and dust from walking in the heat. He didn't ask who she was, just stared at her. Depositing Ensi in the bedroom, Humi smoothed her hair and dropped a kiss on her forehead. The room was cool, being crushed against the second story of another house and therefore windowless. Looking down at the child, Humi thought, *Erene just needs a little push in the right direction. Something slightly different. Something that will get her applause from the people whose approval she cherishes.*

Her instincts screamed out against such a thing, but her loyalty overruled it.

Ensi would be perfect.

Coming downstairs, she stood in the doorway of the back room and said, "Sell her to me."

Hem froze. The boy was kneeling beside him. He grinned in delight. "Father! She gonna take Ens away?"

"Shut up, Meri," Hem said coldly. "Humi—I will overlook that thing you just said."

"I knew I had to come here," Humi said. "And now I know why. I never thought of you before, but this morning it was clear in my mind. How much do you want?" Twin impulses made her smile meanly at him: the desire to coerce him into selling Ensi, and her inner disgust at what she was doing. "You cannot possibly be making enough from the shop to be living comfortably. How much? I am generous."

Hem surged to his feet and seized her shoulders, pushing her back against the doorjamb. In the twilight he seemed even bigger than he was, his eyes like yellow suns. "Do not endanger your soul like this! Gods, Humi, *leave* the ghostiers if this is what they are doing to you! I do not even know you, but I know that you have a *soul*! *Stop it!*"

"You couldn't *take* Tellury Crescent!" Humi twisted away and fled up the first few stairs, whirling to scold him. "The ghostiers were too much for you! You couldn't bear the intimacy! You never understood the bond that makes us die for each other!"

"Mother! Moth—Hoo—hoomi—" Ensi sat down hard on the step behind Humi, banging her head on the banister. One little hand went up to the bump, and the corners of her mouth fell, and she began to cry loudly. Humi twisted around. The baby stretched out her arms and let herself fall against Humi's skirts. Humi scooped her up, pressing kisses over the button nose and wet green cheeks. "There. It's all right. Let me feel—"

She stopped.

Hem stared up at her from the bottom of the stairs. "So," he said measuredly. "So. A true killer."

Ensi kept on blubbering. Belatedly, Humi said, "It's just a little hurt!"

As Leasa bustled through from the shop, her face creased with worry, Humi delivered the girl into her arms. "She's all right, Leasa! I'm sorry, but I think I must say good-bye—I have—I have to get back—".

Hem escorted her to the door in silence. Outside, the twilight was sullen, the sky red-fleeced, black roofs looming against the sunset like predators in silhouette. The owners of brothels and taverns stepped out of doors to poke flaming brands up into their door lanterns. Gaudy signs leered brightly in the lantern light as the street lit up for the second time that day. More beggars than ever appeared to take advantage of the strollers who frequented Temeriton for its nighttime offerings.

Hem stood in the doorway, arms folded. "This is not a good place to raise children. But what can we do? Leasa and I are not rich. There is, as you so correctly observed, a limit to the amount of money one can make from selling knickknacks."

Humi's porter pulled her sedan up to the door. She lifted the curtain aside, gathered her skirt in one hand, and turned back. "Hem—I'm sorry."

"You realized what you were doing in time. They have not completely sophisticated you yet." Hem shook his head. "I can hardly believe that I once lived where such obscene displays are commonplace."

Humi looked at him with curiosity. "Do you still believe in ghosting, then?"

"What do you mean? I am a believer in the gods. And in destiny."

She smiled. "I wish I'd got to know you better. We spent all afternoon talking about Erene."

"That was as much my fault as yours. I suppose it has been too long since I spoke of her to anyone. It accumulates, like a need. She used to come and visit, bringing perfume and laughter and presents for Ensi and Meri . . . I can still tell you the flavor of her scent. Bitter cocoa and honeysuckle." He laughed shortly.

"Yes. She loves that scent, though I don't particularly like it." Humi glanced up at the dark windows. The odor of rotting flesh from the beggar at the doorway drifted past her nostrils. Shuddering, she stepped into the sedan. "Good-bye, Hem. Thank you."

Ensi toddled out and wrapped one arm around her father's leg, waving good-bye as the porter started at a run down the street.

Once they had turned the corner and Humi's feeling of warmth and virtue died down, she bit her knuckles and thought: *What am I going to do? I can't go back empty-handed! What am I going to do?*

As the sedan rattled through Shimorning, the porter cursed and swerved. Humi poked her head out of the curtains and saw a crowd of beggar children. One, a girl of about twelve, carried a toddler on her back that seemed untouched by the dirt on its sister and its sling. Its leaf-green fur glistened with health. It laughed gurglingly at Humi.

She stopped the sedan and got out. "How much will you take for it?" she said, pointing.

It crawled all over the sedan as they rode back to Antiprophet Square. Humi was glad that it was an annoying baby, not particularly endearing. It also helped that she had refused to let its sister tell her its name, age, or sex. She carried it inside under her cloak and left it chewing on the canopy of Erene's bed, with an artfully scrawled note pinned to its garment that said, "This baby's parents died. Take it, milady. It's yours."

When she returned from dinner at the Summers', now disguised as Lady Bonnevine, a Deltan native, Goquisite met her in the hall and enfolded her in a embrace. Her voice was squeaky with emotion as she said, "Erene has gone to Tellury Crescent. She left word that she will not be back for at least two sixdays."

Humi disengaged herself and blinked, hard. Goquisite beamed. Tears stood in her eyes. "Thank you."

"I'll go tonight. To help her with the ghost." Her mind raced. While Erene ghosted, in the total seclusion that was traditional, how would Humi manage? She would have to assist Erene by night and employ a persona whom Erene would believably trust with her business during the day. Lady Falippe Greenbranch might do. Falippe was an heiress and a third-generation noble from Veretry who dwelt in lodgings in the city that (Humi had heard the ladies conjecture) she kept secret because they weren't as opulent as she would have liked.

Yes, Erene would trust her. It was just a pity she wasn't a more pleasant person. Humi had already had to play her often enough to keep her credible; it was going to be an ordeal to act her for several straight sixdays.

And Arity, she thought. *There isn't a chance that I'll get to explain.*

But what is there to explain?

She crossed her arms over her chest. She felt painfully empty.

Eighteen

"So she came back after all," Ziniquel said, looking side-wise at Elicit.

Elicit did not answer. He scraped hard, angrily, at the little ghost of a rat that he was whittling down to nothing. Apprentice ghostiers often made tiny animals for practice; this was one of Algia's that had turned out ridiculously posed. No use for it. He shoved the blade hard with his thumb and made the diamondine squeal.

"You didn't expect her to, did you?"

Elicit turned on the younger man. "Shut up. You don't know what you're talking about."

Ziniquel fell silent. Below their swinging feet, a side channel of the Chrume washed around the stilts of the jetty, creating a brown-and-black-marbled pattern that one part of Elicit's mind noted and stored away for future use. Somewhere amid the waving grasses of the marsh islands were hidden the boats that had set off from Marshtown at dawn. Though the heat of the day had diminished, they had not come back yet; the jetties that jutted out side by side by side all along the marshfront were not crowded. Old men talked, smoked, nodded over their fishing lines. A few women mended nets and clothes. Children dashed around, ostensibly in the care of their grandfathers, their shrill voices rising into the summer sky like smoke.

"I keep thinking of Tessen," Elicit said abruptly. "How could she do such a thing when she has a child herself?"

"It's not exactly an innovation," Ziniquel said. "Maybe for a ghostier who is a mother. But certainly child ghosts are nothing new."

"It ought to be different for a woman," Elicit said helplessly. His gorge rose every time he thought of Tessen—active, alive Tessen, fostered with Soulf Freebird, whose lover he had been for a time when Erene first started to draw away from him. He would have acted as a father to Tessen had Erene not expressly requested that he stay away from the boy. She wanted him to have an ordinary life. You had to give her credit for that. And atheist though she was, she had given him a proper name.

"Emni said that if the child was a born ghost, she would do it." Ziniquel shrugged, leaning back on his hands, his fine-furred throat bared to the sun. Again, the ghostier part of Elicit noted his pose—easy, unconcerned—and stored it away for future use. Zin was far from carefree, of course—none of the *imrchim* had that luxury—but his lithe body managed to give the impression of ease. Conversely, Elicit had heard himself described (by Mory, but it could have been any objective observer) as a knotted bundle of gray ropes.

It had seemed funny at the time. But somehow he had not been able to shake that image of himself as a stooped, careworn old man. Age *did* sit heavy on his shoulders. The conundrum of Algia and Eterneli weighed on his mind. Neither of them was a fit successor to him, not artistically or politically. And he knew it was his own fault. He had made Algia the pale creature she was and had stunted vivid Eterneli's independence until now she took his every word as scripture and dared not go out alone without an older ghostier.

Elicit winced every time he mentally compared her with Mory's dark, passionate Tris or the Southwind twins.

And he knew why he had done it. Subconsciously, he had been afraid of dying. Afraid of being superseded.

Afraid of aging out of his talent and his virility alike. The two things were a good deal the same, after all.

Most of the time he lived each day as it unfurled before him, rejoicing, as Rita did, in the physical things of life. If you looked at it right, each moment was diamondine.

But sometimes (like today), he could not help resenting the young, radiant ghostiers like Ziniquel.

The young, radiant ghostier sneezed. He opened his

eyes and darted a sideways look at Elicit. "You still love her."

"What bullshit," Elicit said solidly. "She betrayed me."

"You love her." Ziniquel's hand slid out over the sun-warped boards of the jetty, stopped a moment, then curled around Elicit's thigh. Bony fingers that had touched him far more intimately than this kneaded the great muscle on the inside of Elicit's thigh until Elicit closed his hand over Ziniquel's, stopping him.

"You can't lie to me, Godsman Paean," Ziniquel said. "You know you never stopped loving her."

Tidal waters surged choppily around the foot of the jetty. Elicit stared down at the brown-and-black foam. He always thought that the grief had died. But then he saw Erene with this baby ghost and he felt a desperate need to protect her from the damage she was doing to herself. The need was corrosive, unending. Sometimes at night he could not bear it, and he crept in the dark to Algia, hating himself every moment.

Humi sat cross-legged on her bed, drinking hot wine. It was nearly midnight. The workshop was silent. Erene had dragged out the process of ghosting intolerably, taking frequent breaks to sit and do nothing or to sleep. It was as if she had slumped down on a soft patch of grass by the wayside and could not bring herself to get up again. And at the beginning she had tortured that baby as no warm-blooded creature should be tortured, simply for the sake of prolonging it.

Humi was racked by a sense of guilt. But had she the child to buy over again, or Erene to let drown in inadequacy, she knew she would make the same choice.

Putting down the mug, she padded through the apartment. The workshop door screeched as she opened it—but the heap of silk skirts and fur that was Erene didn't stir. Beside the armchair sat the baby ghost, blocked in with the subtle washes Erene liked. These light colors had stood untouched for months, while the front of the cupboard became a jumble of Humi's richer pigments. The baby's arms circled above its head, and it rose on its bottom a little, grinning. Too close! How could Erene have let herself fall asleep within the aura of its cold? Already her fur was tipped with frost. How could she have forgotten?

Steeling herself against the chill, Humi closed her arms round the ghost, lifted it and carried it to a safe distance. So light. *You betrayed me,* it cried wordlessly. *You nipped my life out. You, Humi,* you!

Ugh. I hope Erene will provide some good strong emotion to block that *out.*

The torches were sputtering. Rubbing her bare arms, Humi circled the workshop, replacing them. She gathered up the remnants of the meal she'd brought Erene earlier in the evening. By the gods, it felt strange to play the servant again! Strange, but good. She dropped a kiss on the stubbornly creased gray brow. The senior ghostier shuddered but did not wake. Humi stood for a moment, biting her lip, then slid into the chair next to Erene. She cuddled up with her, laying her cheek on Erene's breast, melting the frost with her own body heat.

Nineteen

Black shrouds draped every door lintel in Samaal. Everyone wore black somewhere, often in bands tying up their black hair. The sight comforted Thani. Playing truant while Transcendence slept, drifting along crushed in the crowd, she felt for a moment that she was again the girl she'd been before she prophesied. It was three years; she was sixteen now, and it did not seem likely she would ever prophesy again, the interval had been so long. But that single, garbled flood of words, three years ago, had altered both her and Transcendence's lives. It had inspired in both of them a deep-seated dissatisfaction.

Through her, Transcendence had glimpsed the salty glimmer of Heaven. In her darkest moments, she wondered if he *wanted* her to prophesy again, whether he would give anything to focus the dimly seen door into greatness.

Sometimes she even wanted it herself, so that he'd be happy with her.

Her eighteenth birthday was not so far off now. And she did not know what would happen to her after Transcendence cast her off. Growing up was doing strange things to her. But now their grand circuit had brought them to Samaal. Maybe she would find an answer here.

She leaned on the seawall, looking out over the docks. Almost all the ships had metal hulls and masts. The sun flashed blindingly on them. Piles of rope lay coiled at the base of the seawall. The sea that spread to the horizon was an upside-down night sky, silver constellations swimming as the sun turned on tiny waves. This street, lined behind her with bars and shady, shuttered establishments, was the bottommost of dozens of tiers that lined a natural harbor in the barren coast. Calvary encouraged its people to use stone and metal in building: standing at the top of the whole tin-roofed cascade of Samaal, just as the sun breasted the eastern rim, was enough to blind you for a day.

Thani heaved a shuddering sigh and rested her chin on her hand. She breathed deeply of the racy reek of the crowd: bodies cleansed only by the chafe of the sand in their clothing. "Pardon me, Godsie," a pleasant voice said next to her. "You're not Calvarese? You wouldn't be Domesdian, would you?"

Thàni turned. A young, tawny-furred sailor, hair hacked off short, had spoken.

"I can't tell you how good it is to see a pale face so far from home!" he said. "The sun's got to your fur and hair—or are you Icelandic?"

"No," she said, "I'm from Westshine province."

"Gods! I don't believe it! I'm from Ruche!" Ruche was the next province to Westshine. His delight was infectious. Cautiously, Thani smiled. "Will you sit down and have a glass?" he asked. "It'd be so good to talk of home—"

He doesn't know I'm a leman, Thani thought. *But then, how should he? There are dozens of other reasons for a foreigner to be in the capital.*

She thought of Transcendence, napping in their lodgings on the seventh tier.

She smiled and let the crowd push her closer against the young man.

He took her to a stone-flagged, relatively quiet bar, where sailors from all over the Divinarchy and immodestly dressed Calvarese women sat on stools at small, high tables. A bargirl put shots of sand liquor in front of them. The sailor showed Thani how to empty the glass at one gulp. He laughed when she made a face. "Not used to drinking? How old are you?"

She could have told him then. But she did not. "Oh," she said, "twenty . . . one . . . My father is a merchant. We moved to Samaal three years ago." She felt her face going muddy. She was terrible at lying.

But he did not pursue the subject. He was too eager to talk about his home and family. He was the youngest of thirteen cousins in a saltside hamlet, and there had really been no option but for him to go to sea. But he missed the saltside. Sometimes on deck, he said, he would look up from mending the ropes and think the sea was the salt, glittering. The *yeep* of flying fish sounded like sheep. The afternoon wore away as he rambled on, his voice throb-bing with longing and increasing drunkenness. Thani might have been bored, but she was not. A strange, muted excitement pulsed through her: she knew she, too, was drunk, and she did not care. When, downing his sixth shot, the sailor draped a perfunctory arm over her shoul-ders, she snuggled against him. "Careful," he winced. "I've two cracked ribs, and they're not healin'—"

"Why don't you go see a flamen?"

He shrugged. "They've more 'portant things to take care of than a fellow who can 'eal on 'is own. Don' hurt bad 'nuff, anyhow, for me to go botherin' ... I've ... other things t' do ..." He kissed her face sloppily. A pang of excitement went through her. "You're a swee' girl," he said.

But her training would not let her leave it there. She in-sisted stupidly, "You should go to a flamen! My flamen, Godsbrother Transcendence, would work a miracle for you—"

"Hold u ..." He pulled away. Careful not to slur his words, he said, "*Your* flamen?"

"Yes! He'd be happy—"

"You're—you're a leman." He stood up, heedless of the table, which crashed to the floor, smashing the dozen or so glasses they had emptied between them. "You're a leman ... And you were ... Gods!" He blundered back-ward, his pleasant face a mask of revulsion. The custom-ers stared. "I was ... Get *out* of here!"

Thani did not need to be told twice. Her hands locked over her mouth, she turned and ran out into the last of the afternoon. Her drunkenness made her feel as if she were wading through the air like water. Tears blinded her as she ran up metal-roofed stairway after stairway, until the last vestiges of crowds vanished and she doubled over, panting, alone in a sunbathed, silent street. Over the roofs, the golden orb of the sun was about to immerse itself in the welter of red dust on the western rim. Fine sand drifted lazily in the air. Dogs lay flat on doorsteps, their jowls flapping with their breath.

Thani pulled her jacket about herself. Tears streamed down her cheeks. How could she have gone along with him? Why had she thought she *wanted* it? Why had she thought she could get away with it, in a pious city like Samaal?

She knew of only one cure for misery like this. One she had always known.

She pushed through the lacy metal door. "Transcendence, it's me," she blurted. "I'm sorry I was out so long. I'll never do it again. Never. I'm so sorry . . ." He did not stir. He sat asleep in the only chair, snoring a little, his head pillowed on the stone table, on which stood a half full crate of cactusfruit. They had been grateful when the owner of this house had given them free lodgings, and Transcendence made sure that Thani did not temper her gratitude with even one whit of reproach when they learned that the lodgings were made up of a single room and no bed. Thani dropped to her knees on the floor, burying her head in his robed lap. He stirred and, half asleep, stroked her head.

Gradually the room stopped spinning. She could see under the table, through the pierce-holes in the door to the street. Cobbles and metal doors. All so rigid. She wanted the mutable forms of sand dunes. She wanted freedom. She knew she would never be able to tell Transcendence about her transgression, now that the first flush of self-disgust was gone. Perhaps in the future, when she acted extra pious to make up for it, he would praise her for her renewed fervor. And she would writhe. "Oh, gods," she whispered, "take me back to the desert." The young sailor's kiss burned like a swelling on her cheek. "Take me back where I am safe."

Twenty

Half-sensible, Humi rose on Dividay, threw the curtains wide, and stumbled through her toilette. She was late for brunch at the Summer mansion, but she could not summon a servant to assist her. No one must know that Falippe Greenbranch and Humility were the same person. Blinking, she powdered her face gold, re-dyed her hair deep red, and curled it.

Her maid was truly numb with tiredness. But she did not realize just how numb it was until she was at the Summers', lounging on a sofa, nibbling on quail eggs and seed-toast, and she remembered: *Dividay services.*

"And the conspiracy has a new ally, my dear Lady Greenbranch," Belstem said portentously. "Not being from the city, I don't expect you will have heard. He is a recent accquaintance of mine and Lady Gentle's. Hrrmp!" It was almost midday, and she did not have time to change back to herself if she wanted to catch any of the services at all. Her dress was light violet taffeta, ruffle-skirted in the new style: Marshtowners would think she was an atheist lady come to poke fun; but there was no help for it. She cut Belstem off in midsentence, excused herself, and slipped out of the mansion by a side door. She fled across the square and flagged down one of the porters who lounged around the Ankh mansion's gates, waiting to work.

"Where to, milady?" he asked.

"Circle through Marshtown until you find Godsbrother Joyfulness' congregation." Damn! she could almost hear him raising his eyebrows. As they entered Marshtown, the familiar scents of rotting grass, fish, pig dung, and in-

cense seeped into the sedan. Humi breathed deeply as the
wheels bumped over the cobbles. She knew this district
so well that her mind supplied a street name every time
the sedan swung around a corner. She had come to services here every single sixday since she had arrived in
Tellury Crescent. The ghostiers always came to
Marshtown; wandering flamens preached in the streets
throughout the city, causing blockages in a traffic that did
not stop for the day of worship, but the flamen councillors in Marshtown drew the largest congregations, and for
the ghostiers, demonstrating their loyalty to the councillors was as strategically important as their piety itself.

"We must stand together!" she heard from outside the
sedan. "Above all, we devotees must stand together.
Those with a little to spare must aid those who have nothing."

The sedan slowed to a stop. The porter let the poles
bump softly to the cobbles.

"There has been discontent in the countryside, and all
of you have seen the restlessness in the slums of our own
city. Crying at the gates of the nobility does no one any
good, because the food has all been shipped off for profit.
So we flamens must feed the poor, the weak, and the
young. We are draining the gods' resources. We cannot
save the world all on our own! It is up to you. You must
prove that devotees still have more compassion than blasphemers. You must keep the old ways..."

The porter poked his face through the curtains. "This 's
as close as I can get, milady—"

"Wait for me here," Humi whispered, and got out.
Gathering her pink skirt in one arm, she picked her way
between the seated Marshtowners. Godsbrother Joyfulness stood on a podium made of fish crates, declaiming
with grand gestures. He was telling the parable of Brav-
ery Godgifted's argument with the Third Divinarch: he
acted different parts magnificently, and the salt crystals
seemed to leap about in his eye sockets, glinting in the
sun. He was a big Royallandic man in his thirties, handsome, with fur dappled like sunlight on the leaves of a
beech tree.

Humi sank to her knees by the corner of a ramshackle townhouse. Beside the podium, Joyfulness' leman Flexibility gazed up worshipfully at him. Lexi was a nineteen-year-old Archipelagan, thin and intense. He was Joyfulness' first leman, and in their case everything scurrilously implied about the flamen-leman relationship was true. The sight of him made Humi uneasy. She could not forget the prophecy that the Divinarch had divulged to her three years ago. *You shall receive the highest honor the world can bestow upon you. Yet you shall live a life of deception. Your heart shall be heavy as a rock veined with iron. And the truth is ineffable. The truth is ineffable—*

It had cast a shadow over her future that dimmed, but never went away—a shadow as long as the shadow of a predator standing with folded wings at sunset, with edges as bright as broken glass. It kept receding from her days.

"And so—in the end—we will all become one people again!" Joyfulness smacked his fists together. There was an incredible power in his voice, as if he were drawing on Lexi's adoration, the adoration of all the crowd. He sounded almost godlike as he boomed, "Devotees— blasphemers—all one under the sun, praising the gods, living in peace!" And a murmuring broke out, surging along below the eaves where the sun lay in needles on the thatch. The crowd pressed around Joyfulness in a tradition as old as the flamenhood, each man, woman, and child pushing to touch him once for luck and health. Humi stayed kneeling on the dusty cobbles, her head leaning against a drainpipe made of bundles of dry reeds. She felt as light as if her blood had turned to bubbles. This was the first service she had attended since Arity revealed the true nature of the *auchresh* to her. That night she had, willy-nilly, become an atheist. She had feared that with her childhood illusions about the gods shattered, the flamens' teachings would no longer have the power to move her; but Joyfulness' sermon had pierced her, both stilling her and raising her soul to a silent, clear peak from which she could see for leagues.

At last she rose and crossed the street. In her soft-soled court slippers, she felt as if she were floating. The crowd around Joyfulness had thinned enough that the ghostiers saw her immediately. They always recognized her, no matter what she wore, and they gathered around her, enfolding her in quick, sincere hugs. She envied them their freedom to wear sleeveless summer garments. Nothing marked them out from the run of Marshtowners except the disturbing depths in their eyes, those little shadowy death's heads for which she always looked in the mirror when she was Humility Garden again. Lexi's voice rippled in the background, smooth and ceaseless, as they embraced her: Ziniquel, Rita, Mory, Beisa, Sol, Emni. "I *am* going to come visit you in the square," Emni said. She giggled. "Beisa says just for one day it won't corrupt me. Won't that be marvelous!"

"Wonderful!" Humi said honestly. "I'll show you all around—"

Algia, Eterneli, Trizisim, Owen. "What is that you're *wearing,* Humi?" Owen asked. "Who are you supposed to *be*?" She did not answer. Elicit. As always, his hug seemed a little restrained. "Are you coming back with us for lunch?" he asked distractedly.

"I can't." Ruefully she straightened her hair ribbon. "I have to leave before I am recognized. I shouldn't be here dressed like this. I must just pay my respects to the Godsbrother, then I—"

The cracking, sighing hiss of Lexi's voice came right in her ear. "I see . . ."

Humi twisted. Lexi's features were rigid, eyes peeled so wide the whites were visible, and his hands opened and closed jerkily by his sides.

"Flexibility?" the Godsbrother said. Clumsily, he floundered toward Lexi, pawing the air. "Are you all right?"

A tiny popping noise came from Lexi's lips. His head cracked back, and as he went suddenly limp Humi caught him. "Godsbrother!" Hot and cold sweats washed over her body. "We're over here!"

Joyfulness plunged toward the sound of her voice. He swept Lexi into his arms. "Flexibility! I fear for him, Godsies and Godsmen. This is the seventh time—"

Seventh? Humi thought incredulously, at the same time as a nearby Marshtown woman burst out, "Seven prophetic fits? Godsbrother, how—how is it that he's still alive?"

Unnatural tremors ran through Lexi's body. Joyfulness' head came up, gazing blindly, proudly, around the crowd. "I must ask you all to leave. Now. Some prophecies are too dangerous to be heard by the laity—"

Lexi's mouth snapped open. He began, jerkily and in jarring accents, to speak. "*I see ...*" Rising in Joyfulness' arms, he looked straight into Humi's eyes. She felt her face muddying as all the eyes turned to her. "*She shall not die for many long years. And before she does, she shall receive the highest honor the world can bestow upon mortal or god. Yet she will count it a curse. For she will meet her end alone, forsaken by family, friends, gods, and mortals, in agony.* You will perish in agony!" he shouted at her. "You will perish by your own hand!"

And he went limp. A faint grating sound came from his chest. "*I ... sss ...*" White spittle bubbled up between his lips.

"Lexi! Lexi!" Joyfulness roared. He shook the boy frantically. "Gods—"

"He's dead, Godsbrother," Rita said, reaching to hold him back. "He's dead!" The big man went rigid, then sagged, sobbing, his face pressed to Lexi's thin chest.

"Oh, gods." Humi hugged herself. "Oh, shed the gods' blood." She felt the eyes of Marshtowners and ghostiers on her. Her face was dark under Falippe's yellow facedust. Ziniquel came toward her, hands outstretched, and she retreated, stumbling over the gutter in the center of the street. He had to see—she mustn't be recognized as herself: Red curls bobbed about her cheeks, she had yellow-green fur the color of autumn apples, and her features were pinched but full of sex appeal. As far as the courtiers and socialites and flamens would ever know, Lexi had directed his prophecy at Falippe Greenbranch.

"Humi—" Zin said, quite loudly

Shut up! She whirled away from him. Desperate, she snapped her fingers at the porter. "I'm ready to leave!"

He had to *see*—"I think I have heard enough to tell a fine anecdote this evening at Lady Crane's!"

"Slummers!" a local man with beetling brows said loudly as she passed. She climbed into the sedan and, sinking back against the hard teak seat, discovered that she was shaking. The curtains kept the sun out, but when she wiped her forehead, her fingers came away covered with a slime of facedust and sweat. She grabbed a handful of her skirt and scrubbed her cheeks, her neck, her bosom, frenziedly cleaning off Falippe, cleaning off everything that could link her to this street corner in Marshtown, to this prophecy. Nothing to do with her, Humi! She did not believe in destiny. If she could shift it off onto an imaginary character this easily—*this* easily—where was its power? Nowhere! That was where!

"Where to, milady?" the porter called back respectfully.

The Eftpool? No. Beau is obsessed with destiny. I don't need to hear any more obscure pronouncements today. Have to get away. Where?

Hobnailed footsteps tramped past. The cremators' men, coming for Lexi. It could not have been more than ten minutes since he died, but Humi wasn't surprised. On occasions like this, when a flamen or leman's dignity was at stake, the flamens' all-pervading influence over Marshtown showed like the scheme of a salt-ant colony seen through glass salt.

Humi finished cleaning her face, ripped her dress down the front, and kicked it into the bottom of the sedan. The bodice held her shape, like the discarded husk of a cricket. Air circulated coolly under her slip. "To the Old Palace!" *I'm not going to see Arity. I'm going to see if everything he and Hope and Pati told me is true. I'm not going to see Arity.* "The Quelide entrance. Where no one will see me go in."

The door banged against the wall. Reflex brought Hope's head up. No one ever used doors in the Divine Guards' quarters: like the ghostiers, they let no outsiders enter their domain—a labyrinth of traps and tunnels and cavernous lairs that took up the top five floors of the Old Palace—and besides, *auchresh* who could *teth*¨ had small need of doors. Most of the corridors were full of junk, and so dirty that one could see one's footprints on the floor.

Besides, it was midday. Everyone should be here, if not sleeping, then making the most of these daylight hours when the humans thought they were sleeping.

"It's just Arity making a theatrical entrance, as usual," Pati muttered, pulling Hope back down. "He can't get over how important he is now that he's filling in for the Divinarch. Goes out during the day. Sleeps like a human—*wrchrethri!* Keep on."

Hope caressed him for a moment, then she raised herself on one elbow. "Wait, Pati. It's a mortal. Oh, by the Power. Her hair's full of cobwebs. She must have found her way up the stairs."

Pati peered through the murk. "Can't be—but it is! Silver Rat, Sepia, Val, everyone, look at that!" In one leap he was off the bed. "How dare it!"

The girl stood in the doorway, small and fragile in a violet slip. Hope's heart sank as she recognized Humility Garden, the ghostier's apprentice. She had done her best to forget that night on her balcony when Pati and Arity had, as usual, lost control of themselves and turned a civilized exchange into a disastrous contest as to who could act most undecorously in the fight to cut the other one down. The difference was that they did not usually go all out at each other in front of a mortal. When Arity appeared alone, morose and snappish, the night after the debacle, Hope had thought the thing was finished. But apparently, it had made a deep impression on the Garden girl. Now she thought, *We've unblocked a hole of saltworms. How long are the vermin going to keep crawling out?*

Fury radiated off Pati like sparks. He *teth*¨d across the floor, leaving a sulphuric vacuum at Hope's side. "Milady Garden."

The girls' hands flew to her ears at his voice, though it did not sound especially loud to Hope.

"How pleasant to see you. Might it be too much to ask you to explain this honor?"

The *auchresh* in the sunken pool, the *auchresh* arguing philosophy over in the lamplight, the *auchresh* couples in the darkest corners, all stopped what they were doing. Slowly, on the far side of the room where he had been playing Conversion with Evel and River Grass, Arity stood up. "Have a care, Pati."

"How much of a fool can you be, Arity?" Pati gazed at Humi. "How much will it take to convince you that this was idiocy?"

"I didn't bring her here!" Arity reappeared right behind Humi.

"Damn it, Arity," Hope whispered. "For the Power's sake, don't touch her!" If Arity felt anything for the girl, he would be a lunatic to let Pati know it. She rolled around Silver Rat and stood up, her wings snapping open. Luckily, Arity had seen that, too. He stood stiffly behind Humi, arms at his sides. Humi glanced back at him and moved a step or two away. "I don't know what she's doing here," Arity said.

"However she got here, take her out *now*." This time Pati moderated his voice, but Hope could see anger crackling around him. He was the only *auchresh* she knew who could combine wrath and nudity without losing his dignity. "You were the inspiration for her coming here, if nothing else. Mortals are no use, not to play with or question or nibble on. She's Lady Gentle's nurse-chick, and it doesn't say much for you that that's all you can attract. I should have set my sights on Goquisite Ankh, at least, if I were you."

Arity did not move. "She's nothing to do with me."

"You befriended her."

"She's not my responsibility."

The girl shuffled a little farther away from him. Hope sat down on the edge of the bed platform and let her head fall against Silver Rat's thigh. He stroked her hair without taking his eyes off Humi. The girl looked small and lost, like a rat cowering between two peacocks. But her black eyes were holes in her furry face. Hope could tell she was drinking up every detail of the Divine Guards' private quarters—from the marble floor, scarred as a fisherman's arms, to the ceiling black with incense smoke, and all the *auchresh*-crafted furniture which no human had ever laid eyes on, not since the Old Palace was built.

"I don't need your protection, Arity," the girl said in decent *auchraug*. Every *auchresh* in the room, including Pati and Arity, gaped. "Striver, I did not come as a ghostier's apprentice. Nor as an atheist, nor as a devotee. I came by myself." Implied was, *And I can look after myself.*

"Oh, ho, a fighting chick," Pati jeered. Then his voice went dry and he dropped into the dissonance of harshness and melody that was *auchraug,* speaking fast so that the girl would not understand. "She's seen too much. And she speaks our tongue. Get her out. Now."

"I had no idea that she knew *auchraug.* And I am *not* responsible for her."

"Where could she have learned it but from you? You wouldn't have done that for anyone but a *ghauthiju.* She must be your *ghauthiju.* What I want to know, Ari, is how you found time to have a human *ghauthiju* between your *teth"s* back to Wind Gully Heaven and your bouts of smoking and fucking and arguing with us. We are your *elpechim.* You'd do well to remember that. You are part of *lesh kervayim*—" the cabal—"and you owe loyalty to no one but us."

He meant, To *me.* Hope's heart sank. The tension between Arity and Pati arose from their having spent their Foundlinghoods in the same Heaven, Wind Gully Heaven in the salt of Royalland. As a rule, the Heir had the highest status among the Incarnations, but when Arity arrived fifteen years ago, Pati had already gotten used to lording it over docile old Autumn Rain. Not much had changed since then, except that Arity chafed worse against Pati's control.

Now his voice was steely as a blade. "I owe nothing to you or any of your pigheaded reactionaries. I am Heir, law unto myself, and if I choose to have a visitor then I shall have one."

"My dear Charity, you may have her. You may do whatever you like with her. But she certainly cannot leave."

"Pati!" Hope heard the cry of pain and knew that Arity had backed down. Once again, the king was victorious. "Can you never let down your guard? Never? I saw you just now. You were intertwined with Hope and Silver and Val. They were making love to you. You lay there like a great drone while they worked on your mouth and your nipples and your penis. Yet all the time you had one eye open. I remember you before you went off to Delta City. I was a Foundling, learning to talk, and you were the first *mainraui* of Wind Gully Heaven. I thought your wings were the proof of your maleness, not the signs of a throwback. You taught me how to read and write, how to dance and shoot, how to make love. In those days *you* would make love to *me*. Remember that? You would tell me just to lie there in the starlight falling on the brocade coverlet in your room, and you—" His voice broke.

Through a blur, Hope thought, *Thank the Power the human couldn't understand* that. *She's heard enough secrets already*. Hope had grown up in Divaring Below, in Fewarauw—Pirady. She had not met Pati until she came to Delta City. But then he had been only five years on the job, and still unjaded. Still the noble, compassionate *mainraui* Arity described. That was when she had fallen so deeply in love with him.

Bitter tears stung the inside of her nose. She could hear tears in Arity's voice, too, as he demanded, "Don't you remember? Can't you just ease up now and then?"

"With every word you speak," and Pati's eyes glittered, "you lay another seal on the girl's death."

"They're going to tear each other apart again." Glass Mountain's voice came soft by Hope's ear. He was the oldest of *lesh kervayim*, Divine Guard but not Incarnation. He wouldn't interfere. She knew whose job it was to interfere—and she dreaded it like stepping into a blizzard.

She stood up, fanning her wings. Sheets of veined, leathery gold with claws at each elbow, they weren't just vestiges like Pati's, but genuine wings that could do everything except fly. The inability to fly was the lowest common denominator of the *auchresh* race. And if the cut-off mark had been just a little bit higher—some deviance in the size of the wings, some human roundness in the face, some mutation like Arity's body talons or Val's extra fingers—then Hope would not have been *auchresh*. She would have been kicked out of any Heaven that Found her, expelled as a predator baby. Ever since she was Found she had been painfully aware of this. And since she was such a bad representative of *auchresh iuim*, she would never have become the Maiden had any other young women been at liberty to go: but she had been the only one in the whole world. She and Broken Bird were two of perhaps three hundred female *auchresh* all over the Divinarchy. And the rest were wanted at home.

It was different here in Delta City. The cabal listened to her, but they did not automatically obey her, not unless she joined forces with Pati. That was part of why she allied herself with him, of course. How could it not be? But her relationship with him was not a subject for casual contemplation. It was like her gender, something which she hated and cherished. Like her useless, resplendent wings. Put together, those three things granted her a certain invulnerability.

Naked, she *teth¨d* between Pati and Arity. The Garden girl cast her a beseeching gaze. Hope gave the girl a tiny smile, pushed her away, and said in *auchraug* to Pati, "Let me settle this."

"The Maiden has nothing to do with a quarrel between Striver and Heir. Go away, Hope." Pati had a supercilious smile on his face, but his spine was as rigid as an iron rod, and his gaze locked with Arity's.

"I'm not being the Maiden. I'm a neutral observer who refuses to let you savage each other. This is a quarrel between the Striver and *Arity,* not the Heir. Arity spoke as himself, not the Heir, just now, because his being the Heir takes you both into the realm of safety, away from the bone, where you can hurt each other as much as you like and it doesn't count for anything. That's why you're still insisting on being the Striver, isn't it? You don't want to get hurt."

"Don't be absurd, Hope."

"You're no more a god than I am. But you think you are—and that is the danger. You are starting to think that you can do whatever you like." Inspiration was coming to her, as it sometimes did in these situations. She pushed Humi and Arity away behind her as she faced Pati. "Arity wants to see whether you can overcome the barrier between *auchresh* and *hymannim*. Whether we all can. It's a test, Pati, and you're failing, because of your oh-so-godly stubbornness."

He was a tall white flame in the gloom. His mismatched eyes bored into her. Incense combined sickly with the steam from the pool on whose tiled lip half the Divine Guard sat listening. "Pati, this *does* come down to politics," she said. "You think the way to win our fight, yours and mine against Erene Gentle, is by battling secrecy with secrecy, aggression with aggression. Because we are limited beings, that is the only way we know how to fight. But that is letting her fight on her own ground. And therefore she'll triumph through sheer weight of numbers. We don't need to match her every step. We need our own, innovative politics."

Exactly what the *auchresh,* as a race, had never been able to come up with to save their lives.

So—

They needed humans.

Hope couldn't believe her own cleverness.

She seized Pati's hands. "We'll make this girl part of *lesh kervayim.* We won't protect her from them. We'll see if she can handle it. If she can—then just think! A ghostier's apprentice fighting for us! Her position is unique. She could recruit other humans, atheists and devotees alike, to our cause. It would cut the ground out from under Erene Gentle's feet!"

"She's Erene Gentle's apprentice."

That slowed Hope for a minute. Then she shook her head impatiently. "It doesn't matter. Humans are good at duplicity. You didn't think Arity worked for *lesh kervayim*? Never underestimate him, Pati. This could mean the Throne."

For a moment Pati was still, staring down at her. Then he swaggered round her, grinning at Arity with the infectious charm that the Striver could summon at will, clapping the younger *auchresh* on the back. "Arity, I apologize! I'm truly sorry! I was hotheaded and unforgivably rude!" He swung to Hope. "It's a flawless plan!" And to the human, with impeccable courtliness, as if he really believed her his equal: "Milady Garden, I welcome you to the Divine Guards' private quarters."

Her eyes were like black swamp-holes, uncomprehending. Of course, her head must be buzzing from all the shouting. And even if she spoke a little *auchraug,* she could have no idea of what had just been planned. "Striver." She bobbed her head.

"Call me Pati." A show of teeth. "Would you like introductions to everyone? Or would you prefer to merge in naturally, as it were?"

"Pati," Arity said wearily. "That'll do." He glanced around. "Don't let them ride her too hard, will you?" And he vanished.

Hope coughed as the draft of sulphur hit her face. "What horrible manners!" She smiled at the human.

"Well, well!" Pati turned to Humi. She was peering wildly into the shadows of the room, probably feeling as if she had been deserted in the predators' den, her shoulders hunched in desperation. Again she reminded Hope of a rat in a corner. "He's gone off in a huff," Pati said slowly so that she would be able to understand. "I shouldn't count on him too heavily, if I were you. He's terribly self-absorbed." They moved toward the bed platform, where the *auchresh* who had been playing with Hope and Pati waited, half-hidden in a high sea of coverlets. Some of them had used the time to put on clothes. "This is Glass Mountain." Pati pointed. "This is Silver Rat. This is Val, short for Valor . . . this is Voli, for Frivolity. . . . We use mortal names in the Heavens now, you see. Almost all *auchresh* of my generation or younger are named for virtues." He laughed pleasantly. "My full name is Patience."

Someone was bashing Humi's temples in with a shovel. Gods only knew why: the smoke in the Divine Guards' quarters was no worse than in must human taverns. All the *auchresh* smoked pipes, even gentle, feminine Hope, but their tobacco was only the mild weed that Marshtowners liked of an evening. She had never seen most of these gods before, or else she had never paid attention to them because they were only sentinels. Some of their strange bodily characteristics were enough to make her hair stand on end. Like Arity (Arity who had gone and left her here alone), they were slender as rapiers. Like Arity, they wore earrings.

And they treated each other with a licentiousness that would have made the most extroverted atheist go muddy. Humi was glad of the gloom which obscured her own face. She had thought the night gatherings at Pietimazar's and Belstem's were bad enough—but the *auchresh* had *no* shame! And in between caressing each other, they dropped off to sleep like cats in the sun. And over each other's slumbering bodies, they talked on an on, half in guttural *auchraug*, half in mortal. What she could understand of their conversation, she found fascinating: biting, perceptive, and unfailingly witty, halfway between the impenetrably circular nonsense that the Incarnations spouted in public and the deep tranquility she shared with Arity.

Had shared with Arity. She gazed blearily at Pati and Hope, who were french-kissing while the rest of the circle discussed something with frequent shouts of laughter. Despairing, she thought, *How can I ever hope to treat them as they treat each other?* She felt like a child at a grownups' party. In one night, she'd learned more secrets than she had in three years of slinking around Antiprophet Square under the cloaks of her various personas. But she would never be able to use *these* secrets. She would simply be disbelieved.

"Do you know what? I think we ought to pierce Humi's

ears." Val was heavily built for an *auchresh*, foppish in an
eerie, intense way. His hands each had eight fingers. He
reached over and toyed with her earlobe. "To show she's
one of us now."

Someone else said approvingly, "She has such beautiful earrings, but they're just clamps."

They were Falippe's. Humi would have torn them off
earlier, had she remembered.

"I think we *should* do it." Val signaled an *auchresh*.
"Misty, we're going to give her *wrillim*! You still have
the equipment, don't you?"

"*Wrillim*—is that the *auchraug* word for earrings?"
Humi asked. "Will they hurt?"

Val looked at her in surprise. "No, no, not a bit.
Hope—Pati—everyone! Who has some pretty *wrillim* for
her?"

The gods volunteered various metal loops, studs, and
porcelain ornaments. Humi the socialite bobbed up: she
chose the simplest and most striking, a pair of gold hoops
as large as the circle of her thumb and forefinger.

"Those are mine," Hope said. "I should be delighted
for you to have them."

Val used his steely fingers to close them through her
flesh, slowly. She tried not to wince—first at his touch,
then at the pain.

"There!" He closed Falippe's earclasps in her sweating
palm. "Here are the old ones. They're pretty, but Hope's
suit you much better."

She nodded and tried to smile. Nothing suited *her*, ugly
little greenish-furred human that she was, couldn't he see
that? The smell of the smoke was nauseating. Why did
she notice it suddenly? Was it because her head was hurt-
ing so much? She would not throw up in public. She
would not. The hoops bumped gently against her neck.
She would not throw up—

"In the name of the Power," Hope said suddenly, disgustedly. "Look at her! Just look! Can't you see this is all
too much? I *know* it was my idea, but she's only a human,
and you've been treating her like a Foundling! I'm taking
her home." She scrambled to her feet and folded Humi in

her arms, pushing one knee between her legs, her breath hot on Humi's cheek. Humi felt herself go limp as a mouse in a cat's paws, cloudily aware of Pati's voice sneering at Hope for her softness. Then the room blinked into nothingness, the color of shut eyes. She could not breathe. But this time she did not black out. She thought, *This—is—teth"tach ching*— and held on to those words like a talisman. *Teth"tach ching.*

Her feet hit the floor. Something crunched under her slippers like broken glass, and she was in the workshop in Tellury Crescent. Impossibly, it was still afternoon, and Hope stood facing her, looking diminished in the sunlight, like a skinny, jaundiced teenager. Her wings reached from wall to wall of the long room. She was still naked. But it was her eyes, not her private parts, that she hid with her hands, squinting at Humi in the sunlight from the row of windows. "Ouch, this is bright!"

Humi shook her head wordlessly. She could not assimilate the experiences of the afternoon as rapidly as *lesh kervayim* seemed to have assimilated her. She could not find words for the mixture of exhaustion, nausea, and exhilaration she felt.

"We've accepted you, you know."

"But on what terms? You can't be *rewarding* me for barging in like that! What am I paying for my audacity?"

"Ah." Hope smiled uncomfortably. "You're sharp. But I think I'll leave it up to Pati to tell you. After all, it's his Power-cursed cause."

It sounded suspiciously as if Hope felt ashamed. Humi said nervously, "What is it?"

"Tomorrow. Or rather, tonight. You'll find out tonight." The *auchresh iu* forced a smile. "It's not as bad as all that." She yawned. "It's about four in the morning for me now. When I see you next, it will be four in the morning for *you.*"

"But how am I to get there? I can't traipse up all those stairways again—"

"One of the *kervayim* will come. Be here." And Hope turned into a purple-edged spot on the air that dwindled and vanished.

Humi rubbed her aching temples. Her *wrillim* bumped gently against her jaw. *There's no question of ducking out on* lesh kervayim *the way I ducked out on Arity,* she thought. *And anyway, there's no point now. This is far more serious. Gods, what have I got myself into? What do they want of me?*

The workshop smelled of chocolate and chalk. Familiar, good smells. But Humi could not forget Arity, Arity saying in the mortal tongue, *Don't let them ride her too hard,* as if he *meant* the inuendo, as if he thought some of the gods would *want* her, as if any *auchresh* would *ever* condescend to such a thing—

She remembered Arity, looking at her with troubled, unreadable eyes, looking at her for one moment and then *teth¨ing,* leaving her alone—

Her breath came fast. She whirled. The baby ghost lay scattered in smithereens on the floor of the workshop: a chubby arm here, a button nose there, diamondine slivers in the cracks of the floorboards. Erene was nowhere to be seen.

Twenty-one

In the corner of the bar, a yellow bitch dog danced on her hind legs. Her grizzled trainer gripped her front paws, crooning lovingly to her, displaying broken teeth as he grinned slyly at the crowd. Shimorning was by and large an atheistic district: the working men yelled blasphemies for praise as they tossed coppers. The dog moaned, and her trainer dealt her a blow that contacted her muzzle with a bony smack. "Keeps gettin' above 'erself!" he told the audience. "Gotta keep 'er in line!"

Erene grimaced with distaste. She brought her attention back to the corner table where she, Belstem, and their new allies Gold Dagger and the Hangman huddled. So sordid, this bar, exemplifying the very worst aspects of atheistic culture. But it was all she had now. When Belstem's courier arrived at the Crescent, she had been sitting staring helplessly at her ghost. She had finished the pigment painting, down to the last brushstroke, but somehow the emotion painting had not happened. The baby still wailed with the uncomprehending pain of betrayal every time she touched it. Ghosting was an intuitive craft: Erene had not known how she did it when she could still do it. Now that it had gone, she did not know how to get it back. She had been sitting there, openmouthed with horror, when the call came from the street.

She had greeted the courier as if he were her angel of deliverance. On the pretense of going to get her cloak, she had pushed the ghost onto the floor. Watching it fly into fragments felt good. Childish, but good.

Only now she thought, *Was this how it felt for Molatio?*

Constance? Is this how it feels for everyone when the end is in sight?

I'm thirty-eight. That's not old.

Far more dreadful than encroaching age loomed the possibility that perhaps she was rusty. That her talent had vanished through negligence. That she had not lost the ability to ghost but had forgotten how.

The part of her that did not care, the atheistic part, gazed steadily from one crime lord to the other. "Are we agreed, then?"

Gold Dagger had smeared his blobby features with grime, as he always did when he came out in public. The bright hilt at his belt, winking in the light of the candle that swung over the table, gave the only clue to his identity: Belstem had placed a price on his head which might have persuaded even the Shimorning commoners who benefited from his rob-and-resell trade to betray him. Belstem had promised to cancel the price now that they were allied, but Erene did not blame Gold Dagger for his continued cynicism.

The Hangman sat with his face hidden in a black cowl, hands joined inside voluminous sleeves. "Let me see if I have this clear, milady," he said in a light, ironic voice. "When the Divinarch dies, you want to rid the city of its key devotees: anyone, in other words, who might make trouble for you later on. Prominent merchants, shipowners, and bureaucrats. You do not fear the flamens—but you want to wipe out the entire secular government of Marshtown, and the undesirable elements of the other districts' governments. Yes?"

Erene nodded. Paintpots and brushes, rags and turpentine, waltzed distractingly across her mind. "It has been obvious to me for some time that when we act, it cannot be the clean coup d'état to which we thought we could limit ourselves."

"Other words, you come up with a plan, we come up with the muscle to carry it out," Gold Dagger said.

"Do not be so hasty to commit yourself," the Hangman said warningly. "She needs us."

"And you need us." Erene did not miss a beat. "You

know you cannot stay ahead of Belstem's price much longer, Gold Dagger. And Hangman, what's to stop him from persecuting you too?" She paused. "And quite apart from that, think what it will mean, after the revolution, to be the heroes who helped us implement the change."

"Oh, we are with you," the Hangman said, and laughed. "Never fear."

"'Ow's this?" Gold Dagger leaned across the table, his piggy eyes cold. "Two hundred strong men, immigrants and Deltans both, and twenty women for lightweight jobs. Me and Hangman'll work out the split. Two hundred's enough t' take the Old Palace, easy. The day the Divinarch pops off, they'll all down tools and gather in the streets surroundin' the Palace. It'll be up to you from there."

"Their weapons?" Erene croaked.

"Knives, bows, rapiers."

"Slingshots, cuirasses, blowpipes," the Hangman added.

She folded her hands on the table, nodding, and for a moment she feared she would not be able to stop, that her head would keep dipping and dipping lower, like a mechanical thing. "What do you think, Belstem?"

Belstem had hitched his chair around so he could watch the stage. He laughed richly, clapping his fat hands, as a puppy was coaxed out on stage and sniffed worriedly at its mother's hindquarters. "Make them fuck!" he roared, and hurled a gold crown onto the stage.

"Yes, milady," the Hangman said. "I think you do need us."

This time Erene knew she could hear laughter in his high-pitched voice. She nodded dully, acknowledging his point. His eyes gleamed inside the black hood like smears of poison. She thought of the smashed ghost back in Tellury Crescent, hoping to work up enough energy with self-hatred that she could push herself on for the next few minutes; but the thought of her failure inspired neither exigency nor guilt. The ice was dripping.

In the old days, the flamen councillors of the Ellipse had inhabited five magnificent, plain stone mansions in

Suvret Cat Square. The mansions had been on a kind of permanent loan to them from the people of Delta City. Free men and women who would have scorned the name of "servant" had come from the rest of the city to keep them clean and well fed. The entire district had been so quiet you could hear leman choirs singing.

Those were the days before the market was installed in the square, before coffeehouses and classy brothels sprang up on every corner of the palace district, before Godsbrother Puritanism, the last of the old guard, withdrew from the square and the atheists went wild, planting gardens and carving the mansions into gargoyles and lacework.

But Pietimazar Seaade topped all the rest. He had torn down a thousand-year-old mansion, leaving only the stone skeleton, and filled in the gaps with windows to build his folly. He employed teams of servants whose sole duty was to keep candles burning into every room. The mansion would have lit the whole square at night, if it had not crouched like a paranoid beetle trying to see out of the top of its head in the middle of his topiary garden. The stark shapes of the trees meant nothing to anybody except Pieti and his little adopted daughter; the pair of them spent a good deal of their time among the statues and hedges, ignoring the trimmers and waterers who kept the garden as green, in its austere way, as Goquisite's tropical paradise, even in the height of summer.

But inside, it looked much like any other house. And the same denizens of Antiprophet Square attended Pietimazar's salons as anyone else's. Wine flowed freely. So did money. Pieti approved of gambling, though Goquisite and several other ladies had chosen to frown on it as dissolute. The room was smoky, dimmer than outside; nevertheless everyone was dressed to the nines, and Erene was no exception. Covertly, she checked the other ladies' garb.

"Errie, *relax*," Goquisite said. "You don't seem able to sit still this evening. What is wrong with you?"

Erene leaned her head against a pillar. "It has been a

long day." Desolately, she hoped Goquisite would be content with that platitude.

"Your ghost is finished, isn't it? That sweet little orphan? When can we see it?"

The horror was that she did accept that platitude. "Soon."

Goquisite pursed her lips and laid a hand on Erene's skirt. "Something is *wrong,* Errie."

Erene closed her eyes for a second. "I didn't want to tell you before, for fear you would worry. Earlier this evening I met with Gold Dagger."

Goquisite yelped. "Errie, that man is *dangerous*! Dear Heaven, what were you doing?"

Erene looked tiredly over at the round, worried little face. "Belstem was there, too. We were talking of popular support. The news is favorable: atheism is more popular among the lower classes than ever before. And we were talking of hired knives and cudgels." Goquisite's nose wrinkled. "I know it is distasteful, but we have to consider these things. The Divinarch cannot last much longer. It's six months since he came to Ellipse, and three since any human has seen him. We need to solidify our support."

Goquisite shivered. Her change of subject was so blatant as to be rude if it had not been pertinent. "You're wrong in one thing, dear. Afet Merisand is here. Haven't you spoken to him? He says *he* is in communication with the Divinarch." Her eyes widened. "The Divinarch wants to see you as soon as possible."

A shiver of dread ran through Erene.

Her last audience, which had given her the boldness to make so many of her latter-day promises and alliances and miscomputations, came back to her every day. The Divinarch had assured her in language as plain as any god ever used that she was his golden child. But she had not heard a word to confirm or condemn that since. What did he want with her now? Her mind conjured up a host of dreadful possibilities. At the same time, those possibilities were strangely seductive.

She rose and swung sharply toward the door. Her dress, a puff of sapphire taffeta, frothed around her calves.

"Errie, wait!" Goquisite called.

Erene could not wait. She had to find Humi. Only Humi—who had grown into such a striking girl, tall and long-lashed, sporting a different figure and face every day—could accompany her to this dread audience, could bear her up no matter what happened. Erene needed the lone star by which she navigated this treacherous, uncharted sea.

She saw Falippe Greenbranch perching at one of the gambling tables, laughing, flirting, tossing the dice high in the air. Most men liked nothing better than to win at meaningless sports; the order was simpering losses, then wine, then promises of an even greater surrender. Humi was an expert. Her face was haggard, her fur staring, but no one else seemed to notice. Yet no amount of careful makeup could disguise her exhaustion from someone who, in her deepest heart, still thought of herself as a mother.

Erene caught her eye. Then she excused herself to Pieti and his tiny, ridiculously dressed daughter, and swept out into the night. She stepped between the topiary hedges and waited just out of the light from the arched windows. Five minutes later, Humi emerged, an expectant smile on her face, skirt gathered in one hand as she peered around, still in character. "Psst," Erene whispered.

Humi dropped her skirts and fled to her, hugging her. "Oh, Erene! Where were you this afternoon? The ghost is broken. I was longing to come to you all evening. But Falippe wouldn't look twice at an overdressed, middle-aged ghostier when there are *men* in sight!" She scrubbed her face with her hands, and a cloud of gold facedust puffed out, twinkling in the gleam from the bay windows. She sneezed, and it was as if she slipped out from under a Falippe-shaped piece of stained glass. Her face was bleak, her bosom flat, shoulders slumped.

"Falippe can't be an easy persona to wear," Erene said sympathetically.

Humi shuddered. "This morning—never mind, you'll

hear about it soon enough. Gods' blood, I hate her!"
Weakly she began to laugh. "I'm going to spread the rumor that she got pregnant and found it necessary to go
home incognito. You mustn't ever tell anyone that she
was me. Anyone. Ever. All right?"

"I'm so flattered that you are doing this for me," Erene
said softly.

Humi clicked her tongue as if to say, *Nonsense. Of
course I do it for you.* Erene cast a glance around the
clearing. Typically, Pieti hadn't seen fit to spoil the
minimalism of his topiary with benches, so Erene knelt
on the lush, short grass and pulled Humi down next to
her. "There, child. It's all right. I love you. I love you—"

"Gods, Erene!" Humi pulled away. "Where do you
think we are?"

Erene took a deep breath, consciously avoiding disa-
greement. "The Divinarch has summoned me," she said.
"I need you to come with me to the Old Palace, tonight."
She glanced up at the stars. "Now, in fact."

"Oh, gods." Humi blinked, and seemed to rock on her
knees, catching Erene's shoulder for balance. "I'm sorry.
I have—I have other obligations—"

"What do you mean?" Erene strove to keep her tone
reasonable. "Your only obligation is to me. You just admitted it."

"I know. But this is something different. If I don't keep
this commitment, I will be in danger of my life, I think."

Humi wiped her sleeve across her face. It came away
yellow across the shirring, cleaning her cheeks but leaving her eye sockets golden. "I would if I could, Erene!"

"Then tell me the truth! Don't speak in ciphers." Erene
grimaced. "You look like a raccoon."

Humi glanced upward, as if in an anguished plea to the
gods. "I can't! I'm sorry!" She stood up. "I have to go—I
have to meet them at the Crescent—"

"Then go." The words choked Erene like mouthfuls of
flour. "Go."

"Gods! Don't do this, Erene—"

"Go!" Erene rose to her feet, pointing. "Not another
word! Go! And don't think to foist yourself on me again,

with your half-truths and your—your fair-weather loyalty!"

Humi gave a wordless, disbelieving wail and darted away through the topiary, her skirts flapping palely after her like banners. A crow *craaked* as she startled it. Erene stood still, breathing hard. Love and honesty. The two things went hand in hand. Her eyes burned. Giving in to the storm of desolation within her, she turned her head and spat viciously on the spot where Humi had stood.

Then as fast as it had blown up, the storm died. She sagged, face in her hands, melting, melting.

"All this space discomforts me," the Divinarch said. "Now that I am shrunken, I like smaller rooms. Follow me, milady. I expect you will want to be sitting down anyhow, when you hear what I have to tell you." He laughed. Sliding painfully down from the Throne, he padded toward the back of the great hall. Erene followed him. Silently, like a procession of outlandish ducklings, all the Divine Guards who had been standing on the Throne jumped down and came after her.

The Divinarch reached up to twist a near-invisible wooden doorknob in the wall and waved Erene in. "What ghouls you are. Go away," he said to the Guards and shut the door in their faces. Smiling broadly, he gestured around. "Do have a seat!"

Erene obeyed. A merry fire burned in the hearth. Two armchairs stood on a little rug, the skin of some dappled beast she had never seen. A one-legged table, on which a game of Conversion was arrayed, was made of the nacreous shell of some water-going creature balanced on a white tusk as thick as her thigh. Precious jewels formed the Conversion pieces: rubies for one player, peridots for the other. The room felt as if it might mean home and hospitality to someone so different from Erene that she could not even imagine the way his mind worked.

The Divinarch produced two cups of a cold greenish beverage. It smoked and bubbled in Erene's throat, and the minty taste evaporated fast off her tongue. *"Khath,"* he said. "An Uarechi beverage." Erene did not ask where

Uarech was. She looked down at the gameboard and moved a leman piece two squares ahead, the traditional opening move.

He smiled. "Very well. let us play."

Before they had made ten moves Erene was losing badly. She could not bring herself to care about the game, though she knew that in some incomprehensible way, it was probably significant. Her thoughts flew insolently here and there like a flock of butterflies. Tellury Crescent, Goquisite, Humi, wherever she might be. Humi, whom she had lost. Lost. Lost. She watched as her hand moved a flamen and laid what was left of her position in rubble.

"I think these pieces are damaging your morale, milady," the Divinarch said. With a sweep of one skinny arm, he cleared the board. The pieces fell rattling, glinting like little hot coals on the carpet. "This game is very old. I think we must revise its symbolism." He kicked his Divinarch piece straight into the fire. "There! Much better!"

Erene stared at him.

"I saw only the traditional figures," the Divinarch explained. "A set of Incarnations for each player, a pair of flamens, an army of lemans, and the Divinarch piece." His pinkish-gray mustaches leaped spastically as he talked. He reached under his chair and brought up a double handful of new pieces. "Here. What do you think of these."

The peridot Divinarch piece, a tall, regal woman, had Erene's own face. Unmistakable. The other one did too. She turned them both in her fingers, tracing the faceted features.

"And here are Goquisite and Belstem to stand in for the flamens, and a ghostier or two for good measure. Here is your army of sycophants. Here is mine. Let us play."

"Milord Divinarch," she said, "please don't tease me like this. Tell me what you have brought me here for and let me go."

He frowned. "What do you expect of me? Have I failed to amuse you? Oh, very well. So much for symbols, then." He stood up and tipped the table over. Erene stifled a scream of disproportionate panic as the pieces cascaded over her lap, stinging her legs with sharp little crowns and daggers and syringes. They mixed with the first set on the floor so that the hearth seemed thick with shattered glass. The Divinarch stood erect, breathing hard. The fire seemed to crouch down in the hearth like a frightened animal. Shadows bloomed in the corners.

Erene got slowly to her feet. The shadows seemed to leap up behind the Divinarch, lending him stature so that they were of equal height.

"When a battle starts," he said, "all other rules than the One Rule of combat become obsolete. Councillors must become generals. Voting stones must become whetstones. Or both will be crushed under the battle wagon. I have chosen you, Erene Gentle, because you are a ghostier, because you can kill."

Emptily, she thought, *not any more*. There was a time when this charge would have made her heart race. But she had lost Humi. *Not anymore*.

"I am dying. There will be war after I am gone. So I choose you to be my successor, because you will be able to cut it off short. You will be able to control the conflict and bring the Divinarchy safely into human rule like a ship into harbor. Your hand will be firm on the tiller. For I sense that of all the atheists on the Ellipse, you have both the hunger for power and the ability to keep it."

She shook her head. "Thank you, Divinarch, but no."

"What?" The Divinarch's eyes bulged.

"There was a time when I would have rejoiced to be named your successor. Not any more. I'm thirty-eight." She plucked at her dress, showing him where she had laced her falseribs tighter over her hollow stomach, leaving the front panel slack. "I've lost the ability to make ghosts. I've lost my edge." She drew a shuddering breath. "I've lost my *imrchim*. I think that I've lost the ability to feel."

His mustaches stuck straight out, quivering with fury. "You will be Heir! I have chosen you, and you will do as I order!"

She had to laugh at the irony. "Isn't the idea rather that

I would make a good Heir because in the past I have dared to disobey you? The moment you attempt to orchestrate your downfall, Divinarch, you are defeating your own purpose." She no longer cared how she talked to him.

"I will be known as the Divinarch who ended the rule of the gods!" His voice boomed like a cracked bell. She winced but did not bother to cover her ears. "You will *not* disrupt my plan like this!"

"But Divinarch, I'm not even a good choice. The ghostiers don't trust me any longer. The atheists resent me for doing too much of their work for them. The flamens have not respected me since I moved out of Tellury Crescent. If I tried to assert myself as Heir, my support would crumble like a sand castle."

His grin was mad. "But you have no choice, milady. I have had my sycophants spread the rumors. By the time you return to Antiprophet Square, all the atheists in Delta City will have heard the news. Lady Ankh will already have started to arrange the celebration."

Whirling, dizzying blackness. Erene grabbed the chair for balance. She clung to the light of the fire, that feeble flickering which was the eye of the howling darkness that threatened to engulf her.

Now she knew the truth. This room with its weightless burden floated, like the whole of Delta City, on a spider thread above the howling abyss. It dinned in her ears, tore at her mind. She was sinking through the floor.

Darkness . . .

What else was left for her?

She smiled brilliantly. She must play the game just a little longer. "I can hardly wait. If you would order my sedan, I should be getting back. As you say, Lady Ankh must be impatient to congratulate me."

Twenty-two

Light gleamed on dark swamp water. Reflections of cut-glass lanterns rippled into fragments as the rafts swayed, rising and falling to the thump of dancing feet. There must have been upward of three dozen railinged flatboats, spreading into the channels as if someone had dumped them off the Marshtown jetties like dye. Each raft was a completely different marvel of decoration. Justifiably proud of her accomplishment, Goquisite had invited what seemed like five hundred Deltans and foreigners to the ball. The central rafts held what she called a "buffet" supper; half the assembly thought that eating without sitting down was barbaric, the rest that it was a delightful novelty. At least twenty ghosts watched over the buffet tables, projecting a cold that took the breath away (and kept the hors d'oeuvres nicely chilled).

To the Marshtowners, Shimorningers, and Westpointers who sat in the marshfront taverns, the boats looked like bubbles of light: floating music-boxes where tiny figures circled and glittered to far-off, tinkling tunes. Ostensibly, Goquisite Lady Ankh had thrown this party for the Midsummer festival. Rumor whispered that the nobles were celebrating on a promise of something far greater. But the denizens of the taverns, well versed in cynicism where their lords and ladies were concerned, took neither explanation at face value. "What folly!" the Marshtowners said angrily. "To claim that the Divinarch has willingly relinquished the Throne. Blasphemy!"

"Lucky fuckin' bitch," grumbled the working stiffs in Shimorning, burying their noses in pints of cheap beer.

"Just because she useter be pious, an' changed her mind. Coulda been you 'r me."

"Don't know and don't care, but bet your ass there'll be some loot worth picking up come morning," the fishermen-smugglers in Westpoint sniffed.

To Erene, on the rafts, Delta City looked like a long, low strip of glitter, rising at one end to a dark prow. It might as well have been as far away as her long-lost childhood. She recognized everyone she saw. That was a sign of how far from her roots in Marshtown she had risen. Outlandishly dressed nobles streamed onto the rafts as if Delta City were the boat, and sinking. The other ghostiers were the only people she knew who had not come. And what kind of sign was that? Actually, she felt glad they had not come. Glad. Disguised or not, they would embarrass her. They were anachronisms, country bumpkins, outmoded. Marshtown clung to them like a smell.

Lady Ankh had taken umbrage at Erene's refusal to confirm the rumors of her honor, and had not spoken to her in a sixday. She was holding court on another raft in a childish bid to prove that she was more popular than Erene. She had always been childish: Erene saw that now. Still a leman in many respects, she was devious in her leeching of love and protection from those onto whom her instincts made her latch.

Humi was the one Erene longed for. She hoped the grief wouldn't be too hard on her apprentice. It would not be fair to drag her, too, down into the blackness. *Humi* had not overreached herself; Humi had not committed the unforgivable sin of estranging her *imrchim*. In a real sense, this long night had started when Elicit ended their years of love, that day in the Throne Room, with one word. She missed him so much ...

Not being a ghostier, Erene Gentle was nothing.

Amazing how that nothingness didn't show.

Lady Nearecloud was looking at her inquisitively. She shook herself. "I agree. Absolutely." The lady smiled satisfiedly and began to prattle again. The lanterns lit the raft as bright as day. The new gowns, which sported a ruf-

fle every finger-length from the hips to the floor, glided
and jostled, the women's upper bodies in nipped-in bod-
ices rising like reeds from a tumbled stream. The neck-
lines were so low they revealed the women's armpits.
Erene's shoulders had become better as she grew older,
and her fur was glossy. Well made up, she was one of the
most attractive women here. *Well,* she thought wryly, *the
very least I can do is go out in style.* The men wore
breeches so tight they looked like smooth, furless skin;
their coattails had as many ruffles as their wives' dresses.
All except Bestem's. He wore an ancient green boatman's
coat and a pair of egregiously flowered jodhpurs. "Well,
Erene!" He waddled up to her, massive and imposing.
Lady Nearecloud melted respectfully away. "Where's
Goquisite, then?"

Erene bent just enough to clasp him in a half-embrace.
"She's somewhere over there, I fancy, making the country
nobility feel at home. She has a flair for putting people at
their ease."

"Doesn't she, though!" Belstem hacked impressively
into a lace nothing of a handkerchief, stared at it, wiped
his hand on his jodhpurs. "Bloody useless scrap. It's
Anei's fault. She tells me I have to wear these new ruffles, even on my hankies. I told her, wear 'em yourself!
The girl honestly thought I meant to make her wear a
man's coat. Haw!"

"How old is Aneisneida now?" Erene asked. "She must
be twenty-five or -six—"

"Older than that!" Belstem snorted. "Came to ask you
about this rumor, Erene. Not a grain of truth in it, eh?
We're making fools of ourselves with this party?" His
eyes were piggy. Erene knew he was clever enough to understand that there was a good deal of truth in the rumor
and that he was wondering whether he should take umbrage at Erene for having superseded him in the
Divinarch's esteem.

"Shouldn't Anei be thinking about marriage?" Erene
persisted. "It would be good for her to get out from under
your wing—"

"Couldn't allow *that*!" The worshipers who had gathered around them tittered, but Erene knew Belstem had not meant it as a joke.

"What would you say to Soderingal Nearecloud as a son-in-law? His mother was telling me just this minute that he is in need of a wife's calming influence. And I notice that they seem to enjoy each other's company." She glanced across the raft. As if on strings, the heads of the worshipers turned to see. In a little alcove decorated with a pair of ghosts and floating on an outrigger, a pale-furred woman sat, talking animatedly with a saturine young man. "He is a year or two younger than she, but that should pose no obstacles—"

"Fat fucking chance!" Bestem growled. "Everyone knows he's Gold Dagger's bastard by Halliet!" The worshipers gasped. "If I let her marry *him,* I'd be letting Gold Dagger get his foot in the door of the Ellipse Chamber! The beginning of the end! Swarmed by the commoners! Only us ex-lemans are the *real* nobility!" He turned a complete circle, slowly. "And you lot 'ud better remember it!" Spittle flecked his chin. The lesser nobles were not tittering any longer.

"Belstem," one of them ventured, "shall we go see what Goquisite has provided for supper?"

"No," Erene said sweetly. She flashed a smile, keeping her eyes hard to remind Belstem that he must not reveal his alliance with Gold Dagger. "Bestem, you really must face the fact that the way you use your daughter is intolerable. I like you; that is why I want you to see what you are doing to her. Aneisneida deserves to live." She cocked her head, smiling as he spluttered a rebuttal.

This was a relatively good moment. There would not be many more. She was paddling fiercely to keep herself on top of the whirling, dizzying blackness, but she did not know how much longer she could stay afloat alone.

Dressed as herself, tawny hair gilded just a little to catch the light, Humi glided from raft to raft, dodging burdened servants and musicians, bobbing curtseys to the nobles. They looked straight through her. Not one of them recognised her, and she was profoundly grateful for it. A buzzing nexus of conversation on the middle raft told her where Goquisite was. But where was Erene? This evening was nothing but a tangle of unanswered questions. *I've been lax,* Humi thought desperately. *Too lax. The ghost was broken. I should have made her tell me what happened. I shouldn't have let it slide. Where* is *she?*

Since their argument in Pietimazar's garden, they had not spoken. Every time Humi had called at the Ankh mansion, Erene had been out (though Humi saw her personal sedan by the gate). Eventually Humi had stopped trying. And every night, of course, she had been busy. It seemed that she had been living two lives forever. One at night in the Divine Guards' quarters, learning the ways of the *auchresh,* mastering their speech and gradually understanding what they wanted from her; one during the day, her usual calendar of obligations. She could not have said when she had last got more than two straight hours of sleep. But tonight the unpredictable seesaw of fatigue lifted her high on caffeine and wine and worry.

She wasn't so sure about helping Pati to oppose the conspiracy. But she had no choice. And anyhow, Pati had not asked her actually to do anything for him yet. He had just grown friendlier. His ironic wit stimulated her like wine. By comparison, Hope's standoffishness had blossomed into a warmth that seemed to surprise her as much as it surprised Humi. And there were Glass, Moon, Val, Sepia, Silver, and the other Divine Guards she'd come to know. The affinity she felt with them all astonished her.

Not Arity. Once, when Hope *teth'd* into the Divine Guards' quarters with Humi, he had been there, talking earnestly with Pati, tracing an absent pattern on his leg as he listened to what the Striver had to say. He had looked up, and his eyes had met Humi's through acres of smoke and steam. And she had said something that was lost forever under the din of the Divine Guards' speech. And his face closed and he *teth'd.* His friendship had been a constant presence in her life ever since she made her first ghost. The way she missed him frightened her.

Even worse was the yearning that ran through her whenever she caught sight of him here and there on her

search through the rafts. Leaping up and down on an outrigger to see if he could puncture it with his heel talons;
cavorting with Broken Bird or Pati while a crowd of humans goggled; gobbling hors d'oeuvres under the silent
censure of the buffet ghosts; kissing Bronze Water on top
of one of the flower-arched bridges.

Humi found Erene on the second raft of the northwest
chain, engaged in conversation with Belstem, surrounded
by a circle of sycophants.

She sidled closer. Horror washed through her.

Erene seemed lively, striking, clearly the soul of the
party, and she was charming her admirers no end. But it
was not Erene. To Humi, it was painfully clear that the
senior ghostier had locked her body on automatic pilot
while she went away. Gods knew where.

It kept popping into Humi's mind that the senior ghostier was in the grip of a waking nightmare.

*She is sitting cross-legged, hands over her ears, trying
to figure out how to keep on going when she comes back.
If she comes back.*

*Can that rumor be true? But then why isn't she rejoic-
ing with everyone else?*

Unconsciously, Humi had been twisting the red velvet
of her skirt in her hands. A sizzling rip brought her back
to the present.

*Of course the Divinarch hasn't chosen her for Heir.
Pati or Hope would have told me.*

Would they? How much do they really trust me?

Water lapped on either side of her where she stood in
the corner, as if it were trying to pinch her off from the
crowd of nobles, to set her afloat on her own little raft.
She rose on tiptoe and stared straight at Erene. And met
her eyes. Even at this distance, Erene's eyes were whirling, dizzying vortexes. Everything Humi had ever shared
with her—the laughter and kisses, the ghosts, the bitter
cocoa and honeysuckle perfume, the dresses, the anger,
the lessons in ghosting and in life—reeled faster than
light across her mind.

Humi choked as if she were drowning. Erene smiled,
sadly, and turned her head a little. While she held Humi's

eyes, her voice had not stopped bouncing like a bright ball over the music from the next raft. A splinter stabbed into Humi's hand as she fell against the railing. The black water underneath and the night above her seemed to crush her, as if she were a beetle pinned between two sheets of iron.

She pushed forward between the onlookers, gibbering.

"Who is this strange little person?" Erene asked the group, smiling. "Does anyone know?"

"Just an intruder, milady. I'll get rid of her." A minor lord grabbed Humi and tossed her backward.

She slumped against the flower-hung bridge, sobbing, dry-eyed. Arity stretched over from his perch on the rail and touched her with a talon.

"Are you all right, milady?"

The unwritten code which governed the gods' behavior around humans said that Arity had to *teth* ˮ here and there without warning, perch on the railings chatting snidely with the Incarnations and off-duty Divine Guards, flatten the atheists with sudden displays of wit. Wherever he went he must evoke adulation.

The other complied with the rules more or less freely. But Humi thought that had Arity had his choice, he would have liked nothing better than to tug on a ruffled frock coat and tight breeches and blend urbanely with the human crowd.

Now for the first time in the evening she found him alone.

"Where have you *been*?" she blurted, looking up at him. "You haven't come to see me in sixdays!" How quickly it all welled to the surface. Tears prickled her nose. "You never cared for me! I mean less to you than a rat in a cage might—"

"*Oh.*" He clamped his arms over his stomach, rocking as if he were hurt, hazel eyes blind. "What did you think I meant when I asked you to come to the Divine Guards' quarters? Why didn't you *come*?"

"I had to be with Erene! Couldn't you tell that?"

"Did you know the risk I ran telling you what we are?

Do you know what the others thought when you didn't show up that night? *Traitor*—softhearted throwback—"

"And I *did* come! And you were there. And—" now came the worst grievance of all—"you said, *I have nothing to do with her, She's not my responsibility*—"

"Should I have given them a way to get at me through you?" Arity's voice rose. "And you through me? I was keeping us both safe! Pati suspects already!"

"You're afraid of him."

"*You're* afraid of him."

The world seemed to have shrunk to the little ramshackle bower on the bridge, with the two of them, mortal and god, spilling equally rank, boiling pain out in front of each other.

"You're afraid of us all. Even me. You keep coming because you're afraid of what will happen to you if you don't. You want nothing more than to get out of the whole affair, never to see us again."

Humi took a deep breath. "At first that was true. Gods know I had other things to do with my nights. Like sleep." She paused. "But right now, I would keep going back even if they didn't come to fetch me. Nothing else stimulates me like their talk. I don't feel mortal when I'm around them—I feel unique. Because I'm the only mortal they've ever known, I mean *known*, I am in control of the way they see me. I can be whatever I want. Best of all, I can be Humi. And every night"—she swallowed—"every night, I hope I'll see you there. And every night I feel sick to my stomach when you are not there."

He rocked to and fro, short, violent movements. After a minute he jumped down from the railing. She cringed, but then she saw anger flicker in his eyes, and she straightened her back and stood up, countering his intensity with courage.

"Milady," he said in a caressing voice, "dance with me."

Her heart skipped a beat. "Not—not here."

"What do you mean?" He reached for her hand.

"Not here. Somewhere that people can see us."

For a second his eyes went blue. She had never seen

that before. But it was only a trick of the lantern light. His shoulders twitched as if, had he wings, they would be whirring.

"Come on, then." His fingers dug into her shoulder as he guided her to the largest raft. The other dancers murmured at the sight of the oddly matched couple, but by this time many of the lesser socialites had left, and the palace initiates were accustomed to the sight of gods mingling with mortals, even if not quite like this. The other Incarnations appeared to have left too. Images of black water, the shores of grassy islands, and once a nightsharque fin imprinted themselves on Humi's eyes as he twirled her to a fast waltz. She felt so disoriented . . . it was almost like *teth¨tach ching*. The swamp reeked of mud so ancient and slimy it should never have seen air. In this heat, the water levels were half normal. She fixed her eyes on the blur of other couples spinning past beyond their clasped hands. Their perfumes filled her nose. But Arity's perfume was the strongest. His natural body scent, salt and flowers. She was wearing bitter cocoa and honeysuckle.

"Earlier," she said, "something happened while everyone else was watching Hope and Pati make a spectacle of themselves off the eastern raft."

Arity barked a laugh, and at the startled glances they received, shut his mouth sharply. "They went too far. There are nightsharques everywhere this summer! And it's extremely difficult to *teth¨* out of water! No one dares scold Pati, but I daresay Broken Bird will dress Hope down pretty roundly. You were saying?"

Humi remembered the blackness. She remembered the terrifying feeling of inadequacy that swallowed her when she looked into her master's eyes. She felt the tug of the past.

"Never mind."

With a fanfare, the waltz closed. Panting, the dancers dropped to a halt. A scatter of clapping rose into the night air. "Lords and ladies, in a moment we will play you our final suite of the night," shouted a spokesman for the orchestra.

The couples began breathlessly to chat. Black-clothed servants slipped discreetly between them, relighting the lanterns that had gone out. Humi looked at Arity. He was staring bleakly past her at lord and lady, merchant and merchantees, mortal men and women from every country in the world, with a sprinkling of Divine Guards from the salt who embodied the authority, if not the actuality, of otherworldliness. "Let's get out of here," he said.

Make a ghost. They expected it of her tonight. *Tonight!* The new regime would certainly be well decorated. Ghosts continued to top the list of status symbols among atheists. Didn't they see how ironic it was that as forward-looking, progressive, trend-setting as they styled themselves, they allowed their tastes in such a basic thing as beauty to be dictated by the gods?

Well, Erene wouldn't put it past Goquisite, for one, not even to *know* that it was the first Divinarch, in his infatuation with the only human-created art form, who had raised ghostiers to the Ellipse and turned ghosts into a near-sacred commodity. After all, Goquisite certainly knew the ghostiers' custom of disguising themselves, and she did not care that Erene wasn't disguised.

She couldn't ghost as herself—that was the last, forbidden surrender of the self to which almost no one could stand up. Did they think she could do anything? Did they think normal rules did not apply to her? Well, no matter. She could just catch some little person whose awe of the senior ghostier, twentieth councillor, favorite of the Divinarch, et cetera paralyzed him. She would wrap him in her web of glamour and take him back to Tellury Crescent and kill him and stuff his body under the bed. Then it would be over.

Most of the lesser socialites had left. Too bad. They would have made the best candidates—

"Lady Gentle," the man beside her whispered, "your slip is showing."

She turned on him in anger. Then she stopped. He was a young, smooth-furred Piradean, all silvery fur and eyes that flashed like turned hematites. "You'll do," she said.

"She's drunk," someone whispered.

"You haven't been drinking, have you?" the young man said. "Oh, milady, that would not be wise—"

What right had he to ask her something like that? She hadn't drunk a drop of wine. That was the awful thing. She was stone cold sober and most of the lanterns had gone out and the orchestra was dripping with sweat, playing an endless waltz for the few entwined couples who rocked in each other's arms, and broken glasses and crushed bits of food littered the boards. The lords and ladies stood watching her, silent, the women's hands resting possessively on their partners' elbows, lips pursed.

Deliberately, Erene staggered.

The young Piradean caught her arm. "Ease up, easy," he whispered. "You're as rigid as a ghost. Do you remember when you took an apprentice who was a talking ghost, remember that—what do you remember? Anything?"

"Who are you?" she said. The young man began to lead her away. "Good night, Goquisite!" she shouted.

"Good night," Goquisite trilled. And Erene heard her saying to a nearby lord, in a low, worried voice, "Once she gets him home she will take control, never fear. She's just putting on an act. It is—it is like being disguised, only with words—"

A sedan waited for them on the jetty. "The Ankh mansion, Gentle wing!" Erene called automatically. She only realized her mistake as the porter swung north instead of south. She ought to have taken her ghost to Tellury Crescent. *Well, what the hell does it matter?* The wheels juddered up and down like a drum roll on the Marshstown cobbles. She gripped the young man's arm to keep from being thrown about. His flesh was ropy, the bones prominent; he wasn't that young after all. She looked up at his face. He turned that spellbinding smile on her, and though she could scarcely see the gleam of his teeth, her limbs liquefied.

"Gods," she whispered. "What are you doing here?" Then she wrenched away from him, drove the heel of her hand into her eyes. "No, of course not. I'm sorry. You

weren't even there. None of the *imrchim* were—they have
better taste than to indulge in expensive displays of bad
taste like that—"

"So do you," he said. "Usually. My love."

And he pulled her to him and kissed her deeply, pushing her backward with an arm around her shoulders,
pushing her down on the seat. First she struggled. But she
knew his kiss. She knew the angles of this body. She
reached up and pushed off the curly dark wig, and ran her
hand over short hard fuzz. She knew him: they had once
been a soul in two bodies, a creative impulse split in half,
the twin-chambered heart of the new cadre of ghostiers.

"Porter!" She started out of his arms and poked her
head between the curtains, into the rush of starlight.
"Change of orders! Take us to Tellury Crescent!"

"Don't be a little fool!" Elicit said. He stuck his head
out. "Porter! Ignore that! The Ankh mansion!" Then he
sank down beside Erene again, pulling her over onto his
lap, clutching her close, kissing her every other word.
"It's important to spend our last night there. To change
the way you will remember it in your mind. For your
sake. And besides, the last thing we want is for the ghostiers to come back and find us."

"Come back from where?"

"We all had bad enough taste to attend that expensive
debacle." His voice laughed for a moment; it turned bitter
again. "Except for Eterneli and Algia."

"You went in disguise."

"Those of us who went, yes."

She hadn't recognized them. She had not so much as
known them. The blackness roared up under the sedan,
and juddering became floating, dangerously smooth—

Frenziedly, she curled in Elicit's lap, pulling his arms
around her. "Tear this dress off me, 'Lici," she muttered.
"Rub my facedust off. Rip the earclasps off. Pull the
necklace off my throat. Strangle me with it. Change me,
erase me, take me, lose me, change me—"

"Gods!" He bent over her, closing her between his
knees and chest, holding her so tight she could scarcely
breathe. "What have they done to you!" His mouth

locked on hers, and he bore down as if he would press hard enough that they blended into one being.

In her bedroom in Antiprophet Square on the great silk-sheeted bed, under the starlight billowing in the canvas, they did much more than kiss. After her second climax, Erene lost count. The dark tantalized her with glimpses of sweat-sheened fur, gleaming teeth, a long thigh. Never had there been a more skilled lover than Elicit. Never had there been any lover but Elicit. Hem was a dim memory. She could not even remember the names of the others she had had while she lived in Antiprophet Square, the one-night comforters. Elicit was as considerate as an aged man and as rawly passionate as a boy. How long had it been since she was satisfied?

The room smelled edible. She wanted to lick the air to taste the faint scent of bitter cocoa and honeysuckle. For the first time in years, she remembered why she loved that scent. Pirady in late spring, Grussels city, her father's garden paved with reddish flower beds; a vine climbing up a brick wall; young Erene lying with her hands behind her head staring up at a blue blue sky across which flew a cloud of green buds dipping and dancing on the ash tree.

The bed was a rumpled sea of sheets. Elicit stroked her back, warm, satiated. She burrowed her head into his armpit and wept desperately, nails piercing his arms as she clung to him.

Twenty-three

Arity and Humi stood alone on the roof of Broken Bird's teetering tower of an eyrie. From Hope's townhouse a couple of streets away came loud *auchresh* voices and the thump of a *beleth* drum. The Divine Guards were holding their own post-celebration ball.

"I ought to be with the Old One." Arity leaned stiff-armed on the balustrade. Far below, the Chrume rolled past with an immense, slow rumbling. "He's bedridden most of the time now, so he likes me to report to him every night, telling him about political developments. He told me to come to him after this ball."

"Ari." Humi leaned beside him. "Is there any truth in the rumor that he has chosen Erene as his successor?"

Arity was silent for a minute. Then he said, "I don't know. He met with her about four sixdays ago. I don't know what he told her."

"Would you care if it were true? Pati cares. Of course, he would fight to put you on the Throne no matter what the Divinarch wanted, but if Erene was the legal successor, she could carry a good many of his supporters."

"To tell the truth, Humi, I don't really care," Arity said. He smiled tiredly at her. "Listen how politics pervades our conversation. Was there a time when you thought intrigues would never usurp your heart? When you thought friendship was the only thing worth having? And listen to us now."

"You never think of the Throne, do you?" she said. "After all, you're only the one destined to sit on it."

A muscle twitched in Arity's jaw as he stared down at the Chrume. Humi began to regret what she had said. But speaking again seemed impossibly risky. Finally she leaned against his side.

It seemed that he started. Then, slowly, he put his arm round her. He'd done so a thousand times before, yet this time she was acutely aware of it. The stars shone brilliantly. Right overhead, Skyheart burned a hole in the heavens.

"People were staring at us tonight." He released her. A current of misery swept through her.

"They're not staring now." She picked up his arm and placed it around her waist again. Though she could hardly feel his fingers through the perpetual ache of her falseribs, she knew they had tightened over her stomach.

"Yes. No one can see us now, can they?" He slowly turned her around till they were face to face. In the hollow of his neck, a huddle of claw-tips shone, about to break through the skin. The starlight permitted only the faintest tinge of green in his face. Brown-mauve curls lay limp on his forehead.

Humi remembered. "But they saw us leave together. You know what they will think. Could there be a juicier—"

"By the Power!" Roughly, he pulled her forward into his arms. "Do we *care*? Do we care if the whole world knows?"

She laid her head on his breast. "That . . ."

He stopped speaking as sharply as if he had been stabbed. His breath against her cheek came fast and shallow; she had an idea that he was clutching her rigidly. Damn this dress! She didn't dare lift her face from his shirt. The silk was so thin she could have bruised her cheek on his collarbone, singed it on the heat of his skin.

"Arity, I can't stand this," she whispered.

"What?"

"That I love you."

Moments passed. He shuddered, a long sigh that dizzied her with its fragrance. "How long have you known that?"

"About three hours." She ventured to kiss his neck. Salt sweat sprang out in a nervous reaction wherever her lips touched. Pungent, not rancid. Hot and sweet. Could salt be sweet? "Since I realized why I had been missing you so much. Why my whole body tingled every time I thought of you."

"You humans are less continent than we," he whispered, half jesting, half admiring. "I think now that I have known—for sure—for months. Ever since Pati threw it in my face as an insult. After you came, that first time, he and I had an argument."

"What had that to do with me?"

"We were arguing about you. My relationship with you."

Oh. Humi shivered. "And he said?"

"He insulted me. He accused me of treason to the *auchresh* as a race and *lesh kervayim* in particular. But his evidence wouldn't have been terrible at all if he had put it in other terms. The only reason it hit me so hard was that . . . well, that it was true." Wonderingly, his lips brushed her hair. Then she felt fingernails in the tender flesh under her jaw, lifting her face. Just before their lips met, he shot a wry glance at her.

She burst into giggles, very quickly losing her breath. "Don't *look* at me like that!"

He loosed one arm to run fingers through her hair, lips curving. "Forgive me. It just came to me that I had never looked at you before. No, I don't mean that! I mean that I'd never seen how beautiful you are. Undisguised. Aroused."

"There's never been anyone else. No one but you."

"Not for me, either. Not since Pati, in Wind Gully Heaven." He corrected himself. "*Never.* Never has there been anyone like you."

She wrapped her arms around his neck and kissed him. He responded with skill that was somewhat shocking. She'd burn. No, she'd melt like frost brought into a hot room.

She couldn't stand such ecstasy longer than a second or two at a time. All other worries were forgotten. Time slowed as they stood on the balcony of the spiral-staired steeple high over the Chrume, joined at the mouth by these darting, gulping little kisses. She could not tell which of their hearts was beating harder. Her legs were the last parts of her to melt; as they crumpled, she caught herself on Arity with a gasp. The wicker floor creaked. "Are we allowed to do this?" she whispered. "*Auchresh* and mortal?"

"Is it possible? Is it allowed?" Arity mimicked, kindly. "That's what I have been wondering for two of the most hellish months of my life. We *are* doing it. What better proof?"

"But we haven't given it the ultimate test." Humi attempted to leer. Arity burst out laughing so loudly she had to cover her ears. When he managed to stop, he suggested a shockingly lewd remedy for that situation.

Then he paused.

It came to Humi that he was waiting for her consent.

She kissed him again. Fire and ice bubbled in her veins. "God or not, *auchresh* or not, there is nothing I would like better than to—"

Teth¨.

She *felt* the expanse of night around them contract, the wicker catwalk become a lumpy, glassy floor, the sky shrink to an irregular oblong.

"I used to come here when I was a new Foundling," Arity said, "when I wanted to get away from the overwhelming weight that was civilization. Later, Pati and I used it as a trysting place." His voice echoed spookily, as if the room was very high. "I'm sorry. I didn't mean it that way."

She clung to his arm. "Where are we?"

"In the salt. Your eyes will adjust in a moment." But of course he could see in the dark. With sure steps, he led her to a thing like a large, feather-soft carpet. "It's still here. Good. We are completely safe."

"I hate the thought of you and Pati making love," she murmured. Chills ravished her body as he unhooked her dress and slid it down her arms.

"Because we are both male? *Auchresh* don't have much choice about that, you know."

"No, no, no—it's because—well." She did not know

whether to admit that although the Striver was exciting to be with, she strongly disliked him. She was still not sure whether he and Arity were friends. "Was your relationship anything like his and Hope's?"

"Yes." The first falserib, then one by one the others, gave way under Arity's fingers. Humi breathed deeply. "He treated me like a plaything. I see that now. I was in love with him. But he wasn't with me. Or maybe he found it very easy to fall out of love. When he had to go to Delta City and leave me behind, he took *ghauthiji* after *ghauthiji*, and when Hope came along he swooped her up with no qualms at all over me. He'd always wanted a woman lover—for the prestige which would come to him in the Heavens with being her *irissi*, as much as anything else."

She sighed. "Oh, that feels better . . . Ari, I was used to the idea of men lying with men before I ever came among *lesh kervayim*. My mother, you know, was a lover-of-women—a *kiru iu*. And I think Erene is too—or would like to be. Or she is attracted to both." She shivered as he began the row of infinitesimal pearl buttons down her underdress.

He knelt before her, fingers flashing down the curve of her belly. She could see his face now, frowning in concentration, but not at the buttons. "My Humi," he said in *auchraug*. "She has pushed you so far. Placed such a strain on your loyalty."

She shut her eyes and said in the same language, "I will follow her to the death."

"But there is a conflict of interests. And I'm sure you've seen where it lies." Arity lifted each foot in turn to peel away its stocking, laying them neatly aside. "There is your link with *lesh kervayim*. And if you link yourself with me, it can do nothing but cement that. How can you forward the conspiracy against the Divinarch— against *us*—at the same time as you support us?"

The stark phrases brought the impossibility of it home to her like a knife grating on bone. For the past month she had been pursuing just those interests that Arity described

as conflicting. But she had felt as if she were going to
melt with fatigue.

"Dear heart," he said quickly, reaching up to caress her
cheek. "It's just that if you are involved with me, everything will have more ramifications." He hugged her, tenderly prying her fingers away, drying her trickling eyes.
"I was giving you a last chance to say no."

"While you undress me!" Her head jerked up; she
stared at him in amazement. "From any other *auchresh*,
that would be a cruel joke. But you really meant it." She
searched his face. "You really are concerned that I choose
you of my own free will." *Because what you fear above
all is acting toward me as you think a god would.*

The way he avoided her gaze told her she was right.

A red-hot surge of love suffused her.

"Oh, Arity, I choose you with all my heart," and she
pulled him unresisting to her, curly brown head bowed,
and unbuttoned his shirt. Outside, a salt bird called, its
cry diminishing as it darted over the top of the chimney
to the next night flower.

He smelt of flowers. His nipples were hard as stones.
Humi gasped, then bent her head to them, licking first
one, then the other, darting her tongue over the aureolae.
He shuddered with desire, arching his back, rigid in her
grasp. Then he opened his eyes—such enormous eyes—
and smiled stiffly.

She saw her own body gleam in the starlight, the best
light by which to make love. The pelt of heavier fur at her
groin was wet. She felt it slippery as though she were dripping down there. Arity was trembling, no longer really seeing her, she thought, as he covered her face with kisses.
She could not breathe. His member was a hot hard lump.
She was on her back, he pinning her to the carpet, kissing
her so greedily she couldn't tell when one kiss stopped and
the next began. The air felt like a cold wind on her sex.
She craved him. "I want you. Oh, god, I want you."

He satisfied her craving.

It is unnatural for *auchresh* to sleep at night. Humi
woke before dawn to feel Arity slipping her stockings

onto her feet. In the rosy gray light, she could see that
they had slept in a large cavern at the bottom of a chimney with a narrow, high-up mouth. The air was mild, not
chilly but pleasant. Woody salt debris lay in the corners
as if swept there by rain; a warren of saltmice had set up
housekeeping in the far edge of the feather carpet from
where she and Arity had slept. Tiny transparent-furred
squeakers, they watched her from a distance, peeping.
"Where are we, anyway?" she asked, yawning, just before Arity caught her in his arms and *teth··d* them up onto
the rim of the chimney.

He kissed her neck, turning her so she could see the
whole vista. "Deep in *Kithrilindu.*"

"Royalland?"

"Not really. No human has ever set foot here."

Humi freed herself and walked a small circle, skirt
swishing around bare feet. "Now one has."

The chimney was set like a socket into a brushy, rock-
strewn hillside, its dark mouth insignificant in the grand
sweep of the slope. Far behind them reared a ridge on
which jagged formations branched against a still-dark sky.
The formations grew smoother and more rounded as they
sank toward a flat, glassy plain, the floor of a sea so large
that it spread over the horizon.

The spectacle was the no-color, all-colors of salt, its
opacity ranging from dirt-dark formations to the transparent, glacially quiet plain. Humi could imagine the dazzle
that would blaze from that vast mirror when the sun rose.

"The Sea of Storms." Respect hushed Arity's voice.
"*Writh aes Haraules.* Yes, it looks innocent; you've come
upon it at one of its good times. Do you see how nothing
is moving down there—not even an insect? Now look all
around you." She obeyed—and smiled in delight. Everywhere flickers of movement caught her eye: the saltplants
rustling, the myriad little salt animals that dwelt in the
brush going to ground to wait out the day. Only insects
braved the sun in the salt. The acid scent of growing
things fragranced the breeze. "In the Sea, blizzards can
boil up in ten minutes. When they come up this coast, the
Sea looks like an endless, seething cauldron. And the

storms froth up the Wind Gully like uphill flash floods, white with particles scoured off the Sea, carrying whatever has got in their way. We used to fish for treasure-trove out of the windows."

Humi breathed: "From where?"

"Heaven. I lived here for twenty years." He pointed around the bowl at what she'd thought was a grove of formations, branching and corkscrewing up for fifty armspans, and as she looked, they became Heaven: a fairy-tale castle with spires, crenellations, towers, and a keep the size of a small hill. The turrets were aquamarine-blue, just barely distinguishable from the hillside round about. Now that she knew what to listen for, she could hear *auchresh* voices like bells and trumpets, the words incomprehensible with distance.

She turned impulsively to Arity. "*Teth*˙ us there!"

"Not so fast! Just having been around *lesh kervayim* doesn't mean you understand *auchresh* who have never seen a mortal."

"Tell me the difference, then."

"There is one important thing you should know. At some point in history, we *auchresh* developed a status system." He took her hands. "It has been getting stricter all through the centuries, even as our knowing how mortals lived changed other things in our society. The system is not inflexible, like the castes of pre-Divinarchy Calvary. Rather, one's status changes as one enters into and leaves relationships. You and I used to be *elpechim*. Good friends who are not lovers. Now we're *irissim*." He squeezed her. It was delicious to feel the bone of his hip and the hard curve of his thigh so close, under the fabric, and to remember how the green skin had looked naked.

"What's *irissim*?"

"Two who are bound together as closely as possible. Lovers. Friends. I cannot say it in mortal. It is too deep."

She shivered, resting her head on his shoulder. "Zin told me that the gods have a hundred words for 'friend.' Like *imrchim*. Are all of those status words, then?"

"Yes. But everything in *auchraug* is a status word in one way or another. And the 'friendship' words don't always convey significant amounts of status, and it's not all changeable—in a Heaven like Wind Gully, there is free flow depending on who is in the good books of whom, who is looking after a Foundling, who has become a *mainraui,* and so on. Certain things never change. For example, women automatically have high status. But in a larger Heaven, there will be a limit to the status any particular *auchresh* can gain, depending on who took him in when he was a Foundling. However, if any group of *auchresh,* be they *kervayim, irissim, saduim,* plain *ruthyalim,* or something else, take in enough Foundlings, they move up a little."

"Whew."

"But you don't need to worry about most of that in Wind Gully. Just assume that being a woman, you can say whatever you want to most people. I'll warn you if there's an exception. Oh, yes, just make sure they know you are a woman right away—you are *tith ¨ahu.* Technically, since you are apprentice to the senior ghostier in Delta City, you are *perich ¨hu,* superior to them, but I daren't go that far."

"Ari, you're worried. You don't have to take me if you don't . . ."

Nothingness.

". . . want to . . ."

Wind Gully Heaven leaped and gushed over them like some fantastic, frozen fountain. Carved pinnacles spiked the dawn. Loud, sweet *auchresh* voices, speaking pure *auchraug,* spiraled from window to high-arched window.

Humi gulped and clung to Arity. They waited, two small figures hidden in the tree-height formations which grew against the walls of the keep, until at last they were seen. One voice after another dropped into stunned silence. Someone called out, "Is it the *mainrauim*? Is someone hurt?"

"It's Charity!" *Auchresh* streamed out of a dozen different doors and windows. A bulky, bald male with green-dappled skin came in front. At the sight of Arity, his face lit up.

"Wrought Leaf!" Arity held out his hands, but the man

ignored them, hugging him close in the testing fashion men have. When he was released, Arity waved vigorously at the growing crowd. "*Ruthyalim!* It's been so long since I've seen you!"

"Wonderful to have you back!" the dappled *auchresh* Wrought Leaf rumbled. "We began to wonder whether you had forgotten that we were still here! But—*ahh*— who is this?"

Arity took Humi by the hand and drew her forward. "My *irissu.*"

Thank you for not being ashamed of me. She gave the *auchresh* her best social smile. They weren't bestial, as she'd half feared they would be, ugly relations kept locked away in the salt for fear they would scare the humans. Yes, a few grotesque mutations bobbed above the crowd—but if she focused her eyes just halfway she could pretend they were all human. They stared and whispered like any saltside hamleters would if an atheist lord were to drive into the courtyard and ask for hospitality. But they wore elaborately tattered and slitted garments that no hamleter would dream of donning, and their only ornaments besides their *wrillim* were their bodies within. Most had rudimentary wings. She had to keep reminding herself that they were all males, *kerim:* several smaller ones whom Humi supposed to be adolescents wriggled between them, blinking at Humi from the safety of their "parents' " arms. Foundlings.

"Greetings," she said in her smoothest *auchraug.* "My name is Humility. It is a human virtue-name." *Volunteer your status*—"I'm *tith¨ahu.* You are Wrought Leaf, *tith¨ahi?*" She stepped forward, trusting instinct when she opened her arms rather than offering a hand. For a second the big *auchresh* looked astonished, but then he stooped to clasp her shoulders in a ritual embrace. When the creaking of her bones reached everyone's ears, he let her go, abashed.

"Excuse me, *tith¨ahu.*"

Thank the gods—ah, the Power. That hurt. Unobtrusively, Humi flexed her shoulders to make sure they weren't broken. Lavender . . . cilantro and dill . . .

"*Tith"ahi,* would I be correct in guessing that you are an herbalist?"

He looked pleased. The thick, twiggy *uurthricim*—living mustaches—that half hid his mouth jostled. "How do you know? Yes, I am pharmacist of Wind Gully Heaven, as well as *o-serbali.* Some say I am a master of the craft. But I daresay Arity has told you all about me, and the others." Several other *auchresh* moved forward between the tree-holes. "The other *o-serbalim.*"

Apologizing for her ignorance, Humi shot Arity a quelling look. She did not even know the word that Wrought Leaf had used.

Serbali? "Leader of the people," Arity approximated in her ear, voice strained. "The *o-serbalim* counsel the *serbali,* or in Wind Gully's case, the *serbalu,* Sweet Mouse-eater, an *iu.*"

"Meet the *o-serbalim, tith"ahu.*" Leaf clapped each man on the back hard enough to knock him down, had he been human. "Blizzard Dancer. Red Rat. Curved Steeple. Writhing Snake. We do not have may virtue names here—"

"*Lesh mainrauim!*" a Foundling caroled suddenly, dashing out of the trees. "They return! With good eatings!"

Writhing Snake, an old, shaggy *auchresh,* smiled shyly at Humi. "Excuse the Foundling's loudness, *irissu ae Arity*—"

These young men *could* have been gods.

Lithe and muscular, wing-mantled each in his own way, they loped through the trees from the scrubby hillside, skin glowing with exertion. Sweat dripped down their necks. Their fangs showed in pearly grins of delight.

If one of *these* appeared to her on a deserted hillside in Westshine—

The stories of god-begotten children might be true.

Six of them, stripped to the waist, carried poles on which they had slung a number of scaly, antlered beasts whose fish-eyes bulged glassily. Others bore sacks of what looked like transparent broccoli. Still others carried hunting paraphernalia. "Magnificent deer!" The *auchresh* pressed deferentially around. "Did you find the winkleaf plants for me?"—"I'll go tell Calm Shore you're back, so he can get ready to butcher the escorets—"

Arity pinched her arm. Here amid these rough-carved people, he looked almost human in face and form. (The *mainrauim* weren't human—they were more. They were the Divine Guard before dissolution, orgies, and vice had gotten to them.) "Wind Gully's only claim to fame is that it has somehow managed to produce two Incarnations," he said sourly. He glanced at the *mainrauim*. The exultation of their return had worn off; now as the Wind Gully Heaveners swarmed about them, they stared curiously at Humi. "And Pati and I only occurred because near here—so near that the *mainrauim* must *teth*" to reach safe hunting grounds—is one of he filthiest predator lairs in Kithrilindu. Wind Gully picks and chooses its Foundlings. They adopt only the most intelligent, unlike some Heavens in more remote places, which take whatever they can find."

Humi laughed. "Ari, I believe you're jealous!"

"Of course I'm jealous! These louts have seen exactly two women in all their misbegotten lives, neither of whom can compare to you!"

"Louts or not, they are marvelous specimens . . ." Humi flirted her eyelashes at the nearest one.

Arity growled wordlessly and seized her by the arms and fastened his mouth over hers.

Her spine melted.

At last he broke away, shaking his hair back, throat jumping. "By the Power, I love you, Humility!"

"Don't call me that." Between the silver-leafed branches of the trees, the sky was rosy. The breeze licked through her fur, warm as running blood, warm as a tongue. It would be another sweltering day. She pressed her head against his chest, trying to breast the swell of adoration. "I love you."

Wrought Leaf cleared his throat deferentially. "Arity, would you and your *irissu* care to take supper with the *mainrauim*? We have but to butcher the escorets, and then it will be ready—"

"The *iu* is pleased to accept your offer," Arity said formally. The edge that had vanished when he spoke to her was back.

In the inner fastnesses of the Heaven, they met Wind Gully's own women: Sweet Mouse-eater and Flowering Crevice, the first the Heaven's imperious old *serbalu,* the other a heavily mutated creature with slab lips and four hands' worth of fingers. She and Wrought Leaf (who, were it not for his piebald skin, could have passed for a blacksmith in any Domesdys village) kissed like lovers. "He has higher status than the rest of the *o-serbalim* right now because he's her *ghauthiji,*" Arity whispered. "But she already has her eye on one of the *mainraui,* Running Fox. Wrought Leaf accepts that he will soon fall from favor. When one has so many years and so few lovers to choose among, one ends up trying them all."

"But the Divine Guard aren't like that!" Humi said as the Wind Gulley Heaveners began to butcher the deer. Their kitchen was a dark salt cavern. Down one wall burbled a freshet. "There is true love among them, Arity! I know how Crooked Moon and Unani feel about each other, and they are just one example—"

"People say that living among humans has corrupted them." Arity gazed at the sprightly Foundling boys, their elbows and bare feet callused horn-hard, who were sweeping the blood from the butchering into the freshet. "I do not know. But I do know that the larger Heavens are structured much like human cities. And *that* is corruption! We can rest assured that a thousand years ago our Heavens weren't like Delta City! Here in Wind Gully, I think our civilization is very much as it must have been when the *auchresh* people first cohered out of scattered groups of outcast predators. It feels as if we've been here for ever. And yet on the level of the individual—as everywhere in the salt—there is a transcience, a weightlessness in the air. Do you feel it?"

"I feel it." She shivered. Over eons, the freshet had worn a spreading stain of diamondine in the wall. She pushed her finger along it, releasing a high-pitched ringing sound. The nearest Foundling took fright and splat-

tered her with water. "Eeeow!" it yelped, and bared its
fangs in terror, mumbling incoherent apologies.

"It's all right, Luc!" Arity sidled toward the boy. "He
can't talk properly yet,—he's very newFound—here, Luc,
Luc . . ."

Trembling, the Foundling let himself be won over.
Arity cuddled him. Humi found the picture fascinating: an
adolescent with a man's voice who needed to be reas-
sured like a toddler. "It's only a human," Arity whispered. "A human girl. See, she has fur. Not like you.
Those things on her feet are shoes . . ." Humi let Luc
stroke her cheek and touch her slippers. Then he tried to
kiss her on the mouth.

Hiding her shock, she repulsed him as gently as she
knew how.

"I'm afraid my Lucidity has a long way to go." The
serbalu Sweet Mouse-eater stood over them, supporting
herself on a twisted transparent-wood walker. She
smelled of blood; it splattered the front of her shirt and
breeches, and the wrinkled breasts exposed through peep-
holes. Her skin and hair were as iridescent as Pati's, her
eyes pink. "It will be another decade before he is civilized, I daresay, and I don't know that I'll see that many
more years . . . Are you two coming to supper, then?"

"It'll take a *decade* to civilize that child?" Humi hissed
as they followed her halting steps out of the cavern.

Arity's voice was sullen. "We are not human. We do
not meet our children until they are too old to be shaped
like children. You have no idea what it is to try to tame
a youth who has been feral for fifteen years or more! You
have no conception of how lucky you are to be able to
have babies!"

Humi blinked and pressed close to him.

In a lace-walled tower where the breeze from the hillside blew across the tables, they ate a hearty breakfast (or
supper) of venison cutlets, fried at table. For dessert there
were vegetables (or fruit) which looked like broccoli but
tasted like mangoes. Humi didn't wonder if she could
stomach salt food until the meal was over, but she felt no
immediate ill effects. And anyway, hadn't they always

harvested berries from the salt near Beaulieu, and hunted there when times got lean? The tablecloths were splattered with grease from the frying, but no one seemed to mind the mess. Easy laughter greeted Luc's breakage of an entire set of glassware. *Easy come, easy go, but we will always be here.*

The *mainrauim* clearly held the highest status within the Heaven. While several older men cleared the tables, the younger hunters sat back and talked with Humi and Arity, drinking hot *gherry* (a thick, dark red, bitter beverage), lifting their feet off the tables only long enough for the men to slide the tablecloths out. They thought it hilarious the way they had to lower their voices so Humi wouldn't go deaf when they spoke. In fact, they knew nothing whatsoever about humanity: they wanted her to enlighten them. As long as they remembered to keep their voices down, she was in her element. They asked intelligent questions about Delta City, often outstripping her ability to describe it in *auchraug,* but Arity refused to translate. *Something is wrong with him,* Humi thought. *He's not just jealous. It's more than that.*

It was clear from the way the *mainrauim* treated him that they envied, idolized, and took pride in him. Could that be why he seemed so ill at ease?

Then without warning, visible through the lacy walls of the dining room, the rim of the sun peeked in a fury of gold and red over the *Writh aes Haraules.* The salt sea exploded with brilliance. Humi broke off in the middle of a sentence and scrambled under the table. *Mainrauim* arms came around her, sheltering her face. She felt herself being lifted and carried along. The *mainrauim* ignored Arity's desperate shouts to put her down.

"She's very tender, isn't she? We may not *like* the sun, but we can *tolerate* it."

"But don't you adore how she's furry, like a mouse?" Yellow Twilight fingered her calf.

"Claws off!" yelled Arity.

They set her down in the cool, torchlit stair that spiraled down the middle of the tower. "Do you need us to carry you any farther?" Running Fox asked hopefully.

"Sorry, we have to be going, *ruthyalim*!" Arity grabbed Humi against him. "We'll just give our farewells to the *serbalu*."

Sweet Mouse-eater's bedchamber would not have seemed out of place in Goquisite's mansion, except that the brocades and tapestries that Humi fingered all had the slithery feel of salt fiber. Since time out of mind, Arity had told her, the *auchresh* had been masters of the handcrafts which made this Heaven so beautiful. Treatments for different consistencies of salt, from the granite-hard stonesalt to the cheesy stuff the Foundlings gathered from its hollows; treatments for the tough, fibrous roots of the formations so that they could be woven; for their substance so they could be worked like metal or wood; treatments to reveal one color over another: the *auchresh* were masters of them all. It was not much harder to eke out a living in the salt than in human country, if one was born to it.

Propped on cushions on her bed, Sweet Mouse-eater caressed Wrought Leaf's and Flowering Crevice's heads. "So you are leaving already?"

"Yes," Arity said flatly.

A fluffy salt cat sharpened claws on the rug. Wrought Leaf followed Humi's gaze. "Milky has gotten used to our society, but he's rare," the *o-serbali* said wistfully. "Every human family has domestic animals, so Arity tells us. We are not blessed like that. Animals have an instinct for—*erhmmm*. Our lineage."

"If we didn't always meet in mansions, where one encounters only the occasional poodle to yip and cringe," Arity said, "you would have noticed their reactions to me too, Humi."

"I should like to see those mansions." Wrought Leaf lay flat on his back, one hand linked with Flowering Crevice's over a splash of dried blood on Sweet Mouse-eater's shirt. It was clear they were going to spend the day together. Humi had a sudden, chilling glimpse of something much deeper than she had seen yet in Wind Gully, much deeper than Arity had implied in his flippant dismissal of relationships here. After all, he had said: There is no mortal word deep enough to describe the concept of *irissim* ... She wondered about the *mainrauim*. Would they go to bed with whoever happened to be nearest? And the other *auchresh* with whom she'd spoken—older, younger, and lesser? What about them?

He's wrong about Wrought Leaf falling from favor, she thought. *It's impossible that life be no more than an endless game of musical beds. There has to be love.*

There has to be love.

What good is any honor if there is nothing to sweeten it? What was my life, before I knew Ari as an irissi?

"But the glories of the human world are not for me. Return some time, *tith˝ahu.*" Wrought Leaf's pupils rolled, indicating that he couldn't see her properly. She stepped closer. "Come when there is a storm. Strangers to the Heaven find the blizzards an amazing sight."

"Arity!" Sweet Mouse-eater's voice was querulous and worried. "Can you *teth˝* all the way back to human country from here?"

"Of course I can! Many thanks for your hospitality, *ruthyalu.* Humi, hold on—"

And her feet hit hard cobbles. She staggered, having great difficulty in reorienting herself. It felt as if all the cares she had left behind were settling back onto her shoulders like a flock of lead pigeons. Mora, the daughter of Frivalley the baker, waved cheerfully at her through the steamy shop window. Then her mouth dropped open as she saw Arity. *What does it matter?* Humi thought, a touch wildly. *Everyone will know soon enough.*

All she cared about was that she loved him, loved him, *loved him* with every nerve and muscle. The sounds of humans and animals waking up came to their ears. She could smell the bread in Frivalley's ovens. She was hardly ever up early enough for that. The sky was strangely dark, with a few bright white clouds scattered overhead. Of course, Wind Gully Heaven lay to the east, farther back along the path of the sun. Just the two of them standing in the Crescent, with nothing between them except a thin, cold wind.

He gripped her hands tightly. "Well, that was my home."

"Arity, what's *wrong*?"

"I'd no idea how they would take you! I was afraid of so many things—I was ready to *teth*¨ you away at any moment. But I didn't have to be." Her hands were tingly-numb where he gripped them. "There is hope for our races after all. Oh, Humi, I love you for the woman, not the mortal, that you are, and that I am free to do so is—"

Tears clogged his voice. Humi hugged him roughly, pulling his head onto her shoulder. He let himself be held, trembling. *If I knew half of what he was afraid of, it'd probably be* me *collapsing all over* him. "I love you." It was all she could say, and it was inadequate.

Lifting his head, he smiled, hazel eyes crinkling. "Sundown, tonight. Your boudoir."

She answered with all her heart, in the affirmative this time. "I'll be there."

He brushed fingers tenderly down her cheek, and vanished. The wind swirled away the white-powder footprints he had left on the cobbles.

The hem of Humi's gown was tattered from catching on the salt formations. Letting it drag on the cobbles, she walked slowly toward the Chalice and went in.

Elicit roused Erene at dawn with a soft, insistent shaking. Servants, maids, friends—gods knew who she had gathered about her in this elegant purgatory. Anyone might come in. "Erene, get dressed. We're leaving."

"What ... ?" She raised herself on one elbow. In the light of a new day, squinting with tiredness, she was even more beautiful than he remembered. Elicit's heart nearly stopped before he could get his wits about him, pull her up, and kiss her. She wriggled away, laughing.

"Did you sleep well?"

Outside, the sky was shell-pink, paling to light blue near the top of the great window. The air had cooled off during the night. Elicit watched her pull open chests and closets, clicking her tongue in quiet disbelief at the feathered fripperies that dripped out. Finally she found a plain beige dress. She tied a headscarf around her hair that deepened her gray fur to charcoal and made her eyes snap. "Where are we going?" she asked.

"Not to Marshtown."

Shutting her eyes for a moment, she nodded.

"To the docks. I know it's not the windy season, but there should be at least one ship leaving for Pirady. We'll go to Grussels and then work our way along the coast. There are rocky bays where no one goes. I grew up in one. We won't need money there."

"My father used to take me along the coast on holidays. I know the area you mean."

Elicit could almost taste the salt spray. "White waves ... gray rocks ... trees thick on the tops of the cliffs, spreading inland ... seagulls in the air like bits of foam. We'll build a house in the woods."

She unlatched the window and stepped out onto a wrought-iron balcony. Elicit followed. They stood looking down on a tropical garden walled in by gray stone buildings. Beyond the roots of these buildings, far away, water glinted: the Chrume. *I've had it with rivers,* Elicit thought. *I've spent too much of my life on the edge of a marsh.*

Erene leaned on the rail. Dew darkened the elbows of her dress. "Perhaps we won't have to be quite alone. Do you think I'm too old to have another child?"

He kissed the side of her face.

"I mean, really, I should like to take Tessen with us, but—"

"*No.*" Elicit said, surprising himself with his own harshness. "For the boy's sake, no! He doesn't deserve to be saddled with us."

"I was about to say that once I would have swooped down on Soulf and carried him off without a second thought. Now I never would, though."

"Sorry," Elicit said. "Forgive me." He had meant to flirt, but even to him it did not sound flirtatious.

The sun was coming up.

"You're forgiven," she said in a voice free of laughter. He took her arm. "Let's go."

The bedroom was larger than he had guessed it would be—he had never been upstairs in the Gentle Wing—and strewn with personal bits and pieces. But as they passed through, Erene didn't touch or pick up a single object. Shushing each other's giggles, they crept downstairs. A breath of cold made the fur on Elicit's arms stand up. He glanced around, and saw the ghost of a naked Calvarese girl standing in a baroque-painted alcove. He shuddered. The morbidity of it shocked him. There were no ghosts in Tellury Crescent, nor had ever been. What kind of ghostier decorated her home this way? What kind of pain had she willingly subjected herself to every time she climbed these stairs, when the cold reminded her what part of her life had died?

He turned to her with the questions on his lips. Then he saw her eyes squeezed shut against tears, and her mouth trembling.

He dug her with an elbow. "Race you to the entrance, Erene. Without waking anyone up!"

The loser by two seconds, she fetched up in his arms against the ornate front door, pliant and merry again. The long, hall with its checkered floor was empty, daylit by arrow-slit windows. A torch or two still guttered in brackets. Outside, the air was cool and moist; leaves brushed their faces as they walked down the drive. The market square was still silent, the stalls shuttered. A pig snuffled under a grocer's cart for rotten pomegranates.

"All right," Elicit said, drawing a deep breath. "The docks."

"Do we want everyone to know? We could walk. Or take a sedan."

For a second Elicit's mind rebelled. *You're mad, man! Your career! Algia and Eterneli! Your ghosts, your Ellipse seat, your imrchim!*

Damn me, he thought. *I've never been saner in my life.*

"We'd better walk," he said. "And take the back streets, not the concourses."

Erene turned to glance back at the mansion in the garden. "I wish I had said good-bye to Goquisite. No, I don't! What am I thinking?" She turned in his arms, scrutinizing each of the five mansions which surrounded the square. Their palatial weight oppressed Elicit. "But there is someone I do have to say good-bye to. You know who I mean."

"You still *have* someone to say good-bye to. I envy you."

"Oh, don't," Erene cuffed him gently. "Were she anyone else, we would be on our way to the docks now. But unlike the others, she will understand if we wake her up just to say good-bye."

The dawn came in through the windows of the seldom-used library in the back of the Chalice. It crept palely around the bookcases and woke Humi. She swam slowly toward wakefulness, aching from having slept with her head on one arm of a leather armchair and her legs draped over the other arm. Her facial fur was stiff with tears. After Arity left her, she had sat down in the one place in Tellury Crescent where she knew no one would hear her, buried her face in her hands, and cried her eyes out. Only after the sobs abated had it occurred to her that she had been crying with happiness.

A hand gripped the forearm where her head rested. Gray-furred fingers flattened the silvery puff sleeve, inches from her face: knotted, familiar fingers. Awareness flooded through her; she sat up, rubbing her eyes. Elicit stood over her, smiling kindly. Erene floated near-weightless on his arm.

"Elicit . . . ?" Her head spun.

"Don't ask any questions, darling," Erene said. "We've come to say good-bye."

"Gods, Erene!" Humi caught Erene's hand and pressed it to her lips. "Last night you looked so—unnatural—I was so afraid something was wrong."

"Something was wrong. And for hours I thought it had finished me."

"If something had happened to you while I was with him, I would have killed myself—"

"Who was he?"

She could hardly keep from smiling as she said his name. "Arity."

"Gods!" Elicit flinched back. "Humi, watch your step!"

She nodded as the smile drained fast from her face.

"My poor apprentice," Erene said. "I'm leaving you the twentieth seat. It's not a gift. You'll have to fight for it, and then fight to keep it. If you're crafty, sly, murderous, and underhanded, you could be the most powerful ghostier of this generation."

"What? You're—"

"I'm also leaving you the conspiracy. I'm leaving you the atheists. and I'm leaving you Gold Dagger and the Hangman—Belstem will tell you what we have with them."

"Erene, you're not *leaving* me—"

"Sssh." Erene embraced her, kissing her on the lips. The senior ghostier's heart pounded wildly against Humi's breast, convincing her that she was not dreaming. When Erene let go, Elicit hugged Humi. He squeezed her twice, quickly, and it felt as if some silent understanding passed between them. In three years, she had never understood him as well as she did now. He loved Erene. Just that. He loved her.

"Look after her for me, 'Lici," she whispered in his ear. "The most important thing in the world is for her to be happy." *Can you really say that?* she asked herself. *Whether you mean it, or not?*

If one woman's happiness isn't the most important thing in the world, what is?

Dizzy from the scent of his fur, she accompanied them to the bay windows.

"We'll have to leave this way," Elicit said. "The Crescent's awake now, and we would rather not be recognized."

"The gate to Reedmill Street should be unlocked," Humi said. "Go between the houses—you know the way. Watch out for the pig droppings."

"Now to the docks?" she heard Erene say as Elicit squeezed after her through a break in the fence that enclosed the Chalice's tiny backyard.

"Yes. Let me hold that up for you—"

Humi shut the bay window and rested her forehand on it, undecided as to whether to laugh or cry. As clearly as she had ever felt anything, she felt the drumming of Erene's heart under her hands, like a freed bird's wings. Her palms throbbed against the cold glass of the window. The sun rose for the second time that morning, flooding the sky with white, striking her eyes full of gold.

Twenty-four

The ghostiers' tales of triumph are not like anyone else's. One apprentice slept in the Ellipse chamber for a sixday in order to be there to claim his seat; another gave her master a grain of arsenic every day for a year; another bribed his master with gold to retire. Ziniquel Sevenash's cleverly evoked cardiac arrest also made legend. But unlike other things Humi was to do that year, her capture of the twentieth seat was simple and unremarkable.

All the following sixday, Goquisite assumed that Erene was holed up in her workshop in Tellury Crescent, ghosting the stunning young Piradean man with whom she had left the ball. Only the ghostiers knew what had really happened. Ghostiers rarely abdicated; murder was far more common. The discovery that Elicit had been so discontented with life in Tellury Crescent that he had chosen Erene over ghosting, over his own apprentices, over political power, unsettled older ghostiers like Rita and Beisa. It threatened their monopoly on each other's love and death; even though both of the escapees were *imrchim*, they had been able to leave the rest of the *imrchim* without qualms.

To reassert their solidarity, the ghostiers had to reach a consensus. After a wracking discussion, they accorded Elicit's seat to Trisizim, Mory's apprentice. He was eighteen now, unusually talented, his only drawback his extreme introversion. But he would simply have to learn politics by doing. Biting his lip, he agreed in a mumble, his black bangs falling over his eyes.

Owen was not fit to take on the responsibilities that came with the twentieth seat, so by a series of deceptions,

Erene's and Elicit's elopement was kept from him. It was kept from Algia, too. No one should have the seat but Humi.

For once she had no doubts of her own worth. The fire of Arity's love burned them out of her. She had never felt so confident of her own ability to keep all of Erene's irons in the fire, and her own, too, floating through the days when Erene was still supposed to be in Delta City with a serenity that made people look twice at her and smile.

She spent her nights with the *auchresh*. She seemed to have stopped needing more than a couple of hours of sleep. Arity both nourished and refreshed her.

He worried for her, too. He was the only Incarnation who knew Erene was gone. They had agreed, with the rest of the ghostiers, that it should be kept from the others, lest they tell the atheists. If Belstem knew that Erene was not dead, he would overturn heaven and earth to get her back. Humi was loath to have it widely supposed that she had killed Erene, but she could see that it was unavoidable.

On one of these waiting days, when the city seemed suspended in amber, Humi got a letter from Elicit. The courier dove flew into her hands as she leaned out the window at dawn. She untied the little parcel from its leg and let the bird go. "This is the last time you will hear from us," she read in tiny script. "We have taken passage on a fast clipper to Grussels. The first day out, we were married by a flamen. We think that Erene is pregnant. Tell Algia to look after Eterneli. Luck go with you, *imrchu*."

The Ellipse session was Dividay night. Humi got to the Chamber before anyone else and lowered herself into Erene's seat. On either side of her, Marasthizinith and Puritanism's leman Auspi looked daggers at her. Everyone else pretended to ignore her presence. She waited, the certainty of success cooling her blood, until Arity had officially opened the council "in lieu of the Divinarch, whose poor health deprives us yet again of his company." Then he nodded briefly at her.

She stood up, gripping the table. The torches flared;

soot drifted over the table of refreshments beside the door. "'I should like to make a proclamation. Serenity Gentle is dead. I, Humility Garden, her apprentice, claim her seat and her status as senior ghostier by virtue of three years' training in her workshop."

There was a dead silence.

She caught Ziniquel's eye. He glowed with pride. *Three years to master,* he mouthed. *Nobody has ever done it.*

And through the soundproofed glass of Owen's alcove, she felt his glare of sheer murder.

Then Tris rose to his feet. "And I, Trisizim Sepal, apprentice of Mory Carmine, claim the seat and the status of Felicitous Paean by virtue of seven years' training in Mory Carmine's workshop." He kept his head up, his bangs tucked behind his ears, staring proudly around the Chamber. "Are there any challengers?"

There were not. Humi had the feeling that Tris's claim had been more of an aftershock; everyone was still reeling from her own pronouncement. Silence filled the chamber.

Her triumph rang like a thousand little bells in her ears.

After the session—an absurdly mundane discussion of the laws which had to be introduced to limit free copying of books, yet another of the trivial things which Erene and Goquisite had dreamed up to fritter away the time of the Divinarch's illness—she stayed alone in the Chamber, resting her head on the table. The wooden surface was smooth and black from generations of fingers. The seat of her chair was smooth and black from generations of behinds.

She reached under the table and fingered the "20" carved on her very own voting stone in its little niche. *In three years, you too can become the most powerful human in the Divinarchy,* she thought wryly. *In three years.*

She caught her breath, struck dumb by the sheer odds against it.

At last she stumbled out of the chamber into the silence of the Old Palace's innards. Down the infinite length of the corridor torches flared, one after another until the bright spots fuzzed into a single yellow glow. Here in the very nexus of the human world, she could not smell the sea, though it was so close. Only soot.

She lay with Arity in the Divine Guards' quarters. The great room was nearly deserted, as it was early morning for the Guards, and most of them had to be elsewhere, watching for civil reactions to Humi's pronouncement. "Did you see Pati's face when you stood up?" Arity asked.

She lay flat on her back, staring at the shadowed ceiling.

"He was delighted. He expects your full support— something that he never had from Erene." Arity's voice was low, troubled. "How are you going to manage? Belstem Summer will expect you to dedicate yourself to him, the way Erene did. And now you are senior ghostier, so you will have to dedicate yourself to the ghostiers or lose them as Erene did. Why did you take the seat, my Humi?"

She made her voice bright. "Come on! Do you think I am mad, to turn it down? Or even worse, to let Owen or Algia get it? I think you think Owen could handle it better than I could. Don't you? Huh?"

"I would rather see him die than you—"

She hissed at him, "I had no choice!" Then, embarrassed by her admission, she wrapped her arms around his neck and pulled him down. They lay naked on the big circular bed platform. She smelled tobacco smoke ingrained in his skin. "But as long as I have you," she whispered, "I can do anything."

"You will always have me. I'm not so sure about the other." He sighed, and stroked her thigh. On the other side of the room, someone was quietly practicing the *ouzal*, the lutelike instrument of Kithrilindu. "No one ever said that it's impossible to sit on a fence, darling. I just wish it weren't you who had to do it. That's all." He lowered his mouth to hers, and they made love in silence, for once unwatched.

The Sky Cock tavern seethed with angry voices. Hope perched in the shadows of the rafters, looking down at the calm ghostiers and furious atheists. She supposed the atheists' violent reaction was justified: after all, Humi had killed Erene, who had been both their leader and their prodigy. Not even Hope had expected such a thing from her. But she supposed it was the ghostiers' way. Certainly, *they* seemed calm enough as they watched the fracas. Quailing before his eminent guests, the innkeeper hadn't dared even to offer them drinks. "Wine, you disrespectful slug!" Belstem snarled. "And plenty of it!"

Goquisite paced the room, dark cloak and hair flying as she swung about. "We cannot allow it. It is unthinkable! She must be displaced!"

Pieti gave her a pitying look. "It is the way of the ghostiers, Goquisite. You resent her merely because she murdered your friend." He leaned back in the straw-stuffed chair, cuddling his little daughter, who (long inured to bickering councillors) stood solid as a little ghost against his leg. "In terms of the conspiracy, is there any real reason we need Erene rather than Humi? Is not the fact that we have the senior ghostier on our side the most important thing?"

"*I* think so," the little girl said. To Hope, she was more interesting than all her quarreling elders. The Maiden watched closely as the ghostier girl Eternelipizaran—whose face was still tear-streaked from Elicit's death—smiled at her. It was obviously a tentative offer of communication, despite the fact that Eternelipizaran was a good five years older, but Pieti's daughter instantly quailed, hiding her head in her "father's" lap. Hope's heart ached for both girls. One stunted by the crush of Elicit Paean's expectations, the other pressed transparent by Councillor Seaade's gold-encrusted upbringing. *But if I had a child,* she thought, *not a Foundling, a real child—it would grow up just as warped as either of these little girls, here among the* wrchrethrim. *Who am I to criticize?* And the old familiar pang shot through her heart. For of course it was impossible.

No, Hope, you can't really have a baby, that was just a story your *breideii* was telling you. The female equipment in your body is fundamentally impaired. That's why the predators cast you out. You wouldn't even be a woman, mentally speaking, if you hadn't learned it from the humans. The *iuim* of the isolated heavens are not "feminine." They don't wear dresses or submit to masculine power. They don't manipulate their men with smiles and words. They don't bear children. But it doesn't matter. Mortals are so puny that reproduction has to be the raison d'être of each of their lives, while *we* can devote our time to philosophy and art and having fun. Why should you waste your life tending brats?

Yet the longing for children was something all *auchresh* (and especially, Hope maintained, females) knew intimately, like an inner emptiness.

The room snapped back into focus in her eyes as Goquisite paused directly beneath her perch to glare at Pieti. "Do you dare to call Erene my *friend*? She was the sister of my heart." Her voice shook. "We would have spent our old age together—"

"Don't be cloying," Pieti barked. "You're putting it on. Erene was acting so strangely in those last days that you're as glad as not she's gone. Because she was embarrassing you. Isn't that right?"

"*Oh!*" Goquisite hid her face in her hands.

"Dear, *I* understand." Maras got up and tried to put a consoling arm around Goquisite's shoulders. No one could accuse Maras of piety these days: she was a dedicated member of the conspiracy, and she revered Goquisite, striving to emulate her poise and urbanity. She dressed to the nines. In gatherings of lesser socialites, Hope had seen her shine—but beside Goquisite, she was revealed to be in horse-faced middle age, her veneer of sophistication crumpled. Goquisite flinched from her embrace. Maras had to settle for an anxious gaze into the councillor's eyes. "We understand your sorrow and sympathize with your anger—"

"You do *not* understand!" Goquisite's voice burned. "You are a pretentious featherhead! But at least you agree that Humility must go! It is ridiculous to suppose that an untried girl can cope with everything Errie did! She has severely overstepped herself—"

"I think she has not." Fra's voice came like cool wind. "It would be wise for you to take into account that after Humi killed Erene, we discussed her among ourselves, and we decided that her abilities qualify her. She has been making ghosts for three years. That is more qualification than any of *us* had when we acceded to Ellipse."

"Don't tell them about the ghosts!" Rita hissed.

"It has to come out sometime." Emni's voice was light and strong. "All those ghosts you believed were Erene's—they were Humi's. Did your fur stand on end to feel their emotions? It was Humi who reached into your soul. Did you clamor to be the next to receive one of her masterpieces? In private, Erene and Humi laughed at you."

The atheists were still, thunderstruck. Hope shifted her knee off a splinter. She had known about the ghosts, of course—but of those below, only Goquisite seemed to have shared the secret.

"In other words," said Fra drily into the silence, "Humi is fully worthy of her position. She has already proved herself to you, even if you did not know it. And there is nothing, miladies and milords, that you can do about it."

Silence.

"Well, maybe," Marasthizinith Crane said timidly. "She might be the start of an infusion of young blood . . . this might not be *all* bad?"

"I back the girl," Belstem said unexpectedly. "You ghostiers are all getting old. It's been far too long since any of you killed each other. Unhealthy, as far as my readings into your history show." Leaning on the mantelpiece, warming his haunches, he spoke into his glass of wine. "Pity Erene and Elicit had to be the first to go. Good councillors. On the other hand, the Calvarese kid seems bright, and as for Humi, she looks like the best choice anyone could have made to replace Erene. If she's been making all those ghosts she's gotta be competent." Unspoken was, *I think we've traded a faltering ally for a fresh one.* "Put that in your pipes and smoke it." He turned back to the fire.

But she's not on your side, Summer, Hope thought. *She's on ours.*

Goquisite stepped with brittle grace to an easy chair and sank down. A smell of mustiness rose; she waved it away. Hope stifled a sneeze. "Well, you have made your position clear, Belstem. That being the case, we should perhaps plan Erene's funeral in such a manner that it can double as Hui's inauguration ball." Her sarcasm was heavy. "That is what the ghostiers would do, is it not?"

"You are well versed in our customs, milady," Ziniquel said. He straddled his chair, long legs sticking out, ignoring her sarcasm. "And if you offered to host the affair, I'm sure Humi would be most obliged."

"I have offered, I believe." Hope leaned dangerously far out of the shadows to see Goquisite's eyes. They were dead as rotten wood. "Does tomorrow night suit?" Goquisite brushed away Maras's objections. "I assure you, I am used to organizing *sociales* on such short notice." She laughed humorlessly.

Hope knew where Arity and Humi were. She shut her eyes, visualizing the scarred wood floor, the empty air in the Divine Guards' quarters. She hoped not too many *auchresh* were there. Ugly accidents could happen when one *teth¨d* into crowds. She dropped off the rafter, wings snapping open with a *thump* that brought the humans' heads up, and for the barest fraction of a second she was flying.

Twenty-five

Humi was so deeply in love that for many sixdays she could overlook small things. For instance, the fact that the other two-thirds of the conspiracy did not trust her. Goquisite hated her for (so she thought) killing Erene. Belstem would not divulge his reasons for treating her like an enemy, to be tolerated and used but not trusted. Humi guessed that part of his irritability stemmed from the fact that Aneisneida and Soderingal Nearecloud, Gold Dagger's bastard, were now seen everywhere together, boating, dancing, shopping. They were engaged. But that made Belstem's willfulness no less trying. It was a strange change from the days of her apprenticehood, when, under the guise of various personas, she had enjoyed acceptance and even popularity in Antiprophet Square. But now she had killed off most of them. Sometimes she forgot that Humility Garden was not supposed to be a socialite, a practiced dissembler, but a raw, pious young ghostier, clay for the conspiracy to mold. But she had never been that. When had acting so many characters turned her real self into a persona?

Only alone with Arity could she be what she thought might be her *real* self.

They gave in to wild impulses together. She had never felt so free as when, in the middle of one of Belstem's dinners, Arity caught her eye. She reached under the table and closed her fingers around his hand. "Let's get out of here," he mouthed. "Somewhere wet."

One after the other, they excused themselves, and in the gilded washroom Arity put his arms around her and she felt herself dissolve and they were in the middle of a wide green plain with a thunderstorm rumbling overhead. Rain always pounded Veretry, even when Delta City was cracked and dry. They rolled naked in the grass. The storm needled her bare back, stimulating her to a height far above any place her ghosts' caresses had taken her, in the days when she made hungry love to them rather than coldheartedly seducing them. They lay locked together on the soaked grass, feeding from each other's mouths, she grabbing his buttocks, pulling him deeper and deeper inside her, as if she could fuse them into one being.

The whole city knew about them. From what the *imrchim* told her, they were a scandal in Marshtown, and only the ghostiers' efforts kept the flamens from publicly denouncing her. As it was; the flamens were making strange, impenetrable statements about Arity. It would be unthinkable for them to condemn a god—but prophecy obeyed no such rules. And gossip said that several recent prophecies, both in Delta City and elsewhere, had mentioned Arity's name.

Humi had little time to listen to gossip. Since she was the youngest, Goquisite and Belstem unloaded most of the conspiracy's donkey-work on her. This meant numerous visits to Gold Dagger and his peers—men either puffy or sharkish from too much drink, jingling with money. She detested them.

Gradually, the murderous heat of summer boiled away, leaving the city at the mercy of a dry, brown autumn. Humi envied Arity's fatalistic disregard for politics. Each day, she seemed to find herself deeper embroiled in all her connections. Bronze Water and Broken Bird were the saving of her. She had not really known them before, but now, for some reason ("They want to steal you from Pati," Arity said cynically), they decided that she was worth cultivating. Seasoned diplomats both, they gave unstintingly of their expertise. If not for them, she couldn't have figured out how to play Pati off against Belstem in Ellipse. Certainly she couldn't have prevented the councillors from realizing just who instigated the showdowns that left nearly every session in a shambles. Maybe the tactics were destructive. But Humi could see no other way to avoid being torn in half—if not in thirds, so many people had claims on her, or quarters.

And it seemed to be working, keeping the Ellipse just off the boil, even though floors and floors away, the Divinarch complained through the Guards of being waked up by the shouting. He had deteriorated so much that now he slept at night, like a mortal.

One packed-sand street made up the northernmost town in the world: Juwl, on the coast of Calvary. Juwl's beach kissed the equator. Here the men worked barren fields, not mines. Here there was no mining machinery, nor markets, nor traders. Leather doors flapped in a wind that never stopped. In the evenings, the women walked to the stony strip of beach and called their sea hens. And the hens came flying in flocks, the roosters leading, like flames in their blue metallic feathers, over the black waves that rolled to the end of the earth.

Transcendence stood in the middle of a small herb patch behind one of the huts, staring blindly at the streaked evening sky, his white hair tangled down his back. His weathered throat jumped. His bare feet crushed a pungent scent of thyme from the herbs.

Thani knelt in the back door of the hut, hands clasped in a posture of supplication. Her whole body screamed for her to relax. The stresses of her prophetic fit this afternoon had racked her beyond any pain that she remembered, beyond any pain she had thought possible. She had to regain Transcendence's trust. Behind her, the children of the town shuffled and whispered. *If only the brats would go away!* She checked herself. *Gods, Thani, haven't you blasphemed enough today?*

At that reminder, tears spilled down her cheeks. "Transcendence, I take it back!" she called. "I can be pious again for you, if you'll just let me try!"

"You cannot expect to blaspheme against prophecy and escape twice, leman. When you were fourteen, I excused you because of your youth. This time, the offense is unpardonable." His voice was old, cracked. She winced to hear it. But at least she had got him talking.

"I believe in my prophecy! I believe in the guidance of the gods." If she could only get him to relent—"I'll go to Delta City! I'll do what I said had to be done! You don't even have to come with me, I'll do it by my—"

"Do you really believe, leman, that I would let you go alone?" His voice was cold. "You have already proven yourself untrustworthy."

"Oh, Godsbrother!" She was sobbing uncontrollably. The wind blew hot on her back. She fell face first to the ground, digging her fingers into the dry, sandy earth, breathing in lemon-scented gulps of air. "Please— please—"

She felt him step farther away. His voice throbbed. "Why? Gods, why must it be thus?" She knew he was speaking in the direction of the salt, which lay so close to the sea here that one could see it from the tops of the hills behind the town. "Not only for my leman to be given to prophecy, but for her to blaspheme against her own words! She was once so dear to me. Why must she constantly deny your will? Why can she not acquiesce to the prophecy, which is nothing less than your voices?"

Because it sounds so improbable! Because I'm not yet salt-eyed, and so I can't be sure! For the first time in her life, the salt pilgrimage she might have to make loomed ahead of her like a salvation, not a doom. *I* want *to understand. I want to so badly.*

She stared into the darkness enclosed by her arms on the earth.

Transcendence bent and touched her back with an arthritic finger. There was no gentleness in that poke. "Leman, we will obey the prophecy. He has fallen from godhood. He must die."

"I told you I would—"

"But you are a blasphemer. You will fulfill the prophecy because I tell you to: I will not have you to try to ingratiate yourself with me."

Giving in to the anguish of her body, she flopped flat, rolling onto her back, and wept. The tears ran down her cheeks into her hair. Overhead the clouds ran away from the salt like water into the sky. The black-brown faces of the children intruded into her sight, in a circle like the mouth of a well high above her, asking her in their high, guttural voices if she was all right.

And out of the kissing, as if out of a forge, had emerged a chain whose red-hot links bound Humi and Arity together so powerfully that, Humi thought, looking down at herself as if from a distance as she lay in his arms on the long afternoons when she should have been going about the business of the Ellipse, nothing, she thought, *nothing* could ever separate them. Had Erene and Elicit felt this way? Frightening thought. Could she escape even if she wanted to?

But she did not want to. She hated the thought even of moving enough to be reminded that they possessed two separate bodies. So she did not know if it was possible to get away. Dusty skewers of sunlight pierced between the black drapes with which she had hung the walls of her Tellury Crescent boudoir, blocking out all the sounds from the street, so that it felt as if the room hung in nothingness, suspended on the tips of a dozen swords like a powdery black gourd.

And at night Arity took her harvesting with the *mainrauim* of Wind Gully Heaven. By starlight the salt forest in Kithrilindu looked much like the Chrumecountry around Delta City: fruits like transparent organs strung trees and bushes, and animals crashed away through the undergrowth, and owls' eyes caught the starlight as the caroling voices of the *mainrauim* startled them from their roosts. Humi and Arity fell behind, holding hands, eyes filled with starlight.

"Should we have let so many people know about us?" she asked finally. "Sometimes I feel as if this is too good to last."

Arity pulled a friccas fruit off a bush and sank his fangs into it. He offered her some.

"By the Power, I envy you, Ari!"

His voice was grave as he pulled her close. "It's not that I don't worry. I do. But I don't see any reason to let them spoil our time together. This is all we have in the

world, when you come down to it. The amount of time
we can spend together before we die." Tossing the friccas
fruit into the shadows, he took hold of her face and lifted
her on her toes to kiss her. She tasted the tangy juice.
"What is the Throne?" he said into her lips. "A hunk of
wood and metal. It doesn't deserve so much of your
worry."

"When I'm with you, I know you're right. But as soon
as we're apart—Power, I should be at Belstem's right
now."

"You shouldn't be anywhere but here." They stopped
walking. The voices of the *mainrauim* receded into the
distance. The air was pleasantly cool and dewy.

"It's all right for you," she said. "You don't *care*. People
look at me on the streets and I hear them whispering,
There goes the councillor who fucks a god." Her voice
trembled with bitterness.

"Do you really care what they say?"

"Yes! I do! I can't stand being this vulnerable!"
Around them the forest swayed and whispered. Starlight
filtered down through the trees, and Humi dropped her
face into her hands. "I wish—I wish I had my personas
back—"

Instantly Arity pulled her close, caressing her as if her
misery were dirt to be smoothed out of her fur. "Humi!
Tell me. Tell me now."

"I'm afraid." Tears choked her. She had to get it out. "I
love you too much."

"Oh, Power," he said distractedly. "I love you too
much, too! But do you know how lucky we are to be able
to say that? This is the single best thing that could have
happened to either of us."

She knew. Oh, she knew. And the knowledge dried the
tears in her eyes like a blast of hot wind.

"You can't control this kind of thing."

"No." She let her head fall back on his shoulder, standing
there in his arms. A new cluster of talons on his neck
pricked her ear as she gazed up through the foliage of the
salt trees to the stars. "You can't, can you?" Constellations:
Skyheart. The Wheel.

* * *

"They're too close," Pati said, standing at Hope's side by the wall of the Rimmear tavern. "Too close by far." His tone suggested that Arity and Humi had ventured too near one of the flaming spots on the stretches of fire salt to be found in the middle of Uarech. But they were only laughing and betting with their neighbors by the night-colored arches of the windows, where tables and chairs had been pushed back so that the patrons of the tavern could hold mouse races. "It can't last."

"Five says it can," Hope said. "They're *irissim*. Can't you tell?"

"A god and a mortal, *irissim*? Ha! Arity's infatuated. I can see that. And infatuations at this level are dangerous." He clicked his tongue.

"Pati," Hope said with a sinking of the heart. "What are you thinking?"

He smiled at her with all his teeth.

She quivered her wings in the limited space between her back and the wall. She did not like Rimmear. The heat made her tired. The *auchresh* here talked too much, too fast, and one had to *pay* for a glass of tea or a pipe of tobacco. *Pay,* for the Power's sake! With money! She returned to the salt to get *away* from the ugly, mercenary aspects of Delta City! She wanted to be in Divaring Below right now, splashing through the shallows of the lake under the open stars. She resented Pati for making her come all the way to Calvary on this petty spying trip.

"Arity should be careful," Pati said. "It's quite possible she means to take advantage of him."

"Can't you stop suspecting anyone for one moment? It looks perfectly simple to me. They're in love."

A Foundling passed in front of them. Except for a flapping apron, it was stark naked. It tugged Pati's shirt and pointed to a vacant table. Pati nodded to the Foundling, seized Hope by the wrist and swooped between the patrons to release her over one of the amber saltwood chairs so that she floated down like a piece of silk. She put her thin elbows onto the table and rested her chin in her hands.

"Poor Hope. She knows all about unfair advantages."
Pati smiled, the white skin around his eyes crinkling with
affection and pity.

"I came of my own free will," she snapped, not moving
her head. She didn't know why she kept on trying to hold
her own. Some innate fear of being totally dissolved in
his will. Ridiculous: he already knew all about her, everything she could think of, except maybe her secret desire
to have a child, and *no one* knew that. Apart from that
cavity in the middle of her body, she was his creature.

He signaled the Foundling. "A glass of *khath* for the
iu!" It wrinkled its nose, as if to say that *iuim* got no special treatment here in Rimmear, thank you, but it brought
the *khath* anyhow. Pati tossed it a coin. Hope gulped
gratefully at the clear liquid.

"I think we have to pry them apart somehow." Pati
watched her drink. "Neither of them is as effective in Ellipse as they both were before this foolishness started. And
I don't like the way they have got out of my control."

She blinked at him, that he would sit there and say that.
"Your arrogance defies belief."

"Whenever he comes to the quarters, he brings her.
They're inseparable. It could have something to do with
Councillor Gentle's death—Humility needs someone to
latch on to, if you see what I mean—but I wouldn't bet on
that. No, it's just foolishness, such as Ari has always been
prone to."

Hope turned her head and looked through the fog of
smoke. Humi had just placed a winning bet. The group of
Uarechians with whom they were racing mice erupted in
loud *auchresh* laughter, showing broken teeth in mutated
mouths. Arity pinned Humi against one of the aches and
planted a victory kiss on her lips. Her closed eyelids
trembled, purple with a frighteningly disproportionate ecstasy. Hope hugged herself. Even across the tavern, the
sight singed some tender thing in her. Being excluded inspired both relief and sadness that she would never be
part of something similar. She was too old now.

"They're doing what should not be done." Pati's face
was a pinched white beak. He stared past her, uncon-

sciously gripping the edge of the table so hard that his nails were purple. "*Irissim*. It's blasphemy."

"Stop it. 'Gods'! This would be a better world if that word had never been invented." She glanced around. "Look at this Heaven. Pimps, beggars, *ghauthi keres,* look at that man slapping the Foundling's buttocks, the poor little thing has so many bruises—if your precious flamens *did* come here after they died, what would they think? They'd die again, of shock!"

"It should not be. It cannot be. But they are doing it." He reached out and grabbed her *khath*, drained it in a sucking gulp. "He is Heir. We cannot let him open himself up to scorn and censure this way. The gods must remain ineffable." She heard something crack in his hand; startled, he looked down. A piece of the edge of the perforated stone table lay in his palm, blood welling up round it from a ragged gash. Hope watched curiously as a flush came over his face and he closed his fist around the splinter.

"You understand nothing about human emotions, do you, Pati?" she said.

"Why should I?" A spasm of pain crossed his face. He clasped his good hand around the injured one. "I'm not human."

She felt tiny feet scurry over her toes. Looking down, she saw an escaped racing mouse sitting under the table, lapping the drops of blood that fell regularly to the floor. "We have to remove this distraction, Hope," he said. And she heard that thing she had never thought to hear in his voice again as he said, "We can't let Ari make himself this vulnerable." A tiny transparent creature, the mouse grew solid as it consumed the viscous white blood, as if it were coming into existence. *Power,* Hope thought, *I am weak.*

Twenty-six

"You and Arity make a nice couple," Rita said to Humi one night, "but don't get a swelled head."

"What would I do without you, Rita?" Humi said sincerely.

She knew the older ghostier was right. So the first day that Arity had to go alone into the salt, she disguised herself as her first persona of all: Rosi, who had been Erene's personal maid. Dabbing green facedust on her nose, she grinned at herself in the mirror. *I can still do this! Remember those days ...*

The sun poured in like honey through the windows. The frills she had had put up all over the room, to make it as different as possible from the black *auchresh* nest of her Tellury Crescent boudoir, hung immobile like the petals of flowers when there is no wind. Sitting here disguising herself reminded her of Erene. Dressing to go out at night, nudging each other for space before the mirror ... lazily nibbling chunks of melon for breakfast, those mornings when Goquisite was away ... her sitting at Erene's feet before the hearth, a beauty treatise splayed face-down on her lap, telling her master the irritations of her day ...

Though she had not admitted it to herself as long as Erene "lived," Humi's apprentice status had helped her preserve certain traits of childhood. Now she really had left those things behind. She could no longer hide behind Erene. She had to take whatever Delta City threw at her full in the face, as Humility Garden.

But not today.

She slipped on houseshoes and wandered through the

familiar, soothing luxury of the suite to the door that she had had knocked into the back staircase. Male and female domestics passed up and down all day.

"Hey, Rosi! Ain't seen you in months!"

"Where you been? Goin' down the kitchen? I'll come see you when I finish these fly-papers."

"Ain't seen you about, Rosi—where you been?"

Humi grinned at the last speaker, Goquisite's room valet. "Sick."

He shifted the hot-water buckets he carried. "Pity 'bout Milady Erene, ain't it? Never would've thought that quiet little apprentice of hers 'ud do her in."

Humi winced. "Yeah, well, the apprentice's taken me on now. I ain't complainin'."

"Hah! Nor'd I, if I was you!" He shrugged to readjust the buckets and went on his way. Humi continued down to the back kitchen, where the servants gathered when their duties permitted. "Hey, Rosi!" greeted her when she entered. Grinning, she accepted a seat by the enormous cookfire, where a spit of chihuahuas sizzled for the dinner party she would attend as herself that evening. She felt good. A different kind of good. The denizens of the kitchen were so unlike the atheistic councillors, all of whom had spent their childhoods in similar circumstances before being chosen as lemans. Strange how these commoners weren't resentful of the children of their class who had created a new, elite society around themselves. Rather, they were proud of them. There wasn't a one of these men and women who didn't speak of Goquisite as if she were his or her own daughter or cousin.

Smiling, Humi listened to the story of somebody's sister's wedding. One of the new atheistic ceremonies, held indoors. It sounded as though it had actually been beautiful.

"Hey, Rosi!" It was Deservi, one of the undercooks. "Didja meet Godsister Philanthropy?"

The flamen sat at the big, crudely built kitchen table, drinking a mug of broth. She was a woman of heavy build with turquoise fur, in a linen robe, her leman a butter-braided girl of twelve. It amazed Humi how the kitchen workers bobbed their heads whenever they passed her chair, even though they were mostly atheists. Childhood values were slow to die. "Greetin's, Godsister," she said respectfully.

"It's a long morning we've had," the leman said. "Many miracles. There's a sight of suffering in this city."

From her accent and her pale fur, Humi guessed the girl to be Icelandic. Humi's ignorance of Iceland—and in fact, most of the Divinarchy—was a severe drawback to her as a politician. None of the other councillors was any better off, but almost unconsciously she decided to take this opportunity to learn more. "Godsister? How long've you been in the city?"

"Several weeks." The flamen raised her head. "Cook, have you anything stronger than broth?"

"Wine? Surely. Rosi, you want some too?" Deservi swooped two cups out of the stone sluice where a boy was washing dishes and poured from a stone bottle. The wine was a full-bodied red, light in color, sweet-smelling. As Deservi handed it to her, Humi blinked. The point of contact between her fingers and the mug seemed to have flashed purple. But of course it had only been her eyes. She should stop skimping on sleep. "Cheers, Godsister," she said, and raised the glass and drained it.

Why had everyone in the kitchen gone silent?

She twisted on her stool, trying to speak, staring at their faces. It was as if a cylinder of glass had been dropped around her, thickening by the second.

Darker . . .

Dark, opaque glass . . .

Silence. As if her ears were clogged with wool.

The most curious feeling.

She stirred a little.

A prickling . . . a tingling . . . As if something as thin and bubbly as champagne is running in my veins. I wonder if I should open my eyes? Hmm . . . an interesting challenge. Yes, I think I will.

The heavy-jawed, homely face of Deservi peered at her, green eyes filled with worry.

Humi blinked and said, "Deservi, there's an odd taste in my mouth. I don't think that wine can have been very good."

The cook's face lit up, and she flew out of Humi's field of vision. "She's awright! Talkin' a bit funny, but awright! C'mere everyone, gimme a hand—"

"That's quite all right." But Humi's limbs were shaky. She used Deservi's arms to pull herself upright. She was sitting on the grimy cushions in the chimney-nook. She rubbed her hands, breathing in the familiar scents of roast meat and chopped greens. "What on earth happened?"

"It were the Godsister as saved you." The dish-washer boy pointed reverently to the kitchen table. The robed shape sat slumped, head on arms, with the leman bending anxiously over her. "Me dad says they're nought but frauds, but I'd never seen one of 'em work 'er tricks before. I swear I'll nivver chuck rotten fruits at 'em agin, Rosi. She saved ya."

Scandalizing that any child should reach adolescence without having seen a miracle! Yet for all her saltside birth, and her deep though deeply altered piety, Humi felt awed and a little frightened that a miracle had been finally been worked on *her*. She'd been a healthy child; this was the first time in her life. So *that* had been the sensation. A tickly flood of bubbles surrounding her, flowing through her mouth and nose into her blood, cleansing it. She dropped to her knees to look up into the flamen's face. "Are you all right, Godsister?" To the leman—"Is she exhausted?"

"Aye, she's so. She was already tired but she couldna let you die. You was poisoned, know that?"

Gods! She turned back to the room. "Where did that wine come from?"

"I dunno," Deservi said. "Why? It couldn't of been that. We've been drinkin' it for days."

It could have been nothing else. That flash—

Someone had changed the cup that Deservi extended for the cup that reached Humi's hand. But that person must have been able to *teth*˘. And if they had been here, however briefly, they had seen the flamen. They had known that Humi would be saved. The fire flickered, sizzling with lard dripping from the chihuahuas. Humi needed Arity. She needed his arms around her.

She shut her eyes and clenched her teeth. *Don't wreck your disguise!* As it was, they might put two and two together.

"Aaah . . ." The flamen lifted her head. The salt crystals glowed white against the rare, south-Veretrean turquoise color of her fur. Once, Godsister Philanthropy had been very beautiful. "My child, stand up." Humi got to her feet. "Do you know who would have wanted to do such a thing, and to you, of all people?" She shook her head. The Godsister wrapped her arm around her leman, who helped her to her feet. "I shall leave now, my friends. You have been good to me. I swear, I shall remember the feel of that poison for the rest of my life. It would have taken you like a numbing sleep, kindly, but none the less deadly."

"What was it?" Humi whispered. As a ghostier she knew every poison that could be swallowed, injected, or applied to the body. But many had no taste or smell.

"I would not know it by name," Philanthropy began, but the leman interjected, "A salt poison, Godsister. Those be the worst. Almond-flower."

The flamen smiled. "Why, Ragran, I did not know you were such an expert on poisons!"

"I'd an uncle that was an atheist pharmacist," the girl said as they moved toward the door.

Deservi smiled. "You just sit right back down, Godsister, till you feel better, an' you can have a share of our evenin' meal." She turned to the head cook, fat, elderly Alour. "Can't she, ma'm?"

"O' course." Alour lifted her pine-green jowls. "We always 'elp them what 'elps ours, and Rosi's one of ours. O' course the Godsister can stay."

But Humi clutched herself, thinking, *Almond-flower. What if it had been salt aconite, which kills in a third of a second flat? What then?*

* * *

But she never even told Arity about the incident. It was knocked out of her mind by the happenings of the next day. On a clear jewel of a morning with sharp edges, when the sky over Delta City looked like strong tea and the air tasted of smoke (for some of the fields on the mainland were so dry that spontaneous combustion was occurring), Owen murdered Rita.

It was past two in the afternoon. Nearly everyone in the city was outside—Humi had gone with the other ghostiers to bathe off the Marshtown jetties—when it happened. Owen told them exactly what he had done, afterward, in salacious detail. He came up behind Rita as she sat reading on the roof of Thaumagery House, the book a handspan from her nose, skirts rucked to her thighs so that her withered old legs could feel the sun, and stabbed her in the heart. Straightforward, cold-blooded, and so easy it was almost like cheating.

When he showed off the corpse, washed and dried, it was such a shock to discover Rita had had gray hair that no one could speak.

He claimed the seat—number 12—that very evening. Not a single councillor, neither atheist nor flamen nor ghostier nor god, greeted his claim with applause. Only, perhaps, Eterneli in her alcove, who had started sleeping with him though she was only thirteen. Rita had been a staunch supporter of the flamenhood, and therefore an enemy of the atheists, but not even they could deny that she had seen the fair side of every debate and had had many years of wisdom in the ways of the Ellipse.

Humi felt her loss like a hard blow to the ribs. If it had been within her power, she would have barred Owen from taking the seat and put one of the twins in his place. Preferably Sol. He was chafing to attain master status, and she thought he was getting dangerous. But it was not within her power, and Owen clearly could not care less whether anyone approved or not. He sat all evening with his arms folded, saying nothing, grinning like a cat which has gotten the cream after ten years of trying to knock it off the shelf.

Soon after, the weather broke. With the Divine Guards,

Humi and Arity went to dance in the rain, high in Kithrilindu where the skies opened over mountains that had been worn to lace by years of cloudbursts. They somersaulted over the smooth, wet, white formations and slid down chutes, laughing. The whole day was remarkably free of tension between *auchresh,* and between Humi and the *auchresh.* For the first time since Rita's death, she felt that everything might still be all right.

But when she got home, fluffy-furred and lethargic, wearing someone else's silk uniform, she found the ghostiers crying in each other's arms. Sol had murdered Beisa and Emni.

And I knew, she thought, horror-stricken. *I knew he was becoming dangerous and I did nothing.*

Nothing I could have done.

Oh, Emni!

He sat amid them in the Chalice, elbows on knees, scowling from under his heavy white brows at anyone who seemed to be approaching. Thaumagery House was now empty but for him and Owen. "I wish them joy of each other!" Mory snarled, her nose running as she wept. "He had no need to kill Em too! Not her!"

"She was my friend." Humi hid her face in her arms. *I suppose Emni lay curled around his feet in the womb, after all.*

"You're missing the point," Ziniquel said miserably. "To kill not just the master, but the competition? It's not done."

The breakdown of tradition. Humi knew that that was half the crisis. After all, murder was the ghostiers' bosom friend; they never blanched when it poked its head up in their midst. This was their way of life. But seldom in living history had there been so few ghostiers as there were now. The *imrchim* were used to having numbers to cushion their interactions. Yet the thinning out of Tellury Crescent had a streamlining effect on their vote in Ellipse. Humi's leadership seemed less questionable to Sol, Owen, and Trisizim than it did to Mory and Ziniquel, who had served through Erene's term, or Fra, who had seen Molatio Ash inaugurated. And her reputation for shrewdness fooled Owen and Sol entirely. So they remained loyal.

Their old masters had the last laugh, though it echoed hollowly out of the grave.

And Emni, who was *not* dead, laughed unpleasantly between her teeth. Sol's poison had nearly killed her, but he'd skimped on the dose. That stinginess would be the death of him someday, Humi read in his sister's flashing eyes. Gentle Emni, laughing Emni, nursed secretly back to health by Fra in Melthirr House, wanted nothing more than to kill her brother.

But she would settle for an Ellipse seat.

Preferably a better seat than Sol's.

Perhaps Fra saw what was coming, and took the safe way out. Perhaps Emni, who still had a trace of softheartedness in her, presented him with an ultimatum. At any rate, at the first Ellipse session of winter, when sleet glittered in the torchlight and in wet tracks on the floor, Fra Canyonade abdicated in favor of Emni Southwind. As the Archipelagan woman stepped into the Chamber, demure in a yellow dress, she gave Sol a look of detestation that froze Humi all the way up at the top of the table.

"I could feel it in my bones," Humi said that night. She lay in Arity's arms, in the black-draped, salt-scented nest that was the only place she could get to sleep now. "Ari, I can't have this kind of enmity between them. They're worse than Erene and Zin ever were."

Absently Arity stroked her stomach. "They're beyond your control, love."

She pushed his hand away. "Perhaps. But Arity, if I could only hold them all in the hollow of my palm!"

The room whirled as he pulled her on top of him, clamping her face between his hands. His natural perfume stung her nostrils, rancid with fear. "Don't talk like that! Sometimes I *worry* about you!"

"All right." She lay still. "I won't. Let me go."

It seemed as though these months lasted for years. Humi scolded herself every time she did something reckless. *None of us is invulnerable! And who should know better than you, senior ghostier?* Locked away in a dark closet of her mind: the suspicious incidents, starting with the poisoned wine in Goquisite's kitchen and recurring at more or less regular intervals. The Divine Guard's pipe that had been too strong for her, the fish that hadn't been fresh enough, the syringe that had sprung a hairline crack. The ghost who had tried to retaliate. And a host of lesser things.

But she hadn't time for anyone who wanted her dead. She scarcely had time to be careful. All she could do was ride the crest of the wave as autumn bleached into winter. The icy weather wore on, and on. The stink of refuse hung sharp in the clear, cold air.

Ziniquel and Emni started a passionate love affair. Humi knew that he had always been fond of Emni, but because of her bond with Sol it had been impractical for him to reveal his feelings. Just as the twins had sworn, their bond was unbreakable—but now it was transformed from love into hatred. This was the moment for Zin to declare his love, and Humi didn't blame him for taking advantage of it. The pair became oblivious to the outside world, just as Humi and Arity had. Humi could look at them and smile, even as she wondered uncomfortably just how far she and Arity had come from that state.

Soon after Midwinter, while everyone in the city and the surrounding country was sleeping off their excesses, Algia got out of her narrow bed and crept through the wet Crescent to Thaumagery House. She climbed the stairs to Owen's room. Tears running down her face, she stabbed him in the throat fifteen times, so that his blood soaked the sheet and dripped onto the floor. Then she collapsed on his body, mingling her tears with his blood, weeping fit to wake the dead.

Humi had the story from Eterneli, who'd stood frozen in the door, watching everything. Algia hadn't thought to look around, though she had known that Eterni was sleeping with Owen, and it made perfect sense that she should be there.

Humi hated nothing worse than funerals. Especially when she did not want to admit to herself that she was not sorry for Owen's death. Not sorry to the point that she had had him buried in the pious tradition—easiest to do without making waves—though he had been an atheist.

The Godsbrother droned dolorously on; a Godsister waited nearby to take his place when his voice wore out. It would be hours yet until the coffin was laid in the ground of the great cemetery on the bank of the Chrume. A tree wept droplets down the neck of Humi's black mourning dress. Rowans and willows and hazels crowded among the grave statues, stretching away in the endless disorder of an abandoned statuary yard.

Fissures of self-doubt were beginning to creep over her golden bubble. She was unable to comfort Eterni. It was to Mory that the thirteen-year-old had first fled, weeping for her lover. Only then had Mory sought Humi. When her tears were exhausted, Eterneli went back to Algia in Melthirr House. Now they refused to leave one another. The illogic of it was stunning, but Humi supposed they recognized each other's grief. Algia said she was going to take Eterneli as apprentice.

Well, what difference did one more broken tradition make now? Humi, Emni, Mory, and Ziniquel had agreed that Algia had had to become a master, or else drop out of Tellury Crescent as Hem had done, or go insane. She was thirty-five. "I'm only twenty-eight," Mory said, "yet I'm the most experienced of us all now. It seems only yesterday that I was a new master, struggling to assert myself in Ellipse."

"I remember when you killed Isen. I was apprentice to Constance then." Ziniquel shook his head. "It doesn't seem natural. Five of us, one after another. Who would have said, Humi, that you would be the only one of us to gain the Ellipse without committing a murder?"

"You're forgetting Fra," Humi said forlornly. "He tells me he's very happy in his little house beside the Chrume . . ."

"Keeping bees!" Ziniquel looked as though he would burst with indignation. "How could anyone keep *bees* after having been a ghostier?"

"You're still young, Zin," Emni said tolerantly, breezily ignoring the fact that she herself was not yet twenty.

"Maybe you'll understand why Fra made the choice he did, when it's *your* turn to get out while the going's good." She kissed him. He lifted his eyebrows but reciprocated the kiss. Gradually she pushed him deeper into the sofa, shifting onto his lap. Their affair was still at the stage where passion can attack without warning, irresistibly.

Mory caught Humi's eye, wryly amused. *He* is *still young.*

And Humi felt the panic of a toddler taking its first shaky steps, who looks for its parents and sees them turn once to wave before vanishing into a deep, black, impenetrable cave.

Of what kind of rabble am I senior ghostier now? Where are the wise, kind imrchim *among whom I found myself four years ago? Is it* my *fault everything has changed?*

"In Heaven!" finished the flamen to renewed wails from the gathering. Rain blotted Eterneli's headscarf and trickled down her cheeks, pasting her fur flat. She looked like a grown woman, with her bones showing. "All those whom we have ever lost, we shall meet in Heaven!"

My gods, Humi thought wryly. *I hope not.*

Twenty-seven

"Ari," Humi said, "I met my sister last night."

"Who?"

"Thankfulness. My little sister. She's in Delta City."

"What's she doing here?"

"She's a leman. She's here with her flamen."

"I'd like to meet her." He gazed through the flawed glass of a window in the Chalice, playing with the lace of his open-neck shirt, barefoot as always. His green ankles were dusty. The lead between the windowpanes dented his forehead. Behind them, the ghostiers read and talked quietly; a fire crackled in the hearth under the rudely carved mantel. "Perhaps when it stops raining, we can pay them a visit. Where are they—" he yawned—"where are they staying?"

"Ari," she said in vexation, "I wish you'd go to sleep!" He looked quizzically at her.

"Pati hates it when you don't sleep with them!"

"Pati can go fuck himself. It makes sense for me to sleep on the same schedule as you. Otherwise, you *don't* sleep. And I can't stand it when you don't get enough rest."

She did not want to say that she was afraid Pati might be much angrier than Arity gave him credit for. "Your eyes look funny in the daylight," she said unhappily.

"Well, your eyes look funny *all* the time." She leaned her head on his knee. He tousled her hair.

"Don't," she said. "I gilded it fresh to go to Goquisite's tonight—"

"So now I can't even touch you?" But his voice was

jesting. She pulled his hand down and kissed the clawed fingertips.

Earlier that afternoon—

She was wandering along the Lockreed Concourse, disguised once again as the Deltan maid Rosi, taking a much-needed break from the long-winded, beforehand discussions of the new regime that Belstem insisted on conducting. Delicious scents wafted to her nose from shopfronts and beverage vendors. She bought a cup of mutton broth. These days, she never ate at dinners or banquets, or even at tea parties: one could not know what had happened between the kitchen and one's mouth. But here, she saw the man chuck the meat into the cauldron, stir it, dip the pottery mug in, and put it steaming into her hands. The heat drove the winter chill out of her body. The taste brought Beaulieu back in a rush of memory. And she looked up and saw the flamen and leman standing on the corner of Lockreed and Bowery Crescent, the leman an unusually great distance ahead of the flamen, a sullen, sunbleached blond girl, very thin. She couldn't have looked less Domesdian. But Humi would have sworn—

No. It can't be.

She gulped her broth, keeping her head down. "You seen that white-headed flamen, there, before, friend?" she asked the customer on her left.

He pulled his lower lip, thinking. "Yeah. 'E's new around here. Stayin' someplace Godsbrother Puritanism put him up, from what I hear ... don't know what he's doing in Christon. Name of Transubstantiation or Tranquillity, sump'n like that."

"Transcendence!" Humi yelped, and dropped her broth cup. The canyonlike, terraced buildings channeled the city's voices into a tapestry of sound, woven with scents—cooked meat, fish, toasted bulrushes, offal, ammonia, molten metal—through which she slipped on her way to the corner. She circled a boy carrying a huge stack of dried sandfish and touched the blond leman's shoulder.

The girl spun, brows drawn together. Then her mouth fell open.

The concourse shrank to one small bubble of silence.

"Excuse me, dear." Humi's social voice grated on the stillness. Wrong! Wrong voice—wrong persona—"I couldn't help noticing that you rather resemble—" She scrubbed an arm across her face. *"Thani?"*

"You've changed." Thani's voice was hard, defending against recognition. "You look Royallandic."

"It's only dust!" Humi raised her arm again, then stopped. "But you recognize my face—don't you? Don't you?"

"I . . . think so." Thani reached out and rubbed one finger across Humi's cheek, staring at the tawny smudge. "Yes. Gods! I thought you were long dead."

"So did I. So did I you."

She opened her arms to embrace the girl, but Thani stepped neatly away, leaving her standing there looking foolish. "Humi?" Thani glanced at the Godsbrother. His white brows drew down over the salt crystals as he turned in the direction of their voices, and his mouth fumbled around displeasure. "Can we go somewhere to talk?"

"Surely. Surely. Gods, where do we *start*? But you can't leave him, can you?"

"Him? He doesn't care about me. Fuck him." Thani's voice was bleak. She sounded much older than—Sixteen? Seventeen? A mere child. "Can we go?"

"Ye-yes." *He'll wait here, I suppose.* Putting her hand through Thani's arm, Humi led her down Bowery Crescent, where the carpet vendors kept shop. Tapestry fringes swayed as they passed under the nearest doorway. The cool draft of the passage enveloped them. Smells of wool and leather laced the dark; voices haggled over prices, leisurely, prepared to take all afternoon. They passed on, out into the long, shallow yard where the vendors kept their stock before they cataloged it. Hundreds of rolls leaned against each other and against a few long-suffering trees; secondhand carpets hung over lines, being aired. They created roofless enclosures. Humi led Thani inside one of these plush "rooms" and sank down on the ground, facing her.

"How is it you can come back here?" Thani asked distrustfully.

"Oh, I could walk off with a carpet if I wanted to," Humi said without thinking. "If they recognized me, they'd have been bowing and scraping." She bit her tongue.

"Oh, really? Are you a lady? Are you married to a Royallandic lord?" Thani's face said that that would explain everything neatly but drearily, for if Humi was an atheistic lady then Thani would have to hate her for it.

"I'm ..." *Discretion above everything!* warned Erene, whose disregard of her own advice had brought her to be outcast by her own *imrchim.* Humi closed her mouth. Finally she said, "I'm a ghostier." That meant nothing to Thani, of course: she was safe.

"You don't look like a ... whatever that is. You look ..." A shadow crossed Thani's face. "Twenty-five. Beautiful."

Humi shut her eyes for a second, restraining tears. Why did that blunt assessment mean so much to her? "And you?" she blurted. "You look older too. Grown up. Your hair's so light. Have you been in the sun?"

Thani grimaced guilelessly. She dragged her fingers through her hair, and the coarsely scissored crop stood on end. "Oh, Humi. Yes. We've been wandering. Westshine, at first ... we stayed a long time at each hamlet. I suppose it was so I could get used to the life. Then we went to Delta City, and I learned all the secrets of being a leman. It's not just describing what you see. I hated the city, but I don't remember its being like this, before—not so uncaring and closed-in, nor so smelly. Last time nobody tried to pick our pockets. Last time nobody said she needed a miracle, then when we entered her dirty little apartment, held out a bag of farthings and asked, 'Can you change these into crowns for me?' "

Humi winced. She knew she seldom saw the real underside of Delta City.

"After that we went to Calvary. We've been wandering for about seven years."

"Do you like it?" *Gods, I sound inane!*

"Transcendence says his life's work is Calvary. So is mine. I'd ... I'd do anything to go back."

"Why don't you?"

Thani rubbed her face. "I—I don't think he's going to take me."

"Whyever shouldn't he?"

"We—we have a task to do here. And I'm afraid that he is only keeping me until that task is accomplished. Then he'll claim that I am too old to be a leman and that he came here to find a Deltan child to be his next one." She had, Humi saw, been trying very hard to keep her face impassive. Now, suddenly, she doubled over and hid her face in her rough green skirt, shaking. Her rough-cut hair slid slowly off her neck. Humi wanted to comfort her, but she did not dare. What was it like to·have no one in the world except your flamen, to be bound to him by this devastating dignity that wouldn't allow anyone to see the frailty behind it? All the lemans she had known were so serene, full of inner tranquillity, even poor dead Lexi, who had made no attempt to hide his passion for Joyfulness. The others sublimated it into serenity. But perhaps their flamens' love for them was not a result of this equilibrium, as she'd believed, but the very linchpin of their existence. Would all of them fall apart like this if it were taken away?

How can you just sit here and watch her break? She's your sister! "My dear, I'm so sorry—" Humi tried to take Thani in her arms.

The girl wrenched away, flattening herself against the side of the carpet. It ballooned dangerously behind her. Dust puffed into the air, stinging Humi's nose. "Leave me alone! You're a lady!" So that was what Thani chose to believe. Well, it was Humi's own fault for not being honest with her. "All I want from you is help!" Her eyes grew bleak, cunning. "I'm your *sister*. You have to help me."

"You are my sister," Humi said.

"Do you know any Ellipse councillors? Any important flamens? Anyone you could ask? I know I can't force Transcendence to love me again, but if I could just be with him. That's all I ask, to be with him. Then maybe he would come around."

Humi took a deep breath. She leaned forward, slowly, so as not to present any threat of contact to Thani. The thin ruffles of her servant's dress puffed to fill the space between their knees. "Tell me exactly what it is that you want. I'll see what I can do."

She did not tell any of this to Arity. She did not have time. For a knocking rattled the window, and Arity leaped back. Afet Merisand's face was pressed against the panes among the raindrops, round and frightening as a moon-fish. "Me?" Humi pointed to herself.

The porter nodded and gestured.

"What does he want?" Emni came up and closed her hands on Humi's shoulders. "I wouldn't ride ten feet in that man's sedan if I were you, Humi."

"He's the Divinarch's favorite, Emni," Arity said. He turned to Humi. "Whatever it is, we'd better go."

Gratitude flooded her, quieting the fears that had sprung up to choke rationality as springtime weeds choked crops. He would come with her. He would look after her. But when they got outside, he squinting against the daylight, she clutching an openwork shawl that Algia had thrown around her shoulders, Afet shook his head. He panted, smoking like a draydog in the rain, and he smelled like one too. "Just—Milady Garden."

Arity loomed over the muscular Deltan. Ordinarily slight for an *auchresh,* he seemed truly godly as he boomed, "I am the Heir! And I do not need your pathetic conveyance to go wherever I want!"

"True," Afet said. "But the Divinarch wants to see Milady Garden alone."

Ziniquel gasped, "Gods, Humi—"

"Not a word!" she ordered. Even to her, her voice sounded unusually harsh. "Ari—" she stretched a hand out to him—"I think I'd better go—"

"I shan't let you." he placed a possessive hand on her arm.

She shook it off and got into the sedan. Deferentially, Afet hooked the curtain closed. From outside she heard, "Humi!" Then, "He's gone—"

Then this would be proving to herself that she did not *depend* on him. That she loved him, but did not need him in order to be effective. "Let's go," she said, her voice steely.

Gods, the city smelled pungent today! It was this cold weather. Voices carried on the breeze, too.

But soon they were thudding up the wooden ramp into the courtyard of the Old Palace, and Merisand slowed to a walk. *Where are we going?* Humi wondered, and she poked her head out of the curtain. Darkness surrounded them. Something thudded by in the other direction, brushing her hair with a gust of wind, and she knew it could have taken her head off. The sedan stopped; Merisand helped her out. The floor was of earth, and lumpy. "We are in the stables. Since it is raining. I hope you do not mind, milady."

"It would hardly behoove me to object."

Slowly her eyes adjusted to the darkness. It was a vast, low barn lined with stalls, booming with porters' flying feet. They wove among the incoming and outgoing sedans to a little door tucked between two stalls and passed into a corridor.

"I must guide you myself, milady."

"All right, all right! And stop calling me milady!" She looked sidewise at him. "I think we know too much about each other for that."

"Ah . . . and what knowledge would that be, mi . . . ah, Lady Garden?"

She laughed. Except for a couple of human servants, the hall down which they were walking was deserted. The torches hadn't been replaced. "Oh, things such as that you were the go-between for Aneisneida and Soderingal during the months Belstem tried to stop them from communicating. That you arranged their trysts."

"That's not true!" He darted a glance at her, and tried again. "I was acting on the Divinarch's orders!"

"Mmm." They turned into a lesser corridor. Afet was muddy with anger from collar to hatbrim. "Belstem has called their engagement the beginning of the end," Humi said. "He says that it takes the Ellipse down another rung, from domination by flamens past domination by nobles to domination by commoners. Why on earth would the Divinarch encourage something like that?"

"I do not know my monarch's motives!"

She allowed him that. "Well," she said soberly, "I suppose I have come to find them out, haven't I? I suppose that is why he wants me."

They climbed a shallow spiral stair. Merisand stopped before a plain door. "This is the stateroom. I do not enter unless I am summoned."

Humi pushed the crystal bar and went in.

This room was as large as the Chalice—larger. Checkered tiles covered the floor. Abstract frescoes in a light, rich palette swam in the corners of her eyes, forming fleeting pictures. A few pieces of *auchresh* furniture stood here and there. A high wind surged throughout the room. One entire wall was a pane of glass, a foot thick, with segments swung open, and outside on a wooden balcony a great, wheeled bed stood, its canopies flying like banners.

Humi looked around once more to see if she had missed anything, then ventured outside.

The wind took her breath away, but it was not unbearable. The wide wooden balcony ran the length of the whole sea-front of the Old Palace: the bed was the only thing on it. Vessels of all sizes and descriptions cluttered the ridged green sea, maneuvering in and out of the wharves with the constancy of ants trooping into a hole.

In the bed lay the Divinarch of Royalland, Calvary, Veretry, Pirady, Iceland, the sundry isles of the Archipelago, and Domesdys, et al., dead.

Humi screamed. She scrambled up and kneeled on the coverlet, grabbing the Divinarch's shriveled wrist. "Milord! Oh, gods . . ."

He opened one eye. "Ehhh? What the hell?"

She hugged herself. Gods. Gods. His eyes were protruberant orbs of red-laced milk. Cold urgency took over: she slid off the foot of the bed and began to shove it inside. "Are you all right, Divinarch?" she shouted in *auchraug*.

"I am dying," he croaked in mortal. He appeared to find nothing strange about her speaking his language, although she had never used it in his hearing before. Maybe he didn't realize she was not an *auchresh*. But he must know—he had sent for her. Difficult to imagine this shriveled being in the bed doing such a strenuous thing. He raised himself from the pillows, peering down, his ancient visage contorted with effort. "Aaagh! Do not shut the doors." He was still speaking mortal. "I am fond of the wind—it tastes of salt, and I am homesickly. You— you are Humility? Arity's *irissu*?"

"Yes." She looked at him questioningly.

"I sent for you. I am old ... I cannot constantly be tiptoeing around other people's homes. Not like the young ones. I do not know much of what is happening, except that which Arity and Pati tell me. And of course their reports disagree, so that I am at a loss until Bird and Bronze come and tell me yet another version. My *firchresim* ... such a pity that they are *auchresh*. They are both good men." His speech was punctuated with wheezes.

Humi frowned. "Why is it a pity that they are *auchresh*, milord?"

"Aaah. Human, come sit by me."

Careful not to jolt him, Humi climbed back up onto the bed and sat cross-legged on the slick salt-brocade. His limbs were like sticks beneath the coverlet. His skin looked grubby against the white salt-fiber pillow. She twisted her fingers together. "Divinarch? Why would you regret that Arity and Pati are *auchresh*?"

"Ah ... I know nothing." He wheezed. "I cannot remember."

"Then why send for me?" Surprising herself with her daring, she leaned forward. "Let's be honest. You remember more than you say, Divinarch. Age hasn't diminished you that much."

He laughed. Humi winced and blocked her ears. She had grown used to Arity's modulating his voice. "Teehee! Hee! Hee! Ghostier girl, I *am* clever!" Sparks of fun danced in the cataract-filled depths of his eyes. "But can you tell me why I should not have made you work to learn that?"

"No." The wind skirled through the room. *And I can see you're going to make me work for everything else you tell me, too.* She meant to say, *Have you chosen me to be Heir?* But at the last moment she did not dare. She settled for, "Divinarch, that time you sent for Erene, six months ago ... what did you tell her?"

"We played a game of Conversion. Human, my handkerchief!"

She found the blood-stiff square and stuffed it into his hand. He coughed into it, the force bringing him up off the pillow, but he only flopped back down again. Humi winced. The sound was like metal scraping metal inside his lungs.

"You are ... an intelligent ... human," he said when he finally managed to stop. "There are a great many prophecies including your name. Move closer ... no, put your arm around me. I do not disgust you, do I?"

She settled next to him. The degree of his illness was evident in the cool sponginess of his skin. "No." Then she used the secret weapon Arity had given her, so long ago she could not remember when: "Golden Antelope."

"Eeaaahh!" He spasmed. "I have not been called by that name in a century or more!"

"I'm sorry." She looked out at the sea vista. "Golden Antelope."

For a time he was silent, each breath a victory over frailty and phlegm. The wind carried away the smell of the blood which from time to time he coughed up. "I have not been Golden Antelope since I was young, in Anemone Channel Heaven." Now he was speaking *auchraug*. He seemed not to have noticed the transition. A shiver wriggled between Humi's shoulder blades. "A hamlet, you would call it. On a tributary of the Chrume, deep in Kithrilindu. Back then I was Antelope, *mainraui*. To the first human I ever knew, a young man calling himself Zeniph, I was Gold.

"I will not bore you by telling the story of how I befriended him and was punished by being made to live out my days here in Delta City. The *serbalim* thought that perhaps if I became Divinarch, I could repair the damage I did. They were wrong."

Humi was quiet. The wind seemed almost warm. Perhaps she was getting used to it. At last she extracted her arm and slid down, curling up next to Golden Antelope like a child. Kicking off her slippers, she snuggled carefully under the heavy brocade. "Divinarch? Tell me tales." She rolled onto her back. "Tell me about when you were young. Not about Antiprophet. Anything except him. How did you and the other Foundlings amuse yourselves before he entered your life?"

"We were foolish."

"All children are foolish."

"And because of that, they are carefree." The Divinarch coughed. Then, slowly, he related tales of his life in Anemone Channel Heaven to her. "It was an era when everyone lived for the moment, perceiving the beauty in each other, treating their own existence as a thing to worship and at the same time to laugh at."

Humi was inspired to interrupt, "Being a ghostier is turning that sense of wonder to one's own ends. I suppose we humans were never quite as innocent as you were."

"Oh, no. Never. Because, you see, you have always had children. Without that responsibility, one is free to indulge in a great deal of silly introspection and sheer fun. When I was young, the Heavens still deserved their name . . ."

And he told her of his first lover, his first hunt as a *mainraui,* and the moment when he was summoned before the *serbalim,* when they told him that he was the Heir. Humi got up to shut the portals, and lay back down. Gradually the afternoon dimmed. The ships on the sea ran out lanterns at bow and stern which seemed to toss independently of each other, like fireflies on the dark sea.

"I have failed as Divinarch. But I take pride in my failure." The old *auchresh*'s voice rang out commandingly. "Not everyone can claim the single-handed destruction of a religion *and* of an empire. I think the Wanderer is my only competitor in all of history. You modern councillors do not concern yourself with affairs overseas, other than to make sure your representatives obey you." Humi winced. "But I can tell you, Humility, that when I die, if I am not immediately replaced with another figure of power, there will be war. Calvary will break way to form a state of its own. Iceland and Pirady will band together. Domesdys and Veretry will splinter. The Archipelago will slide back into anarchy.

"Yes . . . I think I have earned myself a place in the histories. My name should loom larger even than Antiprophet's. Do you hear that, Zeniph?" he shouted suddenly.

Humi swallowed fear. "Golden Antelope, do you *want* all this to happen? Is that why you are encouraging the degradation of the Ellipse?"

After a pause, he said, "I want to avoid it at all costs!" He paused again. "That is why I have taken it on me to name a Heir who can represent every part of the Divinarchy."

On no, Humi thought with a sinking of her heart.

But he was still talking. "The last century has proved what I always believed—that your race is equal or superior to mine. I have changed this city from a quiet, pious town where commoners bowed low before the gods to a brawling, crime-ridden metropolis where the gods cover their faces and walk unseen. I wish to see the transformation completed. And so I chose to remain here until the end."

Humi could not speak.

"The Last Divinarch. I should like to be called that."

"It's a good title."

"I do not want flattery from you. If I sicken you," and with a tremendous effort he turned his head, "then by all means admit it."

"Er-serbali?" She had to know something. "That game of Conversion you said you played with Erene—who won?"

The Divinarch was silent for several minutes. His breath labored. "I did."

She sat up, pulling her knees to her chest.

"It had to be, Humility. She was the sacrifice. The cat's paw."

"What do you mean?" Erene had been strong—she had been anything *but* a cat's paw—

"I named her Heir for that very reason. I knew that the first human I named would die of it, and if it were Councillor Gentle, it would make sense to the populace that her title pass down to you. I did not know it would be *you* who killed her—" he laughed—"but things like that happen."

Humi gasped. Out of sheer spite, she longed to tell him the truth behind Erene's disappearance. How could he have plotted so cold-bloodedly? Had she—had she drastically misunderstood his motives?

"You have been my choice all along," he said. "The Divinarchy is yours to keep or destroy. Because in the end, what have we to follow except prophecies? And the prophecies name you."

"Divinarch, the prophecies also say I will be forsaken by all gods and mortals!" she burst out. "And I don't see *that* happening anytime soon! They're contradictory! How can you believe in them?" So much frustration and anxiety growing like white grass in the shadows of those prophecies, tangling up over the years—"They're nothing but the spewings of crazy lemans!" So black, so *insubstantial*—

In a flash of sulphur, Pati appeared beside the bed and backhanded Humi against the headboard. "So you *are* here! Arity was right!" He stared down at the Divinarch. "Old one, what have you told her?"

"Ahhhh. *Firchresi*, meet Humility." The Divinarch grinned, his eyes shut, revealing loose, rotted fangs. "My new Heir."

"Heir." Pati's face darkened and his wings trembled, but he controlled himself. It came to Humi that he had been expecting this. "What about Arity?"

"They are *irissim*. They can make up their differences."

"*Er-serbali*, this isn't about *irissim*! This is about godhead."

Golden Antelope's eyes closed. A trickle of white blood issued from his mouth.

Pati erupted into motion, rolling him over, bending his face to his chest. "Oh, no," he hissed, blinked out and reappeared squatting on the bed, a long-legged spider in breeches and jacket. He chafed the Divinarch's wrists while Humi coughed the sulphur out of her lungs. "If you've let him slip away, I'll kill you—"

The Divinarch's eyes opened. With a wheeze he breathed in. "No—I am not quite slipped yet." Out . . . Sea fog gusted into the room with the wind, curling down Humi's neck. She rubbed bare arms, teeth chattering. "I am glad you are here," the Divinarch said with difficulty.

Pati swallowed. *"Breideii."* He let go of the thin wrists and bowed his head, his iridescent bangs brushing the Divinarch's face.

"My most wayward *firchresi,* and most beloved. Not many revere my name."

"I do," Humi whispered, moved by the first display of real emotion she had ever seen from Pati. "You're a great man, Divinarch."

"That is well." The Divinarch's eyes shone. "And you will make me greater yet."

"But no," Pati said. "My *breideii,* you cannot."

"She is better suited to lead this world than you, or Arity, or any of the others, Pati."

A nimbus of barely controlled anger shimmered around Pati. "She is a human on the foolish side of twenty!"

"Does that disqualify her?" The Divinarch lay still and small in the twilight, eyes closed. "It is prophesied," he croaked.

"A pox on prophecy. Prophecies cannot fulfill themselves."

Cold terror knotted in Humi's stomach. Prophecy or no prophecy, no one could change the Old One's mind for him. Not even Pati. So why had the Divinarch told Pati? He *wanted* this reaction. He *meant* to create a schism between the two of them.

All at once, as if a dark pane of glass shattered, letting her see clearly, she understood his plan. And caught her breath with horror. It depended on her own reluctance and her conviction that she was unfit to be Heir. It had so nearly succeeded! To use Pati like that—to use *her* like that—and Erene—over dozens of years—

"What a note to go out on!" The Divinarch was laughing. Each chuckle cost him a fortune in blood. It smelled rancid, as liquid from deep inside a body nearly two centuries old well might. "What a—note—" A look of alarm crossed his face. "By the Power—"

Concern chased everything else from Pati's voice. "Old One?"

"It . . . is . . ."

"Divinarch, don't go!"

"Quiet!"

"Change your mind, Divinarch! I don't want the Throne! Stay, keep it—"

The Divinarch's face took on a beatific expression. It was clear he had not heard a word she said. "Such a tintinnabulation," he said in lucid *auchraug*. "Like the music of the celestial spheres, heard through a wall of water. Listen!"

The sharp reek of blood pervaded the air.

Humi and Pati raised their heads and stared at each other.

They were alone in the rapidly darkening room.

All over the world, the mismatched machinery of the Divinarchy geared and meshed and clanked, working as it always had. But in the cold, dark stateroom of the Old Palace, its helm swung free.

The world doesn't know it has stopped, and so it keeps on going.

Pati strode up and down. Minutes ticked by. Humi guessed he was wrestling with jealousy, loyalty, grief, and greed. She feared that if she moved, he would leap at her and strangle her.

The Divinarch wanted war. What else could assure him as long a chapter in the history books? He had said that he'd named her Heir because she would satisfy all the warring factions; but in fact he had named her because he knew she could not do so, knew she knew that, and would back out, as in fact she had planned to do. That would leave Arity, who did not want to be Heir either, firmly in Pati's grip. In that situation, the atheists could not do other than rebel. And the Divinarchy would not just be dissolved, it would be torn apart.

All because of Golden Antelope.

A little, innocent, pinkish-gray corpse. She had to thwart him somehow.

"Where is Arity!" she heard Pati mutter, and, "I cannot leave her alone!" She could see where he was only by the flash of his iridescent hair and the screech of his talons on the floor as he swung about. The *auchresh*-built chair she sat in was far from comfortable, but it was the furthest from the dark hulk of the bed. In its tall canopied ornamentation, she saw now that it looked a great deal like the Throne.

And three bright *auchresh* shapes appeared by the window. Heel talons clacked on the floor. Humi started to her feet. Broken Bird, Hope, Bronze Water; and the door crashed open, letting in a wedge of torchlight. It looked like all of the ghostier councillors, with Arity at their head, and Goquisite and Belstem bringing up the rear, the latter puffing heavily—and, gods, the flamen councillors too, and *Transcendence*? What was he doing here? And *Thani*? And why did no one seem to notice them?

"I'm sorry, Pati!" Arity called. "It took me so long to find them all—"

"He's dead," Pati said.

Everyone had been about to speak, but Pati's words fell on the plane of imminent speech and shattered it like glass. Each human and *auchresh* started violently, then fell still. Even the lemans seemed tongued-tied. All of them stood separate, leaderless, like shadows on the pale whirling forms of the frescoes.

"And he has left you—" Pati came forward smoothly, the brightest figure in the room as the door swung closed—"your Heir, Ar—"

Humi drew a deep breath. "Me," she said clearly, making them all turn to look at her. "I am the Heir."

Pati came at her. Spidery hands closed on her chin and nape, no doubt ready to break her neck, and she shrieked, "It's not what it sounds like!"

Somebody grabbed Pati from behind, but his hands remained where they were. "If you had just remained *silent*," he hissed, "then we could have ignored his senile idiocies—"

But it was Pati who had not been thinking straight. *Thank gods,* she thought in a blur, *that he reacted so violently. This way everyone knows I was telling the truth*—"He named—" she was breathing hard, as if each inhalation would be her last—"he named—me Heir—to produce—just this effect, Pati!"

"Let go of her, Pati!" Humi recognized Hope's voice. Her vision was beginning to turn black.

"No violence!" Bronze Water warned loudly.

Pati let go. Slowly, dusting his palms off on his clothes, he stepped back.

Humi turned to face the councillors (*what was Thani doing here?*) and gingerly felt her neck. "The Divinarch gloried in his failure. I thought at first that he just wanted to put me on the seat of power to consolidate his defeat. Then I understood that he wanted more than that. He *meant* for me to back down. And when Arity took the Throne, the existence of the conspiracy—let's not look shocked, we all know about it—would cause a war. A war that would make the Conversion Wars look like a street brawl."

As she stood there in her white slippers and everyday dress, in the gloomy fog with the briny reek of the sea coming in, she had them all in the palm of her hand. Just what she had always wanted. She took a deep breath and used her most persuasive Ellipse tone. "Are we going to give it to him? Or are we going to fashion ourselves a new peace?"

"War . . ." Pati hissed, smiling. "Perhaps that is what is needed."

Panicking, Humi sought Arity with her eyes. Their gazes met across the room in a near-perfect understanding. "Hmm," he said easily, canting his weight to one side. The lemans' voices murmured softly, describing his magnificence. "Let me see how this would unfold. If I took the Throne . . ."

"Then we would fight you!" Belstem cut in, breathing fast with excitement. "We would fight you in the streets, in the countryside, and in the salt! Humi has been named Heir!"

"You prove my point, Belstem," Humi said bleakly. "There would be war. And even if we took Delta City, it would continue. Wouldn't it, Pati?" His face said everything. "Then we would have the power and the police forces, but you would have the common people. We would be even. Worldwide civil war. Can you imagine it? Any of you?" She wished she could see their faces. The dark frustrated her. "There's only one way to avoid this disaster." She took a deep breath. "You must accept me as Divinarch."

And voices broke out, arguing spasmodically in the dark. *Yes—She is the one—don't you see, we can avoid the dying*—The balance swung wildly. The wind had dropped. There was nothing to influence it. It trembled. Then, with a decisive clink of weights, it came down— and doubtful, increasingly cowed, the voices said—*We can't let her—this liberty—this blasphemy—*

"Yes, it is blasphemy," a girl's voice said quietly. Humi did not think any one heard. "But it is ordained. All the prophecies connect with each other." The voice was soft, almost wondering. "It is ordained."

And Arity said in an unmodulated, effortless voice, "It is the only way! We must agree. We must all enforce Humi's right to take the Throne. Then, and only then, are we safe from anarchy!"

Gods, Ari, if it weren't for you—

"The prophecies are nonsense," Pati said flatly. "Get out, all of you. Now."

Argument erupted again, but this time the voices were uncontrolled, violent, and colored with fear. "We will not tolerate this blasphemy," shouted Godsbrother Puritanism, and Auspi dragged him at a run to the Striver's side. Joyfulness followed him. The ghostiers wavered, their voices low but passionate, and then with a terrible sinking of the heart Humi saw Sol and Algia edging towards Pati— *losing faith in her, no faith—*

"Wait!" Arity danced back to frown at Pati. The Striver shone like a candle flame in the fog. The room had gotten very cold. "Striver, speak for yourself! *You* will not permit it? You're not the Heir. I say, for all the *auchresh,* for the whole Divinarchy—"he flung a heedless arm to the room—"we accept her!"

"But it *can't* be ordained," Humi heard the same female voice say fumblingly. Now she recognized it. It was Thani. "If they reject her after all—then how can it be?"

"Shut up, Arity," Pati said in *auchraug.* His voice was deadly. "She's the head of the conspiracy! This would mean the end of our race as we know it!"

"The prophecies are not yet complete, because we have not completed them." Transcendence. Humi turned her head and saw him and Thani on the edge of the loose group of ghostiers, two dark shapes facing each other. Transcendence's voice came low and fierce like a sword. *"Complete them."*

"The end of our race as we know it is already upon us!" Arity shouted. More ghostiers shuffled toward Pati. "If you think you can stem the tide, Pati, you're wrong! All we can do is cut our losses!"

"For you, Godsbrother," Humi heard Thani say—and her hand flashed out of her blouse with a long shining dirk, and she went for Arity. Everyone in the room it seemed saw her at once, and moved slowly to converge on her, but Arity, oblivious, stepped out to confront Pati, and Humi shouted, finally freeing her tongue, "Thani, don't be a fool!" And Arity's stride carried him directly into the range of Thani's thrust and he halted there, turning to Humi to see what was wrong. And Thani's knife caught him in the neck. Blood gouted from the wound and Arity executed a half-circle and collapsed. Thani stooped over him like a rapidly pecking bird, stabbing and stabbing again, sawing the knife in the wounds she made all over his torso.

It was unbelievable how quickly his blood covered the floor.

Humi did not even know that she moved, but she was on her knees in the pool of it, torn between touching him and injuring him further. *"Irissi."* His blood had the fresh metallic smell which comes straight from the heart. She *saw* his heart fighting to beat in the jagged pulp that was his rib cage, pumping his life away.

"I think I'm dying."

She *saw* a shredded lung fluttering, garbling the words.

"I love you."

"Irissi—"

"No," Pati sobbed. "I don't believe it. It can't be. I shan't let it! Out of the way, mortal!" And he shoved her onto her back in the blood, and slipping and sliding, he and Bronze and Broken Bird somehow got all their hands under Arity without letting his heart and guts fall out of his body. Arity's eyelids were drooping, his face bleaching. "I shan't let it happen, not to you! Hope, pull yourself together, we need help!" Sobbing, Hope fluttered to the ground, her wings trembling stiff and wide like a screen behind them. To Humi, struggling to get up in the slippery blood, a white light seemed to emanate from Arity's ruined body, uniting all of the Incarnations with the tears dripping freely from their faces. *"Three—"*

The overlapping shapes of black light faded from the air.

The smell of sulphur dispersed in the fog.

Far below, the sea thumped against solid rock, and the wind keened on the balcony.

Arity's blood trickled slowly into the cracks between the tiles.

A buzzing filled Humi's ears and the night held her like a fly in honey.

Mory had pinned Thani's arms behind her. Sol and Trisizim together had caught Transcendence. Thani's rhythmic, useless struggles, like those of a fly caught in a web, were the only part of the dreadful tableau that was still moving.

Someone touched her shoulder, then quickly withdrew. With an enormous effort, she looked around and saw Ziniquel and Belstem, standing side by side for what must have been the first time in their lives.

Ziniquel said gently, "He's gone. They're all gone. There can be no question of who is Heir now."

"No," Belstem rumbled. "No question."

She stumbled to her feet. As they raised her on their shoulders, the blood on her clothes slicking their fur, she covered her mouth with her hand, digging fingernails into her cheek to keep from vomiting. The other councillors, flamens and ghostiers, went ahead of them, and Sol flung open the door of the stateroom.

Torchlight streamed in. The corridor was packed solid with Old Palace domestics, their faces seamed with worry, and here or there a flamen or a noble.

"The Divinarch is dead," Sol said. "The Divine Cycle is over."

A moan swelled. He quieted it by beckoning Ziniquel and Belstem forward. They displayed Humi over their heads like a prize boar on a platter, the centerpiece of a banquet. *In a moment,* she thought, *they will drive knives into me.*

"Long live the Divinarch!" Sol shouted.

After five stunned seconds, they began to cheer.

Twenty-eight

Far away in Beaulieu, they creak back home after the Midwinter festival in Nece. The carts bump over the stony road to the salt. Merce, and Asure, and Gent's new wife's baby all nod off to sleep in the hay-smelling dark under the stretched cloths that keep the rain off their heads.

Far away in Pirady, Erene is kneading bread on a dark, gnarled table, putting her weight behind each movement. She can see out the window to the roiling gray sea. A storm is blowing up. Elicit sits under the window, carving a leg for the birthing stool that the local midwife has told him to make. Erene stops kneading for a minute to massage her back. Elicit looks up. "It's all right," she says, and smiles. "I just felt . . ."

News from Delta City never reaches them until months after the fact, here in this isolated Shikorn bay.

Far away in Calvary, in the hot, clanking depths of a twenty-four-hour bronze mine, a young man steals a moment to rest on the handle of his pick. *I have to leave this place,* he thinks, watching the bovine profile of his crewmate in the red gleam of slow fire from below. *I have to get out.*

And back in Royalland, the predator's wings flap more slowly as it nears home, winging over the brown expanse of the Chrume that gleams in the starlight as it rolls into the sea.

"I have the girl and the flamen under lock and key." Humi took a deep, slow breath, gazing around the half-empty Ellipse Chamber. Only four councillors were missing—but because they were gods, their absence was as outstanding as if they had been ten. Fifteen people in the room, including Humi herself. When she came in, she had sat down one seat to the left, in the chair which had been empty as long as she remembered. It felt almost like sacrilege. She kept having panic attacks. Everyone looked scruffy and bleary-faced, hair uncoiffed, cravats tied wrong. "The question before the Ellipse is, What is to be done with them? At present they are confined in the lodgings in Christon that Godsbrother Puritanism, so I hear, procured for them."

And guarded by Gold Dagger's and the Hangman's men, who will choose death over failure.

"Kill them," Pati said in a frozen voice. "Never was death better deserved."

As far as anyone knew, the Striver—now Humi's Heir—was the only god left in Delta City. He had arrived back the night after Arity's death. He would speak to no one, not even Humi, and she could not manage to get him alone. He sat apart from the other councillors, knees drawn up to his ears, wrapped in his wings, voice tolling out of the leathery cowl. "Kill them."

"I agree." Belstem had lost weight since the accident. Yellow sleep clotted the corners of his eyes. "They have proved themselves a danger. Their long exposure to the Calvary sun must have damaged their minds."

"No," Puritanism boomed at Humi's shoulder. "I move unconditional death for the leman who struck the blow, for her crime of divinicide. But not for Godsbrother Transcendence. Let him go where he will. He acted according to a prophecy that that very leman made. And painful as it sounds, that prophecy was congruous with a number of others. At first, we did not believe the prophecies because they were so shocking. But nevertheless, Joyfulness and I assisted the pair in following their mandate, and now all comes clear. Charity was a renegade to the gods: he loved human ways, valuing them over his divine remove. He had to die. The tragedy is that his death has only made way for an even greater outrage." His head swung in Humi's direction.

"This was prophesied too," someone protested.

"That is the tragedy," Joyfulness said quietly.

Humi gripped the edge of the table to stop herself shaking. "I can see there is no need to vote. The leman shall die. But how?" At the same time as she hated Puritanism for having enabled Thani to fulfill her prophecy, Humi felt a bleak gratitude to him: she could not have made the decision. Emotionally razed, she could not possibly have given the word to kill her sister, any more than she could have pardoned her.

Ziniquel stood. "Divinarch, the ghostiers have a suggestion." She blinked. Difficult to remember that she was not a ghostier any more, not allowed to ghost, that when she moved to the left her very identity had changed. "We recommend that she be given to us. We will bear her crime in mind—" pious anger darkened his face—"and ghost her in commensurate fashion."

"It is fitting," Goquisite said.

Belstem belched, got up and went to pour himself more wine. He had been drinking steadily.

I cannot do it, Humi thought, panicky. "Shall we vote on that, then?" she said.

"What? What are we doing?" The heights of the Chamber caught Belstem's whisper, amplifying it to an embarrassing volume. He sat down heavily. Wine sloshed onto the table.

Aneisneida touched her father's hand. She glowed with health: her fur was tinted silver so that it looked attractively fair rather than pale, and the torchlight brought out the gold in her eyes. Her wedding with Soderingal Nearecloud was, as far as Humi knew, still scheduled for next Dividay, despite the catastrophe that had thrown everything else in the capital on hold. "Father, we're approving the ghostiers' claim on the leman who murdered Arity."

"Approving? Good. One can never trust lemans—slippery creatures. I should know. I was one. You weren't, girl—you'll never know what it really means to be an atheist, with fire in your belly and Antiprophet's words in your head—"

"No, Father." Aneisneida put Belstem's voting stone in his hand, then opened the plump fingers over the "yes" channel under the cornice of the table.

Humi listened to the subtle rattle-plop as the stones skated through the passageways. The voting system worked by an ancient, mysterious system of holes and slides: each stone was a slightly different size, and the interior of the ancient table conducted them through the channels to two little drawers at Humi's fingertips, one for "yes" and one for "no." The consensus would be unquestioned. A good thing; she hadn't the head to do sums right now. She was well rested, and probably she had eaten something this evening—Mory or Emni or Zin would have seen to that, they still looked after her even though technically speaking she was no longer an *imrchu*—but she felt as exhausted as ever she had at the height of her power as twentieth councillor. Her skull throbbed. She could not concentrate, or rather she could concentrate perfectly, it was just that it wasn't *her*, Humi, doing it. The woman sitting in the Divinarch's seat, the twenty-first councillor, was the Divinarch, a ruler who had lost her Heir, not a woman who had lost her *irissi*. Some of them saw her grief under the shell, no doubt: they would all be poking and prying for it. But she didn't care. Her heart wasn't in the pretense.

Where *was* her heart?

Yesterday she had gone to Gold Dagger's new mansion in Shimorning—without a price on his head, he was easier to find these days than when they were first acquainted—and told him to call off those two hundred men and women with their rapiers, knives, blow-darts, garrotes, and so on. Yes, of course he and the Hangman would still be honored as favorites of the Throne, but their aid would not be needed. The conspiracy had succeeded, the revolution was over. Even if no one seemed to have noticed that yet.

And all the sixday since the catastrophe she had felt as though she were walking in a dream. Accepting that Arity had ceased to exist would be the first, hardest part of waking up to her new role; and she had not even gotten there yet. The worst part of it was that she had no lust for revenge. Not revenge against Thani. Especially if her cruel, ascetic Godsbrother went free, leaving Thani to take the ghostiers' syringes for him.

Puritanism's leman Auspi touched her on the shoulder. Humi startled. To her horror, the girl recoiled as if in fear. "What?" Humi asked as gently as she could.

"Count the vote," Auspi mouthed nervously.

She knocked the heel of a hand against her head. "Oh, yes!" Yanking the little drawers open in haste to cover up her fault, she only just saved the lefthand "No" drawer from falling on the floor.

But it would not have mattered. It was empty.

At first light, as the winter-gray clouds brightened and the sea birds keened around the turrets of the Old Palace, she woke and knew that she had to salvage at least some of her integrity.

She breakfasted on papaya-fried goose in the lacy-walled *auchresh* dining room where no humans had ever come during the Old One's reign. Her roster of noble guests praised the beauty of the architecture and passed the butter. The goose, a hot, filling breakfast suitable for a winter's day, nauseated her. She excused herself.

By eleven o'clock she was in Trebank Road.

It was a twisty, tunnel-roofed alley in Christon where Puritanism had apparently seen fit to lodge Thani and Transcendence. "Good to see you, Divinarch," grinned the gap-toothed guard at the top of the dark little staircase. "She's a bad one, she is! Gonna ghost 'er?"

At his insolence, the bodyguards Belstem had assigned Humi stirred. She stared at the guard distastefully and swept into the apartment. One room, it contained a stained mattress, a window, and a chamberpot. Thani sat slumped on the windowsill, eyes shut, head falling to one side. Tear-tracks marred her grimy fur. At Humi's entrance, she looked up. Her eyes flickered only dully with recognition. "What are *you* here for?"

Humi reached behind her and closed the door. "Do you want to go free?"

Thani stiffened. Then tears welled up in her eyes again. "Humi, don't tease me. They let Transcendence go. But not me. I begged and cried and hung on to him, but they kicked me back in here. They're going to kill me."

Humi's throat filled with pity. She fingered the tallow-crusted candlestick on the wall.

"Why are they killing me?" Thani asked. "Godsbrother Puritanism let us into the Old Palace. He gave us his word that we would be protected—"

Humi clenched her fists at the thought of Puritanism leaning back in his chair, handing down sentence so righteously. *Oh, little sister, did you never hear of a scapegoat?* "I shan't let them kill you," she said. "I'm taking you out of here."

"Oh, Humi—" Thani swung her legs off the windowsill clumsily, as if she had been sitting there all night. She floundered over to Humi and hugged her. Tears flooded from her eyes, but now she was laughing through them and wiping her nose, her body all soft with joy. "I can't believe it."

Between them Humi thought she felt the tension of the terrible deed Thani had done.

"Transcendence told me he would book passage out of the city on Maidensday for two, in case I could get out somehow, but neither of us really thought they would let me go—" Not Arity. Something quite different was weighing on her sister's mind.

"But wait," Humi said. "I thought Transcendence didn't want you anymore."

"Everything's all right now. We didn't want to die hating one another. He said that I had completed the prophecy well, and that he could do nothing other than admire me. We were going to die in each other's arms. Nothing else mattered to us. But then they let him go. He didn't want to go without me, but they dragged him out cursing them—and I can't think how he is faring, blind as he is, alone on the docks—"

Humi had expected Thani to be resigned to death, to need coaxing back to life. She had expected her to have forgotten her childish dependence on Transcendence, to have discarded it like a useless ornament in the face of death. She had thought that anyone who killed a god would be charred to a shell by the experience itself. But Thani seemed to have come out of it relatively unscathed, even healed. Even having lost sight of the deed that she had done, in the greater horror of her separation from Transcendence. She smiled, and wept, and kissed Humi on the cheek. The room smelled of urine. Humi's head spun. The floor rocked under her feet.

On the way back in the sedan, Thani shivered in her thin Calvarese blouse. Humi offered her her mantle, but the leman shook her head, smiling. She looked beautiful with her fur standing up from her goosebumps, showing smooth, dark skin. Fur like frozen streaked light. In the few days of her imprisonment, her cheekbones had gained definition, as had the tendons of her neck. Her tangled crop of hair pleased the eye in its very messiness. Humi the ghostier had no trouble seeing the ghost in her; somebody would have had a field day. But she did not change her mind.

She took the back stairs up to her apartment so that she didn't have to lead Thani through the clutter of syringes, bottles, and pigment pots which was her workshop. No point in frightening her with the fate she had so narrowly avoided. "Do you want something to eat before you go?"

"Yes!" Thani turned and beamed at her quite suddenly, as if she were half submerged in a delicious dream. "I'd better, hadn't I? They didn't give me anything while I was in there . . ."

The scent of porridge still permeated the apartment an hour later, as Humi sat Thani down before the mirror in her dressing room. Hearty porridge, thick enough to stand a spoon up in, with diced ham, and dried pears on the side. While she prepared it, Humi had found herself checking the oats for moths; it seemed years since she had last come here. Lifetimes since she had spent her last night in the boudoir with Arity, just the two of them in the blackness. She had made sure the door to the boudoir was securely shut. She would not take Thani in there. A sixday ago, only a sixday ago, they had made love until the day was half over, and then come downstairs and had sandfish fritters for lunch, and sat together in the window of the Chalice, that fated afternoon—

"I'm going to disguise you so that you can leave the city in safety," Humi said. Thani had a thin, hard body with full breasts. Touching her nearly made Humi vomit, but that had nothing to do with *her*; so she forced herself to relax as she worked darker and darker brown dusts into the girl's bosom. "I'm disguising you as a Calvarese. It *is* Calvary you have to reach, right?"

"I don't know." Thani was smiling. "And I don't care, just so long as I'm going with Transcendence. I thought my life was Calvary. It isn't. It's him."

Why? Why does she care so much? The mirror, a heart-shaped thing that Humi had gotten as a gift from some Icelandic noble, was tall enough to frame both of them against the soft pastel collage of the room. Humi made herself smile into it. Why had she picked colors that would show dust so easily? she asked herself, to take her mind off her jealousy. From time to time, she might want to come back and touch the curtains, and pick up the ornaments, and lie down in the boudoir in the salty sea of black sheets—

Thani grabbed her hand. Thani's was a cold little paw, all bones and calluses. "I could never understand why you ladies want to look at yourselves all the time . . . but see here!"

Humi saw. And nearly dropped the facedust brush. Two faces, one below the other: one framed with messy blond layers, one with a tawny puff of hair; one belonging to a fast-blooming adolescent, one to a willowy woman. But the features were the same. Small, slightly pouted lips, long-lashed eyes, intelligent foreheads. And their expressions identical, to the very self-mocking quirk at the mouth.

"You see . . . ?" Thani let go of Humi's hand, smiling up at her.

Humi drove her fingers into Thani's cheeks, forcing away the smile, dampening her radiance with brown facedust. "Don't worry if it comes off a little on your fingers," she said. "It only has to last until you get out of the city." As she worked sepia through Thani's fur, the likeness vanished. The girl sitting under her hands became a docile dark stranger. "Pick a ship which caters not to nobility but to ordinary people. I'll give you commoner's clothes, and the money to choose your vessel. Keep it hidden."

"You're very generous," Thani said sadly.

Later Humi saw her to the doorway, unrecognizable in some of Mory's oldest clothes. Thani stood in the street, twisting her brown fingers together. "Humi . . . why? Why did you do this for me?"

Humi shrugged, and without thinking, mentioned the thing neither of them had mentioned. "Arity's gone. You're still alive. What good would it have done to let you die, too?"

Thani took a step back. She looked almost horrified. "You'd never have said that the last time I met you. That about its not doing any good. It's done something to you. Oh, gods, if I'd known—" She shivered. "If I'd known—"

Bile boiled up in Humi's throat. For a moment she could not speak. *The effect on me? How much more can we trivialize it?* "Done is done," she said. She leaned her head on the doorjamb. "Now get out of here."

"I wish . . . oh, gods, Humi!" Her radiance was shining through the brown facedust. The Crescent was alive with passersby. People looked curiously at her—perhaps Humi had made her *too* striking: it was unheard of for anyone other than a ghostier to *leave* Albien House, and Thani was definitely not a ghostier—Humi cut her off hastily. "I don't care what you wish! Get out of here!"

"But—"

"Good-bye!"

Thani stayed there for a moment, indecisive. Then, hooking Mory's jacket about her shoulders, she vanished into the crowd. Humi stayed leaning at the door for she had no idea how long, scarcely feeling the cold, wondering what there was left worth living for.

* * *

Pati came to her that night. She was having the Divinarch's suite redecorated to her own, more forgiving tastes as fast as the workers could go, but Palace law prohibited them from working at night, even though there were no more gods to roam the halls, no more forbidden glimpses of *auchresh* life to be caught. She sat alone in the dark, rocking on a wicker chair Emni had sent from Tellury Crescent, her eyes wide and dry as she stared at the mastlights on the sea. The small kindnesses the ghostiers did her reduced her to tears if she dwelt on them. *Trade goes on,* she told herself absurdly.

Pati slipped his arms around her neck from behind and kissed her, his lips dry and hot, the tip of his tongue wetting her fur.

She wrenched away without speaking.

"We almost made a mistake!" He came round in front of her, a narrow silhouette on the fleecy night sky. "What a concept! War as triumph! Golden Antelope meant to drag as many people down with him as possible, didn't he? That's what gave him pleasure. And it took you to fathom it in time."

"Stop it, Pati," she said, too tired to react to his flattery.

He looked hurt. "I'm only trying to maintain a facade of courtesy."

"In that case, you should not slander the Divinarch."

"*You* are Divinarch. Golden Antelope is dead." Pati squatted down in front of her, his white face screwed up, almost human with earnesty. She smelled salt perfume. He must have just come from the salt. "All he cared about was how he'd look in the histories. He only wanted war so that he should be remembered as the one who started it. But he is defeated at last—though not on such a grand scale, maybe, as he planned."

"There is that," she admitted grudgingly. They had peace. That incredible state of affairs, which she had not dreamed possible before the Divinarch named her Heir, shone like the sole bright spot in her personal night. "I think that even without the Incarnations, I can hold things together. I do think it is possible to start a new Divine Cycle with me as Divinarch—after all, the common people never see the gods anyway, it doesn't matter to *them* whether the gods are in Delta City or not, whether a god sits on the Throne or not, just so long as they are there to be worshiped. We are making as little fuss over this reallocation of power as possible."

"Humi," Pati said, "I decided several days ago not to play games with you. I think it only fair to let you know that I don't plan to lose by this."

She felt herself turning the color of mud.

"I wouldn't want to gratify the Old One after all."

She mustered her wits. "What—what do you expect of me?"

"Oh, no more than when you first gained the Ellipse. Your full support. Shall I say that I intend to be the power behind the Throne? Yes, why not? But listen well. This time around, I don't want you playing me off against Belstem. I don't want slander-fights. I want motions. Votes. And Divine Seals."

Erene! Elicit! Beisa! Fra! Rita! Arity!

"Why don't you just put your hands around my neck and kill me right now?" she said in a dry whisper. "Then you'd have everything you want."

For a moment he did not breathe. His face distorted like an illusion in the wind, the flame of him brightening and brightening, swaying toward her. She flinched back. His body burned with energy. She could actually feel his heat on her legs.

Then he rocked back on his thin haunches. "Are we agreed?"

Far below, she heard a rising sea slapping against the face of the island. Voices yelled orders as the sidewash from the Chrume carried ships close to the cliff below the Palace. Sea pigeons cooed from their nests in the turrets.

"I have no choice, have I?" she said bitterly. "We have an agreement."

Twenty-nine

The heavy, wet rain of the last days of winter plopped heavily on the roofs of Marshtown. Humi did not bother to open her parasol as she got out of her sedan and greeted Soulf Freebird. She didn't remember half this many lines on Soulf's face. But of course the woman believed Elicit had died. Strange to think that it was only six months ago that he and Erene had made their escape from Tellury Crescent and Antiprophet Square.

The strongholds of piety and atheism might be named for shapes with corners, Humi thought, but in reality they were knotted circles one had to cut in order to escape. Neither Erene nor Elicit had ever made a wiser decision than to cut them, but they had injured people in their going. Love as powerful as theirs always burned those in the vicinity. Humi should know, for she had once burned the world. And been burned by her sister's even less conventional love for Godsbrother Transcendence. Gods knew where her sister was now. Humi had not heard from her since she and the flamen left the city, months ago.

Soulf's children cowered warily in the door, as though they were used to ducking out of their mother's way. Soulf's husband, Xhil, glowered out of a window, clenching his pipe in his teeth.

"Divinarch." Slowly, painfully, Soulf bowed to the ground. She glanced behind Humi. "Do you wish to bring your retainers in as well?"

"I would not even have brought them this far did they not insist on accompanying me," Humi said. "Believe me, it goes against the grain even to let them know that I come here."

"They're dressed like the gods used to!" piped one of the children suddenly—Mory's younger daughter, a Calvarese-Deltan halfbreed, now seven. Humi essayed a smile at the girl, then winced as she glanced behind her at her guards. They lounged uncomfortably up and down the little street, getting wetter and wetter, cringing under the scrutiny of the locals who had gathered at the mouth of the street to stare and mutter.

"I've changed my mind," she said. "I'm going in alone. Let them amuse themselves here." She bent to the little girl. "See that reddish-furred one in the yellow silk? He might have some sweetmeats if you ask nicely." She turned back to Soulf. "Half of them are Marshtowners born and bred."

"Truth, Milady Divinarch?"

"Absolutely. One atheist Guard is at home today because one pious Guard has winterfever. We go to such lengths to preserve the balance." Failing to bring a smile to the woman's stolid face, Humi sighed and brushed past her into the house. She supposed it should not come as a surprise that Soulf did not trust her. Even if Soulf had liked Humi, the ghostier's apprentice, that ghostier's apprentice was long gone now. So was the master ghostier who had replaced her. Humi had not made a ghost since she became Divinarch. She was not allowed to. And she had not had the time or energy to revise the rules. They provided a convenient excuse.

A Marshtowner like Soulf ought to trust Humi simply because she was Divinarch. But how could you have faith in a Divinarch who supported you in Ellipse, laid the Divine Seal on all manner of bylaws to protect your rights as a devotee, lived as a Divinarch ought in the Palace—yet whose very humanity flouted all your beliefs and traditions? You couldn't. You had to hold back, and mutter with your friends that the yoke she laid on your neck was past bearing.

Reverse those conditions, and one saw why the atheists didn't trust her either. Oh, they acclaimed her in public. They had to. She was the embodiment of their successful revolution, and (publicly) they praised her for warding off the bloodshed which everyone had feared was inevitable. (But secretly, perhaps, they had anticipated it with relish. Humi knew that Gold Dagger, for one, was disgruntled at not having his men made the heroes of the revolution.) And even Belstem and Goquisite, Humi knew, were wondering how much longer it was going to be before the new regime really came in. The very position of Divinarch ought to be abolished, they said, in favor of the rule of the Ellipse. That was what they had planned long ago with Erene. Nothing would have made Humi happier; but there was Pati.

As for the flamens, from oldest to youngest, highest to lowest, they openly reviled her.

"Sooner or later, one of them is going to catch me off guard," she whispered aloud as she walked down the passage inside Soulf's house. "Like yesterday. I don't have time to feel sorry for myself. I shouldn't be here." She slipped through the fleece-lined door of the Eftpool and shut it tightly. Steamy warmth enveloped her. Multicolored lights poured over the fronded plants and the pool. Today, because of the rain streaming down the half-globe roof, the light wavered as though the whole room were under water. Humidity enveloped her, moistening her upper lip and the backs of her knees. There was a metallic tang of green. Dropping to her knees, she lowered one hand into the black water.

The efts were active today, rushing agitatedly round and round. One bit her finger. As the atmosphere began to deteriorate, the light seemed to fade, and the air stirred like a great beast waking. A presagement of the storm disturbed the ribbons at her throat. Even on this leisure jaunt, Humi was dressed as the Divinarch ought to be, in a tight bodiced couturier's creation. "Mell?" she whispered.

He rubbed with naive arrogance against her wrist. *I know you're going to pick me up.* "No, not today! Send me Beau."

With a peevish flick of his tail, he departed. She waited, wondering if her cousin would come. As he wasn't one of her own ghosts, he didn't always oblige.

But she needed him. She had come to see him often when she was an apprentice, but only once or twice after she attained master status; however, now that she lived in the Palace, she was resigned to having a fish for her best friend. "Beau ... Beau ... Here, Beauty!"

With all his old vigor, Beau threw himself at her hand. She thrust her other arm down and scooped him up. Eftpool water soaked her sleeve and splattered her lap, *wetter* somehow than any other water, dark black until the moment it hit. The dress would never be the same, but she didn't care. "Beau! How are you?" She was so glad to see him that she scarcely noticed the smell of decay which accompanied him into the air. He thrashed, giving her a lively glare.

"I'm glad. Oh, Beau—" she caught her breath against losing control—"someone tried to kill me yesterday—"

Who?

"Who wants me dead? An *auchresh*. One of the decorators in the great hall downstairs hurled his glass-cutting wheel at me. One of my bodyguards took it in the face. The decorator said the wheel was pulled out of his hand by something like another, invisible hand."

Beau's face took on an expression of alarm. Minute lips worked. She nearly dropped him. "They wouldn't do that!" *Belstem and Goquisite, Maras and Pieti—betray me? Set up the whole series of attempts on my life to convince me they were perpetrated by an* auchresh? "No. That would be divinicide! It's unthinkable."

His silver gaze penetrated her. *It wouldn't be divinicide. No one thinks you're a god. And anyway, that taboo has already been broken once.*

"They wouldn't have had any reason to kill me before they saw that I wasn't going to do what they wanted! And this is the first attempt since I took the Throne."

His eyebrows capered wildly.

"Well—" Humi felt her mouth trembling. "Maybe it's not, actually." She sat down heavily on the bricks, clutching him to her breast. "Oh, Beau," she sobbed. "I liked being an Ellipse councillor. It was like standing in a high, high place day and night, wondering whether to jump.

But this is different. Being second in the world is so different from being first. I wish I'd never loved Arity! It made everything so perfect for such a short time. And now that he is gone I can't stop thinking about him, and I can't function without him—"

Don't think about him, Humi. It makes it worse. What about the others?

"I wish I'd never known what it is to be an *imrchu* either!" Terrible thought! Yet she did not regret it. She didn't *want* to be *imrchu* of the ragtag company that was the ghostiers now. No one had stepped into her spot on Ellipse, because there simply was no one qualified. Ziniquel had taken over the nominal duties of senior ghostier. But the twentieth seat remained empty! They justified it by saying that since four Incarnations were gone, the number of seats had to stay even. But it flouted all tradition. What was Tellury Crescent coming to? All the ghostiers had taken new apprentices. She could not remember the names of the children. "None of them are my friends anymore except Zin, Mory, and Emni. And not even *they* really trust me—there are too many people giving me unworkable advice, and they can't depend on me. When I talk to them, I feel that we are holding different conversations." She sobbed. "You're the only confidant I have left. And you're an eft!"

Don't blame me for that, his stillness said mournfully.

"But what am I to do? If you're right that I'm in danger from the atheists, it must be because they have guessed that I'm Pati's puppet." She scoured her eyes with her wet sleeve. "I'm keeping the peace. I count that as my greatest achievement. But I don't know how long I can hold on. It could be the flamens attempting my life: It was they who killed Arity—that would explain why the attempts are so inept. They don't have access to my private life. But if it is them, I have no hope of changing their minds. *They're* going to hate me whatever I do, just for being mortal."

Beau flicked his tail at the heavy signet on her forefinger.

"No, Beau. That isn't an option."

Flick.

"I know, I've got myself caught! Tied between a wild dog, a sharquette, and a predator! Where can I go without making everything worse? The city is holding its breath." She chuckled bitterly through her tears. "The only people that I *know* are still supporting me are Gold Dagger and the Hangman. They keep their promises to me, because I pay them. But what use is that, when what I need is a miracle—and all the flamens in the world would die rather than give me one!"

The wind pulled locks of hair out of her jeweled hairclasp. *It's appalling,* she thought blurrily. The Divinarch of Royalland, Calvary, Veretry, Pirady, Iceland, the sundry isles of the Archipelago, and Domesdys, et al., sitting sniveling on the Eftpool floor, hugging a fish. *What would my subjects say if they could see me? They'd be justified in casting me to the predators!*

At that she sat up on her heels. Pride straightened her spine. She marshaled her strength, caressing the filigreed flower on Beau's silver cheek. The wind was getting louder, the water splashing choppily. Beau wriggled, then lay still. Eyes carved of solid silver flesh met hers. Four years in the Eftpool had taught him both humor and wisdom: no longer a raw saltsider, absorbed in the conundrum of his own beauty, with no attention to spare for her troubles, he lived only to hear her troubles. *Follow your heart, Humi,* he said.

"I think I have no heart to follow."

He lay still. Struck by the recurrence of an old fear, she hooked hair out of her eyes, examined his flutter-tailed body.

Beneath one delicate fin she found it. A grey-green eyesore of mold.

"Beau, it can't be."

I didn't want you to know!

"Not you! You're only four years old!"

You've made a lot of use of me. You came to see me even before Erene told you to stay away, and many times afterward. She came *too, many times—*

He gave a buck, a twist, and rocketed out of her grip, arrowing gracefully beneath the surface.

"Beau!" How long would that grace last? How long until he wasted to a skeleton hung with tattered flesh? For a moment, despair threatened. Then she straightened her back.

She was Divinarch.

My last friend. She forced her way through the storm to the door. She paused outside, smoothing hair and skirts. *My last friend.* The Divinarch must look impeccable at all times. In the sudden quiet of the corridor, angry voices came faintly to her ears. Local reactionaries, probably, who had seen her retinue outside and demanded an audience. *My last friend.*

Well, she existed to serve her subjects.

Soulf's children scurried out of her way as she swept toward the street.

Thirty

When Arity was dying, Hope *teth*ᵔd with him to Rimmear. She knew that for some reason, he had liked Uarech, where the night sky looked like the inside of a hammered steel bowl, perforated with stars. It bounced her cries for mercy right back down. Arity tossed and turned like a feverish child when the Striver tried to enfold him in his wings. (And fever set in.) Pati strode out, hurt, and did not return.

But Arity clutched at Hope's dress. So she stayed. She installed him anonymously, with a staff of young *keres,* in a townhouse where he could see the sky through the network of bridges over the chasm. Not that he knew the sky, she thought some nights when she left the sickroom, slumping against the wall, too exhausted and miserable to weep. In the first few days, when delirium made him writhe against the white bandages that stiffened his torso to a sausage, he called for Humi until Hope feared he would do himself an injury. So she climbed between the sheets with him and let him cover her with feverish kisses. He scratched her face and breasts painfully with his talons as he tried to caress her.

When he came back to himself again, he seemed to forget these episodes. Desperation gave way to rancor and second-guessing. It was as if the old Arity had been only a two-dimensional precursor of this bitter, mature *kere.* Hope spent hours lying in the sickroom, holding him to her breast, watching fuzzy shadows creep across the floor as the blazing Uarech sun moved across the curtains. He pinned everything on Pati. She suspected that it was not direct blame for the attack that had so nearly killed him, but a thousand old, fermented resentments boiling to the surface. Pati had bested Arity in everything they'd ever done. And it wasn't that Arity didn't have the authority to order Pati out of his sight. As Heir, his authority had been secondary only to that of the Divinarch. Hope had always wondered at his fundamental inability to defy Pati. Over the course of these days, she learned that his apparent disregard for politics was an outgrowth of that inability, not the other way around. Maybe it was somehow a result of the years they had spent together in that tiny Heaven in Kithrilindu. But she could not guess at anything beyond the jumbled reminiscences.

When he recovered as far as he ever would, he clammed up. His talons had grown out all over his body, so that he looked like a crippled humanoid rosebush with brown thorns. He refused to visit anyone he had known in Uarech. In fact, he moved to lodgings on a lower tier, sinking himself in total anonymity. Sadly, Hope saw he did not want or need her any more; so she went home.

Divaring Below was the largest Heaven in Fewarauw, a veritable city of *auchresh* on the shore of a lake nestled among spiky mountains. On Hope's return, Divaring's *serbalim* presented her with a house by the lakeshore, complete with servants who represented the whole ladder of social status, so that by speaking to her top *o-serbali* she could contact anyone in the city. However, she found that she did not want to. She walked on the shores of the lake at twilight; she attended the social functions put on by Divaring Below's circle of high-status *auchresh;* she suffered herself to be surrounded by a swarm of *keres.* From time to time she took a *ghauthiji.* She even made an *iu* friend or two, and revisited her Foundlinghood haunts with them.

But it was all paralyzingly dull. She missed Arity. She missed Pati. *Lesh kervayim* had scattered all over the world. Despite her misgivings regarding their activities, their visits were the highlights to which she looked forward for days in advance.

And of course Pati's visits were the best of all. Whenever he *teth¨d* to Fewarauw to see her, Hope met him in

a disreputable tavern named the Skeldive, where the
revolution-minded young *auchresh* of Divaring Below
whiled away their spare time. No one knew her here.
Under a male name, she had leased a permanent room to
which Pati could *teth*¨ in safety and rest in afterwards.
Since her return from Delta City, Hope had discovered
that she did many things which were unheard of for
iuim—or in some cases anyone of high status—or in
some cases any *auchresh*. She often had to stop her
mouth before she shocked her honorable elders pink. She
was one of *lesh wrchrethrim:* the corrupted. The human-
influenced. The ancients used it as a derogatory term, but
the young thought it fashionable, at the same time as they
embraced the ideas that *lesh kervayim* sprinkled anonymously in their midst, the concepts of hatred and contempt for humanity.

They sat downstairs at a little table, sipping *skri*. The
multi-arched common room was foggy with smoke as
well as the sulphuric stink of arrivals and departures. The
human vice of pipe smoking, popularized by the Divine
Guard, had recently become all the rage in Divaring Below. The salt herb which low-status *auchresh* substituted
for tobacco reeked—it was a variety of catnip—but the
anonymity that smoking it afforded her was worth the dis-
comfort. When she had a pipe in her hand and *kere*
clothes on, nobody looked twice at her. Pati had an aura
of electric wide-awakeness. When he *teth*¨*d* into the
leased room, he had exclaimed, "I've done it! I've done
it!" She had had no idea what he was talking about, but
she hadn't had time to ask before he pulled her into his
arms, devouring her with kisses. Throwing her facedown
on the foot of the bed, he had taken her with a violence
that was almost rape. Troubled by his urgency, she had
lain awake beside him afterward while he slept like a log.

"So what have you been doing with yourself, Hopie?"
he said brightly. He looked as though he were going to divulge some delicious secret to her and just wanted to enjoy the wait for a few minutes. "Who have you told about
my coming?"

"Nobody."

"Of course not."

"Pati, if I had," she said tiredly, "you would be surrounded by adulators right now. The youngsters down here are all as proud as peacocks. They all speak *auchraug*, they haven't any of those silly conceits about human ascendancy espoused by their *perich¨him*, and they worship your name. They would come to take back Delta City by force of arms if you needed them."

His smile faded. He played with his glass. "Mmm. I didn't know feelings were running that high."

"I myself have tried to explain to the *serbalim* that they may have an insurrection on their hands if they continue to prohibit all *auchresh* from going to the human lands. But I have no influence next to Broken Bird and Bronze Water. The *serbalim* are all listening to them."

"What? What about Broken Bird and Bronze?"

"You didn't know?"

He shook his head. "Hopie, honestly, I've had all I can do to keep my finger on the pulse of Delta City. This is why I need you."

She told him. "Your name may be all over the streets, but the Mother and the Sage are speaking into the ears that count. They're going the rounds of the major Heavens, preaching Golden Antelope's philosophy. And they're gaining followers among the *serbalim*—the *auchresh* that count. Many people think we ought to break off contact with the human lands altogether—that it's done both peoples enough harm already."

Pati swallowed his *skri* at a gulp. His pupils shrank, then expanded, fluttering, as his body assimilated the alcohol. "What can we do about it?"

"*We* don't need to. *Lesh kervayim* are."

'They haven't been reporting to me—"

"They can't, Pati. They told me it worries them that they're acting without your approval, but they dare not break the prohibition on *teth¨ing* into human lands, because the penalty is expulsion from Heaven. So I told them that you would approve of anything they do in your name."

"Within *reason*!" Pati's nails flurried an angry rhythm

on the table, denting the saltwood. "But Broken Bird and Bronze are the highest-status *auchresh* in the world now that Golden Antelope's gone. The cabal can't defy *them*!"

"Not openly, maybe." Hope glanced around. At a nearby table sat a prominent young Divaring Below reactionary, surrounded by friends and disciples. Others threaded their way between the tables, stopping to laugh out loud or plant a kiss on a friend's lips. They wore bright silk shirts and breeches, not traditional Fewarauwan gray. one intimation that Pati was here, and the Skeldive would go wild. "*Lesh kervayim* are going amongst the *auchresh* of the small Heavens," Hope said. "They are telling the story of Arity's death, and the stasis which has gripped the Ellipse since Humi became Divinarch. I know what happened in the state room the night the Old one died: I know the story is a string of extenuating circumstances; but as *lesh kervayim* tell it, the flamens have joined up with the atheists, and Humi was in league with all of them all along, plotting to seize power. Fewarauw is cooking like a lidded pot, Pati. If you wanted an army, you'd have one in five minutes."

He laid his hands flat on the table, turning them as if admiring imperfect works of art. Hope saw the scar he had given himself in Rimmear trailing round the side of his left hand, a purple crease between the bony thumb and index finger. For the first time, his voice betrayed weariness. "This shows how much I rely on you, Hope. I didn't know a whisper of this. Delta City is hermetically sealed." She was quiet. Finally he looked up. "What can you tell me about the other continents?"

"Val and Sepi were reticent, to say the least." Hope recalled their guarded speech and traditional clothes, their broad-brimmed hats, the way they slipped to her door in the middle of the day. "But I gather that things are much the same everywhere, allowing for differences in temperament."

"I could strangle those idiots. Hope, what on earth did you go authorizing them for?"

His displeasure shocked Hope. "What do you mean? They're fighting for *you*! Pati, it seems odd that *I* have to be the one to say this, but maybe you're too closely involved in affairs in Delta City to see that this stasis can't last much longer. The atheists are going to get angry with Humi very soon. Things are going to erupt. And what are you going to do about it? At least *lesh kervayim* are making some preparations!" She felt compelled to add, "Even if I don't agree with their methods. It's foolhardy to inflame the *firim*."

Pati sat back in his chair, gazing at her out of his different-colored eyes. "But here is what you don't know, Hope. I have made preparations. And perhaps I can even make use of these *firim*." He jumped to his feet. "I shouldn't have come here now—I might miss the action. I wanted to fetch you to guard my back; I was about to tell you when you started prattling about our idiot *kervayim*." He glanced around the room. *Auchresh* stared at him, drawing suspiciously on their pipes. The prominent reactionary leaned over to a henchman and muttered something in his ear.

"Do you think," Pati asked, looking down at her, his wings fluttering, "that I really could raise an extempore army?"

Draped over the back of her chair, Hope's wings lifted in an instinctive reaction to danger. With an effort, she stilled them. "Why don't you," she said slowly, "explain why you would want to do that."

"I've arranged for the Divinarch's demise. She's been warned: she's fair game. She knows that I am behind the warnings, for she went so far as to offer me her life. And I should be getting back to make sure that it goes off all right. It's several hours later in Delta City than it is here, but the little ceremony which I plan to disrupt is not scheduled for any particular time. It's a private gathering at Godsbrother Puritanism's, hosted by the ghostiers, for both atheists and devotees."

Hope scarcely heard. Because she had never heard of any attempts on Humi's health or position, she had assumed that Pati had not been serious when he talked about removing distractions. But he had not just been serious; he had been talking life and death. Humi must have kept these warnings quiet, either out of stupid pride or because she really did not know who was trying to kill her. "I never thought you meant it!" she gasped.

"Of course I meant it." Pati's eyes darkened. "And it was going perfectly smoothly, until . . . until . . . the thing with Arity. So I am going to use the groundwork that I laid to achieve a different end."

She hardly dared to say it, in case she was wrong. "To make yourself Divinarch."

"Hope, I have to." His eyes pleaded with her. "You must see that."

"Arity will hate you for this," she said through stiff lips.

"Arity already hates me. If he feels anything, any more."

"I shan't let you do it!" She bounced to her feet on half-opened wings. "Pati, you can't resort to such underhandedness. It's bad enough in Val and Sepia and Silver, but for all our sakes, never mind Humi's, I can't allow it in you."

"Do you think you can stop it? Her death is prophesied!"

"Not necessarily! Prophecies don't come true until someone fulfills them!" Hope felt herself losing the stately bearing which had been her trademark since she came back to Divaring Below. Her voice scaled up, up—now all the *auchresh* in the Skeldive would know she was an *iu*—"I love you, Pati, but I can't let you get away with this—"

He smiled, agonizingly slowly. "Hope, I never knew you to wax so sentimental about a mortal. And it's not as though I didn't give her a chance. After she became Divinarch, I allowed half a year to see whether she could succeed on the Throne. She could not. She vacillates intolerably. Balancing acts are one thing; indecisiveness is another. Her idea of strategy is to degrade the Ellipse into a mud-slinging fight, so that nothing is accomplished. Exactly the same as when she was twentieth councillor. But now that she is the ruler of the human lands, it is unacceptable. In Delta City, Samaal, Rivapirl, Westchasm, K'Fier, Port Teligne, Rukarow, and the other cities, the silent struggle of atheists against devotees has come to a head. You are quite right when you think that soon things are going to erupt."

"Just as the Old One wanted," Hope said with dry lips.

"Just so. I am taking over in a last-ditch attempt to prevent war."

"Pati. I know you. You won't stop there—"

With one foot, he shoved the table with the half-empty glasses away. He stood facing her, arms folded, perfectly relaxed—but it was the relaxation of a predator on the wing. "Be quiet," he said through his teeth. "Come with me."

"Pati?" came a voice from a nearby table. "Pati? *Serbali?* Is that really—"

Pati turned and grinned at the *kere* with all his teeth. "Hello there! What's your name? Want to help me take Delta City?"

"I'm going," Hope said. "Where is she? Tellury Crescent?"

Someone in a far corner dropped a glass. A clamor of voices reverberated through the Skeldive, and the *auchresh* crowded around Hope and Pati's table, touching Pati as if he were a lucky statue. None of them had ever seen their vaunted leader, of course, but no one else would have had the nerve to impersonate him. He smiled past her at them. "My *cujalim!*" Charisma radiated off him like heat.

Hope felt sick. "I'm going," she said, feeling futile.

His brows drew together, just slightly. "She's not at—"

"Your love for me is your weakness, Pati." She kissed him by way of thanks. His lips were stiff. The *auchresh* cheered her; someone pulled off her cap, letting her hair slither down. The tavernmaster jumped on a table, shouting, adding to the clamor as he tried to quiet the chaos. Some Divaringians bawled joyously at Pati, and others brandished their weapons, crescent-knives and projectile throwers. Fewarauwan culture still revolved around its hunters. They were prepared.

"Hope, no one is at Tellury Crescent!" Pati shouted. "I never said they were!"

But she had already *teth¨d*.

Thirty-one

"Good evening. Many thanks for your hospitality." Humi smiled with frozen lips at Auspi as she glided into Godsbrother Puritanism's parlor on Dore Street. A few ghosts on pedestals relieved the formal grouping of chairs and tables. She recognized some of her own. That should have been pleasant, but all she felt was the irony of it: there was Simmel, a Calvarese girl, one of her favorites, sitting smoking on a plinth, proud and self-willed—unable to reach or help Humi, as she felt herself fading like a shadow when clouds thicken over the sun.

She knew the signs for what they were. None of the ghostiers had come near her in days, and though the atheists wouldn't have spoken to her in any case, they'd been avoiding her more assiduously than usual.

But perhaps she had lost track of time. It stretched like elastic. Just when she wasn't expecting it, she would look up and find that a sixday had gone by. At her very lowest guess, it had been several sixdays since she'd had a conversation with another human being: her evenings spent sitting in the rooms of state, alone, or with guests whose puerile small talk grated like gravel on her ears, felt like purgatory. Oh, yes; the Hangman had come to visit her on Sageday. They had talked of Domesdys. The Hangman was really a woman. She had run away from Port Teligne at the age of eleven; for five years she had lived in Delta City as a boy, and then one day she woke up and realized that she was a criminal. After that, she had concealed her gender on purpose. The conversation had served only to remind Humi that other places existed beside the arid garden she had made of the palace and that she could not go there. She had sent the Hangman off sharply.

Such a wide gap between the political and the personal, though the amount of contact one sustained with a person might remain the same! So strange to remember that many, if not all, of the people sitting in this parlor had once been her friends!

She chose a seat in the center of the room. She felt no irritation when the human Guard arrayed themselves in concentric rings around her, closing off her view of all but a portion of the room. She'd finally accepted the guards' dogged companionship; the other day, driven by desperation, she had even tried to strike up a conversation with a couple of them. They had remained silent, martyred expressions creeping onto their handsome faces. Belstem must have told them to let nothing slip. But it would have been foolish to talk to them, at any rate. They reported every word she spoke to Belstem and Aneisneida.

She became aware that the whole Ellipse was here, watching her. She disposed of her gracious smile. The lemans, too, and the multicolored gaggle of children and teenagers who were the ghostiers' new apprentices. Even some garden-variety flamens and socialites! My, Puritanism had taken his nose down out of the air! What were they doing here?

No one was speaking. Hadn't they been, a minute ago? She looked around confusedly.

"Divinarch?" Goquisite gazed coldly at her. "We asked you a question. Why have you ceased to make ghosts? It is disturbing to us all."

"You see, you are so very talented," Algia said sweetly. She wore a ridiculously furbelowed dress. "Tellury Crescent feels the loss of your creations."

"I am no longer a ghostier," Humi fumbled, taken off balance. "I am Divinarch. Why would you want me to make ghosts? That would require me to neglect my other duties."

"Do you not see? Your position requires you both to make ghosts and to govern the land. You are still senior ghostier," Sol said reasonably. "It is not legal for you to stop making ghosts. After all, that is the offense Erene died for."

"Is it my fault that there is no one qualified to take my place as senior ghostier?" Humi asked. Why had she let them put her on the defensive? "I should think that is your fault, as much as anyone else's!"

"Oh, well struck!" Soderingal Summer Nearecloud muttered piercingly.

Gold Dagger was here too, the spring mud from the streets still on his boots, those boots resting on Simmel's veneered plinth. He winked at Humi. The signal of comradeship was like a sip of water to a woman lost in the desert. "It is my own business what I may choose to do and not to do," she said. "I am the Divinarch. And I would thank you all not to question my choices."

"She must've promised the Heir she wouldn't make ghosts any more," piped a young voice. "She does everything he says."

"I perceive," Humi's ringing tones quavered only slightly, "that the purpose of this salon is not to discuss what I do with my spare time. Milady Ankh, could we introduce the topic of the gathering?"

"She thinks everything has to do with politics," said the same high-pitched voice. It was Eternelipizaran.

"Could someone shut that child up!" Goquisite hissed, then cleared her throat. "Yes. Milady Divinarch, we wish to broach a delicate subject: your stand on atheism as a political code. Asking your venerable pardons, Puritanism, Joyfulness. Especially asking your pardon as our host, Puritanism."

Humi grasped the arms of her chair. "My stand on atheism is the same as it has always been. It must coexist with piety: neither doctrine must become militant. I strive to preserve this balance in my arbitration over the Ellipse. Is this not self-evident?"

Belstem coughed. Goquisite tried to suppress a smile. "Milady, I fear it is all too evident."

"Thank you! I favor neither atheism nor piety. I vote

predominantly for neither one nor the other. I bestow equal numbers of Divine Seals on each."

"Milady!" Belstem objected. "You may not favor either doctrine, but that is not wise! You have not bestowed a Divine Seal in almost four months. The scrolls recording the proposals on which you have not yet decided fill half my study!"

Sol said insinuatingly, "Is it not significant that Lord Summer must be the one to file the Ellipse's decisions?"

"*I* haven't time!" Immediately Humi saw she had been wrong to defend herself against a comment which had been meant as a subliminal reinforcement of the mood. Significant looks passed among the guests.

"Divine Seals aside," amended Goquisite. "What is your personal opinion of atheism, milady? That's what we *really* wish to find out."

"Well!" said a local socialite. Apparently her rulebook of etiquette had been breached. *Milady, you'll see a good deal more than that before they're through,* Humi thought.

"I don't think I am at liberty to express a personal opinion," she said. "The Divinarch must be impartial. I cannot admit to a bias which would offend some of you gathered here today, and I wonder at you for demanding it of me, Milady Ankh."

A couple of the other flamens nodded approvingly. Humi gathered she'd scored a point. But Goquisite made a swift comeback. "The Divinarch may always have been impartial. But never before has he had to deal with more than one significant faction. He has always been pious, because that was his only choice. In order for you to follow in the footsteps of your predecessors, you too must declare for one party and one alone."

"But what about my immediate predecessor!" Humi felt herself losing her grip. Her chair in the middle of the room suddenly seemed less isolated. The faces of the councillors pressed in around her, while Goquisite smiled sweetly from an intrusive proximity. "*He* had to deal with the same conditions I face!"

"And his strategy?" Ziniquel said in the clear voice he

reserved for public statements. She could not believe he was speaking. Not against her. "*Laissez-faire!* That is not acceptable any longer! Things have come to a head, Humi. You've got to declare!"

With growing horror, she realized that she was not going to be able to speak for the next few minutes. She shook her head mutely.

The whispers increased in volume until Goquisite said, "I see that the Divinarch is overcome by the gravity of her dilemma. Perhaps we should refresh ourselves while she collects her mind."

The less callous guests greeted her suggestion with gratitude. Puritanism rumbled an order to Auspi, who pattered out of the room along with two of the apprentices to fetch refreshments. The flamen councillors kept no servants.

At last Humi looked up. A ray of weak sun pierced through a window, dispelling the gray drizzle which had persisted all day. It was spring. Back in Beaulieu, her uncles and her father would be deciding which crops to plant to produce the best aesthetic impact from the hilltops. Gossip about the new, human Divinarch must have filtered through the hills to the saltside. Did they have any idea who the gossip referred to? She wished most of it weren't so slanderous. Simmel sat on her plinth, her dark hair glowing auburn in the sun. Humi had gotten her as she was telling her her life story. What a sordid little tale it had been! But Humi had always been attracted to Calvarese ghosts; maybe it was because somewhere deep inside, in some symbolic way which she had not the energy to figure out now, she identified with their rough-and-tumble existence. Raised the third of four children in the bronze town of Hijjaro, in northwestern Calvary, Simmel had gone hungry every day. Sorting ore at three years old, raped by her father at eight, first lover at twelve. How could Humi identify with that?

Time slowed and zoomed, slowed and zoomed. Her ears rang with a tintinnabulation like thousands of tiny bells. Only after a long while (as it seemed to her) did a voice penetrate her trance.

"Gateaux?" Auspi extended a tray of small cakes, each one a masterpiece of the cake decorator's art. "A gateau, milady?"

She must have been repeating the question for some minutes. All the eyes in the room were fixed upon them, and a muddy flush was creeping up the girl's neck. "A gateau, milady?"

"Yes." The word did not come out. Humi tried again. "Yes, thank you." She took the nearest one and bit into it. It was delicious, she was sure, but it tasted like wood pulp. "They are very good gateaux, Godsbrother Puritanism. I compliment whoever gave them to you."

At her words, the councillors relaxed and began to chat again. What had they expected? she wondered. That she would vomit on the floor? She forced herself to finish the cake. "Is there any wine?"

"Wine, Auspi!" Puritanism ordered.

Auspi left the room. The ray of sun wavered and vanished, the drizzle commencing again. Goquisite said, "Milady, have you given any thought to the matter?"

Was there something I needed to give thought to? "I . . ."

"I have an idea! Why don't we put it to the vote?" Maras said brightly, a little too late.

You missed your cue, Humi thought as the last few minutes returned to her. *You need to brush up on your timing, Milady Crane!*

"Put *what* to the vote, do I hear you ask?" Maras continued. "Why, the Divinarch's stance. She seems unwilling to declare for either faction present, and it really is time that she does declare. So if she is impartial, surely that's the best way to decide where she stands."

"An excellent idea," Goquisite said irritably. "The whole Ellipse is present except for the Heir. Belstem, shall we?"

Clearing his throat impressively, rinsing his teeth with his tongue, Belstem stood up and rested his weight on a small secretaire. It seemed liable to give way at any moment. "Since you ask my advice, I feel obliged to give it." He was a worse actor even than Maras. "Our city is in disarray. My police are in constant demand to quell riots before they swamp whole districts. So are the other councillors' men."

Gold Dagger laughed out loud, then caught himself. He transferred his feet to an embroidered sofa and twiddled his thumbs.

Belstem ignored him. "Now, there are two causes for these riots." He looked at Joyfulness. Joyfulness' new leman, a little blond boy named, Humi remembered, Tine, nudged the flamen in the ribs. Joyfulness wrapped Tine's little hand in his.

"One cause," he said, "is that there are more immigrants in Delta City than ever before, and they vie with our indigent poor, so that large numbers of people have no food or work or shelter. And there are not enough flamens to ease their need. Many of them are here in the first place because their homes are uninhabitable: that is, the flamens who have always made their living conditions bearable with miracles are gone. This argues for a return to piety, and a push for more lemans to join the flamenhood."

"Sounds reasonable to me," Humi said.

Belstem glared at her. "*However,* the other, more pressing cause of discontent—and this goes for the Divinarchy as a whole—is that many atheists are disappointed in their Divinarch. The revolution against the old regime has been successful. But where is the new regime? We are caught in limbo. We have not yet been permitted to put economic reforms into effect. We have not yet been permitted to help the starving people to help themselves. Our hands are tied."

"We hold that instead of simply asking a flamen to fulfill one's need, one should work for one's daily bread," Trisizim clarified. Since when, Humi wondered, had *he* been an atheist?

"I could not have put it better myself," Belstem growled. "Now the origin of this problem lies with the Divinarch, who has not permitted—"

Humi stood up. "I think I should be allowed to defend—"

Her guards surrounded her, pushing her back down. Her elbow banged painfully against the arm of her chair. "Jerithu? Skimmeren? Hafi?" she said. They avoided her eyes.

"The fault," Belstem repeated guiltily, "obviously lies with the Divinarch. I propose—in short—a change of Divinarch. Erhmm. The Ellipse—erhmm—has the Ellipse got any suggestions?"

The guards moved aside so that Humi could see him glance ostentatiously around the parlor. Goquisite's lips moved: she must have been suggesting that Belstem himself would make an admirable Divinarch. Humi couldn't hear a word, nor his demurral, the pretty phrases Goquisite used to persuade him, his suspiciously rapid consent. The ringing was back in her ears.

"Who supports Belstem for Divinarch!"

The applause was polite yet deafening.

"Shall we put it to the vote?"

Ziniquel was beginning to look uncomfortable. Straddling a chair, he grimaced and blurted, "Yes!"

Humi watched as with much unnecessary talk, they improvised a system of silent voting, dropping scraps of paper into a basket which Pieti's adopted daughter carried around to each councillor. The voices of the lemans sounded troubled (a near-impossibility); the lesser socialites looked on, round-eyed. Goquisite took the basket from the girl, stood up and smoothed her skirts. She started to pick through the papers, turning each one over, pursing her lips and noting it on a tablet. "This is a farce," Humi said. Goquisite started, and dropped the basket. "I'm sure there is no need to count the votes. Why don't you just get on with . . ." What was she saying again? The room swam. "With . . ." She shook her head angrily. "With . . . with it."

Goquisite could not look Humi in the eye. That felt like a triumph. "I—I feel that after all, we have no need to count the votes," Goquisite said. "The Ellipse chooses Belstem Summer for Divinarch. All that remains is for you to bestow the Divine Seal on the decision, Divinarch. There can be no appeal. The vote was unanimous."

In the dead silence that ensued, Auspi pattered into the room. She hurried over to Humi with silver tray, wineglass, and bottle. "Sorry," she apologized. "I couldn't find the wine. A godsman in the cellars gave me some—"

In that instant, Humi knew exactly what was in the transparent liquid streaming from the mouth of the bottle into the goblet. They had planned everything, even down to this, reinforcing their plot so many times that everything else became unnecessary. Why had they bothered with the elaborate setup, if all along, they planned to resort to this? *When bloodshed starts, laws turn obsolete,* Golden Antelope had said. He had forgotten to mention *absurd.* Humi wanted to laugh.

Then, without transition, she had no desire to laugh at all. The ray of sun reappeared through the window, slanting between Auspi's thin, black-clad arm and body, illuminating the goblet like a giant diamond.

Perfectly clear. She hoped it would be tasteless.

"Thank you, Auspi." She lifted the glass out of the sun. "To your health, my *imrchim*—lords and ladies—Godsisters and Godsbrothers."

She drank.

Her throat seizes up. Numbness races from her fingers and toes toward her heart, constricting it. She cannot feel her body. She cannot see through her eyes.

A door slams against a wall, and there is a smell of sulphur. "*No!* Damn him!"

It must be an *auchresh* voice, to penetrate this blackness that is getting deeper by the millisecond.

"She is dying! That was poison, salt aconite, stupid humans, lethal in less than a minute, *do something*—"

"We didn't do it!" A woman is screaming. Humi can just hear the words. "We didn't want to kill her, just to make her abdicate, we didn't—"

"It was you who killed her, with poison or without! *Godsbrother!* Quickly! Help her!"

She tumbles endlessly into blackness. It is opaque and soft as wool. Cold as a snowy night.

Thirty-two

A man is crying.

Horrendous sound.

Racking sobs.

A woman tries to comfort him.

He keeps weeping.

"Pull yourselves together, idiots!"

No woman has a voice this loud. It is like a faraway gong.

Humi is in darkness. Her mind is working very slowly: she has only just figured out that she is sitting with her head on someone's shoulder, her limbs sprawled out on cushions. She can feel her body, though she cannot move, and the pain is still far away, for which she is grateful. Her eyes hurt the worst. As if they are filled with sand.

She would like to pass out again, but the voices rattle like gravel on her ears, keeping her in the black land on the edge of unconsciousness.

"We killed—let the blaspheming atheists kill her—"

"She is not dead. And they did *not* kill her. Pati did. How else do you think he knew to appear when the confusion was at its height? He got you all into his control masterfully, did he not? Was it not reassuring to see those gods appear with their knives and their crossbows? Weren't you grateful when they started to give orders?"

The man gulps. "We—"

"Zin! Zin! It's all right, love! You knew her best— where can we take her?"

Where has Humi heard this voice before?

"H-h . . . Emni, I can't think. All those dead bodies . . .

Marasthizinith ... Pieti ... even his little *daughter*, for the gods' sake! All dead!"

What has happened? Who is dead? Humi is not. She knows that, although just now she doesn't know much else.

"Never mind!" The woman is near tears herself, but she insists, "Just try to think, Zin!"

With a massive effort, the man controls his grief. "Hem. His name is Hem. He runs a curiosity ship in Temeriton. He used to be Erene's apprentice ... It's all I can think of!"

"Anywhere will do, as long as Pati is not likely to run across her there." The loud voice is cold, irritable. Why does Humi think it should be sweet? "He would be extremely vexed to find out she is alive. I would not put it past him to take steps."

"I hardly see the Divinarch frequenting the worst part of the whorehouse district in the near future!" the woman says.

"Quite right. He will be too busy. Now remember, Ziniquel, and you, Solemnity, keep your mouths shut about this. Only we three, and of course Godsbrother Joyfulness, know that she is not nailed in that coffin in Joyfulness' parlor, too contorted from the effects of the poison to be displayed to the public. We must keep it that way."

"Agreed, Maiden. Gods! Agreed."

The blackness lifts with a bump, and reorientates many times, up, down, and swinging. She recognizes the familiar motion of a sedan. Now and then the voices intrude on the blackness again, but she doesn't try to understand them. She has no sense of direction or time.

There is a jolt. She feels herself topple sideways as the person on whom she is leaning starts up, rapping on the side of the sedan to get the porter's attention. Ziniquel's voice calls, "Stop here."

Cast of Characters

Humility Garden: An Unfinished Biography

The Mortals

Humility "Humi" Garden	
Beauty "Beau" Garden	Her cousin
Faith Garden	Her mother
Strength "Reng" Garden	Her father
Godsbrother Sensuality	A flamen
Mitigation "Miti"	His leman
Godsister Decisiveness	A flamen
Correction "Cor"	Her leman
Cheerfulness "Cheer"	A beautician
Larch	
Ministration "Ministra"	A couturier
Bareed	
Godsbrother Puritanism	A flamen councillor
Auspice "Auspi"	His leman
Godsbrother Joyfulness	A flamen councillor
Flexibility "Lexi"	His leman
Belstem Summer	A lord councillor
Aneisneida Summer	His daughter, also a councillor
Goquisite Ankh	A lady councillor
Marasthizinith Crane	A lady councillor

Pietimazar Seaade	A lord councillor
Serenity "Erene" Gentle	Senior ghostier and councillor
Fragility "Fra" Canyonade	Master ghostier and councillor
Felicitous "Elicit" Paean	Master ghostier and councillor
Nostalgia "Algia" Cattail	His older apprentice
Eternelipizaran "Eterni"	His younger apprentice
Memory "Mory" Carmine	Master ghostier and councillor
Trisizim Sepal	Her apprentice
Obeisance "Beisa" Thunder	Master ghostier and councillor
Solemnity "Sol" Southwind	Her apprentice
Solemnity "Emni" Southwind	Her other apprentice
Ziniquel Sevenash	Master ghostier and councillor
Puritanism "Rita" Porphyry	Master ghostier and councillor
Owen Phyllose	Her apprentice
Afet Merisand	A porter
Mell	Of Djanneh, Calvary
Soulfulness "Soulf"	Of Marshtown
Exhilaration "Xhil"	Her husband
Hem Lakestone	A shopkeeper
Pleasantry "Leasa" Lakestone	His wife
Sensitivity "Ensi"	Their daughter
Merit "Meri"	Their son
Godsbrother Transcendence	A flamen
Thankfulness "Thani" Garden	His leman

The Gods

Golden Antelope	The Divinarch
Charity "Arity"	The Heir
Hope	The Maiden
Broken Bird	The Mother
Patience "Pati"	The Striver
Bronze Water	The Sage
Valor "Val"	A Divine Guard
Glass Mountain	A Divine Guard
Sepia	A Divine Guard
Sweet Mouse-eater	*Serbalu* of Wind Gully Heaven
Wrought Leaf	*O-serbalu* of Wind Gully Heaven
Flowering Crevice	Of Wind Gully Heaven

Sundry family members, ghosts, servants, and gods

Auchraug
THE LANGUAGE OF THE GODS
A BRIEF GLOSSARY

ae(s) of (pl.)

auchresh sing. or pl.: intelligent beings born in the salt, colloquially known as "gods"

auchraug the language of the *auchresh*

be¨leth drum traditionally used for dance rhythms

breideim older siblings (connotes respect)

cujali any *auchresh* (a Foundling, *irissi*, *ghauthiji*, etc.) attached to the *auchresh* in question

denear money (sing. or pl.)

Eithilindre Iceland

elpechim close friends—lovers or not

er- prefix: supreme, over

escorets deer-like salt beasts

fashir v., to force, to compel, to order

Fewarauw Pirady

firchresi younger brother (term of endearment)

firi younger brother (impersonal)

ghauthijim casual lovers

ghauthi kere prostitute (always male in the Heavens)

gherry traditional Kithrilindic drink of a red color and bitter flavor, served hot

graumir v., to go, to leave

haugthirre adj., throwback

haugthule predator

hymanni adj., mortal

hymannim mortals

imrchim ghostiers (occasionally applied to *auchresh* with living arrangements similar to those at Tellury Crescent) *irissim* two bound together as closely as possible, almost always lovers

iu n., female (also connotes high status)

iye no

kere n., male (pl. = *keres*)

kervayim, lesh the cabal

khath clear Uarechi alcoholic drink

kiru iu n., lesbian

Kithrilindu Royalland

kuiros strong-man, criminal (pl. = *kuirim*)

le(sh) the (pl.)

mainrauim hunters, gatherers, suppliers

nem us

o- prefix: below, nearly

perich"hi term of respect used toward an *auchresh* of higher status

Rimmear largest Heaven in Uarech

ruthyalim people of one's own Heaven

saduim business partners

serbalim leaders, usually of a Heaven

skri Fewarauwan alcoholic drink

teth"tach ching instantaneous travel

tith"ahim one not personally known to the speaker, of a different Heaven

triccilim menial servants

Uarech Calvary

urthriccim slender tentacles that look like hair

wrchrethrim the corrupted ones

wrchrethre adj., corrupted

wrillim earrings

Writh aes Haraules Sea of Storms